Julian Lees was born and raised in Hong Kong, attended boarding school in England, and currently lives in Kuala Lumpur, Malaysia, with his wife and children.

The great-grandson of a high-ranking Cossack general who served under the last Tsar of Russia, Julian is a writer who draws from his family's rich history. His novels are set in a world where East meets West, a cross-cultural world which he captures bewitchingly and dramatically in his fiction.

Also by Julian Lees

The Burnings

JULIAN LEES

THE BONE RITUAL

CONSTABLE

CONSTABLE

First published in Great Britain in 2016 by Constable
This paperback edition published in 2017

3 5 7 9 10 8 6 4 2

A CIP catalogue record for this book
is available from the British Library.

ISBN: 978-1-47212-310-7

Typeset in Bembo by Photoprint, Torquay
Printed and bound in Great Britain by Clays Ltd, Elcograf S.p.A.

Papers used by Constable are from well-managed forests and other
responsible sources.

Constable
An imprint of
Little, Brown Book Group
Carmelite House
50 Victoria Embankment
London EC4Y 0DZ

An Hachette UK Company
www.hachette.co.uk

www.littlebrown.co.uk

For Ming

'Things fall apart; the centre cannot hold; mere anarchy is
loosed upon the world.'
William Butler Yeats

Prologue

A wild snarl of nightmare shapes shifted in the blackness. The house with the slanting roof stood at the edge of the *kampung*, a village on the outskirts of an industrial town, shrouded by thick, dark folds of kepuh trees. Isolated in the mouth of the valley, it mouldered like a cracked tooth, the tin-and-wood construction glimmering in the enamelled moonlight. To reach the house, one took a dirt road that snaked through the cassava fields and bamboo groves. It was close enough to be seen by its neighbours but far enough away for them to close their minds to the nightly goings-on.

An hour before *Fajr* prayers, before first light, the rooster caught the first scream; a child's cry of fright and pain that shrieked through the kepuh trees. A door banged. Footsteps echoed down a corridor. A little boy curled his body up tight like a centipede. A minute later the scream came again, more terrified than the last. 'Stop! *Tidak!* No!' Individual yelps. Broken-off sentences. 'Stop! *Henti! Tidak!*'

The village cats tilted their heads at the noise, and switched from staring at the nesting birds to staring at the house with the slanting roof. The child's sobs fell away. Beyond the cassava fields, Javanese fruit bats took flight in the breeze, mimicking the swirl of fallen frangipani that snagged on the damp ground.

As the bamboo grove clicked and clacked, the forest grew quiet. Stilled by an intake of breath.

And then the final wail came, this time muffled by a pillow or a hand. It tore across the *kampung*. As it reached the ears of the village chief, he scrunched up his face and groaned. Barebacked from the heat, he turned in his wicker cot, exposing his spine to the mosquitoes. He wondered whether he should intervene and stretched his hand out to consult his *isteri*. But his wife had already climbed from the cot to make tapioca cake for his breakfast.

'*Tidak lagi!*' he complained, smearing the sleep from his eyes.

'I thought you were never going to wake up.'

'I am going to put an end to this noise once and for all. Every night he is whining like a whipped dog.'

'You should mind your own business, *mah*.' The voice from the wet kitchen was harsh and insistent. In the grainy darkness his wife's shadow looked huge.

'I am the *lurah*, the headman, I should make my approach.'

'Why, ah, so this woman can turn your life to dust?'

'It is my duty, *meh*?' He swung his legs from the cot. He had big, scarred feet from working the plantations for sixty years.

'Duty, *bodoh! Kamu dodol!* Your head is full of coconut fudge.'

'What. You think I cannot be firm and schoolmasterly, is it? Let me gather the council together this afternoon.' As he got up, a stray chicken darted over from its coop and pecked at his toes. The *lurah* approached the window and gazed at the house in the far distance, at the tilting clothes-line pole

2

that resembled an upright corpse. He made a mental note to tuck his good luck charm – a hornbill feather – into his sarong. 'I will gather them,' he repeated softly.

'All you will gather is frightened looks,' she said, trying not to sound panicked.

'You'll see.' The old man played with the rabbit antennae of the family's Sanyo television.

'See my foot.'

And the *lurah*'s wife was right. The people of the *kampung* refused to listen to him. They insisted they would never approach the slanted house and claimed the woman who lived there was *penyihir*. They insisted she was a Chinese witch and smelled of bitter herbs. Some of them even believed that she ate the fleshy parts of homeless young children.

After speaking with the council, the village chief returned home brooding. He took a swig of arak from his secret stash and fell asleep in his cot. His wife found him with his hands gripped to his throat. She had to prise his fingers apart with a wooden satay skewer. He never woke up.

Chapter One

The drive to Schiphol airport took the Sneijders past cheese markets and café terraces and restaurants advertising '*authentiek nasi goreng*'. It was a Sunday morning. The city rang with bicycle bells, church bells and streetcar bells. The air smelled faintly of almonds and batter-fried *appelbeignets*.

Imke sat in the back seat with her arms wrapped around Kiki. She felt anxious.

She had never enjoyed flying.

As the taxi skirted the Hortus Botanicus, she experienced a strong inner stirring, as if something were germinating inside her. She could sense it propagating in her chest, hot and round, about the size of a match head. 'Every time I think about the trip I get this odd sort of heartburn,' she said as she peered from the taxi window.

She saw workmen with newspapers in their back pockets drinking coffee in the sun. Sailors, fresh from the boats, wearing salt on their faces, strolled towards De Wallen with socks full of money.

'But how exciting to be flying in a private jet,' gushed Erica. 'You have the documentation, don't you?'

'Yes, in my bag.' Imke dug them out and handed the envelope to her Aunt Erica and kept her eyes on the road.

Rows of eclectic buildings slouched toward the Prinsengracht canal. She watched the tiny houses flash by and wondered whether it was just Amsterdam homes that had *spionnetje* – tilted mirrors attached to windowsills that allowed residents to spy on passers-by. It wouldn't have surprised her. She'd always considered Amsterdammers the nosiest people on the planet.

Turning her head, she asked her aunt what she was reading.

Aunt Erica moistened a thumb with her lips and flipped a page on their itinerary. 'We have a refuelling stop in India where we are scheduled to pick up the Indonesian foreign minister who is there on bilateral talks. It means we're forced to stay overnight in Kolkata. *Goede God* above. There's no telling what kind of diseases we'll be exposed to there.'

'I'm sure the accommodation will be very comfortable, Aunty Ecks. India is very advanced these days, *hè*?'

'Hole-in-the-ground squat toilets, no doubt. And the beds! What'll be on the beds? Blankets woven from some sort of fabric resembling matted nostril hairs, I bet.'

'We don't have to go, you know.'

'Don't go? Are you mad? This is the pinnacle of my career. The President himself selected me. He could have gone for Veltman, or van Aerle, or Frans Koppelaar, but he didn't.' There was a pause. 'The fact that van Aerle is blind with syphilis might have swayed him of course, but that's another matter altogether.'

Imke handed Erica her iPhone. 'Travel information on Kolkata. See? It's a modern city.'

Aunty Erica scrolled through several pages. 'Oh heavens, no. No, no, no!'

'What is it now?'

'Says here the airport in Kolkata used to be called Dum Dum Airport. Hardly fills you with confidence, does it? Flight 64, this is Dum Dum air traffic control.' She sighed. 'I wonder if I can buy life insurance before flying.'

The match head flared again in Imke's chest. It had been like this for several weeks now, ever since her aunt received the invitation from Indonesia, the letter embossed with the President's gold seal. 'Do you think Yudhoyono will sit for you? Or just give you a photograph to copy?'

'*Copy?* I don't copy. Forgers copy. Parrots copy. Copycats copy. Really, I mean, how could you even suggest such a thing?' She rolled her eyes and glanced at the water. 'Oh look!' She pointed towards the canal belt. 'What on earth . . . ?'

Imke saw a crush of people. They were screaming and shouting, swelling the shores and bridges – a tidal swarm of banners and placards. Police wielding rubber batons held them back. A woman jumped from the embankment into the water and began swimming towards a police boat.

The cab driver shook his head at the chaos. 'Muslims,' he grumbled. 'They all go crazy when a new law is proposed.'

'What law is this?' asked Erica.

'The government wants to abandon the multiculturalism model. They've proposed a new integration bill banning Islamic burqas and outlawing forced marriages.'

Imke watched the boat pass under Magere Brug. The men gathered on the bridge went mad, tearing at their clothes and thrusting signs reading, 'Muslim women eat herring as well!' into the air.

'Well, that breaks my wooden clogs!' exclaimed Erica. 'What is the world coming to?'

'I think they should be allowed to wear hijabs if they want to, *hè*?' argued Imke.

Stupefied, Erica Sneijder fluttered her eyelashes. 'What on earth's a hijab?'

'For a recipient of the Prince of Orange Art Medal you're not very attuned to current affairs, are you?'

Erica fished a magazine from her holdall. It was an issue of *Time*. The cover featured an image of President Susilo Bambang Yudhoyono. 'See? I keep up to date.'

Imke rolled her eyes. 'That issue's from two thousand and eight.'

The taxi headed out of the Museum Quarter. Dog-walkers stopped to chat to one another in Vondelpark. Kiki barked at a pair of muzzled Alsatians. Her tail thrashed between the two women.

'I cannot believe you are forcing this poor animal to come with us.'

'I'm on a six-week sabbatical. Mama's allergic to dog hair,' said Imke, 'and I'm not going to leave her here with strangers, am I?'

Erica jutted her bottom lip and huffed. 'If you had a husband you could leave her with him.'

'Let's not start that again. And anyway, look who's talking!' In all her years, Imke had never met Erica's beaus, never heard her talk about her romances, with either a man or a woman.

'What happened to the bread-bin salesman, the one who used to take you out for rolled pork and brandy-soaked raisins every Tuesday?' questioned Erica.

'He sold kitchen equipment and he lived in Eindhoven. He came to the conclusion that it wasn't worth travelling four hours by bus each week just to get inside my pants.'

'Pity. I could have done with a new bread bin.'

There were certain things that Imke was not cut out to do. A profession in data entry was one. Sharing her life with a man who sold kitchen appliances, Imke strongly suspected, was another. She made a list in her head of her recent sexual conquests and sighed at the thought. Her romantic experiences tended to swing from being depressingly idle to insanely exasperating.

'Did you send him a pebble?' wondered Erica.

'No!'

When Imke decided she liked a person wholeheartedly, she would send them a tiny package containing a carved agate pebble from Indonesia. Erica had received a pebble. Jennifer Lammers from Amstel got one in high school. Danny van Gestel, the first boy she'd kissed, secured one. So too did Piers, her boss at DLHP, and Ellen Jonker, who sold honey and fresh herbs at the Noordermarkt farmers' market every Saturday.

'Anyway, give me the lowdown on this policeman friend you know in Jakarta.'

'His name is Ruud,' replied Imke. 'I've told you about him. His father was Papa's friend when we lived over there.'

'Ugly? Good-looking?'

'I don't know! I haven't seen him since I was twelve. He looks OK from his Facebook photos.'

The taxi driver eyed Imke in the rear-view mirror and smiled.

He drove on, passing Lake Nieuwe Meer. Families picnicked on the grass by the shore. Houseboats drifted alongside as children fed biscuit crumbs to the ducks.

'I still think it's unnatural, getting Kiki to fly. Dogs don't belong in the air.'

8

'The Soviets sent a dog into space fifty years ago.'

'And the Americans sent a chimpanzee. Shall we stop off at the zoo and collect one of them too? It's unnatural, I tell you.'

'It's not unnatural. Besides, Kiki will be travelling in the cabin with us.'

'Yes, at what cost?'

'Who cares, I'm not paying. The Indonesian government is footing the bill. Besides, they've gone through a lot of trouble for Kiki. She's been granted a special diplomatic exemption. It means she doesn't have to be quarantined.'

'You know why, don't you? Rare breeds are a delicacy over there. Our host will be picking bits of roasted spaniel from his teeth for weeks.'

'Don't listen to her, Kiki. Your Aunty Erica hasn't turned into Cruella de Vil just yet.' Imke flicked through the copy of *Time*. 'Says here that Yudhoyono was a former army general under Suharto. He doesn't suffer fools gladly. God knows what he does to artists who make him look ugly.'

'Probably strings them up by their toes.' Erica twisted her torso from left to right and back again. 'Not such a bad idea. This old spine needs a good stretch.'

Chapter Two

Thursday. 5.15 p.m.

My brother thinks that a killer has two faces: a public one and a private one. It is a sensible outlook, I suppose, particularly as he doesn't want to get caught. We all wear masks from time to time. But I worry. I worry that the mask will soon grow so stuck that he will be unable to remove it without tearing the skin from his cheeks.

He lives in a subsidized apartment, built into a maze of narrow alleys and unnamed backstreets. The residents call it *kampung susun* or vertical village. When he leaves for work in the morning, when he emerges from his home, he becomes colourless. His personality turns opaque. Nothing he wears or does is designed to stand out. He is unnoticeable, the kind of person employers look at but do not see. He becomes a figure of insignificance. Outwardly, he is cheery towards his colleagues, a solid if quiet worker; but inwardly, oh yes, inwardly he is like a pariah dog, always hungry, always ready to hunt, always on the lookout for lame prey.

He scares me. *Sih*, how he scares me.

Right now it is still daylight. He watches the woman sweeping her doorstep, sweeping the debris into the open drains. He watches her talk to her neighbour, sneering and gesticulating. She has a busy mouth for gossip, this one has. As she talks she chips at everyone and everything, chip–chip–chip like a knife scraping at a block of salt. So and so did this, so and so stole that. Once in a while she strays from her sweeping, peers up and across the papaya trees, into the market square. And though evening is approaching, we have to be careful not to be seen. She might identify us. Her eyes, as bright and clever as a cat's, might pick us out from the crowd. He waits for her to return indoors, and then he walks round to her back entrance and lifts up the latch. The screen door opens with a creak. And I follow him.

Thick thunder and the approaching scent of rain swells the air. The interior is dim; the day has turned dark quite suddenly. He slips silently into the kitchen and trails his hand across a clothes line, touching a bra strap, a fistful of flesh-toned underwear. His fingers rub against the damp fabric and he slips his tongue into the grooves of the cloth.

He hears a television being switched on. By the window, on a small desk, a fan whirrs. Quietly, he removes the rope from his bag and lets out a slow breath.

Thursday. 5.29 p.m.
Leaning over, at the edge of her bed, he watches her stare up at him. They are like lovers. Their arms touch; his right forearm grazes her left elbow. She wears a fistful of crimson fabric in her mouth. Her nostrils flare then contract, flare then contract. A guttural groan creaks from the base of her chest.

When you subject someone to viol
much more slowly than usual. The same
receive pain. Perhaps it has something to

11

rate increasing. They say children's hearts beat faster than adults'. Is that why children always complain that they are bored, because time moves so slowly for them? I think so. Anyway, it is of my opinion that a fast heart rate equates to time slowing down.

He looks down at the woman by his side. I wonder whether one minute of time feels like five minutes to her now.

I watch as he embraces her throat. One, two, three, four, five. All the fingers of the right hand on her vocal folds. He gives it a squeeze, not a strangler's rough throttle, no, more a father's caress. So tender. First he feels the texture of her skin, which is clammy from all that sweeping in the heat, followed by the thrum of her pulse.

Bup-bup-debup. Bup-bup-debup. As expected, it is beating fast. He adds a frisson of pressure. Mostly from the thumb and forefinger. Her pulse increases. The sweat glands offer an additional film of moisture. He tightens a fraction more and studies her eyes. *Aduh*, so round, how they bulge! Her larynx throbs. The palpitating muscles bring a smile to his face. Eh, now then, what is this, he says to me – a vibration, several vibrations in her throat, tickling the pads of his fingers – is she screaming? Are they her vocal cords singing as she attempts to cry out? She makes the high-pitched sound cars make when they struggle to start. He applies more pressure now on the windpipe. I can see the muscles along his forearm twitch. Fortunately, she is strapped down so there is minimal thrashing about. Her facial muscles strain, her cheeks grow dark, turning from pink to ash.

And then he releases.

She is breathing hard through her nose. Not quite chok- but almost. The crimson mouth gag puffs out her cheeks. Petrified, terror-struck, yet momentarily relieved, her gaze has not wavered from his.

Yes, the learning curve for him is rewardingly steep. But detachment and a careful awareness of his surroundings are paramount.

Strangling someone to death requires a certain amount of discipline.

The same applies to chopping off a hand.

With a theatrical air he rolls up his sleeves and frees her left wrist from its bindings. Like a table magician, he unfurls a red handkerchief and lays it flat on the floor.

And then he shows her the meat cleaver.

Thursday. 5.57 p.m.
Oh, Mother, Mother, Mother! Pinch the right thigh; the left thigh hurts as well. *Cubit paha kanan, paha kiri pun sakit juga.* You used to call him your little pup. But Mother, if only you could see him now: your little pup has grown fangs.

Chapter Three

Ruud Pujasumarta approached on foot. The First *Inspektur* was sweating already. It was a warm morning; the sun in the sky was the colour of an egg yolk. A uniformed policeman waited at the edge of the slum, next to an abandoned truck with its chassis raised and rusted. Campaign posters were stapled to every available tree. Ruud nodded to the policeman and followed him down a narrow path towards a rustic, single-storey house. Two other officers were at hand, shooing the curious away. A few women, faces covered with sago paste to protect their skin, shook their heads in disbelief. This sort of thing happened in Jakarta's Tanah Abang district, they sputtered, or in Usmar Ismael's films, not in their neighbourhood.

'It is through here, *nih*,' urged the policeman. They stepped over a clump of elephant grass to avoid the disused water well.

A rooster, bathing in the dry earth, sprang to attention and scuttled off.

'What's your name?' Ruud asked.

'Hamka Hamzah. We have worked together before. Two months ago on the infamous laundry-snatcher case. What, you don't remember me?'

14

'Tell me what we have, Hamzah.'

'One dead woman in her mid-forties. Mari Agnes Liem.

'She stayed here alone and was not married. But she could have been having illicit relations with a man, living water buffalo style.'

'What else?'

'It appears she had her throat strangled and her left hand has been chopped off.'

'Dismemberment. That's more of a gang thing.'

The policeman made a 'who knows?' face and shrugged his shoulders.

The men removed their shoes at the entrance. They pulled on latex gloves and disposable foot covers. It was a typical two-roomed *kampung* house. The bedroom, which also served as the living and dining area, was at the front; the kitchen, with its electric stove and washing buckets, lay behind.

Inside, a police photographer was snapping pictures of the victim from different angles. Ruud saw a woman tied to a metal-framed bed. She was clothed in a batik *kebaya*. A crimson gag bulged from her mouth like an apple and her mutilated left arm dangled to the floor. A mess of flesh and bone protruded from the stump. Several blood pools reddened the floor.

Ruud stooped to check under the bed. 'Where's the hand?'

'Gone. Together with the weapon he used to remove it.'

'Any sign of forced entry?' Ruud probed.

'Why should there be? Do you lock your doors?'

'Of course I do.'

'People in these *kampung* slums trust one another.'

By the window, on a small desk, a fan whirred and cut through the muggy heat.

'I'd still like to know how he got into the house. Did he knock? Did she know him and invite him in?'

The police photographer, all arms and elbows, squatted down and prepared to take another photo. The flash went off once again. Ruud touched him on the arm and asked him to shove off.

The man gave Ruud a hostile look.

Hamzah and Ruud watched him gather his things and leave. He left through the back entrance. Ruud heard the screen door creak and then slap in its frame.

'Anything stolen from the house?' asked Ruud. 'Apart from the hand?'

A shake of the head. 'TV and VCD player are still here. The jewellery box is intact. Nothing much in it: tin earrings, coral beads, a really ugly necklace with a cheap agate stone. I found a small amount of cash in her bedroom in a wooden drawer. Bloody thing gave me a splinter.' Hamzah glared at his thumb. 'See?' When Ruud showed no interest in his injury he stood on the threshold, lit a *kretek* and inhaled deeply.

'Perhaps the burglar was after something specific. She might have been wearing a gold ring on her finger,' Ruud offered, sidestepping a great waft of exhaled clove smoke.

'So he cut off her hand and took it with him?'

'Maybe she had fat fingers and he couldn't get it off her.'

'Must have been a damn good ring!' Hamzah exclaimed.

Ruud stood by the desk fan and peered out of the window. In one of the open fields, children squatted in the dirt, watching a pair of coconut palm beetles fighting. 'Any witnesses?'

'None.'

'It's a small, close community. Somebody must have seen something.'

'Last night everyone was at the mosque commemorating the Ascension of the Prophet.'

'Everyone but Mari Agnes Liem.'

'She's not Muslim.' Hamzah dragged on his *kretek*. He spoke from the back of his throat, '*Katolik.*' The word triggered a fit of coughing. 'According to neighbours,' he spluttered, 'she was not very popular.'

Ruud's gaze returned to the room. He noticed a crucifix above the threshold and on the walls a pair of colourful Javanese textiles hanging from wooden slats. 'And nobody heard a thing.'

The policeman flicked ash into the palm of his gloved hand. 'There was thunder last night. It might have muffled the screams.'

'Check the bathroom for blood. It's unlikely but the killer might have washed his hands in the sink before leaving. Go over the plugs and drains. Also check with neighbours and family to see if she wore an expensive ring on her left hand. And ask if there are other Chinese and Christians in the village.'

Ruud went through the kitchen and saw a printed note taped to the electric stove. He recognized the words to be part of a recent NGO campaign; launched to tackle unwanted teenage pregnancies. It read:

Cabe-cabean, Cabe-cabean, thin as a reed,
Tosses bread from her door so the goats can feed
Cabe-cabean, Cabe-cabean, goats good and fed,
Strolls to the dump kitchen-garbage on her head

Cabe-cabean, Cabe-cabean, garbage in the fill
Fishes for her supper in the parkland rill
Cabe-cabean, Cabe-cabean, supper on the hook
Takes snakehead in a pan to the fish-fry cook
Cabe-cabean, Cabe-cabean, she eats all she can
But fish swims in tummy like angry Aquaman
Cabe-cabean, Cabe-cabean, tummy full and round
Goes to see the doctor and the doctor frowned
Cabe-cabean, Cabe-cabean, doctor is wild
Rushes you to clinic to pull out your child
Cabe-cabean, Cabe-cabean, did you not see
The father of your child has run off with me.

'Bag this as evidence, Hamzah.'

Ruud yanked at his trouser creases and squatted next to the body, avoiding the pool of dark congealed blood by his vinyl-clad feet. He took several snaps of the victim with his mobile phone. The woman was lying face up; her ankles were bound with twine and secured to the bedframe. Her right hand was tied to the bedpost by her head. There were finger-bruises all along her throat. 'Looks like she was manually strangled. No sign of rope burn. Who discovered her?' He studied Mari Agnes Liem's wide staring eyes.

'Mrs Yahaya from next door. She saw a monkey climbing out of the dead woman's kitchen at dawn. The monkey was clutching a papaya and a bag of prawn crackers. Thought she should come over and investigate. *Berdarah Neraka!* The little bastards steal everything, *meh*?'

Over his shoulder, Ruud saw the signs of a monkey break-in. A sack of rice showed bite marks on it and there were droppings on the floor. 'Is Mrs Yahaya sure the monkey didn't run off with the hand too?'

'Yes.'

First *Inspektur* Pujasumarta patted his trousers. 'Knew I forgot something. Have you got a pen?'

The little policeman unfastened a pen from his tunic pocket. Ruud used it to extract the crimson gag from the woman's mouth.

'You're looking tired,' the little man pointed out. 'Can you not sleep since your wife left you?'

'You heard about that.'

Hamzah took a deep breath and held it before exhaling. 'People talk.'

'Go interview the neighbours, will you?'

The policeman made a face, dropped the ash from his hand onto the floor and went out to make his door-to-door inquiries.

The crimson cloth eventually uncoupled itself from the woman's mouth and her jaw fell open.

Ruud shook his head. Everyone at the force seemed to know his wife had left him for another man.

He dug into his trousers, threw back two Head Start energy tablets and dry-swallowed them both.

The *dokter forensik* stepped through the door, panting, apologizing. He was short and stocky and forever cheerful despite his profession. '*Ma'af!* Sorry, sorry.' His thinning hair was dishevelled and there were sweat stains under each arm. 'It's quite a walk in this heat.' He removed his shoes and pulled on the standard protection. 'I left my car at the top of the main road. All those potholes are bad for the tyres and suspension.'

'You're too late, Solossa, she's already dead.'

'Always the joker.' He laughed. 'And *selamat pagi* to you too, First *Inspektur* Pujasumarta.' Solossa dropped his leather satchel and removed a comb from his shirt pocket. He ran the comb through his scalp, before sidling up next to Ruud. 'Has the fingerprint man come?'

'No, he only does high-profile cases. Unless Mrs Liem here turns out to be the sister of a Supreme Court judge, I don't think the chiefs at Polda Metro Jaya will be wasting money on fingerprint analysis. If it were up to them they'd have this classified as suicide. Still,' he gestured at a ball of fuzz on the floor, 'best to be thorough.' He placed the fuzz ball into a polystyrene bag. 'Just in case there's a change in procedure.'

The forensic pathologist pulled on a pair of latex gloves and sucked air through his teeth. 'Absolute fiasco if you ask me.'

Ever since the National Police ditched Inafis, the fingerprint-based citizen identification system, a network that cost over Rp 28 billion to set up, the bureaucrats have come down hard. Budget purse strings weren't merely tightened; they were throttled.

Solossa's gaze settled on the dead woman's features. 'So! What has happened to you, my dear madam? Looks like you have had a bit of bad luck, is it?' He lifted her clothes and checked for initial signs of sexual assault. 'No scratches or bites or bruises around the breasts and genital area.' He patted her leg like one might comfort a child who'd suffered a bad fright. 'Poor thing urinated involuntarily.'

Ruud still held the crimson gag between his fingers. 'Any idea of time of death? Also, I can't tell if she died from choking, suffocation, strangulation or from her wounds.'

'Madam has been dead a good twelve to fifteen hours.' Solossa surveyed Mari Agnes Liem's face. 'I cannot confirm until I get her on the autopsy table, but I would say she either choked to death or was suffocated. Look at her eyes. Most strangulation victims' eyes are red because the blood has been forced into the whites, or the sclera. When you choke, the windpipe is blocked, there is no blood forcing, and so the whites remain clear, like hers. Also, I see no ligature marks on her neck and an absence of cyanosis.'

'Do you think the hand was severed after she died?'

'Given the amount of blood and the pattern of splatter, I'd say it was most certainly removed before death. Amputation looks clean. Done with a single stroke, most likely a *parang*. But you know what?'

'What?'

'There is no blood trail to the door. So our man didn't simply walk out with the hand tucked under his arm. He had a bag with him and I suspect he laid down some plastic sheeting from the bed to the door to mask any bloody footprints.'

'Confirming it was premeditated.'

Solossa explored her face again, tilting his head to inspect the contents of her mouth. 'Minor bruising to the lips. Nice set of teeth.' He pulled her tongue out of the way. Ah, now, what is this, *loh*?' He pulled away abruptly. 'Fetch me my satchel, Pujasumarta. *Eee-yai-yai!* There is something lodged in her throat.' Ruud handed the pathologist his satchel. Solossa flicked open the catches, fished about inside and withdrew a pair of long, metal tweezers. Ruud grasped the woman's jaws and held them open. Solossa's tweezers entered her mouth briefly and returned with a small rectangle of white acrylic.

'What in hell is that?' asked Ruud.

'A mah-jong tile.'

The men gawped at each other.

21

JULIAN LEES

The pathologist dropped the tile into a collection jar. 'Why would someone do this?' he wondered.

Ruud took the jar and marked it as evidence. 'Dismemberment. Possible signs of torture. I'd say loan sharks were involved. Gambling debts, most likely.'

The day was growing hotter. Ruud ran his finger and thumb along his collar, peeling the cotton from his soggy neck. Goggling up at the sky, he saw a plane passing through the clouds; the 747 was coming in to land. Ruud checked his watch. He had four hours to get to the airport.

Although he hadn't seen Imke Sneijder for close to fifteen years, he still had a clear image of her in his mind's eye. He remembered her well, her laugh especially. Even when she was twelve years old, he believed she'd grow up to be a beautiful woman. There was something about her. She smelled nice, she looked nice and she loved playing jokes on adults. What more could a young boy ask for? And she hadn't been one of those pretty girls who thought too highly of herself either, who'd grow up teasing the neighbourhood boys, making each one feel he didn't stand a chance. No, she was down to earth and kind. And funny. He remembered her being very, very funny. He hoped now, with all his heart, that she hadn't changed too much.

He knocked twice on Mrs Yahaya's door and entered, shoes in hand. He heard music, the airy tones of a small woodwind instrument. A woman, so ancient her yellowed skin looked brittle, like old newspapers left out in the sun, was playing the flute with her nose. She wore a grey shawl that covered her head, neck and shoulders. She sat on a wooden stool with the television flickering in the background.

'Salaam, Mrs Yahaya, I'm *Inspektur Polisi Satu* Pujasumarta.' The crone kept blowing air through her right nostril.

'And this here, you may remember, is Officer Hamzah. You spoke with him earlier.' As a greeting, the little man touched his chest with his right hand and stood in the corner of the room, ready to take down notes in his notebook.

Ruud pulled up a stool and sat. He continued, 'As you know, we are investigating the murder of Mari Agnes Liem, your neighbour.'

The old woman stopped playing her nose flute and gave a little sniff. She scowled at Ruud and then glanced at Hamzah. She gave him the kind of strained smile you might see on a stage contortionist whose pants have split.

'Can you tell me what you saw or heard last night?'

'Why should I tell you anything?' she replied. Ruud heard something rattle in her mouth – her teeth, presumably. 'My father, may the Almighty bless his soul, always said to me, 'Do not ever talk to the *Polis*, princess. They are all demons, demon-spawn of the Dutch oppressors.'

'The Dutch left over sixty years ago, Mrs Yahaya.'

'I know that! What do you take me for, a fool?'

'Is there a Mr Yahaya?'

'There is.' Her expression narrowed. Her voice grew dry and suspicious. 'Why? Do you think my Ahmad murdered the Liem woman?'

'It's strange you should ask that. Did he?'

'I can tell you he did not.'

'How can you be so sure?'

'Because he has been dead since the Japanese overran Sumatra.'

Ruud raked a hand over his chin. 'Is there something you wish to tell us about last night?'

23

'Why should I reveal my secrets?'

'You have secrets to reveal?'

'Don't we all?'

'What do you know about your neighbour's murder?'

'Once you open a box of secrets, it can never be closed again.'

'A friend of yours has been killed.'

'She was *not* my friend.'

Ruud shot an exasperated look at Hamzah in the corner. The policeman was busy worrying the splinter in his thumb. 'Did you see or hear anyone enter or leave her house?' said Ruud.

'Monkeys. I remember it like it was yesterday.'

'It was yesterday. Did you see anything apart from the monkeys?'

'No.'

'Did the woman next door gamble? Did she borrow money from loan shark syndicates?'

'She was Chinese.'

There followed a long pause.

'And?' Ruud prompted.

'All Chinese gamble.'

'So, you're saying she gambled.'

'I have no idea. Did she?'

'Mrs Yahaya, you are not being at all helpful.'

'What, and you think if I answer your questions she will open her eyes again?' She gave another loud sniff. 'She was a witch, you know.'

Ruud got to his feet. 'Right, I've had enough of this.'

'Why are you getting angry?' she asked.

'I am not getting angry, you're talking nonsense.'

'I should warn you, Mrs Yahaya, he has a terrible temper

24

on him,' Hamzah said to the woman, 'especially since his wife ran off with a flat stomach fellow.'

'Flat stomach?' Mrs Yahaya blinked, confused all of a sudden.

'I mean look at me, I have this giant splinter in my thumb but you do not hear me moaning or losing my temper.'

Ruud sank back down on the stool and massaged his forehead. 'Listen, can we just get on with the questions, please!' He checked his watch. 'I've got to get going. There's someone I'm meeting at the airport.'

Mrs Yahaya crossed her arms over her chest. 'I've already told you all I know.' She turned to Hamzah again. 'Flat stomach? I don't understand.'

'So you heard and saw nothing last night?' said Ruud.

'Nothing.'

Ruud got up to leave for a second time. As he rose, the woman reached up and grabbed his forearm hard; she pulled him close so that his ear met her mouth. 'I saw nothing. I heard nothing,' she hissed. '*But I know who did it!*'

Chapter Four

The twin turbine engines of the Embraer ERJ-135LR came to a stop. Imke and Erica extricated themselves from the front of the plane, hurried through immigration and collected their bags from the carousel. Both commented on how clean, calm and modern Soekarno-Hatta airport appeared in the soft afternoon light. When Imke handed in their declaration form, Erica took three quick paces towards the exit but was pulled aside.

'Business or pleasure?'

'Both, I trust.'

She was told to open her luggage.

'Are you sure you want to waste your time with me?' she asked.

The answer was yes. 'Passport.'

'It's not the most flattering picture. I was suffering from a bout of indigestion at the time.'

Erica fumbled with a key and undid the locks.

Imke couldn't believe what the customs officer unearthed from her bags: nine tins of licorice rolls, five cartons of Fruit Juice Bears, nine Ziploc bags of strawberry laces, a sack of Gustaf's Gummy Pink Pigs, Gin Gins in their wrappers, Mars Bars, Yorkies, Twirls, Aeros, a dozen 10 per cent Extra

Free! Packs of Kit Kats, Maltesers, Flakes, Snickers, wine gums and After Eights, boxes of *honingdrop* sweets, tubes of *appelstroop*, a loaf of rye bread, a lump of Gouda, tinned butter, a pound of cured bacon and a pink plastic fly swatter.

'Why you bring all this confectionery?' asked the officer, who was careful to avoid making physical contact with the packaged bacon.

'You don't expect me to survive on the food here, do you?' blustered Erica Sneijder. 'At any rate, I'm afraid of getting lonely. These sweets are my friends.'

The customs man picked up the sack of Gummy Pink Pigs.

They were in the Green Lane and Erica had ticked the 'nothing to declare' box on her declaration form. 'They keep me company at night,' she added.

'A bit overboard on the strawberry laces, Aunty Ecks, *hè*?' Imke whispered from the corner of her mouth.

'Nonsense! Heaven knows I need a nibble or two after that ghastly stay in Kolkata!'

Imke's dog, Kiki, began sniffing the air.

Kiki was a five-year-old cocker spaniel with floppy ears and a black and tan coat. Imke adopted her from an animal shelter in Ookmeerweg when she was a puppy, and even at six months Imke knew Kiki was special. She'd never come across a dog with such extraordinary nose skills. Her scent work, retrieval ability and distraction discipline were off the scale. And because Kiki possessed such talent, it didn't take long for the Amsterdam police department to come calling. But Kiki did not belong to DLHP K-9, she belonged to Imke and was first and foremost Imke's pet, hence the six-week sabbatical.

The customs officer glared at Kiki and then at the women. Imke was dressed in a fruit-patterned shift, looking a bit bedraggled from the journey. Aunt Erica, on the other hand, looked hip, crisp and very Annie Hall in a Dickensian Rag & Bone suit, crimson blouse and bespoke men's brogues. 'Why do you suppose he's staring at me?'

'Maybe he thinks you're Martina Navratilova's dad,' said Imke with a grin.

He picked up the tube of *appelstroop*.

'I use it as medication,' Erica told the man.

The officer went away briefly to discuss matters with his colleague.

The man returned, thumbing his documents. 'Can I see your import certificate?'

'Oh, heavens, we weren't told we needed one.' Aunt Erica batted her eyelids at the customs officer, who suddenly looked very pleased with himself. Then she turned to Imke. 'I think he likes me.'

She batted her eyelids once more at him.

'You have to pay fine,' he said abruptly.

'Pay a fine? *Goede God* above! What for?'

'Too much chocolate, *tss-tss!* Must be for commercial use. You not pay, we *menyita*. Take from you.'

'It's my cocoa therapy, you rapscallion. Don't you *menyita* me!'

The customs man began quoting numbers. 'You pay five hundred thousand rupiah.'

'Five hundred? That's absurd!' She turned to Imke again. 'How much is five hundred thousand? God knows it's probably the equivalent of three euros, but I'm going to argue willy-nilly.'

'OK, you give coffee money,' countered the man. 'Coffee money. Two hundred thousand.'

'You can roll your coffee money into a bundle and shove it up your rear end.'

Just when a trip to the interrogation room seemed imminent, a man brandishing a security pass pushed towards them. He was dressed in a pale grey suit, chauffeur's cap and driving gloves. He salaamed the ladies, thrust a piece of paper at the customs official and waited for him to read the missive. Moments later, the luggage was marked with orange chalk and cleared without further fuss.

'My name is Nakula,' the man in the grey suit volunteered, addressing them both. 'President Yudhoyono has sent me to collect you. I will be your driver.' He piled the bags onto a cart and pushed it to a waiting colleague. 'This way, please.' As they strode through the arrivals hall, a man with a camera took several snaps of them.

Nakula escorted them outside, where a blanket of heat smothered Imke like a warm coat. She tugged an enormous sun hat down over her ears and sucked in the tropical air.

By the taxi rank, a street hawker was cooking satays over a charcoal grill. A *kretek* dangled from the corner of his mouth as he fanned the flames with a newspaper. Almost immediately Imke picked up a memory-scent from her childhood – thin wisps of wood smoke, the greasy perfume of peanut sauce. It was a strange sensation, realizing that she and her parents had once shared these sights and smells.

They skirted the long line of Toyota Vios with Blue Bird taxi stickers on their windscreens.

Nakula led them to a black Mercedes S-Class that was parked in the shade of the terminal.

He opened the passenger door. 'Your luggage will be taken to Bogor Palace separately. More room for you to stretch out your legs. Please,' he gestured with his hand, 'make yourselves most comfortable.' Erica climbed in with Kiki.

Imke was about to follow when she saw a man jogging towards them. 'I brought you some iced Milo!' he shouted. 'Sorry I'm late!'

Imke recognized him immediately. The dark flop of hair was shorter, the stark face softer, but he was undoubtedly Melchior Pujasumarta's son. 'Ruud!' She hugged him. 'It is so good to see you.'

'You too.'

Ruud handed her a polystyrene cup, laughing. 'Wow! You're still a helluva looker!' He couldn't believe he'd just said that.

Flattered and embarrassed, Imke beamed.

'How was the flight?'

'It was fine.'

'Excited to be back?'

'Of course. Crazily so.' She took his arm. 'Ruud, let me introduce you to my aunt.'

The policeman dipped his head and leaned into the car to shake Erica's hand. 'A pleasure to meet you.'

When he stood up straight again, he seemed a little flushed. 'Listen, Imke,' he said, 'I know you've just arrived and you're tired, so why don't you head off and I'll call you once you've settled in. I'll take you out for lunch later in the week. Sound good?'

Sipping iced Milo, Imke looked at Ruud, noticeably charmed.

'Sounds good.'

He looked at his watch, reluctantly. 'Christ, I'm such an idiot. I have to run. Police work.' He gave her another hug and jogged off in the direction he'd come, retreating and waving.

Imke waved back. She paused for a second and watched him melt away into the crowd. She turned and saw Aunt Erica in the back seat of the Merc, working her way through a Yorkie. On impulse, Imke pulled out her mobile, took a selfie and did a victory dance, and because nobody was watching, she did a quick pirouette with her arms in the air. 'Yes! Jakarta!' she mouthed. 'I'm back!' With that, she clambered into the car and flopped down next to Kiki and Aunt Erica.

Aunt Erica kicked off her brogues. 'Martina Navratilova's dad, indeed,' she sniffed. 'I'll have you know it's very chic for a woman my age to dress as a man.' She ran a hand through her short-cropped mane. 'It's a style favoured by many French movie actresses.'

'Very Victor/Victoria.'

'So that's your friend, is it? He didn't hang about for long. Talk about ants in his pants.'

'He had to get back to work. It was very sweet of him to come and see me.'

The car pulled away from Soekarno-Hatta airport.

Imke noticed Ruud had written the words *Putri Salju* – Snow White – on the polystyrene cup. She smiled to herself. 'He hasn't changed much.'

'Oh good.'

She leaned over and gave Kiki a hug. Kiki climbed on her lap, gave the Milo a cursory sniff then pressed her cold nose to the window.

31

As the car made its way through small neighbourhoods on the outskirts of Jakarta, Erica drank in the sights. Everywhere she looked she saw a paradox between the wealthy and the poor – bicycles and *ojek* taxis vying with BMWs and Porsches; sparkling malls next to shantytowns. Everything was either blossoming with rot or concreted over. Most people wore Western clothes, but Imke spotted a few men dressed in *teluk beskap* and *kopiah*. There were also women returning from market wearing embroidered blouses, batik sarongs and long stretches of cloth, called *selendang*, draped over one shoulder.

She'd never seen quite so many motorcycles in her life.

Imke, on the other hand, stared at building sites. There was construction going on almost everywhere; every fifth block was either going up or on the verge of falling down. The place is booming, she whispered.

Nakula slowed the Mercedes at a junction. Election banners and campaign posters lined the streets. Every tree, every wall, every lamppost, carried the image of a politician's face. Erica nudged Imke and pointed out the crocodile of young schoolboys in *peci* hats too big for their heads. 'On their way to the mosque,' she said.

Vendors with long poles on their shoulders jogged by. Some carried crates of papayas; others transported wicker cages full of live birds.

A man in baggy shorts approached with a bouquet of flowers in each hand. He tapped his fingers on the windscreen. Nakula shooed him off.

Eventually, the car made its way through the nest of humanity; it skirted several grand colonial-era buildings, gleaming white in the sun, and headed for the countryside.

'Would you care to listen to local classical music, mam?' the driver enquired.

Imke replied that she would. Nakula tuned the car radio to RRI, and the distinctive sounds of a gamelan ensemble. The sacred melodies flowed and resonated. Without warning, Imke was overcome with nostalgia. It was the music she'd heard as a child. She listened afresh to the metallophones, *kendang* drums, gongs and bamboo flutes. And once more she thought of her parents.

'Your first time in Indonesia?' asked Nakula.

Typically, Imke would deflect such a question, not subscribing to the idle chitchat of strangers, but she liked Nakula's tone, and the way he rolled his Rs in that uniquely Indonesian way. 'Actually, no,' she conceded. 'I was born here. I left in 1998 when I was twelve.' Suddenly reluctant to reveal any further details of her past, she held her iPhone to her ear and pretended to receive a call.

'Your *ayah* was a businessman here?' continued the driver. She did not reply.

Her father ran coffee estates in South Sulawesi.

Hazy impressions took shape before her eyes. Scattered memories loomed out of the smoke. She saw thatched huts and lush trees and village women in bright clothes moving through green *kopi* fields. Picture postcards in her head.

The Sneijders lived in a luxury condominium in Jakarta, but every fortnight Mathias would spend four days in Toraja to oversee the plantations. He sometimes took his daughter Imke with him, to meet the estate manager, to walk the fields and visit the sorting warehouses, where rows of women, fifty-long, sat opposite one another grading coffee beans, picking the highest-quality cherries for export. Since she had no siblings, her father gave her his undivided attention and they found genuine pleasure in each other's company. Once, he took her to pick red rambutans in a *kampung* half an hour's drive away. The rambutans were firm and juicy, and the manager's wife, Ratna, stuffed them with garlic and crushed coriander roots. She served them to Imke for lunch with minced chicken and roasted peanuts. Every time Ratna saw Imke she would comment on her prettiness and how she had inherited her father's features and table manners. This always made Imke grin with pride.

Her mother, Ardy, a typical *totok*, or Dutch-born wife, never went along; she'd stay behind in Jakarta to enjoy her afternoons at the country club, shopping for Surakarta silk dresses at METRO, or getting into a state because the local supermarket didn't stock feta cheese. Imke didn't mind. She enjoyed the quality time spent with her papa in the Sulawesi highlands; she loved following him about as he strode confidently, amboyna wood walking stick in hand.

Life was good to Imke. She went to the British International School, grew up speaking English like Kate Winslet, Dutch like Famke Janssen and Bahasa Indonesia with the subtle inflections of an expat. She made solid friends. Each year she auditioned enthusiastically for the Christmas pantomimes; she joined the Brownies and played knee ball with her Girl Scout pals, and although she dreaded her piano lessons and never practised, she could bash out a version of 'The Pink Panther' if called upon.

When not in South Sulawesi with Papa, excursions to KidZania or the water park took up most weekends. Afternoons were sometimes whiled away at the 21 Cineplex. Evenings meant barbecues and pool parties. And every summer the family returned to visit Aunty Erica in Europe. But then the Asian financial crisis struck. The Sneijders, keen to avoid the ensuing riots and violence in Jakarta, fled to Holland. A month later Imke was at her new school in Amsterdam, doing jumping jacks in *groep 8* PE class in her shorts and black plimsolls, pulling Wilma Wentink's braid.

Imke's gaze took in the passing scenery, and without warning she found herself longing for her father. The red-brown earth, the shacks made from wood and scraps of tin, the scuttling chickens, the roadside fruit, all snatched at her soul. Everything reminded her of him and her idyllic childhood.

She looked at her iPhone and made a call.

'Papa!' cried Imke when he picked up.

'_____'

'Yes, we've landed. It's just as I remember!'

'_____'

'We're on our way to Bogor now. On the verge of a new adventure.'

'_____'

'About an hour's drive, depending on traffic.'

'_____'

She looked at Erica. 'Right, yes. I'm sure she will. Ha, ha.'

'_____'

'How much rain?'

'_____'

'Wear a hat when you go out. Or at least take an umbrella. Don't go walking in that old Burberry trench coat without a hat. Dust off that ancient deerstalker of yours. Promise?'

'_____'

'You don't want to catch a cold with your birthday coming up.'

'_____'

35

'Say hi to Mama. OK. I'll call again soon.'

'____'

'Oh, and Aunty Ecks says to remember to go to her place on Sunday night and take out the rubbish. The bin man comes Monday morning.'

'____'

'Did you separate the potato peelings from the plastic, he says.'

Erica made a cluck of disapproval.

'Love you.'

'____'

'Bye.'

The car progressed at a stately pace.

'He sends his love and says it hasn't stopped raining since we left.'

As they passed through a small village, Aunt Erica began humming Whitesnake's 'Summer Rain'. She waved at the villagers with a stiff hand, like a dowager in a carriage. Occasionally someone would wave back and shout, 'Hey *bule!*'

'How charming. Are they shouting "*buur*", the Dutch word for neighbour?' asked Erica with a smile.

'*Bule* means foreigner,' explained Nakula.

Her face dropped. 'Preposterous, isn't it? You don't see me hanging my head out of the window and shouting, "Hey yokel!" at everyone who passes.'

A small plump man with a large plump face greeted them at Bogor Palace with a salaam. Imke thought he had to be the roundest Indonesian in the world. He wore a cinnamon-coloured safari suit that did nothing to hide his roly-poly *nasi goreng* belly. '*Selamat datang!* Welcome!' he chimed, bowing with a dramatic flourish and introducing himself as the head of the household staff. 'You may call me The Captain.'

They stood in the foyer of the magnificent white mansion, amongst the polished pink marble of the pilasters, capitals and festoons.

'You will be staying at one of the private bungalows on the estate grounds.' He pointed to his left. 'Just over there, by the lake. A personal housekeeper will attend to your needs. And if you wish, afternoon tea can be taken here, at the Istana, each afternoon at 4 p.m. Usually, we are open to the general public, but not whilst you are here. The only interruption will be the Cabinet meeting SBY is hosting next week.' He hopped on his toes and his belly wobbled. 'Apart from that, the grounds are yours. Oh, and Mrs Erica, all requested art materials and equipment are awaiting you at the bungalow.'

A page brought in a tray of drinks, followed by others offering moist, scented towels. Each moved about dozily, as if they'd just climbed out of a hammock.

'*Bajigur*,' announced The Captain. 'A beverage made from crushed-ice, coconut milk, pandan leaves and ginger.'

'And here was me expecting a Kir royale,' mumbled Erica.

Imke sipped the *Bajigur* and dabbed her face with the moist cloth.

'When will I be meeting the President?' asked Erica, cheerily.

He bowed his head. 'When it suits SBY's busy schedule.'

'Ooooh, look!' exclaimed Erica, gesturing through the air. 'Wouldn't that view make a wonderful backdrop for the portrait! What a beautiful lake. I can see it now, dark lounge suit, red tie, shiny hair, strong eyebrows, medals pinned to his chest. I presume he wears his medals. Does he have them on his chest or on a necklet? Anyway, we'll just have to see, won't we? And I can drape him in a yellow scarf to bring out his inner child!' The ideas rattled in her head like seeds in a gourd.

The Captain's eyes darted towards the main entrance. Outside, a mild commotion surrounding an invasion of toads broke out.

Imke heard a noise that sounded like croaking – a loud *grooook!* – followed by a chorus of *grooookup!*

A knot of warty amphibians had apparently taken over the palace's fountain. 'You must excuse me,' said The Captain. 'We have an infestation. Somebody is threatening to throw petrol on the water and set the toads alight.' He rushed away to give the gardeners a scolding.

'Or perhaps he ought to be darkly lit in sharp chiaroscuro,' deadpanned Erica. 'No. Too harsh, too baroque.'

Imke rubbed the red indentation left by her sun hat.

A quarter of an hour later the portly man in the safari suit returned, twirling a silver pen between his fingers.

'We have many toads here,' he divulged with a shake of the head. 'But we also have several hundred beautiful deer that graze in our gardens.'

'I'm sure we will get to know the Istana and all its glory in due course,' Imke held her floppy hat in her hand, threatening to use it as a fan, 'but we've had an awfully long journey.'

The Captain's eyes widened, as though snapped from a trance. 'But of course, of course. You must rest in your bungalow.' He spun his pen and glared at his staff, and with an accusing voice asked them why they had foolishly kept the *Eyang Putri* waiting.

The bungalow was a short walk from the palace, standing back a little from the road. On the left side was a small bamboo thicket, and on the right ran a lane leading to the staff quarters. They entered the white stucco bungalow and Erica clapped her hands in delight. A wooden crate welcomed her. One side of the pitch-pine planking was levered away, revealing multiple-sized canvases, easels, brushes, paints, sketchbooks and pads. In the sitting room, she flopped onto the leather sofa. 'Look how bright it is inside! And don't those wonderful cabinets contrast well with the turquoise cushions.' She sprung to her feet, peeked inside the cabinet and was delighted to find a DVD player with a selection of Hollywood films to choose from, and a 56-inch flat-screen Samsung television set into the wall. 'Oh, I do hope the verandah catches the morning sun off the lake,' she cried, sliding open the patio double doors. 'Don't you just love it here, Imke? It smells of lilies and old teak floors warmed by the sun.'

In her suite overlooking the water and sprawling lawns, Imke unpacked her things, listening to the lingering bird tweets coming from the nearby trees. The room was bright and airy and decorated in a neutral colour palette complemented by rich blues and daffodil-yellow hues. And it was vast; it took her nine long strides to cross from her bed to the en-suite bathroom. Imke approved. The art on the walls was fetching too. She especially liked the framed lithograph of Arie Smit's *Balinese Boy* hung above the bed. She hummed to herself cheerily, unfolded her nightgown and laid it out on the chaise longue. Next, she removed her shoes from the suitcases and lined them up against the wall. Seeing them all in a row made her feel at home.

Minutes later, she was at the washbasin arranging her creams, serums, lip liners and eye shadow in a long column across the shelf. She grabbed one of the Body Shop bottles and dabbed a pea-sized dollop of lotion onto her hands and elbows. A few moments afterwards, she removed the vase of lilies from her room and placed it in the corridor, on a table beside a vintage Bakelite phone. She shrugged apologetically at Erica. 'Gives me an itchy nose.'

Imke undressed and slipped into some long shorts and a coral plunge-neck top, checking in the mirror to ensure that her cleavage wasn't showing. Have to be respectful to my hosts, she decided, best to dress modestly. She brushed her lifeless hair. Was that a pimple forming on her cheek, she wondered? Better daub some Vitamin E oil on it later. And what was the story with those eyebrows? They leapt off her face like fuzzy caterpillars. Talk about a bloody monobrow! What on earth had Ruud thought? Frida bloody Kahlo! No wonder he ran off like that. Be thankful you don't have her thin little moustache too! She decided to pluck them there and then.

Five minutes of torturous plucking and pulling later, she dabbed at the tender pink flesh between her eyes and put her tweezers away.

With Kiki curled under a bureau, busily chewing one of her squeaky toys, Imke went to place a photograph of her parents beside her bed, when she spotted an envelope on the bedside table addressed to her. She tore it open and read the note, which was written in a hand that would have given a graphologist a considerable amount of trouble. It read:

'Welcome to Istana Bogor, Imke Sneijder, daughter of Thys Sneijder. May your short-lived stay in Indonesia be fraught with enlightenment.'

It was not signed.

How odd, she thought. Imke reread the message. Something about the phrasing made her feel uneasy. The use of the word 'fraught' was patently a translation gaffe, and the presumption that her stay would be 'short-lived' grated, but there was something else. How did they know to call her father Thys? Nearly everyone knew him as Mathias. Only her mother ever called him Thys. Had The Captain written the note? Had President Yudhoyono?

She sat on the edge of the bed, sifting through a slow rush of thoughts, feeling suddenly alone and amiss. She stared at the palms of her hands as if they held a secret that would help her. Eventually, after several minutes, her hands formed into fists and she struck the tops of her thighs. She read the note one more time.

Chapter Five

The sun was dying.

Ruud's office was on the second level of the Central Police Station on Jalan Kramat Raya. The walls were the colour of an unwashed parsnip and carried a feint aroma of root vegetables; on them hung a large map of South Jakarta and a portrait of General Sutarman, the Mighty Overlord.

Outside, on the streets, drivers pressed vigorously on their horns. The noise of the traffic seemed never-ending.

He removed his shoes and cooled his socked feet on the smoothed concrete floor.

'Not some common curry-sauce variety homicide, are you?' he said to himself, leafing through Mari Agnes Liem's file.

Through the gap in the half-open door he saw a woman emerge from the elevators. The sight of her made him straighten up with a jerk. The woman was marching towards him. She wore a silk *kebaya* and generous smearings of Tiger Balm, which he could smell at twenty yards. Like many Indonesian women, she did not wear a headscarf.

'Your mother-in-law is here!' someone yelled.

She burst into the 12×12-foot room.

'How can I help you this evening, *Ibu mertua*?' Ruud said with a strained smile.

'My daughter's running around with some young playboy and you ask how you can help? Go talk to your wife. Tell her to stop making the family look bad, that's what you can do.'

'My *ex*-wife. We're divorced. She left me for another man, remember?'

'Remember? No way can I forget. Now she running around with some playboy!'

'I'm in the middle of a murder investigation.'

'Good! Why not say the playboy did it and throw him behind bars. Hit two flies with one slap!'

Ruud smiled politely. He could almost hear the muscles in his jaw tightening. Talking to her was like chewing on a hot pepper; it was just a matter of how much he could take. 'Why do you keep coming here, *mak*? Your daughter and I are separated. I mean, no offence, I like seeing you and all but . . .'

'Where you find body? In culvert?' She spoke over him. 'Body must be full of worms, *meh*?'

'I'm afraid I cannot disclose any information about the case.' He shuffled the papers on his desk and checked emails in order to look busy.

Police Commissioner Joyo T. Witarsa shambled into the small space. He was a grumpy, growling man, about 6 feet tall, with a bloodhound face and a splayfooted walk. He brought to mind a cheap Walter Matthau.

'Who', he asked, looking around without turning his head, 'is this?'

'My ex-mother-in-law.'

The woman gave a nod. 'You may address me as Nyonya Panggabean.'

'Pleasure . . . to meet you,' drawled the commissioner. He

often spoke this way, emphasizing the first word of a sentence and then mumbling the remaining words under his breath.

'I hear there is big murder investigation. My son-in-law tells me body found in culvert.'

Ruud clenched his jaw.

'Face bloated and full of worms is what he say.'

Ruud's lips tightened. 'I *never* said that! And for heaven's sake stop calling me your son-in-law!'

The commissioner opened a can of Calpico, tasted it and then drank with a vague air of annoyance.

'His wife and her playboy lover make loud sex in my house every night. You should hear the noise.'

'OK!' blurted Ruud. 'I don't know why you would want to share that.'

'So loud it makes neighbourhood dogs howl.'

The older man bent forward at the waist à la Oscar Madison and mumbled something under his breath. Ruud didn't catch it but his ex-mother-in-law did; she tossed her head back and laughed with complicit delight.

Ruud felt the heat rise in his cheeks.

Some women when they laugh can make a man feel like a simpleton. Mrs Panggabean was such a woman.

'Is there something you wanted to see me about?' asked Ruud, gazing at his boss.

'Mari Agnes Liem.'

'What about her?'

'I've got the whole department leaning on me.' The commissioner took a long sip from his can. 'Do you have any leads?' He took another long swallow. 'Theories?'

'My son-in-law said body found in culvert was murdered by a playboy he knows.'

'No, I did not!'

The chief let out a bemused grunt.

Mrs Panggabean's phone rang. She answered it.

Ruud grabbed his chance and fled the room.

7.05 a.m. Jagakarsa, South Jakarta.
The first pinpricks of daylight.

Below the neon HERO signboard, two detectives took statements from the supermarket manager and several of his employees, mainly cleaners and delivery staff.

Ruud Pujasumarta was in his kitchen brewing coffee, dressed in boxers and his 'Conserve water, drink BEER' T-shirt, when the call came in. It took him just under fifteen minutes to reach the crime scene.

Having climbed out of his Toyota Yaris, he stood on the pavement sucking in lungfuls of air, steeling himself for what lay ahead. He'd seen it all in the last seven years: machete attacks, street stabbings, parking-lot shootings, husband killings, boyfriend bludgeonings, gangster garrotings, clergymen cooked in their cars, decapitations, poisonings, hit-and-runs, drive-bys, executions, electrocutions and eliminations. The rope, the gun, the chain, the knife, the axe, the lead pipe; scissors, hammers, kitchen knives, golf clubs, snooker cues, screwdrivers, wrenches, Samurai swords; he'd seen the lot.

His mind burned.

He was rarely spooked. As a kid, he'd walked past the Islamic cemetery every day to school and felt nothing. He'd sat through his cousins' midnight ghost stories and experienced not even a shiver. *The Exorcist*, albeit a dreadfully dubbed version, had bored him, and the 2007 blockbuster *Angker Batu* almost sent him to sleep. In fact, the whole idea of living demons, Sumatran forest devils, spiked ghouls and spiny monsters was ridiculous to Ruud. But murderers were different. They spooked him. They spooked him because they were palpable and solid. Their spikes and spines were all too real.

And the body that lay mangled in front of his eyes was testament to this.

Ruud approached the cordoned-off back alley, straddling the yellow *Garis Polisi* barrier tape, towards the exit door that flashed *KELUAR*. The miry street was slippery from overnight rain. Instinctively, he began to trace every line, every length and configuration of the crime scene, like an animal marking his territory.

He saw Hamka Hamzah dealing with the media circus, talking to reporters, keeping the press vultures at bay, forcing the camera crews behind the demarcation line.

He pulled the officer to one side.

'Same situation like before, *nih*,' said the little man, scratching the scalp beneath his beret. Ruud noticed for the first time that he wore his hair parted down the centre. 'Two female victims in seven days.' His voice was raised to counter the Jakarta traffic noise. Already, the city was in full cry. Motorcycles buzzed along like droning Flymos. The booming bass of a passing car bent its own windows. 'Two women, both with their left hands chopped off.'

Ruud patted his trouser pockets. He wanted to make notes. 'I forgot to bring a pen and paper. You got a biro?'

'I gave you my pen last time. You still have it.'

Ruud dismissed the accusation with a shake of his head. He slid towards the mass of reporters and borrowed one from a *Globe* correspondent to jot down his observations clumsily on the back of a credit card receipt. 'Removing the left hand . . . strange. It must be punishment for a crime, or for violating some sort of trust.'

The dead woman stared at Ruud with a predatory gaze. Face fixed in a grimace, her teeth as white as maggots' flesh.

She lay broken; an avalanche of hair and limbs amongst jutting bottles and jagged fishbones. 'Do we know who she is?'

'No KTP card or any form of ID on her apart from a cell phone.'

'She was found dumped amongst the garbage?'

Hamzah nodded. 'One of her legs was hanging out of the industrial-sized refuse bin. We tipped it over and she fell out. Nobody touched anything.'

All of a sudden the second verse of the 'Cabe-cabean' ditty popped into Ruud's head.

> Cabe-cabean, Cabe-cabean, goats good and fed,
> Strolls to the dump kitchen-garbage on her head

'Who called in the crime?'

'One of the cleaners. A woman called Amira.'

'Has she been isolated and questioned separately?'

'Yes.'

'I want you to contact the local taxi companies. Check if any of their drivers saw anything. Same with the buses that travel this route. And the *bemos* and *mikrolet* cabs.'

In the sky above, the clouds bumped together, dark and bruised.

Ruud and Hamzah hovered over the corpse. They waited for Solossa, the forensic pathologist, to arrive. Ruud got down on his haunches and took a snap of the victim with his mobile phone.

'When you interviewed the old crone,' he asked. 'The mad one claiming she knew who killed Mari Agnes Liem, what exactly did she say?'

'Mrs Yahaya? She didn't make any sense. First she said it was the *Bugis*. Then she said it was the demon *Wewe Gombel*. Finally she said it was someone with a black hood who carried young ones away in a sack. Something about him punishing children who suck their thumbs by cutting off their hands.'

Ruud searched his pocket for his energy tablets.

'You believe in devils?' asked Hamzah.

'No.'

'I believe in devils.' His voice took on a serrated quality. 'I bet he's here.'

'Who?'

'The killer. I bet he's watching us right now from some dark crawlspace. I bet he's somewhere close by, checking us out.'

Ruud felt himself grow cold. The hairs on his scalp prickled and rose.

What is it that alters the atmosphere when people become frightened? Does it have a scent, a taste? Does the air literally warp with the altered vibrations? Ruud caught it – the dread – spreading from stomach to legs. And by the way Hamzah stared at him he knew that he felt the same.

Ruud held his breath and scanned the streets. He looked up at the buildings, at their long thin shadows, his eyes darting from window to window. He wondered if anyone had seen anything. Somebody was watching from behind a doorway; another from a rain-flattened hiding place. He was acutely conscious that dozens of faces were looking at him, sneaking glances from the shelter of curtains, from behind pillars, from the sanctuary of their cars. He could hear their silent voices.

'He's getting bolder.'

'How do you mean?' said Hamzah.

'He left this one out in the open.'

'So?'

'Someone could have seen him. Sooner or later he'll make a mistake.' Ruud repeated this several times to himself. He kept saying it over and over like a protective charm.

An officer came over and passed Ruud the statements. No eyewitnesses. Ruud gave them a cursory glance and handed them back. He wiped his mouth with a swatch of toilet tissue. His face was as pale as the paper.

Hamzah flicked a thumb over his ear. 'Look who has finally decided to turn up.'

'*Selamat pagi* to all!' cried Solossa cheerily. 'Is that rotting flesh I can smell?'

Solossa dropped his leather satchel and removed a comb from his shirt pocket. He ran the comb across his scalp, before sidling up next to Ruud. 'Has the fingerprint man come?'

'I'm getting an acute sense of déjà vu.'

'You are looking unnerved, First *Inspektur* Pujasumarta. A bit peaky. Are you feeling ill?'

'No more than usual when a corpse shows up before breakfast.'

Solossa had a stain on his shirt collar. It might have been blood. Most likely it was curry sauce. Ruud considered telling him, but decided against it. The stain looked a stubborn one.

The pathologist went to work.

After a while, Ruud asked if it was as he expected.

Solossa got to his feet. 'Same MO as last time. Signs of being manually strangled. But the cause of death points to choking. Left hand removed with a cleaver. Mah–jong tile lodged in the throat – the two circles – exactly as before. Except,' he paused to take a closer look, peering at the acrylic piece through the polystyrene bag, 'this time the bottom circle has been scratched away. See that? The blue circle's surface has been scraped off.'

'And like Mari Agnes Liem, the victim is Chinese.'

'Looks like it. Or at least part Chinese. Dead about twelve hours. No initial signs of sexual interference. Can't be sure yet if this is the primary crime scene. No sign of the missing hand?'

'We'll comb through the crime scene once you've signed off, but I'm pretty certain it's not here. I'll send a formal request to Polda Metro Jaya district command. It's time we got forensics involved, no matter the cost and lack of budget. Fibre and hair study, DNA analysis, the works.'

The police photographer reappeared and adjusted his angles. The flash went off.

Hamzah lit another *kretek* and inhaled greedily.

Ruud looked down at the victim's face once more. A thin line of ants drew a black syrup moustache across her mouth. Each ant carried a crumb of dried blood in its jaws. Ruud rubbed his own face with his hands and wondered again if someone dangerous was out there watching.

Someone was.

Chapter Six

The setting sun, so bright on the walls of the palace, turned the interior light golden.

Imke exhaled a loud sigh as her aunt, scowling, read the note. There was a long silence. Erica folded the note in two. She was dressed in the black top and jeans she always wore when she worked. 'Well, it's an imaginative welcome message, I'll give them that much. Not quite the usual invitation to the manager's cocktail party.'

'So you didn't get one too?'

'No, no note for me,' said Erica.

'I thought you ought to see it.'

They sat alone in the Teratai Room, relaxing under a grand chandelier, taking afternoon tea. The plush silk settees were especially comfy. 'Are you OK?'

'I'm fine.'

'Sure?'

'Of course.'

'It's just that you have the same face as when you eat Brussels sprouts.' This made Imke roll her eyes. 'You look so much like your father sometimes,' observed Erica. 'It makes me smile. I'll have a word with The Captain if you like. Find out who left it.'

'No, please don't, Aunty Ecks, there's no need.'

Erica nodded. On a plate with a doily were some local treats. 'I assume it's a case of lost-in-translation, cows that say boo and that kind of thing. God above only knows what would happen if I were to write a note in Javanese. It would probably instigate a coup d'état!' She took a sip from her bone-china teacup and inspected the plate of snacks. 'What did they say this was?'

'Those are fried soy beans. The round ones next to them are *kerupuk*, deep-fried tapioca crisps. Hard and crunchy.'

'Sounds great.'

Imke smiled again. 'You can't say the word "great" without being sarcastic, can you?'

'Probably break my teeth,' mumbled Erica.

'Go on, try one.'

'Do you think I should?'

Imke shrugged good-naturedly.

Erica took a tentative bite of *kerupuk*.

'*Hee hee hee!* Look at your expression!'

Crunching, Erica raised an eyebrow. 'Not as tasty as sour cream and onion but can't complain.'

They rose from the sofa and meandered into an adjoining drawing room, cups and saucers in hand. Kiki followed them from one room to the other. 'It's odd staying in the bungalow and not at a hotel. So different in many ways. I mean, what are you allowed to raid for free?'

'I noticed all the soaps and shampoo in your bathroom have already gone.'

'Well, it is Acqua di Parma, what do you expect?'

'So how was your first session with the President?'

Erica draped an arm over Imke. 'You know, he's really quite cultured,' she whispered, as though telling a secret.

'I'm sure he is.'

'And very knowledgeable – he revealed all manner of things. Did you know that chewing tea leaves quenches thirst? He also explained how to spot a genuine Affandi from a forgery, and said we must visit a town called Jelekong in Bandung. There are five thousand people living there and thirty-five per cent are artists.'

'Did he reveal any juicy gossip?'

'Oh, this and that. He confessed that George W. Bush was so blundering at the G-Twenty summit that he . . . actually I promised him I wouldn't tell a soul.'

'Liar.'

'And he has quite a collection of hand-drawn maps from the nineteenth century, mostly of the Dutch East Indies, Batavia and Celebes. I asked him what he hoped to do when his term ends this October, and do you know what he said? He's thinking about opening a fried rice restaurant! Can you imagine? He's really quite amusing to chat with.'

'You sound like you fancy him, *hè*?'

'What nonsense! Although, admittedly, he is gruffly hand-some in a blunt, edgeless sort of way.'

'How much painting did you get done?'

'How much *painting*? *Goede God* girl I'm not a handyman priming his kitchen walls!'

'All right then, how many brush strokes did you leave on your precious canvas?'

'Why, none at all.'

'I knew you'd say that!'

'One must sacrifice days, weeks even, to get under the subject's skin. I can't create the way I do unless I can give a shape to my emotions. I made some preliminary sketches of the way he moved, where he placed his hands, that sort of thing.'

'So you spent two hours scrutinizing him.'

'You make him sound like a laboratory rat.' Erica paused and glanced out onto the lawns. Several dozen policemen and security staff in military fatigues and dark glasses milled about, mobilized on account of the President's visit. There were camera crews there too, hoping for a newsworthy photo op. 'No, as I say, he is really rather chatty. I was surprised to learn that he tries his hand at writing love ballads.'

'You *do* fancy him!'

'Oh stop it! But I hasten to add that we do share a kind of forced intimacy. Imagine two strangers being stuck in one of those tiny Parisian elevators for three hours.'

A gong reverberated in the distance. Imke and Erica dashed to the main entrance and stood in the foyer with the household staff, which had all lined up to say farewell to the President.

'He's going?' whispered Imke out of the side of her mouth.

'Spending a few days with his family at Cikeas.'

The President swept past. Everyone, including the two Dutch women, bowed, inclining their heads, like flowers turning toward the sun as he withdrew into a waiting black vehicle.

Moments later everyone dispersed.

'Oh look, here comes The Captain.'

The round man waddled over. He was dressed in uniform today, a black blazer with shiny embroidery on the cuffs and silver pins on his lapel. The front buttons on his blazer strained as he offered a quick bow. 'Salaam. Your request has been granted,' he announced.

Imke regarded his large, circular face. Her eyes lit up. 'To see my old home? The apartment where I grew up? You've got permission from the owners?'

'Yes. I have arranged for you to be driven there by car tomorrow morning. Nakula will take you. The current tenants are out of town so you will not be intruding.' He turned to Erica. 'Good news. SBY informs me that he enjoyed his time with you today. He will spend the weekend at his Cikeas residence, but has allocated two hours of his time for a sitting next Tuesday. I hope that pleases *nyonya yang kita sayang.*'

Erica's mouth broadened into a smile.

Imke shot her an amused, knowing look.

'You look nice.'

Imke twirled to reveal her colourful outfit before climbing into the Mercedes. She waved from the car window. 'See you later!'

'Enjoy yourself!' cried Erica, waving back and blowing a kiss.

She was on her way from Bogor to central Jakarta. An hour later she was still in the car. The traffic jams on the Jagorawi Toll Road were relentless. Imke kept her window open for a while. She liked to take in the smells and sounds of the city, but only if the car was moving, with the asphalt rushing by. She breathed in a lungful of diesel exhaust and wound up the glass.

'Have you worked long as a driver, Nakula?'

'Only six weeks, mam.'

'And before?'

'Not easy to get a good job in Jakarta. So I do this and that.'

Imke nodded, gazing at the road ahead, hoping to draw memories from her surroundings. 'Are we almost there?'

'Soon,' replied Nakula.

'Good.'

She was exhilarated. She'd waited so long for this. Unlike the other day, when she'd felt guarded speaking to Nakula, today she was unrestrained. While she remained mildly suspicious of any new person she met, she was equally eager to find out more about life in Jakarta. For a while she felt like a little girl again, asking about everything: the food, the weather, the new buildings under construction, the old buildings that were demolished. The chauffeur responded as best as he could, his voice passive in the morning heat. Imke felt she already knew the answers to most of the questions but she enjoyed hearing verification. After a while, like a child coming down from a sugar high, Imke fell quiet. She stared out of the window and took in the city.

Imke grew up in a condominium along Jalan Gajah Mada. She could see the waterway from her bedroom on the fifteenth floor. Long ago, fishermen threw their weighted nets into the conduit to catch shrimp and crabs. But the latter half of the twentieth century was cruel to the Molenvliet; it succumbed to the demands of the metropolis; rubbish accumulated and drains became blocked. On bad days, when the wind was not in their favour, the Sneijders could smell the sewage drifting across. It seeped in through fastened windows and shuttered balcony doors. The real estate agent had failed to highlight this particular unpleasantness. No doubt the stench became one of the reasons why Imke's mother spent so much time at the country club.

Imke, on the other hand, didn't mind the smell so much. Her *babu*, Pini, used to tell her that people from the shanties

56

often washed their clothes in the canal, but Imke didn't believe her. Surely, the water was too black, she would say, the clothes would come back dirtier. Those people had no choice, said Pini, they could not always rely on rain water to clean their washing.

As Nakula's black Mercedes cut through the Jakarta traffic, skirting the muddy escarpment, Imke sat alone in the back, recalling this conversation. She wondered what had happened to her *babu*. Pini had worked for the Sneijders for twelve years, practically raising Imke. She was from Yogyakarta and had a smiley face with big cheeks. She cooked a mouth-watering *bubur ayam* (chicken congee) and always ate them with *emping* crackers. She associated Pini with the smells of freshly inked batik, with satays, with *gado-gado*.

They passed the Hotel Grand Paragon – or the Grand Pull-the-plug-on, as Erica liked to call it. Imke smiled. Erica always managed to make her smile. Earlier, she'd asked whether she should come and see the condominium too, but Imke insisted it was something she wanted to do alone.

Erica was pleased to hear this. 'I have a lunch appointment with my man Cadbury.' She held her elbow at 90° and bit into an imaginary giant Creme Egg. 'So no need to hurry back. And don't worry, I'll keep an eye on Kiki.'

She checked her phone. There was a text from Ruud asking her for lunch. She smiled and pictured his face, the eyes demanding contact. She tried to remember how they'd met. He was Melchior's son. Melchior Pujasumarta worked for the Association of Indonesian Coffee Exporters. His wife was a Dutch-Australian who taught English at BIS. They had two boys, Ruud and Arjen. Was it Arjen? Imke couldn't remember. All she could recall was that Ruud's brother had a few behavioural problems, hated green vegetables, despised cats and liked to keep to himself. Whenever she talked to him he refused to look her in the eye. The Pujasumarta family came over for barbecues at least once a month. And now Ruud was all grown up; tall, handsome, energetic, and a police detective no less – and not at all strident or angry as some policemen tended to be.

Her fingers hovered over the dial button. 'Not yet,' she said to herself. 'Call him later, *hè*?' She tucked the phone back into her bag.

A young boy falls in love with *Putri Salju* – Snow White – that was what Ruud used to say to her, half-jokingly. It always made her laugh.

The car stopped at a set of lights, behind a lorry exhaling huge puffs of oily smoke. A little further along, where the road met the canal, a police cordon was set up. Three marked vans had parked against the water's edge and several policemen shouted instructions to a group of divers on a barge. Not far away, young boys from the squatter settlement jumped into the shallows. They wore goggles made of rubber bands and the ends of soda bottles. There were about a dozen of them, excitedly dipping in and out of the filthy channel.

'What are they searching for, Nakula?' asked Imke.

The chauffeur eased the Mercedes alongside the marked vans and lowered his window. He leaned his head out and spoke to one of the officers. At first, the policeman seemed disinclined to answer his questions but, on seeing the presidential licence plates on the car, he offered an explanation.

'There has been a murder,' Nakula said, speaking into his rear-view mirror. 'The police say that something was thrown into the canal. They are trying to recover it.'

'You mean the weapon?'
'No. *Tangan, tangan.*'
'Tang–nan?'
'A hand. A human hand.'

One moment Imke was living in the city of her birth. Laughing with Pini, dancing to the sounds of the local radio, laughing like it was a sacred thing, her breath throbbing and retreating.

And then . . .

The relocation people were in her apartment, all dressed in Allied Pickfords orange. They took books from shelves, wrapped pots and pans in newspaper, placed crockery in bubble wrap, and with deft professionalism they packed everything in cardboard. It took them eleven hours to strip her home. She wasn't even allowed to say goodbye to her school friends.

Nothing had prepared Imke for this. This void. This leaving Indonesia behind. The country had really got its fishhooks into her. 'You'll love your new home and you'll get over it in time' was what her mother kept saying, but what Imke felt as the plane took off was a collapsing within herself. As if the scaffolding of her ribs was set alight, as if something hot and dark had burned a hole inside her and torn everything down. She missed Pini. She missed the hubbub of the streets, the ABBA songs blaring in public places, the lush vegetation. She missed the food. She missed everything. Especially Ruud. But most things are forgotten over time, rubbed away to a murky smudge and, as Nietzsche wrote, 'Without forgetting, it is quite impossible to live at all.'

She received sympathetic pats on the head from her father

and hugs from her mother, but the feeling of loss persisted. Her father bought her *poffertjes* to make her feel better. After a while the smell of the pancakes and the sugary butter made her feel sick.

The first week in Holland was the worst. Imke found it difficult adjusting to her new school. The students, already in their own little cliques, viewed her with suspicion, particularly when they discovered she was from Indonesia. 'Are you from the jungle?' they teased. She looked them in the eye and laughed. 'Yes,' she said, 'I was born in a tree house on the foothills of Krakatoa.' It sounded good and some of them believed her, but nobody extended a hand of friendship.

Papa, who was protective at the best of times, started treating Imke as if she were a rare porcelain vase. If he could have wrapped Imke in Allied Pickfords bubble wrap he would have. But the more he fussed the more she resented it. She hated being seen as the little girl lost. So Imke, like so many children looking for escapism, turned her attentions to the gogglebox. Each day following classes, she ran home and glued herself to *Animal Planet* with a plate of Jan Hagel cookies. She ended up watching so many episodes that by the age of fifteen she knew the repeats by heart. When she saw her first episode of *K-9 to 5*, a show about Alsatians and a Belgian Malinois with everyday jobs, she knew what she wanted to do in life.

She left school at eighteen and her passion saw her enrolling at the KNGF Geleidehonden where she learned to train guide dogs for the visually impaired. She met a few boys, dated several of them, but never appeared to be in love with them, or even remotely infatuated. Was it because, unlike her, they hadn't been third culture kids? Was it because none of them had spent any significant time outside Holland? She couldn't be sure.

Five years later, having qualified and then excelled as an instructor, she joined the Police Dog Service (DLHP), training canines to recognize single specific scents. She first took a house on the outskirts of the city, a rural neighbourhood with fields of flowers and snags of wool on wire fences. Later, she moved to Westlandgracht to be near its people and parks.

Yet something about Indonesia still nipped at her. The scratch that it left behind itched her chest like a ravenous tick. It got so bad that even the smells from the Javanese kitchen on Nieuwe Doelenstraat put her in a funk. So, in order to unwind, she went for long rambles in Vondelpark. Each night she led her dogs, striding confidently, walking stick in hand, feeling the lines of her father's cane, the one he'd carved himself out of amboyna wood. And for some reason this placated her. But she was never truly becalmed. It wasn't as if she was unhappy; she surrounded herself with people who made her laugh, who helped her when she needed them. It was just a feeling deep inside her, a feeling of something unresolved.

She suspected she knew why. As a third culture child she didn't quite know where she fitted in the world. She was Dutch but she didn't feel completely Dutch. She didn't even feel completely European. She was quasi Asian with a drizzle of Nederlander and a sprinkling of Englishness. Dutch pea soup with a side order of *sambal* and HP Sauce.

Is that why she lived in Westlandgracht, an Amsterdam suburb that increasingly attracted Turks and Moroccans and Indonesians? Is that why she sometimes felt so messed up and lonely? If she were to take out a personal ad in *De Telegraaf* it would probably read something like:

Java-born daughter of Dutch Christian/Calvinist parents living amongst Muslim community would like to meet dog-loving, footloose, well-travelled man with an insatiable desire for squeaky toys. Must be able to cook *nasi goreng* and mix a mean *jus alpukat*. Sense of humour optional.

Yes, there was no denying it, Indonesia had claimed her – and then lost her. And, ever since, she'd been mourning that loss, that sense of rootlessness. Hers was an unresolved grief of leaving something behind. It probably explained why she'd returned, because she certainly hadn't come for a holiday. Imke was in Indonesia to find something far bigger than a holiday.

What she'd come for, she decided, was closure. Though, truth be told, she didn't know how she was going to find it. She supposed the important thing was to come and look for it, no matter what form it took. But what if closure didn't exist, thought Imke. Didn't everyone have a few tangled loose strings that couldn't be tidied up? Perhaps nothing is ever over.

The car came to a stop by the guardhouse. A large brass sign read: 'Majestic Heights'. By now, Imke was bursting with a mixture of curiosity, trepidation and excitement. It was the same kind of feeling she'd experienced as a little girl when her mother first took her to see the reptiles in Ragunan Zoo.

She stepped out of the car. This was the place of her earliest memories.

There was a raised pond and a fountain in the centre of the driveway. She saw the tiny square of grass where she had jumped rope. It was here that she'd dozed in Pini's arms; here that she'd sat eating peanut butter biscuits; here that she'd learned to ride a bicycle.

She could still remember the feel of the pond water through her fingers, the tangy smells of the gardener's Gudang Garam cigarettes and the colours of the trees. This little spot she'd once called home; its fabric remained engraved on her soul.

Imke took the elevator with Nakula to the fifteenth floor. The square number buttons that lit up when you pressed them had been replaced. She hesitated at the entrance for several moments before ringing the doorbell. There was a jumble of children's shoes by the door. An Indonesian helper greeted them. It wasn't Pini, of course, but Imke felt a stab of disappointment nonetheless. The helper invited them in. The smell of pine-scented air freshener was cool and sharp.

Imke's eyes swept over the apartment. The living room was smaller than she remembered and the dining area darker, but this was it. The epicentre of her childhood, where the sound of her tiny feet echoed, barely skimming the floor as she ran along the corridor each morning. Dream-trails from that long-ago time.

The helper offered Imke a glass of water and informed her that she was free to look around.

Imke went from room to room.

The place had been completely redecorated but she still recognized parts of it.

'This is where my old height chart used to be,' she

beamed excitedly. 'Scribbled on the hallway wall.' She bounced on her heels and laughed in sheer delight. 'And this used to be my bedroom!' She remembered it was once pink. She saw it all, a collage of images: the *My Little Pony* bedspread, the *Madeline* stickers Blu-Tacked to the cupboard doors, her Little Lulu dolls on the window ledge. And later, posters of the Spice Girls and Hanson on the walls, her *Sabrina, the Teenage Witch* pyjamas tucked under her pillow with matching furry slippers on the bedside carpet. All gone. The room was now beige and white, turned into a home office and full of IKEA furniture. In years past her parents had filmed her first wobbly steps in this room, watching her career around on her glider in her striped romper suit, bringing them random toys with a jubilant 'Naaah!'

Her head was full of Papa: the great bear hug he gave her when he came home from work; her returning as big a hug as her small, skinny frame allowed; her head crammed between his bicep and chest, nose rubbing against his neck, the smell of Paco Rabanne on his skin, then being lifted up onto his shoulders.

Imke dropped to her haunches and reached down to touch the woodgrain of the floor. She was struck by a pinwheel blur of memories: tinkles of laughter. Giggling squeaks. Polly Pocket dolls. Mama in her Surakarta silk dress. The tasty slurp of chilled Ribena straight from the carton. Mouthfuls of French toast leaving powdered sugar on her chin. Sick in bed with chickenpox and being bored to death. Treasure hunts in search of whistles and tops.

She set off for the kitchen. The kitchen tiles were new. She saw a stranger's family photos pinned to a bulletin board; school notices and a child's artwork adorned the fridge. 'I used to feed my Barbies in here, nudging French fries to their plastic lips. And over there', she opened the back door that led to the fire escape, 'is where my father carved his initials. Look!' She pointed. Nakula and the helper looked. 'I think I can still see it.' She ran her finger against the surface.

There were so many emotions pulling at her heartstrings she felt a bit giddy. She retrieved her mobile phone and rang Erica. 'Aunty Ecks! Aunty Ecks! Aunty Ecks!'

'Imke! Imke! Imke!'

'I'm at the condo.'

'And?'

'I feel happy and excited and more than a little sad.' She knew she was talking too quickly but she couldn't help it.

'I told you you would.'

'Everywhere I look I see a tiny part of me, the way I used to be.'

She went into the master bedroom. The bed was where it used to be. The bed she used to bounce on every Sunday morning. The bed, her mother liked to tell her, where she was conceived. There used to be a wine stain on the rug. Imke bent down and touched the re-laid carpet.

'Just remember to breathe, OK? And Imke?'

'Yes, Aunty Ecks?'

'Love you.'

'Love you, too.'

A little later Imke stepped out onto the balcony and cocooned herself in a tiny circle of silence. A superfine haze blanketed the city.

She had longed for this, longed to return to where she had been at her happiest. She had this one thing left of her childhood, this aging expat condo with its teak cabinets and round rattan loungers and IKEA chairs. And she no longer wanted it. It was no longer her personal sanctuary.

Imke stood, stared unseeingly for several minutes, her face pink from the heat.

And then a man, his hand gently on her elbow, steered her to a chair. He offered her a glass of chilled water. He smiled. It was a smile that said I know how you feel. I understand. She smiled back. Seconds later the man she knew as Nakula dipped his head and took his leave.

Chapter Seven

Friday. 6.09 a.m.

I can sense his agitation.

He is a dry river, thirsty for a deluge.

Every morning he wakes with a sense of panic in his chest. I know because I am there to witness it and I see him wake with a jerk, his muscles tense, his defences on high alert. He has been like this for as long as I can remember. *Sih*, ever since the trouble started with that man.

It was dark. The call for *Dhuhr* prayers was still hours away. The man entered our room, smelling of stale alcohol. There was an unholy lustre in his eyes. He was Mother's friend, the 'gentleman caller' with the greedy laugh. We were small then, no more than five or six. Oh yes, I remember it as clear as day. The man was tall; the light from the hallway outlined his nakedness. He hovered over my brother, standing at the side of the bed. My brother pretended to be asleep as the man pulled back the blanket. He didn't dare open his eyes, but he was conscious that the man was stroking himself. It went on for a long time. As long as it took to sing the entire 'Nina Bobo' lullaby in my head. My brother kept his eyes clasped shut all along, even as the man gave a low grunt, splashing something wet by his feet. My brother thought it was the sap from a coconut palm.

He has not slept properly since that night.

Friday. 5.41 p.m.
I have to stop my brother. His actions have become intolerable. I plead with him. I threaten him. *Aduh*, but what a joke! He is not scared of me. My words, my actions, repeatedly fall on deaf ears. It is like pouring a cup of fresh water into the sea.

I try to reason with him. I change tack. I say, 'At least place crystals over her eyes to give her unimpeded vision in the afterlife.' I hope this will make him think of heaven and hell. Make him think of his actions and their consequences.

Not surprisingly, he dismisses my words. Perhaps he is already in hell.

He looks down at the woman by his side and removes his glove.

I watch as he embraces her throat. The same routine: one, two, three, four, five. All the fingers of the right hand on her vocal folds. He applies pressure.

She makes an awful noise. A small dark patch spreads steadily by her crotch. And then he releases.

The crimson mouth gag puffs out her face. I smile at this. I cannot help myself. Her jowls balloon like Louis Armstrong's cheeks. She breathes forcefully through her nose.

He frees her left wrist from its bindings and leaves the blade cooling on her flesh.

Seconds later the cleaver comes down hard. He pulls the gag away to admire her expression. The woman's mouth forms a round black hole.

There is blood in his hair and on his clothes. Her blood.

His hand returns to her windpipe. Violently this time.

Yes, I confess that my brother has a perpetual thirst. And it will not be quelled.

Friday. 11.05 p.m.
The air in the room is humid; the walls damp enough to cultivate mushrooms.

My brother is annoyed.

Fists clenched, he pounds on his head, beats them against his thighs. It looks like he may froth at the mouth.

In front of him, on the floor, is a 3-inch-thick urethane insulated box. He fills the bottom of the box with dry ice. I help him pack the empty space with wadded newspaper, lining the inside with sheets of Styrofoam.

He places the woman's hand inside. He covers it with more dry ice and closes the lid.

There are seven other boxes pressed up against the far end of the room. Six of them remain empty.

My brother is annoyed because the police are not doing their job.

He has left them the mah-jong tile as a clue, not once but twice, and still they cannot see what he wants them to see. He screams a jumble of words, laughing, giggling, yet angry at the same time. A sequence of words, like a cacophony of biblical tongues, shouted repeatedly over and over again. He slams the flat part of his hand against the table.

Then he grabs a pen, holds it like a dagger and scrawls images into the wall. The pen snaps in two from the force.

He works himself into a fury. So crazy he would set his own hair on fire.

He bangs his fist against the wall. This goes on for several moments. When he is calmer he stares at the bruised knuckles. He settles. The space around his rage is perfectly still.

I manage to pacify him. It is one of the advantages of being his sibling. I rub the skin of his knuckles and quieten him down. He needs me, he tells me. I am his second skin.

I keep rubbing the bones in his hand.

On a nearby table a mobile phone begins to vibrate. It is a text message from his work, giving him instructions for the following day. He scrolls through the pictures taken on the phone. There are about twenty recent photographs. I see the two victims. I recognize the crime scenes. There are several before and after shots.

'What do the *polisi* know?' he demands.

I tell him they know nothing. This news does not please him. He says it is up to me to steer them in the proper direction.

'All idiots. Pecking at the ground for clues like half-witted chickens. The commissioner,' he says, 'he spoke to those trash reporters and turned it into an alarmist carnival. He is the problem. He is clouding the issue, blowing smoke in everyone's eyes.' His face distorts as he says this. He pulls his lips back and shows his teeth, but it is not a friendly smile. It is the smile of a man pulling the wings off a fly.

My brother says he wants to maim him, lop off his *kontol* penis. But I am sure he will not. Nobody deserves to lose a penis, and I know that, despite all his bombast and bravado, he will not become distracted. He will stick to his plan. He will kill all the women first.

Chapter Eight

Ruud affixed photographs of the victims to the corkboard on the wall. Earlier, he'd written on an adjoining white-board, using the same red marker, the names of the victims, their addresses, approximate times of death and the first responders at the crime scenes. Now he put up a map of the city and, with the same red marker, drew a line connecting the two locations where the crimes occurred. Next, Ruud arranged the plastic chairs in a circle. He found people spoke more openly when seated that way. As he did so, Police Commissioner Witarsa shambled into the small space, his tall frame bent forward as though battling a stiff wind. He moved clumsily, his flat feet slapping against the floor.

Three male detectives followed Witarsa into the Incident Room. One of them was a Sumatran in his late thirties called Vidi, who wore a *Sunnah* beard and square bifocals. The other two were Aiboy Ali, ten years younger and clad in a black Megadeth T-shirt, and Werry Hartono, the child of the unit. At twenty, Hartono was straight out of the Police Academy at Semarang, graduating with a sub-second lieu-tenant rank. Untried and untested, he was a little pompous and not, in everyone's opinion, very bright. What's more, he insisted on speaking English to Ruud in order better to learn the language of his heroes, Benedict Cumberbatch and Martin Freeman from *Sherlock*.

Werry was undeniably one of those uptight fellows who ironed his underpants. What was the point of ironing your underpants, thought Ruud, if you spent the majority of your day kneeling beside a gunshot victim in 32°C heat with the sweat running down your back?

And to Ruud's dismay he wore a pinky ring on his right hand embossed with the logo of the Indonesian National Police.

Vidi, who always opted to wear his brown police uniform rather than civvies, pulled up a chair and sat down, squeezing a pair of spring-loaded finger strengtheners in each hand.

Ruud thumped the man's upper arm and said, 'Morning!' with a wide grin.

'You come to work so happy all the time, izzenit,' grumbled Vidi.

'It's your angelic face that fills me with joy, brother.'

'So?' Witarsa took a sip from his coffee cup. 'WHAT do you make of it all, Pujasumarta?'

'To be honest, very little, sir. The second victim has been identified as Shireen Zee, aged forty-five, worked for PT POS Indonesia, widowed, no children. Suffered exactly the same fate as Mari Agnes Liem. Everything points to the same perpetrator. Both died from choking. Initially they were manually strangled and then had their left hands amputated before clinical death. The same weapon made the cuts on both women. No signs of sexual assault. There's not much background data. Neither had criminal records or underworld links. Neither had any business conflicts or known enemies. Of course we are still looking into their lives, their relationships, friends, lovers, bad habits and bad debts, but right now all we have are two premeditated murders without any obvious motives.'

'There's always a motive.'

'At present, we can find little to connect the two victims – they had different jobs, went to different schools, had no personal or family connections. Phone records going back five years show they didn't call one another. One lived in the *kampung* slums, the other in a public housing block. They looked nothing alike. Their hair and clothing styles were not similar. One was small, the other heavyset. The only thing that links them is their age – they're both forty-five years old – and the fact that they were Tionghoas.'

Vidi retorted. 'Indonesia's got what, three million Chinese-Indos, izzenit?'

'COULD . . . the killings be racial?'

'It's possible, sir. I've sent a couple of the boys to Glodok market already.'

'And forensics?' asked the detective with the beard.

'The lab analysis came back with nothing consistent. We've searched both of their homes and haven't come up with anything. There's a pending toxicology report to see if the women were drugged, but other than that we've drawn a blank.'

'Not surprising really. He dumps the second victim in a pile of filthy rubbish, making it so contaminated with soil and plant material, fibres, mucus, broken bits of glass and God knows what types of chemicals that it's almost impossible to glean much from the lab work. Having said that, we found no trace elements, no body fluids and no fingerprints – visible, latent or moulded – at either crime scene. Everything was wiped clean. And the only hair and fibre evidence we discovered at Mari Agnes Liem's house is garbage.'

'Why?'

'The hair we found was monkey hair.'

Vidi squeezed his finger strengtheners.

Witarsa paced splayfooted around the circle of chairs. 'You still think this is the work of loan sharks? Someone like Susanti?'

Slack-mouth Susanti was a gangster, a 'preman', and a member of the Betawi Brotherhood Forum, Jakarta's most notorious underworld gang. He owned the Leopard Karaoke Club on Hayam Wuruk and ran a number of gay bathhouses on Jalan Talang Betutu and Protocol Street.

The Leopard Karaoke Club was a multistorey entertainment complex. It employed a bevy of young women and had VIP rooms with 'locked doors', offering its clientele a guarantee of privacy and security. Everyone in the force knew it was a front for a brothel.

Ruud shook his head. 'Looking more and more unlikely. The killer's no paint-throwing *lintat darat*, that's for sure. And then there's this strange ditty he left us. I'm sure you're all familiar with the recent Cabe-cabean campaign, launched to tackle unwanted teenage pregnancies.'

'Still,' countered Vidi. 'Slack-mouth Susanti has a longtime history of maiming those who do not pay their debts, izzenit? We should bring him in for questioning.'

'I,' Witarsa took a long swallow of coffee, 'have to agree.'

'And what about the missing hands?' asked Vidi.

'We've dragged the canal by her house. So far nothing,' said Ruud.

'We've found nothing,' Aiboy Ali interjected, 'because he keeps them as souvenirs.'

Witarsa shifted his stance so that his flat feet were even wider apart. 'We need to get on top of this! I *need* results!'

he bleated. Ruud studied his boss's hangdog face. There were more stress lines than usual – perennially paranoid about getting the sack, he'd recently developed a tiny nervous twitch, a tic that made his left eyelid jump. Tetchy, mistrustful, insecure, he came to work each morning believing he was the victim of some elaborate political jostling and intra-divisional pettiness, that his walking papers were being drawn up, that he'd spend the rest of his days doing mall security at Grand Indonesia Shopping Town.

The police chief's cheeks quivered. 'There must be a connection between these two women. Look for cousins, boyfriends. Damn it, I don't care if they share the same newspaper boy! Get me something!'

'We're doing all we can, sir,' said Ruud. 'However, the question remains – why? Why is he doing this? And why does he keep the hands?'

'Like an Apache collecting scalps,' mused Werry Hartono, stroking his puppy-fat cheeks.

'Profile?' Aiboy Ali was in his late twenties, a year older than Ruud. He had long hair and wore 6-inch black leather biker cuffs on each wrist. Ruud liked his spicy aftershave smell and his playful nature, and he didn't mind that he often called him *Gajah* – meaning elephant – on account of his forgetfulness. Besides, humour during the ugly moments kept the unit sane. Nine times out of ten, when working a case, Ruud found himself without pen and paper to take notes. Sometimes he'd forget his warrant card, having left it in another pair of trousers. Once he even misplaced his car keys at the crime scene. The nickname both irritated and amused him at the same time.

Aiboy Ali was born to a Madurese family of cattle farmers. He had become a good friend. Initially the only thing Ruud knew about him was that he was a heavy metal freak and had a thing for some ungodly local band called Burgerkill. He would blast their horrendous clatter from his car stereo first thing in the morning and went out of his way to lend Ruud Burgerkill's entire discography, which Ruud did not even pretend to enjoy.

Ruud's neighbours across the hall had a teenager learning to play the drums, and the occupants of the flat above had a crying baby. He decided if he mixed together the combined din and threw in the sound of dishes crashing to the floor he'd produce something resembling his colleague's taste in music. Ruud was more of a Blur, Arctic Monkeys and Smashing Pumpkins fan, and although he sometimes discussed the merits of a good song, he drew the line at arguing and discussing who made up the top-ten greatest death metal groups of all time.

A joker and a prankster, Aiboy Ali also owned the filthiest of filthy laughs; a guffaw that suggested it rolled about in muck every so often. But he was a policeman first and foremost, so he kept the laughter to a minimum during work hours, as though he had a small latch in his chest to secure it shut.

'At this early stage,' reasoned Ruud, 'I can only give you a generic profile, but I'm confident he is not a visibly insane person with a weird hairdo and crazy eyes.'

'Assuming it's a man, *Gajah*,' said Aiboy Ali.

'I'm sure it's a man. Women do not dismember. Men do.' He paused. 'Expect a normal person. A loner perhaps, most likely an introvert, but at the same time controlling in relationships. No outward signs of perversion or sadism. However, I imagine he is somewhat withdrawn. Autopsy reports suggest both victims were strangled almost to the point of death, with severe pressure bruising to the leftward slant of the throat, indicating a right-hand bias. Given that neither woman was sexually assaulted, it's possible he could suffer from penile dysfunction and kills out of frustration.'

Ruud clenched his jaw. 'The question is, does he leave a signature, like a red rose or a calling card? And if so, why?' Ruud turned away from his audience.

Removing two 8×10 photographs from a cardboard folder, he pinned them to the wall side by side. 'This is the only real clue we've got.'

Ruud paused for a second to allow the room to take in the image. Everyone stared at the picture of the mah-jong tile.

Aiboy Ali spoke up. 'The mah-jong pieces from the two crime scenes are exactly the same.' He balanced an iPad on his lap. The Iron Maiden wallpaper flipped upside down as he jostled his knees.

'Yep. The circle tiles are known as *Tong zi*. In Cantonese the two circles tile is called *Leung Tung*, meaning literally 'the same', or 'two-of-a-kind'. The interesting thing is that one of the circles has been scratched away. By a knife or something equally sharp.'

'Why leave us clues?' said Vidi. 'I suppose you are going to tell me this gila-boy wants to get caught, izzenit.'

'No,' argued Ruud. 'It's not that he wants to get caught. He leaves clues because he feels he can't get caught.'

'SO, you are confident he will kill again.'

'Yes.'

'I have a question,' piped Hartono. 'Was Shireen Zee murdered at the crime scene or was she taken and dumped there afterwards?'

'Solossa and his pathology team believe the alleyway

behind HERO was the secondary crime scene. They think she was first killed elsewhere then moved.'

'Which means the pattern is different. Why not leave her to be discovered at her own home? Like Mari Agnes Liem?'

'Shireen Zee lived with her mother in a busy apartment block. There's no evidence to suggest she was murdered at home. My guess is the perpetrator thought it too risky. This fellow likes to take his time over his victims. He finds pleasure in the ritual torture and killing. Most likely he abducted Shireen Zee and took her to a deserted warehouse or abandoned lot and killed her there.'

'What about the security cameras at HERO?'

'There are surveillance cams at the rear of the supermarket. They only cover the rear exit and the manager's parking space. The alleyway behind and the rubbish bins are not in view. There is no visual confirmation showing anyone coming or going.'

'Pujasumarta,' beseeched Witarsa, his grumpy Walter Matthau face screwed up in quiet desperation. 'You have to give me something. Something to tell the generals. Going back to the mah-jong pieces. Is it possible the two circles reflect the perpetrator's state of mind? That by scratching one out it means he . . . may have been betrayed. By a friend. By his partner.'

'It's possible.'

'Maybe an ex-boyfriend or lover.'

'We're already looking into it. The tech boys are searching Shireen Zee's mobile phone records. We've also gone through the victims' calendars and diaries but found nothing to suggest they were meeting anyone. The same goes for Facebook and their email accounts. Neither woman had much of a social life.'

'CHECK if either registered with any online dating sites,' Witarsa said.

Vidi ran a palm over his scraggly facial tufts. He looked pale all of a sudden. 'Any prints on the tiles?'

'No prints whatsoever,' said Ruud. 'They were wiped clean. But we know they are part of a set known as 'China Green'. Manufactured in Guangzhou. Very common. Available to purchase on tokobagus.com.'

'Well, that's just bloody fantastic,' spat Witarsa, fighting a rear-guard battle to maintain his composure.

Ruud continued. 'So our first priority should be to find out why he stuffed these pieces into the victims' mouths, and their significance. Does he have a desire to be identified? Is it a cry for help? Or is it a simple red herring to lead us astray? The pattern of the crimes shows he is organized. That he is patient and pragmatic. This suggests the killer will display similar traits in his personal life.'

Aiboy Ali lifted the iPad from his lap. 'Says here on Wikipedia that mah-jong means 'the game of sparrows'. Shuffling the tiles at the start of a round sounds like twittering birds.'

Ruud scratched the back of his head. 'Gang bosses sometimes have sparrow tattoos inked into their arms.'

'A man with a sparrow tattoo is a person that is unbeholden to rules and is the master of his own destiny,' said Aiboy Ali.

'*Alhamdulilah!*' Witarsa's tired face grew animated, like a bloodhound picking up a scent. He karate-chopped the air with an arm. 'I knew this had something to do with those loan-sharks.' He bounced on his flat feet. 'Vidi, get off your arse and find out how much these women owed Slackmouth Susanti! And Pujasumarta, you're a First *Inspektur*. You have pebbles for eyes? Jackfruit for brains? There's your suspect. Bring him in. That's an order!'

Werry Hartono raised his hand. 'May I remind you, sir, that we should use the term "possible suspect", as declaring Susanti a suspect is an official judicial process in Indonesia.'

'Shut up, Hartono!'

80

Chapter Nine

Loo roll lay strewn across the wet floor.

The plastic dipper overturned.

The man tore off his bifocals and concentrated on the blank, white wall in front of his eyes. How he managed to reach the toilet cubicle without attracting attention was beyond him. Did they see him trembling at his desk? Had they seen him stumble in?

Nobody must know. Nobody must see him this way.

Here it comes!

The shakes. And the sweats. And the headaches.

He could feel himself changing.

He ran both hands through his *Sunnah* beard and muttered a silent prayer. His face grew taut.

Bent over on the toilet bowl, he began to count.

Seventeen, eighteen, nineteen, twenty . . .

When even counting became a struggle, he slapped his face several times.

He listened to his heartbeat thrumming in his head. The rate was increasing.

How could he be so careless and forget the kitbag? He could die without the kitbag, without the tester, without the clear plastic box of medication.

His fingers untwisted the ends of the sweet wrapper. The crumpled cellophane fell to the ground. He sucked on the boiled sweet.

He swallowed whatever saliva remained in his mouth and slid off the bowl. He fell back, resting his bottom on the floor and his head against the wall. The tiles were wet. He wanted to stretch out his legs but there wasn't enough space.

Deep breaths. Take long, steady deep breaths.

He felt his lungs fill with Clorox-tainted air.

The sweat had soaked his collar. He loosened the buttons of his uniform. Withdrawing the wallet from his trouser pocket, he seized the plastic insert and ripped it free. He screwed up his face to glare at the photograph of the woman.

He cursed her once, twice, then kissed her image.

A minute crawled by.

His hands stopped shaking.

But the headache remained sharp and pronged. A porcupine puffer fish swam behind his eyes, bumping against his frontal lobe.

A shriek of rubber startled him. The door to the men's room shuddered open.

He heard voices and footsteps.

The police commissioner entered and stood in front of a urinal. He was speaking with Ruud Pujasumarta.

The man with the *Sunnah* beard held his breath. He grabbed a wad of loo roll and wiped his brow.

Nobody must know. Nobody must ever see him this way.

Chapter Ten

The thinnest of moons lit the driveway of the bungalow. Toads hopped across the lawns. House lizards made small *chik chak* calls as they hunted mosquitoes and other insects.

Half asleep in bed, Imke lay drifting somewhere between dreaminess and waking. She turned over onto her face. Her shoulders stretched and loosened. Her left arm was numb. She shook it to force blood into her fingers. Her body relaxed. She began falling into the folds of a dark tunnel. Her breathing grew shallow.

In her sleep a sound came to her. Like a clink of metal dragged over stone.

A black shadow grew close. It hovered utterly still over her, its long white hair cascading down like poisoned milk, blocking out the light. A hand pinned across her face. Wind howled. Fingers pushed into her mouth. Her muscles froze.

'Wha . . . dhupp!' Imke jerked awake, her eyes wide. For several befogged seconds, she wasn't sure where she was, or how she'd ended up in a strange bed. She strained at the darkness and slowly recognized the contours of the room. A nightmare, she said to herself. Just a bad dream.

But something had woken her. A sound. A scratching. A footstep. A light, uneven tread. Something sharp, metallic, followed by a footfall and something flitting past. It came from outside her window. She blinked and blinked again. The heavy drapes were not drawn, but the net curtains were. The window was a faint charcoal rectangle in the dark. And something had scraped against it. This wasn't a dream. She sat up. Her heart pounded. She held her breath and for a long time she did not move. She wondered if the dream was still with her. She waited. When no fresh sound came, she breathed out and dismissed it as her imagination.

Half a minute later she heard a small branch breaking somewhere close. Her flesh shrank against her bones. She didn't dare switch on the bedside light but fumbled for her watch. The luminescent green hands glowed three o'clock. She got out of bed and, feeling her way, approached the far wall. Kiki growled, her black lips drawn back.

Imke placed a hand on a butterfly pleat and parted the net curtain to one side. There was no moon. The window-pane felt cold against her forehead. A smattering of starlight reflected off the surface of the lake. Black masses and shadows shifted amongst the distant woods. Her eyes darted from tree to tree. Nothing.

She listened. Silence. She took a deep breath and decided to return to bed.

Instinctively, she retrieved her phone and called home.

'Papa, it's me.'

'_____'

'Yes, it's late. The middle of the night. Three a.m.'

'_____'

'No. Nothing's wrong.' Her words sounded strained. 'I couldn't sleep.'

'_____'

'Yes, jetlag. I just wanted to hear your voice.' She thought of the note by her bed. She hesitated. 'Papa, did anyone apart from Mama ever call you Thys?'

'_____'

'I know it's a strange question.'

'_____'

'I'm just asking . . .'

'_____'

'No reason.'

'_____'

'Not everything has to have a reason.'

'_____'

'No one in Jakarta?'

'_____'

'No. I didn't think so.'

'_____'

'Papa, I wish you had come with us.'

'_____'

'I know. What's past is past, but . . .'

'_____'

'All right. I shouldn't have brought it up.'

'_____'

'Yes. OK. I'll go back to sleep.'

'_____'

'Me too. Bye.'

'_____'

'Bye.'

Imke exhaled and rubbed the side of her head. She'd pressed the phone so hard to her ear the rim ached.

She sat at the end of her bed and looked at the phone in her hand. She had an empty feeling in the pit of her stomach. Her relationship with her father had always been easy. He, rather than Mama, was her emotional bolster. When she was growing up in Amsterdam, following their return from Jakarta, Mama was responsible for everything in the house. She did the clothes shopping, prepared breakfast and supper, drove Imke to her sports days and music gigs and lessons. Papa, meanwhile, oversaw the emotional stuff, like the time when she was sixteen and her boyfriend Danny van Gestel snogged Cornelia Paumen at the school dance. It was Papa who'd sat anxiously in A&E at BovenIJ as doctors treated her injuries after she'd fallen off a moped while stoned on hash; he that gave her the stern talking to about drugs.

He was also in charge of museum tours and trips to watch Ajax play at the Amsterdam Arena.

At KNGF Geleidehonden Papa was the one she phoned whenever her self-confidence wobbled or if the course work became too hard or if one of her dogs fell sick. He'd always been there for her. Papa anchored her.

But ever since she'd decided to join Erica on this adventure, the mere mention of Indonesia caused friction. Why? Was it because he'd been forced to leave behind a job he'd loved? Was it because he never scaled the same professional heights again? Did he miss the trappings of an expatriate lifestyle so much that he loathed talking about it? Imke shook her head. None of it made sense.

God knows she'd tried to get him to join them on this trip, until in the end she'd given up hope and stopped bringing it up entirely. But now she wanted to bring it up. She called him back.

'Papa, what's the matter?'

He did not answer straight away. Several seconds ticked by. And in those seconds Imke analysed the silence. What was he hiding? What was it about Jakarta that sent him out of kilter? What wasn't he telling her? But he didn't give her the answer she wanted. Instead, he said he was just a silly old man and she wasn't to worry. He asked if it was hot, if the smog had lifted, if the rains had come. Anything to fill the silence.

After a while she hung up.

Bird song. The gentle clatter of cutlery.

A silver water-heated dish containing beef sausages and turkey bacon rested on the sideboard.

Imke sat at the breakfast table with a bowl of freshly cut papaya that she didn't intend to eat. Clad in a fuchsia dressing gown, bare ankles beneath, her feet nestled in a pair of soft Turkish slippers, she gazed beyond the verandah, at the lawn and distant woods. The air was fragrant and mild, the sky an expansive blue.

Erica sat opposite Imke. She passed her niece a cup of tea.

The ceiling fans whirred. Erica glanced at the morning paper. The headlines in the *Jakarta Post* were all about the elections.

Kiki lifted her head off the floor and nudged her with a wet nose.

Erica extracted a tube of *appelstroop* from her handbag and smeared some on the tip of her finger for the dog to lick.

Imke kept staring at the trees beyond the lake, at the damp shade of the banana plants.

Kiki tried her luck with Imke, who absentmindedly fondled her ears. The dog thumped her tail in response.

'You're probably missing your own bed. It's never easy sleeping in a strange house. I often have these awful dreams, and when I wake up I'm sure the threat is still there,' said Erica. 'Aren't you going to have your breakfast?'

'I'm not particularly hungry.'

Erica was unperturbed. 'Is there any toast?' She looked towards the kitchen.

Imke tightened the sash of her dressing gown and crushed a fork into her bowl of fruit. She played with her food for several moments and stared at the porcelain milk jug shaped like a Garuda, a bird-like creature found in Hindu and Buddhist mythology. 'Let's go and do something different today,' she said eventually, more cheerfully. 'There's a village I want to visit outside Jakarta. The Badui are a hill tribe who've turned their backs on the modern world. There's no electricity, no cars, no phones. It's a barefoot existence.'

'What? Are you mad?'

'I feel like getting away. We can stay overnight in a hut built on wooden stilts. The villagers bathe in the river. We can do the same. It will be fun.'

'Bathe in the river? Why on earth would you want to do that?'

'Just because.' She tore off a bit of fruit and fed Kiki under the table. 'It's only a couple of hours' drive from here. Think about it, a place completely frozen in time.'

'Sounds like a new means of torture. I don't like being part of all this traditional native stuff, not since I witnessed oil wrestling in Istanbul.'

'This is nothing like that.'

'I had terrible dreams for days after. It was akin to watching two fat men tussling in a molasses barrel.'

'You're acting like a pantomime dame from *Downton Abbey*.'

'Oh, I *do* hope so.' She sipped her tea. 'What I'm trying to say is I think we should do something a little less, well, how should I put it,' she waved a hand about frantically, 'a little less adventurous. Somewhere I won't act as a meal for mosquitoes. None of this toes-planted-in-the-soil nonsense. Can't we go to a spa? I could do with a facial or a salt and seaweed scrub.'

Imke shook her head. 'You can take me to the Intercontinental spa next week. How about a puppet show, instead, *hè*? Would you be interested in visiting the shadow puppet theatre, *wayang kulit*?'

'That sounds so much better. Something that doesn't involve bug swatting and jungles and things swimming into your underpants. Speaking of getting into your underpants, you should call that policeman friend of yours and ask him to join us.'

'His name is Ruud Pujasumarta and I don't think he's interested in my underpants.'

'Oh, I wouldn't be so sure of that.' Almost smiling. Knowing. Erica gazed longingly towards the kitchen. 'Are you sure there's no toast? Whole wheat would be nice.'

Imke refilled Erica's teacup. 'I guess I could ask him along.'

Erica's teaspoon clinked down. 'This really isn't good for my blood pressure, you know. Why serve us butter and jam but no toast? Not a croissant or bread roll in sight. Look at that houseboy over there. He's half asleep, enjoying a vertical siesta. I've seen mannequins more energetic than the staff in this place. Is there a bell I can tinkle? I don't particularly want to shout.'

Imke didn't respond.

'You're miles away.'

'Am I?' she said cheerily.

'Still thinking about Ruud getting into your underpants?'

'No!'

'Looks like you are.' Erica clutched the sides of her dress, her eyes filled with mischief.

Imke took a bracing sip of tea and scrolled through her iPhone address book, then dialled Ruud's number. Their exchange was a little stilted, which wasn't surprising. He said he was in the coroner's office, and made a joke about it. There was forced hilarity from Imke, a few gaps in the conversation, but Ruud agreed to meet her for lunch.

'Right, we're all set,' she declared, putting the phone down. She drizzled Erica's *appelstroop* onto her fruit, fingered a piece of papaya and popped it in her mouth.

'I'm sure the two of you will have a smashing time.'

'You're coming too.'

'No, I shouldn't.'

'What, and deprive him of meeting Maggie Smith's evil doppelgänger?'

Erica chuckled. 'You do say the most appalling things to me.'

When she finished breakfast, Imke inspected her sticky fingers. She went though the double doors onto the verandah and rinsed her hands under the outdoor tap. Then she went to inspect the grassy area by her bedroom window. Beyond lay the woods, all blue butterflies, wet heat and hostile undergrowth. A path bent to the left, skirting the bungalow, and she noticed how the tufts of dead weeds growing in the cracks in the stone had been trodden down.

The bamboo clicked in the breeze.

She saw shoe marks in the soil. One set of heavy heels with pointed toes.

On her way to meet Ruud for lunch it began to rain, so Imke had no choice but to sit in traffic with Erica for over an hour. The rain came down so hard she feared the windows might leak; she wished she'd worn plastic or rubber shoes instead of her trendy Bally flats.

Motorcycle *ojeks* sped past, some perilously close to being sideswiped by buses, their passengers casually leaning back, texting, not holding on to either bike or driver. As the deluge worsened, more and more riders stopped to gather under bridges and flyovers. Here they removed their windbreakers and wore them back to front to keep out the wet.

Nakula deposited them on the periphery of an outdoor market. By now, it had stopped raining but the ground was wet and sludgy, the mud and mire sticking to Imke's flats. She felt water seep through the soles of her shoes.

As Erica climbed out, she almost buckled from the heat. A man grilling satays on an open coal fire, his radio blaring Indo pop at full blast, offered her a smile. Erica exhumed a handkerchief from a sleeve to dab at the corners of her mouth, exhaling irritably. 'More foreign smoke and foreign music.' All the vendors stared at her. 'I feel like a rotisserie bird shoved into an oven to sweat and bake with everyone watching.'

Imke asked for directions from a woman with a bunch of bananas tied to string and dangling from her hand. Languidly, the woman pointed at a line of wet washing hanging between windows.

The sound of the market was unlike anything in Holland, thought Erica. Voices screeched out prices like cries from threatened crows. 'It's chaos,' she said to Imke. 'Look at it. Like the first morning of the Harrods sale.'

A vendor held a frog by the throat and thrust it at Imke. 'Cheap!' he trilled in Bahasa Indonesia. 'You buy five kilo I give discount.'

'I don't need five kilos of frogs today, but thank you all the same.'

He deposited the frog in a reed basket where it joined a knot of similar tail-less amphibians.

They found the small café by a little cluster of men, squatting on their haunches, just watching the world go by.

Inside, over a dozen people waited for a table. Loud music blasted from the overhead speakers. Imke and Erica stood in line, under the air conditioning, savouring the respite from the heat. They read the list of house specials tacked to the wall.

'He's not here yet,' said Imke. She had to shout to be heard.

'I wonder if they serve chocolate milk here.'

'They might have Milo.'

Erica's arm shot up into the air. 'Two Milo please, waitress.' The waitress ignored her.

'I don't want one,' Imke protested.

'They're both for me.'

Imke glanced at the menu on the wall. 'Looks like boiled beef offal is their speciality here, *hè*?'

'No wonder it smells like a tannery.' She extracted a tube of *appelstroop* from her handbag. 'In case I have to smother the taste.'

Imke cast her a withering look as the door burst open.

'Sorry I'm late!' sputtered Ruud. He gave Imke a hug. 'Traffic.' He seemed decidedly flustered. He noticed the line of people and approached the counter, returning a few moments later. 'My apologies. I swear I made a reservation.'

'They take reservations?' asked Erica.

'Apparently not,' observed Ruud.

Imke was beaming. 'That's OK, we only just arrived.' The water in her shoes squelched as she gave him another hug. She scrutinized him and pointed at his groin. 'What happened to you?'

Ruud looked down. 'I spilled Pepsi on my slacks. Fortunately they're an old pair.'

'Uh huh.'

Embarrassed. 'I'm always doing stuff like this. I seem to be getting clumsier by the day.'

'It's a big stain.'

Ruud caught the waitress's eye.

The waitress nodded and led them to a table.

'And I keep losing things,' he continued.

'So do I,' said Erica. They sat down.

'I put my keys on the hall table; the following morning they're gone. Next thing I know I'm going through every pocket, every drawer.'

'It's called old age, my dear,' said Erica.

'He's not even thirty, Aunty Ecks.'

'I call it being an idiot. They should hang a sign round my neck: "Numbskull at large. If you find his car keys, mobile, house keys or brain, please call the following number."'

Imke looked around 'This is a nice restaurant, hè?'

'Yes, I like it here. The food is good and the ice is made from bottled water. I thought you would prefer it to those hotel coffee shops where everything smells of coconut and maraschino cherries.'

'And menus with pictures of the food. That always sets the alarm bells ringing,' commented Erica.

The waitress passed them laminated menus with high-gloss photographs of the dishes.

'Oof!' sputtered Erica with a wince.

They sat watching the other diners for a while. It was an odd silence, but soon Ruud and Imke started talking again and slowly they fell into a familiar tempo, one shared between them all those years ago.

'When did you two last see each other?' Erica asked.

'A long time ago.' They answered in unison.

'Do you remember the lobster derby?' said Imke. 'Your father brought over some live lobsters for lunch and we painted numbers on their backs with nail polish and raced them down the kitchen corridor?' Ruud nodded and smiled. She went on, 'What about the Norwegian neighbour who swallowed the wasp?'

Ruud covered his eyes at the memory. 'Boxing Day brunch. Lars Ringstad. It was swimming around in his glass of beer. We watched transfixed each time he took a sip.'

'It was still alive when he gulped it down!' Imke guffawed. 'I can't believe neither of us said anything to warn him.'

'We were only seven. Anyway, it didn't do him any harm.'

The waitress returned, notepad in hand. Ruud exchanged a few words with her. 'She says the liver today is very fresh. They serve it with a type of fava bean.'

'Hannibal Lecter would be pleased,' deadpanned Erica.

Ruud ordered *coto makassar*, a beef offal stew made with ground nuts, ginger and turmeric, and a plate of *gado-gado* swimming in peanut sauce. He also asked for some fresh pineapple. 'The natural sugars in the pineapple give the body stamina,' he explained.

'I get my stamina,' said Erica, 'from Mars Bars and Twix.'

'I'm not really into chocolate.'

Erica looked quietly horrified at the thought of someone disliking chocolate.

When the food arrived, Erica viewed it suspiciously.

'I hope you can take Indonesian spices, Mrs Erica,' said Ruud.

'What's that oozing from the depths of the boiled egg?'

'Aunty Ecks, you're being difficult. I *know* you like *gado-gado*.'

'Try not to eat the eyeballs, Mrs Erica, they're just for flavouring.'

Imke took a bite of raw vegetables in peanut sauce, moaning with pleasure as she chewed.

'You're having sex with your food again,' whispered Erica.

Imke closed her eyes. The Indonesian salad brought on a nostalgic reverie. 'I used to have this as a child.' She raised the fork to her lips again. 'Mmmmhmmmm!'

Laughing between large mouthfuls, they chatted freely as they ate, and then Imke asked Ruud about his wife.

Ruud sat forward in his seat, his vulnerability showing. 'She left me a year ago. We're divorced now.'

'Oh, I'm so sorry. Was it mutual?'

Ruud realized he must have had a crushed expression on his face because Imke quickly apologized. 'Sorry, I don't know why I said that.'

'It's OK, I don't mind talking about it; in fact, I think it's good that I do. Since she left, I seem to talk a little less, brood a little more.'

Imke took his hand. 'But you're all right?' There was a brief silence.

'Apart from the bags under my eyes and an empty bank account, I'm great.'

Erica took a long swallow of Milo and looked at Ruud almost apologetically. 'Imke tells me your mother isn't from Indonesia.'

'Yep, I'm half Australian.'

'Ah, well that would account for a great deal.'

He laughed and squeezed Imke's hand affectionately. 'Mum's Australian-Dutch and Dad's from here. They met when she came to teach at BIS in the mid-eighties. Dad used to follow soccer on TV, but she's managed to turn him into a true blue Aussie who now enjoys watching aerial ping pong and sipping Bundy rum. My parents moved down under five years ago. They have a house in Berwick, just outside Melbourne.'

'I haven't been to Melbourne. I'd like to see it one day,' Erica confessed.

'I'm told I still speak Bahasa with an Aussie twang.'

'You don't sound all that Australian,' countered Imke.

'Don't encourage him, dear,' whispered Erica, 'otherwise it'll be strewth this and fair dinkum that before you know it.'

Imke rolled her eyes. She wasn't subtle about rolling her eyes either. 'Do you live alone now?'

'I live with my brother, Arjen. My parents fly over every Christmas to see us.'

'Yes, I remember you had a brother,' said Imke. 'What does Arjen do now?'

Ruud struggled to define what his brother did. His home life was becoming appallingly dysfunctional. His ex-mother-in-law's face popped into his head, and he was about to say something scathing about her when his mobile rang.

It was Aiboy Ali. '*Gajah*, it's me.'

Ruud excused himself from the table. His thoughts were still with Imke as he went out onto the main street to take the call. God, she's lovely – talkative, witty, eats with gusto. And what a face!

'I have something for you,' said Aiboy Ali.

'What is it?'

'The toxicology reports have come back.'

'And?' said Ruud.

'There's a reason why no skin or fibres were discovered under the nails of the victims. Neither put up a fight.'

'Go on.'

'Both women were drugged. They found hypodermic puncture marks on the backs of their necks, just above the hairline.'

'He would have grabbed them from behind and injected them with a tranquillizer. Any idea what?'

'Xylazine.'

'Never heard of it.'

'Neither had the forensic boys. It hits the central nervous system pretty quick. They use it to castrate horses.'

'Shit.'

'Like everything else these days, it can be bought online from America but you probably need an import certificate.'

'Is Hartono with you?'

'Yes, he's standing right next to me.'

'Put him on,' insisted Ruud.

'Second lieutenant Werry Hartono speaking,' he announced in English.

'Hartono, get me a list of all registered vets in Jakarta and find out if any of them have had their practices burgled in the last year. And check with the riding and polo clubs to see if they keep any of this Xyla-whatever in their medicine chests.'

'Do you think the perpetrator could be a vet?'

'Frankly, I don't have a clue. Listen, my mobile battery is about to die, so take this down carefully. I need you to contact a Dr Diaz Prasasti at UI campus. He's Head of Faculty for Agronomy and Veterinary Medicine.'

The phone went dead.

On their way back to Bogor, Imke asked Erica what she thought of Ruud.

'He's a strange one,' Erica decided.

'Strange in what way?'

'He's too enthusiastic. Too friendly.' She offered Imke a digestive biscuit out of the packet. 'An introvert pretending to be an extrovert. And he doesn't like chocolate. I'm always suspicious of people who don't like a finger of fudge.'

'How can anyone be too friendly?'

'He reminds me of Jan Schtucks.'

'Who is Jan Schtucks?'

'A hideous bore from Limburg I once knew who tried to persuade me he was an amateur gynaecologist. He smiled like Liberace all the time. I had to douse him with a glass of cold water.'

Silence. 'Well, I like him.'

'Obviously you do, with all that eyelash fluttering going on. He didn't really respond, though, did he? Do you think he might be a bit King Lear?'

'Oh, please.'

'I'm only asking. He did seem a little weak in the wrists. Not that there's anything wrong with being a *poot*. The more people that wave the rainbow flag the better, in my opinion.'

'You do say the most ridiculous things sometimes.' It's fine, Imke said to compose herself. Don't react. She's just trying to wind me up. Anyway, why am I acting as if I'm even remotely interested in Ruud? His job should put me off for a start. She made a list of his faults. Sporadic contact. Divorced. A homicide policeman. Dodgy Aussie accent. Horrible trousers with a stain on the front. Silly smile.

Actually, as it happened, she liked his silly smile.

At least he wasn't some seedy-looking Columbo with terminal dandruff or a Chuck Norris lookalike sporting a hairstyle dangerously verging on a mullet.

Best to stop thinking about him altogether, she decided. It'll just drive me potty. The last thing I want is a man messing with my head – thinking about what he's doing, what he's not doing, what he should be doing, fantasizing over his hands, his lips, his legs.

Imke's phone chirped out the *Benny Hill* theme.

When she heard Ruud's voice her hand moved to her mouth to conceal a smile. 'I thought your mobile phone battery had died. Ha ha! Really?' She could hear the laughter in his voice; she looked out of the window and listened for several moments, squinting, as though struggling to follow what was being said. 'Kiki. Yes. Well, yes she's very good at what she does. Mmm. Usually disarticulated dead bodies, often buried underground. Yes, there was a severed limb once in Rotterdam.' A pause, followed by a growly chortle, derisive of herself. 'You're not serious. My God, you are serious! You really want me to come and help you?' She nodded. 'Hmm. Well, if you think we can add something then . . . I see . . . No, no that's fine.' Her eyes were brilliant. 'All right. We'll speak again later. All right, then, OK. Bye.'

'What was that all about?' asked Erica. 'If he was asking you out again he certainly has some rather curious chat-up lines.'

'He was calling from a call box. There was quite a bit of

static so I didn't catch everything he said and he was running out of coins.'

'What did he want?'

Imke, wide-eyed and boundlessly game, couldn't contain herself. 'Kiki.'

'Kiki? Your Kiki?'

'Yes,' she said, tantalized. 'I mentioned she was a human remains detection dog, that she's received advanced specialist training.'

'And?'

'A double murder inquiry has been launched. He wants me to go and register my name at the station and get a card. He wants my help. Something about finding a missing hand.'

Chapter Eleven

The birthday celebration took place in a cosy Italian restaurant on Reestraat that fizzed with music and laughter. The waiter refreshed everyone's glasses with sparkling water and scraped the tablecloth for breadcrumbs. Mathias Sneijder checked his mobile for the umpteenth time, then looked up, gesturing his thanks to his wife and friends with a balloon of brandy. He sat at the head of the table, amongst a party of eight. They'd all opted for the six-course tasting menu, washing down the antipasto and pasta with a crisp Pinot Grigio and pairing the veal with a 2007 Barolo from the Rocche vineyards.

It was nearing midnight and he was neither tipsy nor tired. '*Proost!*' he sang. The brandy, rough against his tongue, brought a smile to his face. He felt happy. He *was* happy. Strictly speaking. Apart from this odd sensation of loss that circled like a soft voice, mingling with the others. It was Imke's voice. *Imke*. His *engeltje*, his little angel. Earlier when he spoke about her it was with the energy of a child recalling a wondrous fairground attraction. He talked excitedly about her self-sufficiency, her language skills, her ability to mimic British regional accents and her specific dislike for

Brussels sprouts, before regaling them more softly with stories of her kindness towards stray animals.

He touched his drink again, caressing it with his fingertips like he would his daughter's cheek, wrapping his palm around the balloon, and suddenly he was pierced with guilt. *Imke.* He missed her. Birthdays just weren't the same without her smiling from the other end of the table. But it wasn't her absence that bothered him. It was something else. Something he hoped to God she would not find. Something he prayed would not find her.

He felt a quickening. His feet curled in his shoes, the arches of his insteps tucked up – a sure sign he was anxious. His feet bunched up when he peered down from rooftops, when he had blood taken by a nurse, and nowadays whenever he thought about Imke doing whatever she was doing in Jakarta.

Ardy glanced his way. She smiled at him and he smiled back. Though Ardy would never have guessed it, a knot tightened in Mathias's stomach. His ability to hide anxieties from his wife was not a new phenomenon, but the realization that he'd lied to his daughter struck Mathias more tellingly than ever.

Mathias fixed his phone with the kind of expression Kiki gave Imke when the dog required her supper. He wanted to call her. Should he call her? He looked to Ardy for encouragement but she was deep in conversation with Rozamond van der Pols. Perhaps Imke would call him later, or better still, Skype him when he got home. She'd left him a card and a present – a pair of Santini Cinelli cycling gloves – before jetting off to Indonesia, and she'd texted him earlier. But he so wanted to speak with her and hear the love in her words. Her absence made him feel as though he had rocks in his pockets.

He thought briefly of the cycling gloves. They were brightly coloured track mitts, light and breathable and perfect for gripping the handlebars. He would take the Raadhuisstraat bike route on Sunday morning, start in Westerkerk and head north to Keizergracht before turning back along Herengracht. Hopefully, the fine weather would hold.

On impulse, with his free hand, he played with his phone. He read the text message again – a sweet message wishing him a wonderful day with all her love – and a strange tremor settled behind his eyes.

Then all of a sudden the room around him grew dark. And several male waiters were singing. The cake arrived and Mathias's red hair, greying at the temples, became redder in the flare of the candles.

He sucked in a breath and held it, leaning forward, eyes closed, making a wish.

The heat of the candles reached his chin.

He repeated the wish more deliberately in his head. And a shiver ran down his neck. May she never discover the truth. Because the truth will cut through her like a serrated knife.

And with a whoosh, the candles went out.

Chapter Twelve

Erica spent the next few days sketching, doing colour studies, consulting reference photographs and correcting. As Leonardo said, 'Drawing is the art of correction.' Erica was constantly correcting.

The Bogor skies grew bruised with the coming of the rains. The humidity was playing havoc with her gesso primer, making it thin and runny, and when it dried it dried with a dusty, gritty appearance.

Imke, meanwhile, made arrangements with the police department and collected her temporary warrant card. Erica questioned the wisdom of getting involved with a local murder investigation, but as far as Imke was concerned she was flattered to be offered the opportunity to demonstrate her talents outside Holland.

A bundle of nervous energy, she practised addressing Ruud's homicide team, speaking the words aloud in front of the bathroom mirror with fierce concentration.

'I have been invited here as your . . .'

No.

'I am a dog trainer. I have been invited here . . .'

No.

'*Inspektur Polisi Satu* Pujasumarta has invited me here to . . .'

No.

The roll of a cadaver detection dog is to find very recently deceased persons in various urban, rural, wilderness and water environments. Dogs like Kiki, however, have been trained specifically to pick up scents of body parts in various stages of decomposition. Kiki is trained to detect scent sources from a distance of half a kilometre or more . . .'

No, that doesn't sound right either. She was going to address a roomful of police detectives, not schoolchildren. She had to get the patronizing tone out of her voice. Imke shook her head and her hair fell, screening her face. She thought she had awful hair. It wasn't curly or wavy or spiky or styled in any way. Her hair was flat. She had flat hair and she hated it. At least it wasn't dark orange like Papa's – thank goodness! She went into the loo and grabbed her bottle of Pureology Strength Cure Shampoo. 'Gives your locks body and shine!' she mouthed, before tossing it in the bin.

On second thoughts . . . she fished it back out. No point in wasting seventeen euros.

Mechanically, she combed a knot out with her fingers and rehearsed again what she was going to say to Ruud and his homicide unit.

She swilled the remains of her Calpico Soda around in her glass and drained it in one. The sugary residue stuck to the enamel of her teeth, making her feel queasy. She cursed herself for getting addicted to the stuff and decided to fetch a glass of water.

She found Erica in the drawing room flopped across the broad wooden floor planks, lying amidst a higgledy-piggledy mess of magazines and sweet wrappers.

'You get such a different perspective from down here. Looking at the world as if you were an ant.'

Imke crumpled onto the leather sofa and heard the cushions hiss under her weight.

Silent. Preoccupied. 'Aunty Ecks, can I ask you about Papa.'

'I assume you're referring to my brother.'

'He's clammed up on me.'

'Nothing new there. When he was seventeen he hardly spoke for weeks on end. The longest sentence I heard from him was, "I'm in the bathroom."'

'Do you know why he was so unenthusiastic about me coming here? It's been bothering me for a while.'

'He's like that sometimes. You should have seen him as a boy. Taciturn doesn't even come close to describing it. Poor fellow did have a mullet the colour of pumpkins, though.'

'Did he ever mention anything to you about Jakarta?'

'Look, your Papa can be a funny old bird now and again.'

'I asked him about it a few weeks ago.'

'What did he say?'

'That's just it. Not much. It was evident he was holding something back but he wouldn't tell me what. I asked him if something bad had happened to him in Jakarta, but he just shook his head and kept reading his paper. I could tell he was lying by saying nothing at all.'

'Well, that's your father. Even as a teenager he was never sentimental about his past. We moved house twice when we were young, once from your grandpa's town Dokkum and a few years later to Amsterdam. Both times he didn't long for the friends he'd left behind or miss his old neighbourhood. In fact, he would say he hadn't really liked them much in the first place.'

'Do you think it's a kind of self-preservation mechanism?'

'Let's just say he's good at burning bridges.'

'But you're still close to him, aren't you?'

'Of course I am, I'm family.'

Imke stretched her arms behind her back until she felt her shoulders crack. She peered out beyond the verandah and blinked at the darkness. 'Something must have happened to him here,' she surmised. 'I'm sure of it.'

She felt it. Sensed it. The way only a child can sense a parent's disquiet.

'Well, Nancy Drew, if you find out, be sure to tell me.'

'You know what?' said Imke. 'I should send him an email. Lay my cards on the table.' She mimed typing on an invisible keyboard. "What's the matter with you? Something doesn't add up. What are you hiding? Did you steal the neighbour's BBQ? Are there bodies buried in the back garden? Spill the beans." Clickety-clack, clickety-clack. Send.'

One thing her father had always been good at was honesty. If Imke asked him a question she always got a straightforward answer or a rational explanation. At least that had always been the case until recently.

The problem was that if he was misleading her or concealing something, she didn't know how she was going to react. Towards him or towards herself.

Erica crabbed her way off the floor and her fingers probed a sack of gummy bears. 'Fancy one?'

'No, thanks.'

The houseboy showed up and handed each of them a glass of chilled orange juice.

Imke went outside and sat on the verandah steps. She lit the candle in a hurricane lamp. A wind blew across the lawns. It carried the rich, musty smell of rain. Imke watched the candlelight surge from the draught; the flames jumped wildly.

Something touched her back. Imke turned. It was Erica. 'Storm's approaching.'

The wind died to a stop.

The silence felt unnatural. The only sound was the pulse of the rain. No more, no less.

Ruud placed the whiteboard pen back into its rack and eyed what he had written.

Reasons why hand gets chopped:
> ROBBERY *– i.e., attached to a briefcase of cash*
> PUNISHMENT *– e.g., serial bag snatchers in Saudi*
> RELIGIOUS *– In the Christian Bible. Mark 9:43. 'If your hand causes you to fall into sin, chop it off. It is better for you to enter into life crippled than to go away with two hands into hell, where the fire never goes out.'*
> TROPHY

He underlined 'TROPHY' and added an exclamation mark. He took three steps back. Seconds later, he took a red marker to re-underline it.

He read the words again with rising incredulity. He grabbed the eraser and scrubbed the board clean.

Moments later he was in the corridor about to enter the interrogation room. 'We have to ask ourselves why these murders started when they did? What triggered them?' said Ruud.

Aiboy Ali rubbed his chin. 'And why were all the victims killed on Friday? What's the significance?'

'Perhaps he gets off work early on Friday.'

'Well, strictly speaking he kills on Thursday night. We only find the body on Friday.'

Ruud eyed Slack-mouth Susanti through the slit window. 'A face that launched a thousand car alarms.' Earlier, Commissioner Witarsa collared Ruud and asked him how he was going to proceed.

'I'm going to watch him closely and listen to what he has to say.'

'Watch and listen? *Watch and listen?*' His nostrils dilated. 'My career is on the line here and you are just going to watch and listen.'

'The investigation is progressing.'

'Yes, at the speed of a bloody tortoise!'

'OK, you're right. Let's see what happens when I twist the leopard's whiskers.'

Aiboy Ali held the door open and Ruud entered. Slack-mouth Susanti stumbled from one end of the interrogation room to the other, loose at the knees and heavy at the heels. He was dressed like a lorry driver, his undershirt diesel-stained and tatty. Ruud watched him and wondered if he was made from spare parts, with legs that didn't seem to fit.

He was a thickset man who moved with unsteady, leaden feet, as if he'd filled his pockets with stones. Ruud often thought he resembled a drunkard wading armpit-deep into the sea.

'Sit,' ordered Aiboy Ali.

Susanti did as he was told, fists planted on the table. He eyed Aiboy Ali's black leather biker cuffs with suspicion.

'Who's the Hell's Angel?'

The detective smirked. Aiboy Ali was used to this. A lot of people, including his superiors, resented his look. They called him an XTC heavy behind his back. But he'd worked

109

undercover narcotics for twenty-two months, blending in, acting the part, so frankly he didn't give a fuck.

Susanti spat on the floor. He hated bikers and tattoos and piercings with a passion that was unusual for a gangster. But then as far as he knew he was the only gangster in Jakarta who'd had two toes amputated because of an infection resulting from a dirty needle.

'Where were you on the night of Thursday twenty-third?'

'Out and about.'

'Do you recognize these women?'

Ruud tossed two photographs in front of him irreverently and concentrated on the gangster's eyes. 'For the record, I am placing photographs six-two-three A and six-two-six A in front of Mr Susanti.'

One image showed Mari Agnes Liem with her left hand removed. The other was of Shireen Zee in a similar pose. They drew the kind of emotional response Ruud expected. Susanti laughed. 'You're not pinning this cock-shit on me.'

Ruud shone the Anglepoise in his face. 'Mari Agnes Liem. She owed you money.'

'You're crazy.' He laughed again. 'They should strap you in a straitjacket an' pack you off to Magelang.'

Aiboy Ali stood and gripped the back of an empty chair.

'They say you have a touchpaper temper. You look like a man who likes to harm women,' said Ruud.

'An' you look like a man who's been watching some feller poke your wife with a bigger dick.' Susanti's mouth widened. 'Yes, we hear things on the streets, too. Your wife leave you?'

Ruud kept his face impassive even though it felt like a punch in the stomach.

'You beat up women who don't pay on time,' snarled Aiboy Ali.

'I don't deny it,' he said wryly.

'You're an extortionist, a blackmailer and a thief.'

'I am many things, but I am not a thief.'

'You'd steal the air from your own bicycle tyres if you could.'

'I did not kill these women.'

'Well, let me tell you how this is going to play out. You are going to be charged for murder. A judge will probably sentence you to thirty years at Batu. And then one night you'll be woken up in your cell and taken to a remote palm oil plantation, where they'll string you up against a tree and pump three bullets into your chest.'

'You have nothing on me. Talk to me when you have some proof.'

Susanti was staring straight ahead now, eyes level with Ruud's chin. The laughing had stopped. His eyes lifted.

They held each other's gaze for a magnified moment.

The gangster looked as though he wanted to reach over and take a swing at Ruud. Then deliberately, almost sarcastically, he pursed his lips together and leaned back. His shoulders inched lower as he slid down the chair, snapping his fingers twice. 'Where is my lawyer?'

'Probably in gaol for corruption, collusion and nepotism.'

'You want a little sweetener? No problem. How much salary supplement you want.'

'You think I want a bribe? I'm not interested in *suap* or *cuci uang.*'

'What you want?'

'To find out who killed these women.'

'Ask me the question again.'

'Where were you on the night of Thursday twenty-third?'

Susanti contemplated the wall, eyes hooded, face blank. 'I was at hospital.'

Aiboy Ali's knuckles had gone pale on the top of the chair. 'Visiting one of your victims?'

'Receiving treatment.'

'Treatment for what?' Ruud peered under the desk at Susanti's shoes. 'Step on a pet scorpion, did you?'

'Bowel cancer.' He pushed his hand out, as if to push the tumour away. 'I stayed overnight in Graha Medika. You can study their register.'

'Cancer.' Aiboy Ali repeated. Ruud could almost hear him chewing his lip.

'Yes, and if I find out you've told anyone on the street you're dead.'

'Worried it will make you look weak?'

'Fuck you.'

Aiboy Ali released his grip on the chairback. The interview was over.

The moment Ruud marched out of the interrogation room he was seized by Hamka Hamzah. They advanced between the desks, each one screened by cheap melamine partitions. 'The call log shows the last phone call Shireen made on her mobile was at seven fourteen p.m. on Thursday. It was connected to the mobile phone tower at Sunda Kelapa.'

Ruud's hands signalled 'give'. He studied the list of numbers. 'When did you get this?'

'Just now.' The little man removed his beret and ran three fingers through his centre parting. 'I got it from Hartono here.' Werry Hartono clicked his heels and bowed his head.

112

'Sunda Kelapa. The old docks? That's a hell of a distance from where her body was discovered in Jagakarsa.'

'Thirty kilometres, give or take.'

'What was she doing there?'

'I have zero idea,' Hamzah conceded. 'Shireen lived on the other side of town in Depok district. And she worked at the POS Indonesia office in Central Jakarta City, several kilometres away.'

Ruud scratched the back of his head. 'So, she last used her mobile phone at seven fourteen p.m.'

'And Solossa determined that Shireen died between seven and eight p.m.'

'Which means she must have been abducted somewhere near Sunda Kelapa. Who was she calling?'

'Her mother.'

Ruud eyed Hamzah.

'What are you looking at?'

Ruud cocked his head. 'Do you know what you remind me of? Those little plastic men they put on wedding cakes, with the silly little moustache and shiny hair. Don't you think, Werry?'

Werry Hartono remained impassive.

Hamzah sniffed.

'I suppose not,' reflected Ruud. 'Anyway, let's go pay old mother Zee a visit, shall we?'

'Are you going out like that?' enquired Werry Hartono in English.

'What do you mean?' Ruud looked at the clothes he had on.

'That shirt first saw the light of day in nineteen eighty-five. Look at the state of it. And there's a stain on your trousers. You are our commanding officer. At the academy our officers were always well tuned out.' He kissed his pinky ring.

'I spilled some Pepsi. And the word you're looking for is *turned* out.'

'That is what I said,' Hartono countered with a nasal whine.

Hamzah butted in. 'Who does your ironing now your wife has gone? You?'

'My brother.'

'Your brother irons your shirts . . .'

'Yes.'

'Your *brother*,' he scoffed.

'Can you please stop talking about my family and concentrate on the case. And Hartono, stop hanging around like a bad smell. Go do something useful.' Werry Hartono skulked off to his workstation.

Ruud tucked his shirt into his trousers. By the water cooler, he saw the police photographer perched on Vidi's desk. Vidi typed something on his keyboard. When he noticed Ruud watching, he changed the angle of his screen so that Ruud couldn't see what he was doing.

The photographer put his fingers together and cracked the joints. The knuckles snapped like dry twigs. He stared at Ruud. Pale skin, dark menacing eyes.

'What is he doing here?' Ruud asked, turning one-eighty to face Hamzah.

'Who?'

Ruud looked straight at Hamzah. 'Who do you think I mean? Behind me.' He held Hamzah's gaze. 'What's-his-name, the camera guy standing by Vidi's desk. Old Crackpot Eyes. We saw him at both crime scenes.'

The little man made a 'who knows?' face and shrugged his shoulders.

Rudd was maddened. 'He was staring at our crime chart in the Incident Room just now. He shouldn't be privy to that information. He might leak it to the press. What is he doing here? Why did you let him in?'

'How do you mean *let him in* . . . ? I don't even bloody work here! I'm a Sabhara street cop assigned to your bloody case.'

'Yes, sorry, I forgot.'

'Anyway, what are you talking about? There's nobody chatting with Vidi.'

Ruud turned round, his face tautened.

The man was gone.

Hamzah strolled across and shut the door to the Incident Room. As he did so, Vidi hastily slammed closed his desk drawer, but not before the little policeman caught sight of what the detective was hoping to hide – a small clear box of disposable hypodermic syringes.

Ruud dug into his trousers and threw back two more energy tablets, rattling the plastic container they came in. Shit, only one left. Must remember to buy some more.

The two men took the elevator to the car park. They both climbed into Ruud's blue Toyota Yaris. 'Arief,' said Hamzah curtly. 'The fellow you saw, the police photographer? His name is Arief.'

An hour later, Ruud emerged from Shireen Zee's bedroom and gently swung the door shut. He skirted the dark, narrow kitchen and approached the seated woman in the corner. He placed his right hand over his heart. 'Thank you for speaking with me, Mrs Zee, and allowing us into your home.'

115

'Did you find anything of interest in my daughter's bed-room?' The woman was in her sixties, dressed in black, and had a plump, grey face; her mouth was tight and thin.

Ruud's smile was flat. He tucked his plastic binder under his arm. 'Just gathering information.'

'I already spoke to a policeman. Answered all his ques-tions.' She shifted her large bottom. Ruud pulled over a stool and sat next to the woman in the wicker armchair. He ran his eyes over her tired face; it looked like all the air had been let out of her body.

'I'm aware of that, and thank you for talking with my colleagues, but I'd like you to tell me a little more about Shireen, if you can.'

At the mere mention of her daughter's name, Mrs Zee's eyes began quivering. She pulled a tissue from a box and motioned for Ruud to look away.

'Do you have a child, First *Inspektur*?'

'No, I don't.'

'You can count your lucky stars then that you won't have to suffer what I am going through.'

Ruud hung his head. Waited a beat.

She shot him a furtive look, like a patient with toothache sneaking a peek at the dentist's teeth, in some misguided hope of reassurance.

Witarsa once told him that a homicide detective's demeanour ought to be assured and steady – like a surgeon's hands. There were times when he had to be delicate, and times when it was necessary to wield the scalpel.

Right now he was obliged to be delicate.

'How would you describe Shireen?'

Mrs Zee took a deep breath and stared at her hands. 'She was a happy person. Musical. She loved J-Rocks and ADA

116

Band. Bought all their CDs. Strong-willed too. She was highly strung as a child, but she grew out of it.'

'You say she was happy.'

'Happy, yes, but she had a few regrets, too, wishing she had done better at school, that sort of thing. Sometimes she wished she could have got a degree, gone to work in medicine or something.' She looked about the room, at the armpit of an apartment. 'You couldn't blame her.'

'She was a good daughter?'

'I tell you how it was. She did everything for me. Cooked. Cleaned. She was a good daughter. She liked watching soap operas on the television, principally Islam KTP. You know, with that tall man with the eyebrows. But I'm afraid to start watching them. I have an addictive personality.'

'Have you always lived together?'

'Ever since Azri died.'

'Her husband.'

Mrs Zee nodded her head once. 'She married Azri Zain, a foreigner. A Malay. He converted her to Islam. Nice man. But he had a heart attack. Died aged forty-seven. So young, but such is life. That was six years ago.' She took another deep breath.

'Any children?'

She shook her head. 'Shireen did not like children.'

Ruud considered this for a moment. 'Surely you mean she didn't want children.'

A beat.

'Yes, sorry.'

Ruud looked hard at Mrs Zee. 'When did you last eat?' he asked.

'Me? Oh, *tidak lapar*.'

'No, really, you must keep your strength up.'

'Shireen used to do all the cooking.' Her voice trailed off.

Ruud got to his feet and pulled on an apron from behind the kitchen door. He turned on the water tap, washed his hands, opened cupboards.

'What are you doing?'

'Making you lunch.' He stuck his head in the fridge and pulled out some tofu, an egg, some beansprouts and half a cabbage. 'Did she start seeing other men following her husband's death?'

'No.'

He found a packet of Kobe savoury mix in the cupboard and a bottle of Indonesian Bango sweet sauce – the one with the stork on the label. 'Did a man stop by at any time?'

'No. No men. Sometimes I worried that she might never find herself another companion, but it didn't bother her. Being alone. But, she did not like being known as 'the widow Zain' so she changed her name back to Zee. She continued to follow Islam, but not in a strict sense.'

She kept staring at her hands. 'Poor Shireen. She never thought she was very pretty, but to me she was beautiful. Recently, she felt she was putting on too much weight. She liked her sweets.'

'I see.' Ruud began shredding the cabbage. 'Did her weight affect her mood?'

'No. As I said, she was a happy person. But it caused her concern. She did not want to die young like her husband. She wanted to get healthier. She began walking and cycling.' Her brow trembled at the memory. 'Long distances. "In this heat?" I'd say to her. But she said the long walks gave her time to think. She had a busy job. It never gave her time to think.'

'Where did she walk? In the parks?'

118

'Sometimes in the parks, but usually after work she would change into exercise shoes and walk around the neighbourhood.'

'Bowls?'

'Top shelf. So good of you. What are you preparing?'

'Crispy bakwan. Did Shireen ever walk around the old docks to look at the boats?'

'The old docks. I don't know. She never mentioned it.'

'You mentioned she also had a bicycle. May I see it?'

Mrs Zee blinked hard. 'The bicycle was with her when she . . .'

Ruud made a mental note of this as he beat the egg, mixing all the other ingredients into it. 'Can you describe the bicycle? Big, small, colour?'

'White. Red plastic seat. Locally made.'

'I see. Anything else you can tell me about Shireen?'

'She didn't care for eggs.'

'Eggs.'

She stuffed another tissue under her eyes. 'They disagreed with her. Made her break out in a rash.'

'Same thing happens to me with prawns,' said Hamzah from across the room. 'And my throat gets itchy as heck.'

Ruud glared at him.

Hamzah made a face. 'What?'

Ruud's gaze returned to Mrs Zee. 'Did you notice anything different in Shireen's recent behaviour? Did she seem agitated?'

'No.'

Ruud filled a pan with oil and lit the stove. 'Was anyone threatening her?'

'No.'

'Do you know anyone who held a grudge?'

She pulled herself up straighter. 'Mr Bimbom. The egg man.'

'The egg man.'

'He sells her eggs at the market.'

'I thought she was allergic to eggs.'

'She is. The eggs were for me.'

'So why did she have a problem with Mr Bimbom?'

'He swindled her.'

'How?'

'She bought a dozen eggs from him last February and most of them were stinky-bad. Do you know how you can tell if an egg's gone bad? Place them in a bowl of water. The fresh ones sink to the bottom. The bad ones float. Nearly all of his eggs floated.'

'I see.' He dropped his voice slightly. He moulded the tofu-shrimp-egg-cabbage-sprout mixture into oval shapes, then dropped them one at a time into the hot oil. 'So they had a row?'

'Yes, she went back and demanded her money be returned.'

'But he refused.'

'Why, yes! How do you know that?'

'He's a First *Inspektur*,' Hamzah proclaimed drily from across the room.

'Do you think Mr Bimbom would kill Shireen over this dispute?'

'Bimbom kill my Shireen? Impossible. I've known old Bimbom for twenty years. He's my second cousin.'

Ruud emitted a tired sigh. 'Anyone else who might hold a grudge?'

'Not that I can think of.' She put her hands to her mouth. 'Why would anyone want to harm her? I cannot understand it. She was a good woman.'

Ruud made a *mm-hmm* sound in agreement. 'Did anything unusual happen in her life lately? Did she lose a lot of money? Did she come into money? Anything out of the ordinary?'

'Well there was the post office robbery. She worked at the payroll office for PT POS Indonesia. She was on duty when it was robbed last month. Men with guns charged in. She said she was terribly frightened. The crooks got away with cash. Good luck nobody was killed.'

Ruud made a mental note of this. 'Can you remember how much was stolen?'

'Quite a lot, according to the newspapers.'

Ruud went quiet for a few moments. He watched the bakwan carefully, as they browned and crisped. 'I'd like to find out more about her social life. What was her religion?'

'Islam. We both converted from Christianity when she married Azri.'

He drained the pan and laid the bakwan on some kitchen paper. Moments later he plated up and placed the dish on Mrs Zee's lap. 'And when was that?'

'Nine years ago. I go to *masjid* each Friday and every day during Ramadan.' She picked up a fritter and blew on it before tasting. 'So good of you,' she repeated.

'Tasty?'

She smiled as she chewed. 'Tasty.'

'Did Shireen own a laptop or home computer we can inspect?'

'No. She couldn't afford one. I think she was saving up for an Acer.'

'Did she keep any old photographs of her ex-boyfriends or school friends? Of her work colleagues?'

Mrs Zee got up and returned with a stack of Kodak

photographs in a box. They were all slightly faded and had dates digitally stamped into the bottom right corner.

Ruud wiped his hands on a dishcloth and took his time going through them. He stopped when he was about a quarter of the way through.

Ruud's eyes narrowed a fraction. 'Where was this one taken?'

Mrs Zee leaned in and regarded the image. 'Oh, that was their Friday evening get-together. She and a few other girls used to meet at a *kampung* house to play mah-jong. One of them owned this old, slanted tea-shack of a house in the country. This would have been, what, fifteen years ago now? I never knew who the other women were, but Shireen,' her eyes quivered at the mention of her daughter's name, 'she supposedly enjoyed their company. It went on for a few months but then she stopped going. There was a disagreement over something. I don't think she kept in touch with them.'

'Mah-jong,' observed Ruud, looking pointedly at Hamzah. He turned the photograph over. Nothing had been written on the back. 'Mrs Zee, I'm going to have to borrow this.'

Ruud promised to return it soon and tucked the photo into the folds of his plastic binder.

They took the concrete staircase to the ground floor. Somewhere in the apartment block, a baby wailed hysterically. From every tenement, pro-government pamphlets jutted from letterboxes like sly tongues.

Ruud opened the rear doors to the building and there was an instant rush of heat and traffic noise. Dust and exhaust fumes thickened the air. The little policeman coughed a bronchial cough and immediately lit a cigarette.

give his image power and height. She pulled herself back up and arranged her paints in an uneven line along the bench. More than half the tubes carried no markings other than a circle of colour on the cap.

She blinked in the sunshine, at the pewter glint of cloud. Her eyes had begun to ache.

Erica Sneijder was passionate about being an artist. Some people were passionate about skiing holidays, or playing golf, or recycling aluminium cans. Some had a thing for golden *patat frites*, or white asparagus swathed in brown butter, or vintage model trains. But Erica wasn't like that. She craved only two things: art and chocolate.

When asked by *Modern Painters* if there was anything she was nutty about, she replied in a deep, growly Cookie Monster voice: 'Choco-late! I looooove choco-late,' before reverting to her normal tone. 'I devour it, demolish it, lay waste to mountains of cacao. But my nourishment comes from painting. The sense of being enwrapped and over-whelmed by pigments intoxicates me. Tones and texture make me giddy. Colour is what I live for, intuitive colour.'

'I'm not dealing with flesh tones and half tones and dark tones. I'm dealing with emotions. Yes, of course I have to get the eyes transparent, and yes the mouth must be painted with soft edges, but that simply comes down to technique. What I require is a subject with a tungsten will to match my own. A personality who can hold my attention long enough for me to use that strength as an outlet for my own emotions, free of self-censorship, free of inhibitions, mixing and separating life with spirituality.'

Perhaps she over-romanticized her calling, but hey, she said to the journalist, throwing up her hands, this was how she felt. She was on a creative quest. She had a thirst for it.

But to her, painting was not the same as sipping water – drinking more when thirsty, less when not. It was a constant. The thirst was never slaked.

Sometimes, however, Erica needed to get away and think through the artistic process. She did this by doodling, going for a walk, examining a weed growing in the park, day-dreaming on a long train journey, listening to music, or just surrounding herself with people who didn't mind her being flakey. The worst thing was to spend too much time staring out the same window, ensnared by the same objects. The fact of the matter was that she had to do something new and fresh each day and not be scared of failure – anything so long as the wellspring of creativity didn't run dry.

'What inspires you?' A busybody German woman once enquired on a beach in Corsica. 'I'm not sure,' Erica replied, drawing the coastline, tightening the rubber grips on her easel. 'Rembrandt's *The Night Watch* at the Rijkmuseum gets my juices flowing. Sometimes I go and spy on the local artists sketching by the canals. Often it's something completely ridiculous, like watching a plastic bag blowing in the wind.'

Abstract expressionism, Blossfeldt's *Art Forms in Nature* and Barcsay's *Anatomy for the Artist* all held a sacred place in her heart, as did her books on art history. She owned shelves and shelves of them, many with hand-coloured or colour-printed plates. In fact, she had so many she was forced to stash some of her books and binders in the oven due to lack of space in her pokey house.

'Also, please, your favourite artists are who?' asked the same, rather prying, lady, hovering at her shoulder.

'In the seventies Kandinsky, Kupka and Pollock were my artists of choice, only to be replaced in the eighties by

Warhol and Jasper Johns. I actually started out by drawing pencil illustrations, à la Norman Rockwell, graduating to charcoal, then to acrylics and finally to oils.'

The nosy parker pointed at Erica with her ice lolly. '*Gut*, one day maybe when you are famous you paint me, OK?' Erica had merely nodded and carried on with her sketching.

Fame. Erica didn't care for the word. She certainly had no desire to be a celebrity, or at least not one of those celebrities on the cover of *HELLO!* Recognition was nice – such as receiving the Prince of Orange Art Medal – but she didn't want to be famous, especially the show-all, tell-all insanity of contemporary fame.

How could anybody, she wondered, possibly want to live like Kim Kardashian? Why would anyone choose to lose his or her freedom? All those eager hopefuls on *American Idol*, desperate for that smattering of stardust, were on a hiding to nothing. *Goede God*, they must be mad! What with the shutterbugs camped on your doorstep, the camera lenses mounted on your neighbour's balcony and the carloads of trailing paparazzi. It was absurd. And if you reacted by bouncing your shoe off a photographer's head as Justin Bieber did, you ended up doing 100 hours of community service. What was the fun in that? No, it definitely wasn't for her. Although she wouldn't mind being snapped sipping champagne on a yacht with her arms draped over George Clooney's tanned torso.

No, she was ambivalent towards fame.

Money, on the other hand, was something she definitely took a shine to. Long ago, a journalist asked her what she would do if she won the lottery. She said she'd pile all the cash into a swimming pool and dive in like Scrooge McDuck.

Erica used a rag to wipe the excess colour from her brushes, rinsed them in Sansodor and dunked each one in a bucket of water.

As she did this, she regarded the recent press clippings sent to her by her agent. There was one written a few months earlier and published in the *Jakarta Post*, announcing her appointment to paint SBY, commissioned by the Arts Council of Central Java. She glanced at another cutting, a photograph, this time of her and Imke at Soekarno-Hatta airport. She really didn't enjoy seeing her face in the news.

Yes, she was passionate about being an artist. But sometimes she wanted more. Sometimes she wanted just to escape from it all.

Erica shaped up her brushes and rested them, bristles up, in a large glass jar.

She rubbed her aching eyes again. She needed to take a break – a lengthy amble to mentally sketch some local colour.

Besides, the toad chorus of *grook-groookup!* was slowly driving her mad.

Across the sweeping lawns, somewhere beyond the lake, the music still played. Erica removed the art apron she always wore when she worked and hung it in the wardrobe. With two squirts she covered her arms with sunscreen and left the Nivea SPF 40 on the workbench. Lou Reed's 'Walk On The Wild Side' suddenly popped into her head. 'Doo doo doo doo doo doo doo doo doo,' she sang while rubbing in the cream.

She laced her Solillas sandals, grabbed Imke's amboyna wood cane, and strode out onto the grass, following her ears.

Her black-clad figure in full sail, she took the faintest of trails that led to the main road, past the succession of bronze statues of naked ladies (a throwback to the Sukarno era) and the avenue of Banyans.

Through patches of sunlight, engulfed by a sea of green – emerald, lime, pea and sage, flames of beryl and jade and rainforest moss.

A man, a stranger, appeared through the greenery. He beckoned her from beyond the tall grass, towards the acacias.

The music rose to a crescendo.

She maintained a steady pace.

The man smiled. She smiled back and headed his way. She wondered what that glint of metal was in his hand. Like the flash of a kingfisher.

Erica expected he was a wayside walker or groundsman of some sort.

He waved her closer. There was nothing for it but to go over and say hello.

He slapped his hand against a low tree branch and raised it high, allowing her to duck beneath. She lost her footing. He lunged at her.

Nobody saw her go down.

The Incident Room was foggy with cigarette smoke. It was standing room only. Imke, with Kiki sitting obediently by her side, was nearing the end of her presentation when Commissioner Witarsa tapped on the glass. Ruud rose from his chair, raising an apologetic hand, and stepped out of the room, into the corridor.

'WHY didn't you authorize this with me?' Witarsa rubbed his hand furiously across his face. 'She cannot be part of this.'

'Says who?'

'You cannot have her on the team!'

'Why? Because she's a woman?'

'Don't try to find a racial or sexual bias, Pujasumarta. She is an outsider. A civilian.'

'We've used external professionals before.'

'She doesn't have security clearance.'

'Oh for God's sake! When has that ever been an issue? You're the one complaining that the investigation is progressing too slowly, at the speed of a tortoise. I'm the one being proactive here.'

'Our own Animal Police unit would have done.'

Ruud knew this was coming. The Jakarta K9 unit was capable of sniffing out drugs, explosives and DVD bootlegging factories, but their two cadaver dogs, two Weimaraners, were very young and raw. 'Just let me get on with it.'

'What are the chiefs going to think?'

'What are the families of the victims going to think when I tell them we could have solved the case but Commissioner Witarsa was too small-minded to bring in an expert?'

The clock in the corridor counted off another half-minute. 'You honestly expect me to believe that she can help.'

'Yes. Imke Sneijder is good at what she does. In Holland they think she's one of the best.'

Next door, Imke's penetrating voice grew quiet. Chairs scraped along the floor and the door to the Incident Room burst open. A disgruntled hubbub swept through the hallway as detectives came streaming out, some in uniform, many in civvies.

Aiboy Ali, Vidi and Werry Hartono filed past him.

Ruud made for the elevators.

'NOT so fast,' Witarsa drawled. 'The office pantry needs a new toaster.'

'What the hell are you talking about?' said Ruud.

'A Kenwood Kmix. Two-slot, adjustable browning control.'

'I'm not Kitchen Warehouse.'

'Peek and View function. I like Sun Kissed Yellow.'

'You're serious.'

'Get me a Kenwood and I'll give the dog woman three days,' said Witarsa.

Ruud slipped off towards the elevators, his right arm extended in a valedictory wave.

Below the neon HERO signboard Kiki sniffed the ground, her tail rigid with purpose.

Imke and Ruud moved towards the door that flashed *KELUAR*. They each drank hot coffee from plastic bags. 'You take it with sugar, right? I asked for medium sweet.' He took a bite from his *roti bakar* with cheese. 'You sure you don't want some of this brecky?'

'I'm fine, thanks,' Imke said. She sucked on her straw.

'Right then!' He bounced on his toes. 'Let's get started.'

'Are you always this bloody perky in the morning?'

Ruud laughed. 'A lot of people ask me that. It's just the way I am, I guess. No point coming across as a wet weekend. You know how you hear about comedians with dark personalities, they're paid to make people laugh but they're all tragic and gloom-ridden inside? Well, I'm the opposite. I've got a pretty dark job. I see horrible things almost every day. But I've got to stay positive. It's my way of keeping myself light. Breezy. Upbeat.'

She looked at him and cocked an eyebrow.

'As buoyant as a blimp.'

'With about the same amount of hot air, I'd say.' She smiled.

'How about a little singalong of "Always Look On The Bright Side Of Life"?'

'Now you're starting to annoy me. At least you're not a cliché.'

'What do you mean?' He took another meaty bite of the *roti bakar*.

'One of those disillusioned cops whose idea of nourishment is a Silk Cut and a shot of bourbon.'

His cheeks bulged with bread and cheese.

Had a bystander been gazing down from the apartment block across the road, he might have observed two young people sharing a morning stroll, rather than investigators on the scene of a murder inquiry.

Imke wrinkled her mouth. 'Well, so long as you don't start singing "Whistle While You Work".'

'Hi-Ho! Hi-Ho!'

'Enough already!'

'OK! OK!' He laughed, arms raised in surrender.

'So, back to the case. Shireen Zee was discovered over there, *hè*?' She pointed at the industrial-sized refuse bin.

'Correctomondo.'

'Please place this rubber cone at the base of the bin.'

Ruud obliged. 'How did you get on last night? Did you stay in and watch a movie?'

'I shared an early supper with Erica, then surfed the net for a bit. What about you? Go over the case files? Did you have dinner with Arjen?'

Usually Ruud did not discuss his private life with people. He didn't talk about the holidays he took, or the books he read, or whether he should buy a Sony TV or a Samsung. But today he wanted to share all these things, and more, with Imke.

He told her a little bit about the meeting with Shireen Zee's mother, then added, 'There's a photograph. It has this group of women who got together to play mah-jong. We need to find out who they all are.'

'Perhaps one of them is your killer.'

'Or related to the killer.'

'Here, Kiki.' Imke slapped the side of her leg. Kiki came running, tail wagging. 'Sit, good girl.' Imke gave the dog a treat from her biscuit pouch. 'Where was the coroner's van parked when it arrived to collect her body?'

Ruud took twenty paces to his right and stopped. He was standing in the middle of the cordoned-off back alley. Imke followed him and placed a rubber cone by his feet. She took several more steps back, straddling the yellow *Garis Polisi* barrier tape.

'And you say the local taxi drivers saw nothing. Same with the buses and *mikrolet* cabs that travel this route.' She took another step back. 'Which makes me assume the killer is mobile. He has his own car or the use of somebody else's vehicle.'

'Unless he lives across the road.'

'Yeah, right,' she scoffed. 'Here,' she said, handing him her bag of coffee. 'Hold this, will you?'

Imke turned and retreated through the door that flashed *KELUAR* and emerged with a stepladder in her hands, which she erected by the nearest bin. She clambered up and took a tentative step onto the metal lid.

'Watch your footing,' he said.

Sunlight sliced off the windscreens of passing cars. She shielded her eyes, took another step and fell down with a crash, still managing to stay atop of the container.

'Slippery,' she said, rubbing her bottom, laughing. 'I must

confess when I woke this morning, balancing precariously on a giant wheelie bin wasn't at the top of my to do list.'

'Perhaps you should come down from there,' suggested Ruud.

'Course not!' She got straight back up. 'This is nothing compared to six hours of wading through Amsterdam's sewers.'

Ruud patted his trouser pockets for his Head Start pills.

'Back at the station,' said Imke, 'who was that jowly splay-footed fellow? She had her sunglasses high on her forehead in the peak of her windswept hair.

'My boss.'

'Thought so. He's a bit of an arsehole.' Imke crossed her arms and surveyed the scene.

'He has the cork in too tight – liable to blow anytime – but he means well.'

'Aiboy Ali seems nice.'

'He's a good guy.'

'What's it like?'

'What's what like?'

'Being a homicide detective.'

Ruud shrugged. He looked beyond her and when he spoke his voice was quiet. 'It's not easy.'

'I'm sure.'

'You're forced to think on various levels. There's a family's grief and anger to deal with. Someone's father, mother, sister or brother's been killed. Which means I have to show a certain dignity. It's hard finding the right words to say to someone whose heart has been torn out. But at the same time I have to ask the difficult questions. You see how tenuous and frail it all is. Life, I mean. There are some of us, Vidi for example, who struggles with the concept of happiness, he distrusts it, because he's seen how, when a good thing enters your life, it's only a matter of time before it's snatched away from you.

'Then there are the lies. After a while you realize it's hard to trust anyone. It's a cynical thing to say, but it's true. You're talking to a person and within a minute you start spotting inconsistencies and ploys. Changes in their breathing pattern. Shoe shuffling. Just little details. And you figure out that all the eye contact, the sincere tone, the apparent helpfulness, is a sham. Everyone has something to hide.'

Imke nodded.

Ruud laughed. 'God, I sound like a jilted agony aunt.'

'Is it true?' she asked. 'What they say about people looking to the left when they're visualizing a remembered event? And looking to the right when they're fibbing.'

Ruud looked to his right. 'Yes, it's true.'

'Do you take anything seriously?' she chuckled.

'Yep. My job.'

'Ruud?'

'Yep.'

'How long were you married?'

'Three years.'

'That's not too bad.'

'It felt bad enough when she left me.'

'No, what I meant was if you're married longer the knots are more stubborn; there's more cutting required to free yourself.'

'I never really thought of it like that.' He paused. 'Shall we get to work?'

'Sure. Tell me about the CCTV cams.'

Ruud pointed them out. 'They only cover the rear exit and the manager's parking space. The rubbish bins are out of range. The same goes for where we're standing now. There's no visual evidence showing the perpetrator coming or going.'

'But he must have parked his car somewhere along this back alley.'

She shielded her eyes from the slanting sun then raised a finger, aiming it at the far corner of the supermarket. 'See that?'

'See what?'

'There's a traffic mirror to the left of the manager's parking space.'

'So?'

Imke climbed down from the top of the bins. 'It might be in line with one of the cameras.'

Ruud dropped both bags of coffee, ran to the mark below the convex mirror and looked up.

'My God, you might be right. The reflection. The camera might have caught something in the reflection.' His head steamed with castigation. How did he fail to spot it?

'If you can enhance the image, we might be in luck.'

Imke crouched and looked Kiki in the eye. She whispered something into the dog's ear and stood up. Kiki's body elongated, her tail grew stiff. 'Find!'

Kiki sprang up and dashed left and right, tail wagging, nose to the ground, twisting and turning.

'She is quite effective as a trailing dog too, searching for a specific person by following tiny particles of dead tissue or skin cells dispensed during relocation. Most likely she will pick up on very minute pieces of cadaver or blood residue.'

'How good is she?'

Kiki came to the refuse bins and plopped herself down. 'The best I have ever worked with. Kiki can detect human remains through concrete or even at the bottom of a lake 50 feet deep, can't you, *hè*? Who's a good girl? Good, Kiki.' Imke gave her a treat. 'OK, she found the location where the body was discovered. Let's move on.' The dog's attention focused unwaveringly on Imke's voice and hands. Imke snapped her fingers and signalled. 'Find, Kiki, find!'

A few moments later she came to a halt by the cone where the coroner's van had parked. 'You see? She's picking up tiny trails of skin cells. Good, Kiki.' She handed Ruud a treat. 'You try.'

Ruud snapped his fingers once and shouted, 'Find!'

Kiki was off again, twisting and turning. This time she headed away from the supermarket car park towards the dead end. Initially, she went as far as the brick wall, then the monsoon drain, but quickly double backed. She came to a stop and plopped down in the middle of the alley, beside some discarded KFC boxes. Imke placed a third rubber cone by the dog's tail and gave her another treat.

'You learn quickly,' observed Imke.

'Tell that to my old schoolteachers; they used to say that filling my head with knowledge was like filling a bucket full of holes.'

'I'll bet this is where he parked. He opened his trunk, pulled Shireen Zee out and dragged her body from here to the refuse bins.'

'But why dump her here? Out in the open for just anybody to find? Why not hide the body?'

'At some point the body's going to be discovered whatever happens, so why try to hide it. Digging a hole leaves clues and takes time. Best to just throw it on the garbage. The crime scene's already contaminated and in his mind the victim is trash anyway.'

'But if he took the body into the forest, say, and weighed it down, threw it in a swamp, that would give the body time to degrade, eliminating all sorts of evidence.'

'Maybe he dumped the bodies immediately because he wanted them found, *hè*? He's making a statement. Look everyone, look at me, this is what I do! I kill middle-aged women. I hack off their hands because they're dirty and unclean and because they all played mah-jong.'

'Why did you say that?' demanded Ruud.

'Say what?'

'The thing about the hands being dirty and unclean.'

'I don't know, probably because in this society people consider the left hand to be unclean.'

'Yes, but dirty can also mean lewd and depraved, can't it?'

Imke shrugged.

Ruud snapped his fingers. 'A high percentage of serial killers were abused as children, either sexually, physically, or psychologically. I read it's something like seventy per cent. And a high percentage of the abusers turned out to be their parents.'

'And?' Imke pulled her sunglasses down from her forehead.

A picture emerged in Ruud's head. He saw a young boy locked in a dark closet, sitting on the floor, knees drawn to his chest, hands pressed over his ears. He is crazy with fear. The person on the outside terrifies him. There is a switch in her hand made from thin bamboo. When she beats him it leaves red welts. The closet door opens and he tries to run, but her fist is in his hair.

'He's killing his mother. Every time he kills one of these women, he sees her in his head. She was the one that abused him. All these victims are substitutes or surrogates for his mother-rage.'

'Imke made a concessionary face. 'Possible.'

He swiped at the air. 'It's just a hunch.'

Ruud got down on his haunches. He examined the ground to the left of the KFC boxes. Rain fell the night before. Despite this he could make out very faint, and very small, discolourings in the crushed stone, secretions of fluids from the body onto the ground.

Ruud pulled out his mobile and spoke to Aiboy Ali. He told him he wanted the forensic unit recalled to HERO. He also asked him to find someone who could enhance a CCTV still frame to reveal a car number plate.

'Yes, as soon as possible,' urged Ruud. He paused to listen as Aiboy Ali spoke. 'What? When? I don't understand, how could she . . . Right, I see. But how can he be sure? I see. Yes, I will tell her.'

Ruud ended the call and looked at Imke.

'What is it?'

'The palace staff called looking for you. Your aunt. She has disappeared.'

Chapter Fourteen

The bungalow was deathly quiet. The clock in the hallway read a quarter past ten at night. The vase of lilies in the hall shed another petal, leaving a crown of corollas on the floor.

Imke slid open the verandah doors. The easel, the canvas, the brushes, trowels and painting knives were how Erica would have left them. Perplexed, she stepped out into the evening warmth. The paint-spattered sheeting on the floor rustled as she trod on the plastic. On the workbench she saw a tumbler of half-finished water and a blue tube of Nivea SPF 40 sun lotion. Beside them sat a plate of chocolate biscuits covered with a glass dome to keep the ants away.

She considered the situation: her Aunty Ecks had gone missing; the last person to see her was the houseboy at 11 a.m., almost twelve hours ago. He'd cleared the breakfast table and brought her a tray of Assam tea. She made a fuss about the Carnation Milk in the Garuda milk jug and asked for the fresh kind, drawing a picture of a pink-uddered cow on a sheet of A4 with her coloured pencils to emphasize her point.

Not long after, when he went to make up her room, she told him to leave it until tomorrow.

She did not appear distraught at the time.

When she did not show up for lunch, the houseboy

thought little of it. However, when she ignored the chocolate cookies the cook left her an hour later, he alerted the
head of the household staff. And when, later still, she failed
to materialize for afternoon tea, the palace staff decided to
contact Imke.

According to The Captain she must have gone for a stroll
as her walking cane was missing; but she couldn't have gone
far because she forgot her phone, her wallet and coin purse;
there was no record of a local taxi being called and all the
palace chauffeurs and their cars were accounted for. The sen-
tries at the gates and security kiosks saw no one. And at the
back of the estate, behind the orchard where the staff's
recreational quarters were located, nobody had seen a thing.

All of which, thought Imke, made no sense at all. And it
was my walking cane she'd taken, father's cane, the one he'd
carved out of amboyna wood.

Should she call for a search party? Surely, it hadn't come
to that yet? Lines of people beating the grass with sticks?
No, not yet.

Erica was a grown woman. A responsible adult. Gone for
a stroll? Perhaps she had. But where could she have walked
to? Where would a friendless woman in a strange country
without a rupiah to her name go?

Imke went indoors and shut the double doors behind
her. She didn't last more than a minute inside. She needed
air. Back outside, her bare feet pattered around the wet
verandah floor, across the slippery tiles. She stared into the
darkness. Gathering her hair into a loose knot, she went out
onto the lawns. The rain was lashing down.

She walked out to the lake, and for a brief crazy moment
she thought she heard Erica calling to her, from beneath the
water.

★ ★ ★

Half an hour to midnight.

The Captain pitched up, armed with a notepad.

It was still raining. The Captain's shoes were wet from walking through puddles. He removed them in the hallway.

Imke followed The Captain, who in turn followed his *nasi goreng* belly, moving busily from room to room in the bungalow, opening and closing the wardrobe doors. The portly man retrieved his silver pen from a pocket, gave it a twirl and scribbled something in his notepad.

He entered Erica's bedroom. Imke cringed at the mess. Biscuit crumbs ground into the sheets, Flake wrappers discarded on the carpet, booklets, pamphlets, pencils and sketchbooks strewn about willy-nilly. A tangle of scarves and bras hung from the desk lamp.

'Untidy, but no obvious indication of a struggle,' observed The Captain.

Untidy didn't quite do it justice, thought Imke. The floor looked like the morning after the Battle of Hastings. When the houseboy turned down Erica's bed each night, he probably found doughnuts in it.

'No valuables missing. Her clothing and belongings are undisturbed. No sign of a robbery and no evidence of an intruder. When in Holland, does she often go missing like this?' he demanded.

'Not without saying anything or leaving a note. She has a bit of a sweet tooth so she occasionally runs out to the late-night convenience store.'

The Captain shook his head. Imke couldn't tell if this was from frustration or out of concern.

At any rate, thought Imke, she still has two untouched boxes of honingdrop sweets, some Astro Belts and a mound of uneaten Kit Kats on the bedside table. If she had gone out voluntarily it wasn't in search of a snack.

'May I go in your bedroom?'

'Yes, of course.'

Imke fetched a pan and brush. Mechanically, she swept up the lily petals from the floor. When she entered her bedroom she caught The Captain hovering by the clothes cupboard, stuffing something awkwardly into his trouser pocket. She swore she saw a scrunch of white fabric disappear into his pocket – a handkerchief maybe, or, God forbid, a pair of her knickers. No, please no, not her knickers, she couldn't cope with that right now.

He cleared his throat and quickly folded his arms across his chest. 'Do you know what your aunt would have been wearing?'

'I found her art apron hung up in the wardrobe. Underneath it she'd have worn a black top and black jeans. She always wore black when she worked.'

As if dressed, thought Imke, *for a funeral.*

It was now two o'clock in the morning.

Imke watched the shadows play out by the lake.

Her mind's eye enacted different scenarios over and over in her head, which was thick with worry.

The rain had stopped, but the eaves continued to drip a percussion of water.

'The guards at the main gate did not see her, but we assume she must have passed through unnoticed.' It was The Captain's voice. 'However, one of the palace maids was beating a carpet on the west lawn and she recalled your aunt walking down the gravel path and leaving the grounds. This was around noon. We have checked the nearby farms and plantation houses, searched a radius of ten miles and made several phone calls to hostels and town lodgings along the trunk road. Nothing. No sightings.'

He tapped his belly.

'Unfortunately, we cannot view the security cameras as they were not on yesterday. Maintenance work.'

'Maintenance work,' she repeated dismayed, the words falling from her lips lifelessly.

'So, I suggest you rest, Miss Sneijder, she will return when The Creator deems it so.'

Imke stared into the darkness. She had stopped listening.

The Captain half-nodded, half-whispered to himself. The President, he sputtered, would be alerted in the morning.

Sunrise.

With the night giving way to bright daylight, reality reared up like a snake. Imke could think only of Erica. She sent Kiki to search for her aunt, but whenever the dog picked up a scent it was quickly lost in the myriad of tall grasses.

It was galling. Imke could no longer hide her confusion, fear and rage. For years she had subconsciously inoculated herself from her aunt's eccentricity. But this disappearance was unprecedented. Had she been kidnapped? Was she injured, or sick, or even dead? Imke's chest grew hot with panic. Her eyes were swollen from lack of sleep. She went out onto the verandah and, leaning on a supporting post, shielded her face from the climbing sun. A rooster strutted past. Imke eyed the bird accusingly.

'Where,' she cried softly to herself, 'where the hell are you, Aunty Ecks?' Her fingers dug into her hands. Angry fear burned in her throat until she thought she might choke on it. She repeated her aunt's name, uttering it over and over as though she was hurting her.

144

Chapter Fifteen

'*Inspektur Polisi Satu* Pujasumarta?'

'Who's asking?'

'*Salaam.* Sorry to barge in on you homicide boys during your lunch hour. My name is Timur Djamin.' He removed his peaked cap and clasped it in the crook of an elbow. 'I'm a lieutenant colonel attached to Brigade Mobil Twenty-seven, armed robbery.' He showed Ruud his warrant card and badge. Both his thumbnails were well over an inch long.

Ruud had just stepped out of the elevator. He cradled a brand-new Kenwood toaster in Sun Kissed Yellow under his arm. He deposited the toaster in the office pantry and led Timur Djamin into a small conference room that looked onto the street below, but the room was busy. A number of people set out their prayer mats and directed themselves to the east, bowing and prostrating. Those that were too busy to perform *Zuhr* carried on working at their desks unapologetically.

Ruud directed him to his office and sat him down. 'How may I help you, Lieutenant Colonel?'

'I trust you are aware of the post office heist that took place last month?'

'The one at Sawah Besar? I heard about it, yes.'

'How much do you know?'

'Only what was in the papers.'

'Well, let me fill you in. How it happened was, roughly a tenth of the twenty-six thousand POS Indonesia employees are paid in cash from the Sawah Besar office. On the last Friday of each month, twelve armoured vehicles arrive at nine a.m. and transport the money to the various POS locations around the city and the Greater Jakarta area. At eight fifty-five a.m. on this given Friday, as soon as the electronic locks on the vaults flashed green, six robbers stormed the third floor and overcame the two security guards by the iron grille, as well as the three guards standing by the vaults. They wore full-face Balaclavas and heavy boots, and wielded handguns. They also had on Seven Continents Movers overalls.'

He paused to make sure Ruud was taking it all in.

'The first thing they did was to shoot the director of payrolls in the back of the knee.' He made a pistol out of his thumb and forefinger. 'And how it happened was, this shut everyone up and stopped any potential cowboy heroes from hitting the panic alarm. The raiders then snatched a guard's radio and, pretending to be the head of security, informed the waiting Armorindo Artha vans at street level that the service elevator was broken, the armed units should wait by the front lobby. All the while, the staff in the basement eyeballing the security monitors saw nothing but grey on their screens. Thinking it was just a loose cable, they put in a call to the IT department. Seconds later, the gang triggered the fire alarm. From the higher floors, two hundred employees, oblivious to what was taking place on the third floor, left their desks to file down the stairs, leaving the service elevator free.

146

'This gave the raiders an extra few minutes to fill their specially designed containers with cash. When they were done, they disengaged the CCTV cameras in the service elevator, pulled off their Balaclavas and made their getaway via the back exit and into a waiting removals van. Witnesses say they saw several removal men in brown overalls pushing wheeled metal boxes out of the building. Nobody thought it was suspicious at the time.'

'How much did they get away with?'

'I am not at liberty to say.'

'Fair enough, but what's this got to do with my investigation?'

'I tell you for why. It went too smoothly. Why did the CCTV cameras on the third floor stop working at precisely eight fifty-five? Because someone in the vault room knew the internal layout and cut the Cat-five-e cables.'

'You're saying it was an inside job.'

'We're considering it.'

Ruud looked thoughtful. 'And you think Shireen Zee was involved.'

'Again, there is a chance.'

'And her murder?'

'Perhaps she was asking for a bigger cut. Maybe she threatened to spill the beans.'

'So they killed her.'

'Could be.'

'I take it you've had access to her file. How do you explain the mah-jong tile?'

'Just to throw us off balance, confuse us.'

'Get us looking left when we should be looking right. And what about Mari Agnes Liem? How is she connected?'

147

His expression grew hard. 'That part has got us all mixed up. Why do you suppose I'm here talking to you, First *Inspektur?*'

The lieutenant colonel rose from his chair and Ruud took that as a signal to do the same. The two men sauntered into the corridor. They advanced between the desks, each one screened by cheap melamine partitions. Ruud led Timur Djamin to the water dispenser, filled two paper cups with cold water and handed him one. 'It's an interesting theory, but I can't see it myself. Nevertheless, we'll cross-reference Shireen Zee with anyone with a history of armed robbery on the database and see what the computer spits out. She may have been some gang member's girlfriend, or aunt, or sixth cousin once removed, but I doubt it. Shireen's death isn't gangster related.'

'How so?'

'We're hunting someone with a very different profile. This isn't about intimidation, or blackmail, or about keeping someone from talking. It's about revenge. Whoever killed Shireen Zee wanted her to acknowledge her crime and he wanted to send a message to the others.'

Timur Djamin brooded over this. 'Others?'

'I think Shireen Zee and Mari Agnes Liem were part of a club. A group of women, most likely, who met sporadically. My guess is he's picking them off one by one.'

'But you won't catch him unless he kills again, is that what you are saying?'

'It would seem that way.' Both men squeezed out a tight smile. Outside, muezzins fell silent. The prayers were over. The lieutenant colonel looked at Ruud a bit longer, then turned for the door.

★ ★ ★

Ruud saw Timur Djamin to the elevator. They shook hands and Ruud promised to pass on any relevant information that came his way.

The elevator door had only just closed and Ruud was halfway to his office when he saw her. His ex-mother-in-law. She was dressed in a dark mauve *kebaya*, brandishing a stainless-steel tiffin carrier.

'Oh God, no! No, no, no, no, no,' he hissed.

'Look-see, I bring you nourishment!' she yelled. Several detectives peeked out from their cubicles. 'Look what your loving Mumsy-in-law Panggabean has for you!'

He ushered her into his office and shut the door behind him.

The stink of Tiger Balm was overpowering.

'Why have you brought me food?' he asked.

'What? I cannot feed my son-in-law lunch?'

'Ex son-in—'

She stopped him. 'Just because you and your wife are no more does not mean I cannot feed you. And there is nothing in court documents to say we cannot be friends?'

'But I—'

She took his hand in hers. 'I feel guilty for what she has done to you. Guilt she obviously does not feel. This is my way of atoning for it.' She smiled into his eyes. 'Look at you, *meh*, you are too thin. Must eat!' She set the carrier down and released a small catch on either side of the handle. '*Gulai Bebek!*' she enthused, placing the top container on his desk. 'Your favourite ducky-waddle curry.' She went on her tiptoes and pressed his shoulders down with both hands. He sat.

'But I'm really not hungry,' he lied. He had not ingested a proper hot meal since his lunch with Imke and Erica.

'Eat! Eat!'

She laid out the cutlery on the desk and the containers of yellow rice and sweet potato *pilus*.

He stared at the steaming food. Everything looked delicious.

'My daughter running around with that playboy and you ask why I bring you nourishment?'

Ruud knew there was little point arguing; she never listened to reason; she only heard what went on in her head. The moment she made up her mind about something, everything else became white noise. He grabbed a spoon and fork.

'You go talk to your wife. Tell her to stop making me look bad, *nuh*?'

He mixed some of the dark spicy sauce with the yellow rice.

'Neighbours now complain. I have to turn TV on loud-loud. Your wife and bloody playboy making love noisier than two skeletons dancing on tin roof!'

He took a mouthful, closed his eyes, sat back and smiled.

Ruud lifted the plate to his nose. The curried duck, smelling of tamarind, lemongrass and galangal, always took him back to his childhood and a succession of summer evenings spent at his grandmother's house.

He was about to take a second mouthful when he saw a man approach the front desk and speak with the duty sergeant. Ruud's interest in the curry vanished. He rose from his chair, not taking his eyes off the man.

Mrs Panggabean used a finger to flick him on the ear. 'Eat!'

Ruud swiped her hand away.

Ruud took a step forward and stopped abruptly when he saw the brown package cradled in the man's hands. It was the size of a shoebox.

The man wore a black windbreaker, the type motorcycle couriers wore, and his face was pale. There was a wild, confused look in his eyes.

'What is it you are holding?' Ruud heard the duty sergeant ask. Ruud could almost hear the sergeant's thoughts – there's something suspicious in there. What is it? A gun? A home-made bomb? 'Please, *neh*, open it up for inspection.'

The man, looking even paler now, shook his head. His mouth opened monstrously wide to form some primal, silent scream.

The sight of this chilled Ruud's heart. His feet and ankles went stiff, almost freezing him to the spot. Ruud gave a shout of alarm and the man swivelled to face him. They locked eyes. The man's frenzied expression did not change. Realizing he had to act swiftly, Ruud dashed up to the man, pinned an arm behind his back, and frogmarched him out of the building.

A few minutes later, Ruud returned with the parcel tucked under his arm.

Commissioner Witarsa was there to confront him, fists planted on hips. He pulled Ruud to one side. 'What was that about?'

'It was nothing.' Ruud felt his entire body stiffen.

'Nothing?' The word exploded across the room. 'The duty sergeant almost hit the station alarm. What with the suicide bomber at Pojo then the blast at the Rajapolah headquarters—'

'It's not like that.' Ruud talked over him. He ignored the tight, balled feeling in his stomach.

Witarsa stared at him, demanding an explanation.

Ruud cringed; his first instinct was to shrink away, but the big man stepped across him. 'All right, all right. If you must know, that was my brother.'

'Your brother?'

'He has emotional issues. He doesn't like speaking to strangers. I was supposed to meet him outside by the coffee shop at noon but I forgot. And the new medication he's on makes him panic when things don't go as planned.' Ruud held up the parcel. 'It's a shoebox.' His hand moved over the lip of the box protectively to ensure the contents would not spill out. A mirthless smile stretched his face. 'I was going to play a game of badminton tonight. He was lending me some trainers.'

The commissioner tipped his head back suspiciously, eyebrows up, eyelids down. 'You share the same shoes?'

'We're the same size.'

Witarsa's jowly face grew dark. He rubbed his hands furiously across his brow. 'The investigation has not moved forward an inch and you're going off to play badminton.'

A tiny nerve rippled under the chief's eye.

'It helps clear my mind.'

'First your mother-in-law and now your brother. What the hell is this, a bloody Lebaran family festival?'

Mrs Panggabean stuck her head out from behind Ruud's door. 'I heard that! My son-in-law is a good policeman. He has more arrests underneath his belt than anyone in whole department.'

'Get these people out of my bloody station!'

Ruud turned and made for the restrooms, concentrating hard on walking normally. Behind him, Witarsa's voice took on a higher, more insistent pitch.

Ruud ignored Witarsa and tried to hide the fact that his hands were shaking. It took him twenty hurried strides to reach the men's room, where he locked himself in a cubicle and challenged himself to examine the parcel.

The package was sealed with tape, the name and address printed by hand:

INSP. POLISI SATU RUUD PUJASUMARTA (Iptu),
POLISI RESORT JAKARTA PUSAT,
61 JALAN KRAMAT RAYA,
JAKARTA

Ruud slowly cracked open the lid of the box and peeked inside.

His face turned pale.

He saw a wad of tissue paper and cotton wool. He peeled the tissue to one side and touched something spongy and soft. It was a pink tongue. And it was swaddled in cotton wool. Everything was coated red with dried blood.

He doubled over, trying not to retch.

For a moment or two everything went blurry.

153

Chapter Sixteen

Ruud held the shoebox in his hands.

He'd been in the toilet cubicle for ages.

He was breathless, panting audibly as if he'd run up several flights of stairs, three steps at a time.

Christ almighty I've got to do something. Take him to see a doctor. But he's already seeing a therapist every week. Get him to talk to somebody new then, somebody with better qualifications. I can't just ignore this . . . this behaviour. I've turned my back on it for too long. Magelang. I should take him to the psychiatric hospital in Magelang.

Now wait a minute. Have you thought this through? They'll institutionalize him. They'll say he's crazy. In a sense I suppose he is a little crazy but . . .

But what?

Shit. There's someone coming.

Voices from the corridor. Two men entered the restrooms, talking loudly. It was Vidi and Aiboy Ali. They took a piss and left without washing their hands.

Ruud came out from the cubicle. He scrubbed his hands with soap, ran his wet fingers through his hair and examined himself in the mirror. He put on his professional face.

'Don't', he said to himself, 'let this get to you. Just don't.'

He shut his eyes.

What the hell am I going to do? First things first: get rid of this fucking box.

Ruud stood under the shower. He'd fled from the station and returned home to confront his brother, but the flat was empty. The place still smelled of scorched coffee and the percolator was warm, so he knew Arjen had only just managed to give him the slip.

Once again Ruud scrubbed his hands with soap. He noted they were still trembling with the shock. A tongue. A fucking tongue! On the way he'd chucked the shoebox into a builder's skip, contents and all. He knew the rats would eventually get to it.

In a way he couldn't really blame his brother for his actions. But he certainly wouldn't condone it. The question that kept snatching at Ruud was why? Why would Arjen deliver a severed tongue to him in a box? Was he seeking approval? A reward? Was it meant as a trophy?

Ruud rubbed his face in frustration.

The stray cat had kept them both up for weeks, wailing and screeching each night by their first-floor window, squalling like a tortured child. It also left the vile smell of tomcat piss all over the place. Ruud imagined Arjen had lured the poor animal into the kitchen with a saucer of milk. Probably strangled it with a cord before severing the poor thing's tongue. Gruesome. Disgusting. Completely sick. What worried Ruud was that this might have happened before.

Yet, the flat itself was undisturbed. There were no signs of a struggle, no cat hair, no blood, no ruction whatsoever. Perhaps he did it in the back alley, out in the open. Just like that. Ruud shuddered. He shook off the thought. He'd have to report this to Arjen's therapists.

But Ruud already guessed what conclusions the shrinks would come to: more medication, stronger dosage and shinier pills. Where would Arjen be without the pills? What would Ruud do? These pills had become a beacon in Ruud's mind in the same way a marine buoy offers hope to the sea-tossed sailor.

It came to him then that his brother's illness was like a bushfire, moving with the wind, constantly changing direction, spreading quickly, always threatening to outflank him. Turn one way, it follows; turn the other, it chases.

The water stung Ruud's cheeks and throat, sandblasted him until he felt stripped of everything. Stripped of his mother-in-law's nagging voice, of his ex-wife's face, of the stories of her noisy lovemaking. Stripped of his brother. His crazy, crazy brother and the mutilated cats. Stripped of the cemetery smell of Mari Agnes Liem and Shireen Zee. Stripped of all the blood, horror and ugliness that came with his job.

He turned the taps off and wrapped himself in a towel.

Pinching the skin above his nose, he gazed at his reflection in the mirror and sucked in his upper lip. He looked awful. His eyes were swollen from overwork, his complexion blotchy and strained. He pressed two fingers to his throat, beneath the jawbone, probed the lymph nodes for soreness. Was he coming down with something? he wondered.

Down, up, down, up. He executed five quick thigh lunges, and then sank to his knees to perform ten push-ups, hands flush against the floor tiles.

He paused afterwards, straightened up, collected his thoughts, did one last thigh lunge and decided he was hungry. A slice of buttered bread with a little Vegemite on the side wouldn't go amiss.

Towelled dry, he scooped up his dirty clothes and threw them in the basket, then he entered his bedroom to get dressed. He flipped the switch on the radio and began snapping his fingers. The station was playing a funky R&B mix. He turned up the sound, clicked his fingers and bobbed his head, loudly singing the chorus to himself, jutting his chin to the rhythm. The phone rang. The caller display showed it was Imke.

Then it came to him again, the joyous expression on Imke's face when he greeted her at the airport. It was absurd, he thought, how easily she managed to make him smile.

'Hey,' he said, pulling up his trousers. 'What news of your aunt?'

'She hasn't turned up. I'm really worried, Ruud, I can't think where she's gone. Something has to be done, she's been missing for over twenty-four hours.'

Frowning, Ruud buckled his belt, clipped the handcuff pouch in place and secured his Heckler & Koch 9mm into the belt holster. His head tilted to support the handset between his chin and shoulder. 'Do you want me to come over?'

'If you can.'

He continued to dress in fits and starts, listening as she described her sleepless night. At the same time he checked his laptop for emails from Witarsa or Aiboy Ali. He knew he ought to return directly to the station. There was so much that needed to be done: the security cameras from the HERO alleyway had to be re-examined; there were calls to be made to the Prosecutor's Office, reports to be typed; he had to cross-reference Shireen Zee with anyone with a history of armed robbery; the women in Mrs Zee's photograph needed to be identified.

He entered the kitchen, grabbed some bread, butter and Vegemite. The electric clock on the oven blinked 1.14 p.m.

Ruud squeezed his eyes shut. 'I'll be with you in an hour.'

The lunchtime rush-hour traffic was already backed up to the bottom of Taman Bunga. Ruud ran the hard shoulder, fastened the magnetic blue light and turned on the siren. Lights flashing, he sped up the ramp and hit the Jagorawi Toll Road ten minutes later. His eyes slid past the highway signs and advertising billboards.

It was a quarter to three when the unmarked Toyota Yaris reached the bungalow. Ruud had called Imke on the way to ask after Erica – still no sign of her. He told her not to panic.

Imke was standing barefoot by the door as his car drove up. She wore no make-up and had her hair pulled back in a scrunchie. She crumpled her eyes against the glare of the sun.

'Thank you for coming all this way.' Imke reached for his hand and cradled it in her own, leading him inside with a tug.

Ruud paused in the sitting room, trying to get his bearings.

The bungalow was silent and empty. Ruud stepped out through the double doors onto the verandah. He stretched his gaze to the left and then to the right; along the base of the bamboo grove a security guard rested on a plastic chair with his baton by his ankles. Lolling against the shrubbery, his head was tilted back, mouth open. He appeared to be fast asleep.

Ruud examined the easel and looked at the canvas, at the abandoned brushes, sticks and trowels. The smell of oil paint, turpentine and linseed oil hovered thinly. He scrutinized the Nivea SPF 40 sun lotion and replaced the tube on the workbench. 'Have you tried Kiki?'

'Yes, but no luck. I used the night gown Erica slept in, raised it right up to Kiki's nose.' Imke bent at the knees and stroked the dog's head. 'We ran outside together – she's not allowed out unrestrained because of the deer, so I had her on a lead – but she came across as confused. The rain didn't help either. She got as far as the lake then lost the trail. My God, do you think Erica drowned in the lake?'

His voice was gentle. 'I know this isn't easy for you, but I don't want to speculate. Can I see her room?'

Imke nodded. Her face was flushed and a nerve jumped in her cheek.

All the drapes in Erica's room remained closed against the tropical light. Ruud stepped into the semi-darkness.

'Apart from me, have the police been here?'

'The Captain, he's the head of the household staff, didn't want policemen traipsing through the palace grounds. The President wouldn't like that, he said.'

'But he doesn't mind me being here.'

'I told him you're a friend.'

Ruud took in the queen-size bed, the silk damask headboard, the silhouettes of furniture, the general clutter of the disarranged room. 'Nothing's been touched?' he asked.

Imke shook her head.

He stepped across the threshold. Slivers of light crept through the cracks in the curtains. He went over to the bed. A sweet smell of marshmallows rose up from the sheets.

Digging into his trousers, he whipped out a small plastic

container and threw back an energy tablet. 'Anything missing?' He dropped his voice to a whisper.

'I don't think so. Why are you whispering?'

His forehead creased. 'I don't know.'

He flipped on the overhead lights. Together they leafed through Erica's possessions, looking for a clue to her whereabouts amongst the wreckage of Aero wrappers and jellybean tins. They found nothing of note. He made his way into the adjoining bathroom, picking up the crumpled towel on the floor and hanging it on a rail. When he returned he slid a chair over and sat. Imke was already seated on the edge of the bed; her shoulders slumped forward.

'Erica's toothbrush is still here,' he said.

After several moments, Imke made a noise in her throat. It sounded like a suppressed whimper.

'Are you all right,' he asked.

'Something terrible has happened to her, hasn't it?' Imke looked at Ruud for confirmation.

They locked eyes.

'She's been kidnapped,' she said quickly, fearing the awful truth. 'Hasn't she?'

'It's too early to say, but usually if someone is taken we would have heard something by now. The kidnappers would have made contact.'

'But what if they don't want anything in return? What if this is politically motivated? Or the work of a single madman?'

Ruud didn't reply. He crossed his arms and tried not to think of the worst outcome to all this, but all he could see were emergency vehicle lights, yellow barricade tape and a dead body in a ditch.

Ruud gave Imke's arm a reassuring squeeze. He wondered when would be a good time to ask Imke if her aunt knew either Shireen Zee or Mari Agnes Liem, or whether she ever played mah-jong.

'Jesus.' Imke shifted her legs, wanting to stand up, to get up onto her feet, itching to move. 'Sitting here is doing Erica no good whatsoever, Ruud,' said Imke. She banged both fists against her hips in frustration.

'What do you propose we do?'

'We should get into your car and go and look for her.'

Ruud sighed and ran a hand through his hair, then dropped it quickly. 'Come on then. We good to go?'

It took only a moment to get Kiki's harness on.

The car headed east on Jalan Kapten Muslihat. Ruud drove as far as the Cibalok River before doubling back.

He stopped every few miles to show pedestrians a picture of Erica. Nobody admitted to seeing her.

Imke pressed her forehead to the glass. The sun beat down. The window glass was hot to the touch, yet Imke leaned so hard against it her left arm went numb.

They took a minor road and made for a rural town to the south. Despite the recent rains, the town square was dry and dusty. Ruud parked the car and Imke cracked open the back windows for Kiki. She got out. Her left arm tingled. She shook her fingers vigorously to coax the blood back into them, shivering the silver bracelet on her wrist. Cicadas shrilled at full volume. A swarm of scooters swept past, kicking up grit. The dirt in the air left her teeth grainy.

She approached a small family shop where two tinsmiths sat hunched over a table. One man blew into a little pipette.

The other used a rawhide hammer and a pair of small pliers to form intricate bits of jewellery.

Imke pulled out her mobile and asked the tinsmiths if the *bule* woman in the photo looked familiar. They said no, she did not look at all familiar, before offering to sell her some earrings on the cheap.

Just then Ruud's phone rang. He spoke quickly, then dipped his head and blew out his cheeks.

'What is it?' demanded Imke.

The folds of skin around his eyes crumpled. 'There's been a development. I have to go.'

'What is it? What are you not telling me?'

'They've found another body, Imke. Not far from here.'

'Is it Erica?'

'I haven't got any firm info.'

'What did they say?'

Ruud hesitated. 'They said she's a foreigner.'

Chapter Seventeen

Wednesday. 11.47 p.m.

A moderate earthquake struck Serang this morning. People may not be aware of this but we experience at least one per day in Indonesia.

The earth rumbles.

My brother rumbles.

He is as excited as a little boy at a birthday party.

I urge him to calm down. 'One moment you're like a goat butting a fence, the next you are hopping about resembling a fly.'

My brother looks at me. Smiles. Loosening the draw-strings of his mouth.

There has been a shift in him, you see, a delirium threatening to bubble over. But I know that smile. *Aduh*, it is a dangerous one; a temblor rumbling just below the sur-face that contains the potential for horrendous violence.

He shakes with new-found excitement, venting like a sulphur chimney. He has a new victim. An older lady. One he did not expect to find. The one he calls the poisonous foreigner – *bule beracun*.

A vein on his temple throbs and thrums. It is not unlike

watching a volcano spill or an earthquake unfold before my eyes. A great, swelling *terra mobilis*.

They say that several hours before the earth trembles dogs run into the open howling for the dead. Cows buck and rear, kicking down the walls of their sheds. Birds fall from the sky. Often, water will rise up out of the soil, throwing bugs from their holes and earthworms from their chambers. Even crocodiles, the most cool-headed of coldbloods, clutch their offspring in their mouths and flee for their lives. If I were a crocodile, I too would flee for my life now. But I do not. I cannot.

Instead, I regard him.

He unfurls the red handkerchief and lays it flat on the floor and positions the meat cleaver at its centre.

Carefully, almost reverently, he picks up an insulated box and places it by the handkerchief. The box is packed with dry ice and has a padded hole in the middle, shaped to house a single hand.

As eruptions go, this is on the Krakatoa scale.

Thursday. 2.30 a.m.
My mother, may the fires of hell forever burn her, once told me we were conceived from fevered sperm. My father had been ill with the shivering for some days and she'd nursed him back to health. She claimed that as soon as he recovered he thrust his seed in her, but she knew the seed was bad. Charred black from the sickness, she'd said.

Two seeds. One egg. The single zygote that splits to form two embryos.

There are numerous stories of the ungodly twin on Indonesian television. Even Hollywood uses the device at times.

Yes, the TV tells us we must always fear the evil twin, and if the TV says this then it must be true. Why? Because omnipresent television has replaced God in our lives.

Please forgive me. I am meandering. I may also come across at times as light-minded, but people are wont to hide their fears in different ways, no?

Thursday. 7.25 a.m.
They call Bogor the rainiest city in Java. Now I see why.

We are both soaked to the skin, but it is he who does the heavy lifting.

The phlegm gathers in his throat. My brother is panting. Fifteen minutes. He has dragged the old lady by her feet across a field, in the rainstorm, for fifteen long minutes, taking 889 steps. He counts as he pulls, her ankles tucked under his armpits. The sodden earth sucks at his feet. He is pleased that it's raining. The downpour will wash away his trail and a good part of the blood and trace evidence. But he is careful. His body is swathed in a grey bed sheet, like a vagabond, concealing his identity from any curious onlookers gathering for a pre-dawn stroll. He has covered his shoes in rags tied on with string. This has altered the shape of his footprint. Later, he will go over his tracks and fluff up the earth with a tree branch.

He selects a spot, hidden by thick foliage, and sets her down on her back, securing her arms with rope. He squats and waits, watching the woman wake from her induced sleep. He passes the mah-jong tile from gloved hand to gloved hand, studying her, savouring her. She stirs. Her eyelids flicker to life. A smile stretches across his face – a grin like the Garuda – and almost tenderly he thrusts first the tile and then the red handkerchief between her teeth, pushing it deep into her mouth. Her breath whistles through her nostrils. He shows her the meat cleaver and gazes into her saucer-wide eyes.

Her throat emits a thick gurgling noise that sounds like yesterday's leftover, lumpy custard clogging up the drain.

His fingers gouge at her throat.

She howls through the gag.

He squeezes. Watches the colour of her cheeks turn an impossible purple, hears the last tiny pocket of air expel from her lungs. Then releases.

She is still conscious.

He rolls up the left sleeve of her top. First he caresses the five long, thin metacarpal bones, then he tickle-touches her forearm and feathers his way up, all the way to her shoulder. Tracing slippery S shapes across her collarbone. Now he is stroking her chest, feeling her heart thumping against his palm. Another grin. He likes what he sees. She is large breasted. Just like Mother.

Six, seven, eight. He counts out twenty beats, leaning in so close their noses brush.

The first of the day's little green *angkots* clatter through the streets, a mere mile away, heading from the minibus depot to God knows where. I can even hear the clip-clop-clop of a horse-cart taxi hurrying along.

He removes a glove. He likes to touch them just as they die. But he is careful and makes sure he leaves no prints on the solid areas where he thinks they will show – fingernails, teeth, eyeballs and bits of clothing. He only ever touches the skin.

I sing the 'Nina Bobo' lullaby in my head and wait.

He strokes the knob of her chin with his thumb and tells

her she is about to go to the other side, below the earth's surface where she belongs.

Like the other two, he will remove this one's hand whilst she is still alive. He raises the meat cleaver high in one seamless motion and blood spatters all over his waterproofs. It's a good thing he is wearing protection.

Nobody shouts. Nobody screams. The only witnesses are the starlings rustling in the trees.

The trees, towering above us, rise 30 feet into the pewtered sky. Dawn is near. A silver-and-grey hour. Over there is Mount Salak, in the far distance. And over here, by my feet, a dying, petrified woman lies shaking and twitching, her pants clogged with the stink of her own piss.

Alive, for now.

He takes a celebratory breath. The air is fresh, or as fresh as can be hoped for in a city of 11 million.

I see him grinning in the dawning light, see him wipe the sweat and rain from his eyes. Raindrops streak down his chin. He smells of leaves. Not leaves basking healthily in the sunshine, but leaves left to rot on a damp soil bed.

Thursday. 5.48 p.m.
The television news channels carry reports of a body found in the woods. The fear and anticipation threaten to possess me.

Possession: what a fascinating word, don't you think, conveying something tangible, carnal and haunted.

My brother is possessed. He has demons.

No. You do not understand. I am not being fantastical here. There are real demons inside him. I saw them take him. I saw it with my own eyes. The *pocongs* fighting for his soul. They were black and churning the air cold. There was one

167

in particular, hanging over him with its blood-red face and protruding fangs, whispering: 'Here are the corpses, here are the corpses.' For the briefest moment its yellow eyeballs studied me sideways, hungrily, before returning to my brother.

I wanted to scream out, but the air had been drawn out of me. And there was this smell. Of hot embers and burned chicken feathers. It is the smell of the seven gates of *Jahannam*. The place that is blacker than tar.

They've breeched his defences already, you see, and they are busy supping on his soul.

The terrifying thing for me is when people look at me they see an imposter.

They see my brother.

This is why I have built my little shrine without him knowing. I want people to understand that we are different. The Zoo Man, you see, was exactly like me. And he got away with it.

Chapter Eighteen

The weather had altered considerably by the time Ruud and Imke arrived at the crime scene. A torrential downpour lasting fifteen minutes left the entire landscape waterlogged. Culverts and storm drains grew choked, so much so that Ruud was obliged to park the Toyota Yaris on high ground, forcing him to make his way down to the wooded area on foot. The rain continued to fall in long sweeps.

'Stay put,' he instructed Imke bluntly.

'I'm coming with you.' She was clipping Kiki to a lead.

Ruud signalled to a policewoman in a white headscarf pinned under her chin.

'No. Imke, you shouldn't even be here.'

'She's my aunt.'

'All we have is a body. There's nothing to indicate that the body is Erica's. Stay here until further notice. I mean it. And don't let Kiki off her lead until the forensic team give the all-clear.'

He left Imke under the supervision of the female police officer.

The rain eased up. Ruud negotiated the high shelf of the road and slithered down the hill and across the muddy floodplain. Aiboy Ali, donning a rain-lashed Metallica vest, intercepted him and led him to a police 4×4. He had a word with the woman seated in the back who'd found the corpse. She'd been out walking her cocker spaniel. It was one of the few places in the neighbourhood, she said, where dogs were permitted to roam. She called 110 as soon as she realized what she'd stumbled upon.

Ruud thanked her, told her to leave her details with Aiboy Ali and made his way to where the tall acacias formed a copse. He ducked under the crime scene tape and saw several of his fellow detectives smoking busily as they talked into their mobile phones.

He discovered Solossa on his knees picking bits of earth from the victim's mouth with a pair of long tweezers. 'I'd say she's been dead ten, eleven hours, Pujasumarta. On display for all to see. MO is the same as the others. Left hand gone. Hacked off crudely but cleanly. I still can't work out if he wants the hand as a trophy or some sort of fetish object. Anyway, I suspect we'll find out soon enough.' Solossa paused to allow Arief, the police photographer, to take a snap. A shoo of the fingers unsettled the flies crawling in the slicks of blood. 'We pulled the red handkerchief from between her teeth and sure enough, abracadabra, there it was. A mah-jong tile. It's all been bagged and labelled. Oh, and she's a foreigner all right. See this thing round her neck?'

The woman's corneas peered blankly at Ruud, her tongue exposed at one corner of her mouth. Raindrops fell on her cheekbones but her doll's eyes kept staring. There were leaves in her hair, stuck to her neck and throat. The backs of her clothes were stained green.

His stomach muscles drew in. He found it hard not to gag. He took in the contours of her waxy face, her torn outfit, the mutilated left arm, before turning immediately to

170

traipse up the muddy slope to his car, wanting to be the one to break the news to Imke.

A light shower had begun to fall again. A second spell of heavy rain was nearing. Ruud looked up and saw Imke watching him.

Imke was standing by the car. The anxiety in her face was obvious. Her hair partly shielded her eyes, which had a barren quality. Her nose was running. She wiped it with the heel of a hand. The desperation in her movements masked a crushing certainty. She tried to look resolute.

As Ruud drew close, the female officer moved to one side, the static from her police radio filling the silence.

He wrapped his arms round her and held her tight. He held her as if to keep her from falling. She fought to break loose.

'It's not her,' he said.

She felt as if she could hardly breathe.

'Say that again.'

'It's not Erica.'

A rush of unfathomable relief coursed through Imke. 'Oh God. Are you sure?' she said, in a voice that steadied as she spoke. 'There's no mistake?'

'Yes, I'm sure.'

'Who is she?'

'I don't know yet. I didn't ask. All I know is she's wearing a pink jogging suit. We think she's from Thailand. She's wearing a locket round her neck containing a picture of the Thai King.'

Ruud let go of her. Imke felt her legs weaken. Both she and Ruud leaned back against the bonnet of the car as if to catch their thick breaths. Behind them, a cloud of insects formed. Hundreds upon thousands of winged ants rose and sank in the fading light.

'I'll get someone to drive you back to Bogor.'

'No. You wanted Kiki's and my help. Let me work the surrounding area with her. Someone can take me home later.'

'Erica's still missing.'

'Yes, she is. But the ground disturbance is fresh. We should get in there before it becomes diffused.'

'Are you up to it?'

'Of course I am.' It was important for her to do this. She reached into the car and grabbed a bottle of water. She unscrewed the lid and tipped the contents over her head. 'I wanted to plunge my face into a basin of cold water, but this will have to do.' She smoothed back her wet hair and wrung it out. With the colour back in her face, she clicked her tongue at Kiki and led the dog down the slope.

Back and forth, men in padded headphones swept the ground with handheld metal detectors.

It was wet. Tree boughs rustled, shadows moved with a liquid flutter. Imke turned up her collar even though the rain had slackened. They'd been at the crime scene for almost an hour waiting for the forensic team to finish their job. A white tent was set up but only the technicians were allowed anywhere near it. Imke wasn't sure how much more of this she could take. She could tell Kiki was growing impatient, straining at the leash one moment, lying down and whining the next. Imke, too, felt agitated, strung out. She looked at her watch and did a quick calculation. Her aunt vanished some thirty hours ago.

Her nerves jangled. 'How much longer?' she pressed Ruud, her tone unnecessarily sharp.

Strange, she thought. Before today she'd witnessed numerous crime scenes, come across many decomposing bodies, but now she found herself shaking. Was it the sight of the victim that had spooked her? Because it could have been Erica lying there? Or was it just tiredness causing this jitteriness? Imke reminded herself that she hadn't slept at all the previous night. She was running on adrenaline.

'Won't be long now,' said Ruud.

Imke looked across to see the tech team trudging off, removing their gloves and masks like surgeons after a successful appendectomy. Some of them turned to glance at Imke, giving her a curious stare. She could read their thoughts: What's this Western woman doing at a crime scene? Must be a journalist. Probably CNN. Wonder if she'll come over and interview me?

She could still see the corpse in the near distance, the face white, waxy. A thin black centipede skittered across the dead woman's nose. Even from here, Imke could identify the victim's trainers as Nikes. In her line of work she saw trainers of various styles, but Nikes were the most common: Zoom Vapors, Air Max Lites, Low Tops, LeBron Lifestyles, even old timers like Rifts or Epics sometimes made an appearance. She could never remember the dead people's faces or their names but she always remembered their shoes. Three months ago, from the bottom of Kloveniersburgwal Canal, they fished out a six-year-old boy in brand-new Puma Drift Cats. He'd probably only just learned how to tie up the laces.

When Ruud went over to talk to Solossa for a second time, Imke checked her phone for messages and found her inbox empty, so she called The Captain and was put straight through to his voicemail. Exasperated, she hit redial, only to get the same result.

She looked up. Some teenagers skulked, smoking in the distance by the Bank Agris billboard, chucking stones in the river, sending showers of earth into the air. The wind carried their voices back to Imke. She knew they hoped to catch a glimpse of the corpse, something grisly and exciting to tell their friends. A burst of light made her turn her attention to her left. Imke saw the police photographer squat down by the victim, snapping pictures of the deceased from different angles, twisting his lens. He was all arms and elbows. The flash bulb popped every few seconds. Sated, the cameraman got to his feet and turned to glare at Imke, bristling with menace. Imke felt a niggling sense of disquiet. She'd felt his eyes on her a few times. She wanted to ask the two questions that had been on her mind since the outset. Who are you? And why do you keep staring at me?

Moments later he approached her. 'Need a lift home?' he asked in Bahasa Indonesia. He mimed turning a steering wheel.

She shook her head. He put his fingers together and cracked the joints, snapping them like dry twigs, then turned and made his way up the slope.

Aiboy Ali came and stood by her side with an umbrella. His Metallica vest was matted with rain and the fine hairs on his arms stuck to his skin. 'I wouldn't get in a same car with him either,' said Aiboy Ali, the umbrella held away from him to shield Imke. 'Gives me the shivers that one. He makes copies of all the dead he photographs and sells them online to sickos. Heaven knows what else he does with them.'

'Charming-looking fellow,' she said. 'He's got tombstones for eyes. Reminds me of a predatory bird.'

Wind buffeted Aiboy Ali's umbrella. He shook a cigarette out of a packet and offered her one.

'I don't smoke,' she said, yet she took one from the outstretched packet nonetheless. He leaned forward conspiratorially and lit it for her. 'You and *Gajah* known each other a long time, is it?'

Her nerves settled following the first drag. 'Nearly all our lives.' The smoke made her lightheaded.

'What was he like as a boy?' probed Aiboy Ali with a naughty Cheshire cat smile, his entire body sprouting mischief. She could tell he liked nothing better than to wind Ruud up and that he was a terrible tease. 'I bet he was a – how do you say, in England – a person who always wears an anorak.'

'A geek.'

'A geek! Please tell me he was one.'

Amused, Imke suppressed a laugh. From what she recalled, it was she who'd been the geek. It was Imke who'd memorized the first ten digits of Pi; Imke who'd played chess at recess; Imke who'd drawn maps of fictional storybook realms.

'Yes, he was a huge geek,' she lied. 'The biggest.'

He did a fist clench, his long hair falling over his face. 'I knew it! Wait till I tell Vidi!'

It was just getting dark by the time Witarsa arrived. He had a raincoat over his arm. 'DO WE,' he cried out the first two words before mumbling the remaining ones under his breath. '. . . have a name?'

The police commissioner's eyes appeared red and rheumy,

as if he'd been rubbing his face with curry leaves. He wore the usual basset-hound expression of doleful disdain.

'Not yet. All she had on her was a set of keys. The victim was wearing a jogging suit and running shoes. Early morning stroll by the water, I should think,' said Aiboy Ali. 'No phone, wallet or ID.'

'House keys?'

'Yes, looks like it, but certainly not car keys so she probably walked from her home.'

'Get a dozen or so uniforms to go door to door and see if she's from the neighbourhood. Do we know the time of death?'

'Only very approximate.'

Witarsa shrugged on his raincoat. The coat was old and curling at the lapels. He spotted Solossa and waved the pathologist over.

The *dokter forensik* approached. His thin hair was dishevelled and there were sweat stains under each arm. Solossa dropped his leather satchel and removed a comb from his shirt pocket. He ran the comb over his scalp before extrapolating. 'Twelve hours at a guess, but we will only know once we have her on the slab. We'll get the most accurate reading by establishing the concentration of potassium in the vitreous humour.' He snorted. 'That's the fluid in her eyes.'

'What else?'

Aiboy Ali plucked at his black vest, peeling the skull from his sticky back. 'A man selling breakfast buns from his *bemo* said he thought he heard a woman's high-pitched shout.'

Ruud joined them under the streetlamp, pulling his windbreaker hood tight to keep out the rain. 'When was this?'

'About seven this morning,' said Aiboy Ali.

'Did he see anything?'

'No, *Gajah*, he was setting up shop. The sun wasn't up. And the makeshift stall selling sweet tea, just over there,' he pointed, 'they saw nothing either.'

'So she was abducted here and then dragged over the grass to where the trees are,' affirmed Witarsa, pacing.

'About half a mile. If you look carefully you can see the impressions made in the turf, but he's covered his tracks well. The rain has washed a lot of it away too. Good thing we had the dog.'

Kiki had done her job well. With Imke's guidance, she had led them from where the body lay all the way to the edge of the river.

The forensic unit was now working on the nearby picnic tables, wooden benches and rubbish bins.

'What else do we know?' asked Witarsa.

'There's a needle mark on her neck, so I suspect he used the same veterinary sedative, Xylazine. A small controlled dose disabled her in seconds, putting her in a paralysed state, immobile but conscious,' said Solossa.

'Any sign of the used hypodermic?'

'We're still searching,' said Aiboy Ali.

'He's a lunatic,' Witarsa proclaimed.

'I'm not so sure he is, sir,' cautioned Ruud. 'That title implies he's mentally impaired and acts in an unpremeditated way, that he's somewhat unprofessional. Everything I've seen indicates that he is careful and methodical. The ditty he left at the first victim's house advertises where he's going to leave the bodies. Think about it, verse three of the note reads:

Cabe-cabean, Cabe-cabean, garbage in the fill
Fishes for her supper in the parkland rill

And the third victim, here, is found in a park by the river. Do you see what I'm getting at? This guy's no lunatic. It's all been deliberately planned out.'

Ruud pulled a photograph from the plastic binder tucked under his arm. 'Which brings me to this.'

Witarsa glared at the photograph. It was the one of Shireen and her mah-jong group, taken at the *kampung* house.

Ruud unbuckled his penlight and shone the beam at the image. 'This one here is Shireen Zee. Next to her is Mari Agnes Liem. Now, look at the woman standing on her right,' said Ruud. 'That's her lying dead over there. Three of these women have been murdered. Sir, you have to get this photo to the press. It's the only way we're going to identify the other two women. We have to warn each one before it's too late. The clock is ticking for them.'

'But the papers will have a field day with this.'

'You'll have every middle-aged biddy huddled, fear-stricken in her home, refusing to venture out,' said Aiboy Ali with sarcasm.

'Sir, we need you to deal with the media.'

Vidi came over, holding his mobile in his hand. He was in his dark brown police threads with the shiny studs on the sleeves. 'I just got off the phone with the tech boys. They've come back with enhanced CCTV images from the HERO alleyway. You were right. He used a car. But I have good news, bad news and very bad news.'

'Let's hear it,' groaned Witarsa.

'The perpetrator drives a black Toyota Camry. That's the good news, izzenit.'

The commissioner gave Vidi a rallying pat on the chest.

'What about the driver?'

'The driver gets out of the car and removes what

resembles a body from the boot; he's wearing a hoodie so his features are hidden.'

'So we've got nothing?'

'Nothing. The data was corrupted.'

Ruud swore.

'The lab used Genuine Fractals 6, but as the images were captured through a convex mirror the coverage is patchy at best and they could only pick out the first letter of the number plate – B.'

'Jakarta plates,' said Witarsa. 'Look, I want this fucker found. Top priority. Tell them to outsource if they have to. I don't give a damn about the budget cuts. There's an Australian firm we've used before. The one based in Sydney. Send them the footage a.s.a.p. Get me visual clarity, facial mapping, enhanced stills, the works. I don't care how much it costs. Anything else?'

Vidi opened his notepad and repositioned his square bifocals to read out the figures. 'I made a few calls to the Ministry of Transportation and did a few calculations. There are thirteen point one million authorized vehicles in the greater Jakarta area, two and half million of them are cars with registration code B, and an estimated hundred thousand are Toyota Camrys.'

Ruud swore again.

'But the really bad news is the licence plate is not white on black,' Vidi's voice gave a little tremor, 'it's yellow on red.'

Ruud's shoulders went rigid. He exchanged glances with Vidi and saw the fear in his colleague's eyes. It was the look of a captured animal.

'What are we going to do?' asked Aiboy Ali, rattled.

After a moment's thought, Ruud realized there wasn't much more they could do.

'I don't believe this,' sputtered Witarsa. 'This is the last bloody thing we need.' He puffed out his jowly cheeks and lifted his face to the sky. 'If this gets out it's going to cause a media shitstorm.'

At the top of the hill Ruud pushed through the scrum of news people. He was withdrawn.

'How are you?' asked Imke.

He looked around at the mass of reporters and whirring cameras. 'Popular.' Held back by a line of traffic cops in yellow jackets, a dense crowd of jostling onlookers and press had gathered, men and women with microphones, SLRs and questions.

'Tell me what that means,' urged Imke as they got into his car. 'Yellow on red.'

Ruud shifted the blue Toyota into reverse, turned the steering wheel and heard the mud shoot out from under the tyres. There were leaves and grass stuck to the bottom of his shoes.

As the car splashed through the potholes, Ruud didn't take his eyes off the road.

'Car licence plates in Jakarta can be distinguished by their colour. White letters on a black background are for private vehicles. Black on yellow for public transport. White on red for fire engines.'

'What's yellow on red?'

'Ministry of Defence.'

'No way.'

'Yes way. For once I'm worried what we might uncover.'

Imke stared at him. 'You think the killer is a government minister?'

180

'I don't know what to think right now.' Headlamps on full beam to see through the rain and swarms of motorcycles, the car found its way onto the Jagorawi Toll Road, linking Jakarta to Bogor.

Ruud made a call on his mobile. 'Vidi, how long before the Australian firm comes back with enhanced surveillance footage? No, not good enough. Yep, OK, tell them to make it three days. Also I want you to use your phone and discreetly film the onlookers, film every face in the crowd. If we're lucky our perp may be watching.' He hung up.

Seconds later he made another call, this time to Aiboy Ali. 'Do you have access to a laptop and wireless connection?'

'Yes, *Gajah*, we're set up for it in the van.'

'I need you to get me some information.'

'Hold on.'

'How long will you be?' Ruud did not get a reply, but he could hear Aiboy Ali's footsteps clomp through the mud and the van door sliding open.

'OK. I'm at the laptop.'

'The Ministry of Defence is split into two sections. ABRI is responsible for the armed forces and HANKAM looks after the administrative end of things, but has no say when it comes to military command. I bet if you do a search you'll find that most MOD-registered Toyota Camrys belong to HANKAM, while ABRI have a pool of Land Rover LWBs.'

Ruud stepped on the accelerator and overtook a lorry.

Imke sucked in her breath as he narrowly missed sideswiping a Honda Integra. She made sure her seat belt was securely fastened.

'Listen to me, I want you to look up HANKAM and tell me everything you can find. I'll stay on the line.'

Ruud reached into his hip pocket, took out a box of Head

Start pills and swallowed one. He turned away a fraction, trying to hide his anxiety from Imke.

He waited as the windscreen wipers swished. Silently, they listened to the rhythm of the rubber blades as they moved in an arc.

'*Gajah*, you still there? OK, I have some info.' Aiboy Ali read out the names of the minister, the secretary general and the three directorates-general, before expanding on the organizational structure and number of support staff.

Ruud made a mental note of his colleague's tenacity and ferreting abilities, and wondered if he had any weasel blood in his DNA.

'Great. See what else you can dig up. Also, check if a black Toyota Camry assigned to HANKAM was reported stolen, then call me straight back.'

Aiboy Ali exhaled over the phone. Ruud knew exactly what he was thinking: this case was going to take up all of his time – and the Football World Cup was about to get under way. Aiboy Ali loved watching World Cup games almost as much as he loved thrashing and banging to a Megadeth solo.

'Keep at it, OK?'

'Yes, *Gajah*.' He rang off.

Ruud stared ahead at the road, squinting at the glare of the oncoming headlights, preoccupied. Trying to work it out.

Imke turned and scrutinized him. He looked tired round the eyes. Aware that she was watching him, he raised his eyebrows and shot her a sideways glance.

'What's the matter?'

'There's something about the police photographer I don't like. He gives me the creeps.'

Ruud felt the same way but didn't say so.

'Was he at the crime scenes before anyone else?'

'Why do you ask?'

'It's just a question.'

'Imke, this isn't some TV crime drama, the suspect isn't one of the cast of characters.'

'I'm just saying.'

'I know what you're saying.'

An uncomfortable silence followed.

'What are you thinking?' she asked eventually.

'What am I thinking? I'm thinking I could do with a very strong coffee.'

A long beat.

'Our perp is going to go after the other women, isn't he?'

'Yep.'

'He'll make a mistake, Ruud, and when he does you'll catch him.'

'I know. I know. But what I don't understand is why now? He's kept his anger and urges under control for so long ... and then suddenly this, one after the other, three victims in a fortnight. Boom! This explosion. Projecting all his hate, frustration and self-loathing onto these women. What's triggered it?' He was thinking out loud. Speaking quickly as if time was not on his side. His voice was low and close. 'Something's pushed him over the edge. Was it a death in the family? The full moon? Some weird magnetic pulse in his brain? A chemical disorder? Like some kind of psychotic imbalance. Perhaps the severed hands are an allusion to the fists that beat him as a child.' Ruud drummed his fingers on the steering wheel. Imke wasn't sure if he was talking to her or to himself.

'I thought you said he was killing his mother. That every time he kills one of these women, he sees her in his head. That she was the one that abused him.'

183

'I'm not discounting it.'

'But you're right,' agreed Imke. 'Something triggered him off.'

'Conceivably, somebody has come back into his life, a special someone who left him and hurt him. He might be seeking approval.'

'From whom?' asked Imke. 'His parents? An ex-girlfriend? A childhood sweetheart?'

'I don't know, but one thing's for sure. He's looking for a response.'

Ruud drove at speed. 'Cutting off the hands and taking them induces a feeling of power. As does leaving the mahjong tiles. They're a symbol.'

'A symbol for what?'

'For what that someone did to him.'

184

Chapter Nineteen

At the security gate Ruud flashed his police credentials, stretching his arm through the car's open window. The rain had stopped falling and only the occasional needle-tip of mizzle prickled the air. The guards in the kiosk raised the barrier and Ruud continued along the driveway, passing the small bamboo thicket to the left before parking by the lane leading to the staff quarters. Along the exterior walls of the bungalow, garden snails clung to the stucco to keep from drowning.

Ruud removed his muddy shoes and held the front door open for Imke and they entered the bungalow. She removed her shoes too, but that didn't prevent Kiki from leaving mud-tracks all over the floor. The lights were already on and the ceiling fans whirred overhead. The houseboy must have switched on the drawing room lights and the lanterns on the verandah. Imke flopped into a sofa, exhausted. 'God, what a day.' The leather cushions hissed under her weight.

'Do you want anything to eat, *hè*?'

Ruud checked his watch; it was well after eight. 'No, I'd better head off,' he said, standing in his socks, rubbing the back of his tired neck with his hand.

'That reminds me. I should feed Kiki. Poor girl's been on the go since morning.'

'She did a great job today.'

'I've got a bottle of duty-free brandy. You sure you don't want to stay for a drink?'

'Did somebody say drink?' A fluting voice rang out bell-like across the room. 'I'm going to ban the use of that word! Abstinence should be the order of the day. Abstinence!'

They heard a clicking sound from the verandah, and in that instant the doors slid open and Erica barged in.

She perched on the threshold for several seconds and slapped at a bug on her arm, before hastily sliding the doors shut behind her. She stood stiff-legged with her Solillas sandals dangling from her fingers and walking cane under her arm. Both Imke and Ruud stared at her in utter shock and amazement.

'An awful word, I know! Brings up such awful images of Calvinists and puritans on their ducking stools. And besides, it's so damn difficult to spell – is it 'ence' or 'ance'? I can never remember. But if you'd had the kind of night I've had you'd be off the sauce, too, I can assure you.'

Stupefied, Imke rose very, very slowly from the sofa. The first thing she felt was a fug of bewilderment, quickly followed by a flush of relief. Relief gave way to curiosity. And abruptly, curiosity gave way to anger.

'What on earth's the matter, Imke dear? You've gone all pale. Hello Ruud, are you well? Yes? No? Why is everyone gawking at me like I'm a freak escaped from the circus?'

Erica opened her mouth to smile, and on her tongue a red cherry drop glistened, bright as a ruby.

Calmly, Ruud took a deep breath and said, 'Mrs Erica, I think you should tell us where you've been.'

★ ★ ★

Kiki, tail thrashing, rushed over to sniff Erica's trousers and feet. 'So this man waves me closer. He has this metal object glinting in his hand. Naturally, I'm intrigued. He slaps his other hand against a low tree branch and raises it high, allowing me to duck beneath. I lose my footing, and he lunges and, fortunately, catches me by the elbow, so I don't fall. "Thank you," I said.'

Propped against the sideboard, Erica paused, hunched her shoulders and threw her head back. A joint in her neck cracked. She said she was knackered. She certainly looked it, thought Ruud, with her short hair in jagged disarray and a queasy colour greening her cheeks. If he didn't know better he'd say she resembled a bulldog suffering from distemper.

'He told me his name was Yohanes. "A pleasure to meet you, Yohanes. My name is Erica," I say. "I see you're a musician." He brandished his metal flute. "From China," he said. He drew a bamboo flute from within his sash. "This one made in Indonesia." He tightened and set his lower jaw, pulled his top lip over his teeth and played this beautifully melodic section of a Javanese folksong. Then this lovely lady comes over. She's in traditional dress and explains in broken English that they're all part of a travelling band on their way to perform at a wedding. *Gamelan*, she says, tapping herself on the bosom with her right index finger. She took my arms in both of hers and squeezed. "*Assalamu alaykum*," she says in greeting. And before you know it she's invited me to join them. She holds out her hand quite unselfconsciously and leads me to an open-topped lorry.

'At first I can't quite fathom why the troupe is in the palace grounds, but I soon gather they're here to collect their *rebab* player, who's an apprentice pastry chef in the royal kitchens.'

Erica suppressed a yawn. 'Sorry, it's been a long day. So, to

187

this wedding we go. The reception was in a vast community hall where about eight hundred guests came and went as they pleased – eating, gossiping, milling about, taking photos, climbing in and out of cars, materializing from neighbouring houses. I got the impression that every adult man was drawing on a clove-scented cigarette and every adult woman had a child on her hip. And here's me with a borrowed shawl slipped over my head, tossing flower petals in the air and greeting people like they were long-lost cousins.

And the wonderful thing was that everyone welcomed me with warmth, including the bride and groom who were both enveloped in silk and batik and silver thread, with jasmine blossoms draped over their shoulders.

The band played for hours. Guests arrived with potted orchids and wicker baskets laden with fruit, offerings of uncooked rice, sugar and raw noodles. When they departed, they all left white envelopes of money, which they dropped into a box by the door.'

Erica flexed her right knee. 'Blasted knee's acting up again. Doctor says it's rheumatism.' She paused to regain her thoughts. 'Where was I? Oh, yes, so darkness falls and as the night progresses the real festivities kick off. If you thought Glastonbury or Lowlands was a party,' she gasped, 'you ain't seen nothing until you've been to a Javanese wedding. I mean, where do I start? Everything was a blur of colour and noise. There were fireworks and firecrackers.

'I'm a bit embarrassed, to be quite honest, gatecrashing it the way I did. But it was such fun! I only wish I'd brought the happy couple a gift. And the food! Mountains of it. You can't imagine. There was this squid dish they served that had a hint of something sweet in it. Quite delicious. And it's utter nonsense about them not drinking in this country. They do, but they do it discreetly. Homebrewed Iban *tuak* rice wine. I must have quaffed a couple of bottles of the filthy stuff.'

Erica coughed at the memory.

'And if that reality-twisting rice wine wasn't bad enough, one of the band members passed me a herbal cigarette, which got us all giggling. There's no point being an artist,' said Erica, 'if you can't be a dash outrageous, is there? He called it Shabu but it certainly wasn't cannabis, I can tell you that much. Made me dance for hours. There must have been something mildly hallucinogenic in it as I had the most ridiculous dreams afterwards – something about teaching vegetables to sing and dance. Big, fat tomatoes in little buckled shoes. Truly horrific. Anyway, needless to say, I woke with the most awful dry-mouthed hangover in some villager's thatched hut, covered in mosquito bites. First thing I see when I open my eyes is a picture of Dr H. Susilo Bambang Yudhoyono's face on the wall. My watch said it was three in the afternoon. I didn't know where the hell I was. Didn't recognize a soul around me. Four men were sprawled on the floor snoring like warthogs – fully dressed, I might add – and it dawned on me that I had no means of getting home.'

Erica continued talking, but Ruud could tell that Imke now categorically did not wish to hear any more about the wedding.

'In the end I got a ride on the back of a cigarette-seller's scooter. I offered to pay him in Mars Bars but he didn't quite understand.' She looked at Imke and Ruud and let out a huff. 'So that was my little adventure in a nutshell. Everything all right with you? Good. Well, there's nothing like a near-psychotic episode to get the old appetite going. Anyone know where the biscuits are?'

★ ★ ★

Imke's jaw clenched. Her voice was sharp and combative.

Ruud shrank into himself. Feeling intensely uncomfortable, he wanted to get out of there, right now. He knew better than to involve himself in someone else's family feud, so ever so slowly he started backing out of the room towards the front door.

'Biscuits?' screamed Imke. 'To hell with the bloody biscuits!'

Ruud let out a low, slow whistle. 'OK. I'll leave you both to it then,' he said, forcing the muscles in his face to form a tight smile. 'I'm going to make tracks.' He murmured a polite goodbye.

Imke glared at Erica briefly and then marched out of the door after Ruud. She saw him to his car.

'Go easy on her,' said Ruud.

Imke's pupils were large and liquid, her hostility on temporary hold. She kissed him gently on the mouth. 'I'm just glad she's safe,' she murmured. 'But she still deserves a bloody earful from me.'

'Talk tomorrow.'

'Tomorrow.'

She planted another kiss on his lips. 'Thanks for everything today. And drive carefully. Promise?'

He nodded.

Then she whirled round and stormed back into the bungalow to continue her verbal assault.

Kiki tilted her head to one side. She rarely heard Imke raise her voice like this. She wagged her tail a few times, confused, thinking it might be a new game, before crawling under the bed to hide.

'What the hell,' cried Imke, 'were you thinking? How

could you simply go off like that? It's so irresponsible. Did you not think for a minute that I'd be worried?'

'I'm sorry, Imke.'

'I wasn't just worried, I was frightened sick. And it wasn't just me. You had The Captain, the palace staff and Ruud freaking out. They even informed Yudhoyono. What the hell got into you?'

'I simply wanted to get some air.'

'You were gone for a day and a half!'

'Yes, I realize that now but . . .'

'But what? There are no buts. Don't shake your head.'

'Imke, I'm fifty-eight years old. I can take care of myself. I have done all my life.'

'That's not the point.'

'I'm afraid it is the point. I'm a grown woman. I need space sometimes. I need to get out and see the world. Take in its colours and textures. It's what I do.'

'You're not listening to what I'm saying.'

'I think I've been berated enough for one day.'

'You could have been killed!'

'Stop overreacting.'

'I'm not overreacting!'

'Yes, you are. You sound like a hysteric whose trousers are on fire.'

'A third woman has been murdered. I thought it was you. I saw her corpse. Her corpse!'

'I was never in any danger.'

'How was I to know? It's so bloody selfish of you, flouncing off like that.'

Erica twisted her mouth and looked away. She headed for her room.

'And now you're going to bugger off and sulk in your bedroom, is that it?'

'I'm going to lie down.'

'God, I don't know why I bother.'

Erica wanted to hold her tongue, but the bitterness in Imke's voice touched a nerve. She stopped and turned. 'Remember who you're talking to, young lady. Your father was right. You should never have come on this trip. Never! He said you'd start doing this, getting all inquisitorial.'

'Inquisitorial?'

'From day one you've had this bee in your bonnet about his past. "Papa, what's the matter? Papa, why are you behaving like this?" It's all I ever get to hear.'

'What is your problem?'

'I'm just saying, sometimes you have to leave things alone.'

'What are you talking about?'

'Your father. Yes, he had a past. Yes, it got him in trouble. Let it be!'

'You think I don't know he did something wrong? That he left with his tail between his legs? Of course, I know. It's bloody obvious.'

'I just . . . I think you should stop claiming to be all concerned about something when you're not. Pretending to . . .'

'I'm not pretending! How can you say such a thing? Where is this coming from?'

'I'm sorry, Imke, that was below the belt,' she apologized. 'I know you're not pretending.'

'Then why did you say it?'

'To deflect . . . to repel . . . I don't know. A part of me is trying to protect you.'

'Protect me from what?'

'I don't know. I . . .'

'What?'

'The thing is, questions can never be unasked, accusations never retracted. What I'm trying to say is the truth sometimes comes in God-awful flavours. And you have to be prepared for the aftertaste.'

They stared at one another for some time.

'You're talking about Papa, aren't you?'

Erica nodded.

Eventually, Imke took her aunt's hand and held it between her own. 'You said he got into trouble. What did he do? Tell me. I really want to know.'

The bungalow was a pool of light in the gloom. Inside, the words toppled from Erica's mouth, raw and unfiltered. They came spilling out like prisoners held too long in a hellish gaol, tumbling head over heels, one after the other.

A secret. A black secret.

Imke held her breath and felt a drop of acid splash her stomach walls, first scorching then spreading like fire across her gut. Something inside her felt toxic and bloated. Her blood grew hot, but behind her eyes everything went cold. She put her head between her knees. Erica's words crackled white and harsh in her brain like radiation frost. For a few befuddled moments Imke wasn't exactly sure what she heard. But then, as the story began to sink in, shocked comprehension swiftly turned to denial.

This isn't right. Erica's got it all wrong. The story can't be true. It has to be a mistake. A lie. Papa couldn't have done this to me. He couldn't have!

Her face crumpled and she ran out on to the lawn and threw up.

Erica watched from the verandah and hung her head. When it came to Imke, instinct told her that her niece had to solve this particular problem by herself.

Chapter Twenty

The roads were busy.

Ruud drove like a man who hadn't slept for two days, staring drowsily at the red tail-lights stretched ahead. The promise of a hot meal followed by bed spurred him on.

Bone-weary, he needed downtime, plenty of downtime. He just wanted to clock off work, drive home, kick off his shoes, quaff a Pepsi, climb into his 'Conserve Water, Drink BEER' T-shirt, play ten minutes on the PlayStation, then fall asleep till midmorning with the aircon on full blast.

All along the dual carriageway, Ruud thought about Imke. He had been surprised when she'd kissed him, but he wasn't surprised at how good it had felt. Her lips were buttery soft. He wanted desperately to hold her close and run his hands over her body, and he daydreamed about exactly that for several miles.

When Ruud got home Arjen was there, stooped over the ironing board. Arjen looked up momentarily from his pressing, nodded, then spritzed the yoke of the shirt with his spray bottle.

'Did you go to the food market at Putra Raya like I told you?'

His brother grunted a response. Ruud checked the fridge; it was well stocked.

Ruud kicked off his shoes. Ever since the kiss he walked with a lighter step. He uncoupled the handcuffs from his belt, stashed his Heckler & Koch in the GunVault, changed into a T-shirt and fixed dinner, careful to avoid including anything green in his brother's diet. Arjen hated to see anything green on his plate; he said it made him think of slime and mould and phosphorous poisoning and the skin on the back of a toad. He also said that it sounded like the word *gangrene*, and that made him think of rotting flesh. This meant that all vegetables consumed in the household had to be either carrots, cauliflowers, radishes, turnips, parsnips, tomatoes, red peppers, yellow peppers, white cucumbers, red lettuces, aubergines or purple asparagus (which their mother brought over every Christmas from Australia).

He also struggled to ingest anything triangular shaped, no matter how small, owing to his dread of pointy bits.

Ruud watched his brother set the iron on its stand and fold the shirts, smoothing out puckers and wrinkles with the flat of his hand. He wondered when he should bring up the matter of the cat's tongue. Probably best if he waited until after they had eaten.

Following dinner, Ruud made Arjen dab the scratches on his arms with iodine in case they got infected. Who knew where that cat had been?

'You know, they look more like human scratches than a cat's,' observed Ruud, passing him the purple bottle and bag of cotton wool. His brother kept his stare locked on the floor. 'You shouldn't have killed it,' scolded Ruud.

Arjen reasoned that nobody would miss the stray cat and that its awful midnight yowling kept the entire building awake.

'You wanted to stop all that horrible noise. Nothing wrong with that,' said Ruud. 'Serious word now. You can't go around killing cats. It's just not allowed and it's cruel.' Ruud told him that everyone made mistakes but he must never do that again. What he'd done was wrong.

And then, sheepishly, Arjen apologized. He admitted it was something he shouldn't have done.

Ruud asked him why he'd brought the box to his work place.

'Can you imagine what Witarsa would do to you if he found out? He'd have you locked up.'

Arjen didn't meet his eyes. All he could do was examine the floorboards.

'I'm going to make an appointment for you to see Dr Jayadi on Wednesday.'

His brother made a face.

'Yes, I know you think all he does is give you pills, but they'd work if you remembered to take them half the time. And don't tut at me.'

Arjen's expression remained sour. He asked what colour Wednesday was.

'Days don't have colours.'

He insisted that they did.

Ruud was anxious about him, but there was also something morbidly comical about the whole affair. Ruud sighed and saw the entire story unrolling in front of him. Loony tunes brother of decorated homicide detective flips out at a police station, carrying mutilated animal parts in a shoebox. Animal welfare groups throw a fit. The Indonesian Cat

Association calls for Ruud's resignation. There's a cover-up. Disreputable things happen, whereupon some enormous tragic saga unravels.

'Why did you do it?' he persisted.

Arjen squirmed and replied that he thought it would please Ruud, especially as Ruud had banged on the wall and screamed out in the middle of the night: 'Please someone, anyone, wring that bloody thing's neck!'

Ruud looked at Arjen for a long while. And in those moments he felt a twinge of sympathy and understood just how fragile his brother was. He also understood once again why his wife had left him: it wasn't because she'd fallen for another man (although she had); it wasn't because of his job and the antisocial hours he worked; it wasn't because he sometimes came home with blood on his clothes; it was because of Arjen. He was the elephant sitting on Ruud's chest. The glaring truth was that she couldn't cope with sharing their apartment with him.

Ruud tidied up the dining table and piled the dishes in the sink while Arjen began washing up and scraping the frying pan. Faint clinks of plates and pings of cutlery followed Ruud into his bedroom.

Ruud cricked his neck left and right. This part of the job – the downtime – was hard for him: going home, switching off from the case and leaving the dead behind so he could live his life normally for a few hours.

As Ruud settled down for a round of golf on the PlayStation, his mobile rang. '*Gajah*, the victim has been confirmed as a Thai national. Her name is Supaphorn Boonsing and she was forty-seven. She used to live in

Jakarta, but left to live with a man in Denmark; she separated from him and returned only last month.'

'OK.'

'Also, we've got something on that drug, Xylazine. Werry Hartono spoke to Dr Prasasti at UI campus, the head of Veterinary Medicine, and together they came up with a list of all the registered vets in Jakarta who'd had their practices burgled in the last two years.'

'I'm listening.'

'There were eleven reported break-ins during that period, all of which had drugs stolen from their pharmacies. Ketamine, Oxytocin and Diazepam were the most common targets. Only one practice, the one on Jalan Kecapi, reported Xylazine missing, quite a lot of it too. I spoke with the veterinary physician. He's pretty sure it was an inside job. A couple of guys that were working there started acting sheepishly after the incident, so he let them go, claiming he was downsizing the clinic. He was too intimidated to make a formal complaint.'

'OK.'

'Now get this. One of them has a police record that would make Baekuni blush.'

'Name?'

'D.W. Soeprapto. Born in Bengkulu. Aged twenty-eight. Spent six years in Tanjung Gusta prison for drug charges, one year for extortion, and arrested but not charged for indecently assaulting a woman in twenty thirteen.'

'Why on earth did the clinic hire him?'

'Prisoner Rehabilitation Programme.'

'Yeah, right,' he scoffed. 'As if that ever works here.'

'There's more. Guess who he had previous links to?'

'Tell me.'

'Slack–mouth Susanti.'

'You couldn't make this stuff up.'

'I'm going to ask him a few questions. Werry's coming with me.'

'What about Vidi?'

'He's spending the evening with a sick cousin. He'll join us later.'

'I'll meet you in ten.'

'I'm texting you his last known address now. And *Gajah*, after this we both need to get some sleep.'

A light drizzle fell. The windscreen wipers stuttered and warbled.

A harrowing squall of sludge metal blasted from the car stereo courtesy of Aiboy Ali, who headbanged to the guitar riff.

Ruud turned the music down and switched off the wipers. 'Tell me a bit more about this fellow.'

'He had a fancy job title at the clinic: Animal Transport Coordinator,' said Werry Hartono.

'More like Drug Transport Coordinator,' laughed Aiboy Ali. Ruud smiled too. A faint hint of his colleague's spicy aftershave remained.

Ruud scrutinized his watch. 'So let me get this straight. You want to roll up at his door at ten forty-five at night like a Jehovah's Witness.'

'If he has nothing to hide, he has nothing to hide,' parried Aiboy Ali.

The three men fretted in Ruud's parked car. Aiboy Ali shoved a fresh ammo clip into his handgun butt and pushed the slide back. Ruud looked quizzically at his colleague. 'You think we'll be needing that?'

'Just business as usual.'

Aiboy Ali carried a Glock 17, but Ruud didn't like the fact that the Glock had no external safety catch, so he got special permission from Witarsa to handle a Heckler & Koch.

Ruud thumbed the safety of his 9mm and checked the magazine.

Werry Hartono could hardly contain his excitement. 'The game is on, Mrs Hudson!' he yelled.

'Bloody hell!' Aiboy Ali reared back. 'Don't shout like that! What is he talking about?'

'Something from *Sherlock*, I'd imagine,' said Ruud. 'Won't be long before he's wearing a deerstalker.'

'What's a deerstalker?'

'Forget it. We good to go?'

'Rock and roll.'

They all bailed out of the Toyota at the same time. The night was a little fresher and cooler than usual. The rainstorms had rinsed the air of the stink of city buses. Ruud crossed the street and hesitated, stopping to look at Werry Hartono. 'I want you to stay here.'

'Why?' came the familiar nasal whine.

'Because I say so.' He tossed him the keys. 'Keep the air-con running.'

Werry skulked back to the car and crawled in, slamming the rear door hard behind him.

The two detectives climbed the three flights of stairs and made their way down a long corridor with tenement flats on either side. The jaundiced ceiling lights blinked and popped every few seconds, and the sounds of their shoes echoed off the exposed brick walls.

'Number three four four. This is it,' announced Aiboy Ali.

Ruud slow-scanned the deserted passageway. He heard arguments coming from his left, children shouting loudly from somewhere above.

Aiboy Ali rang the bell, stepped to the side of the door and banged hard.

Ruud braced himself, the way a child braces before plunging into a pool of cold water.

No answer.

He tried again.

'Guess nobody's home,' said Ruud.

His colleague brought out a penknife. 'I can break the lock.'

'Bad idea.'

'Listen, this might turn out to be nothing. Let's get a warrant and come back in the morning, what do you say *Gajah*?'

'Sounds like a plan. I need to get my head down, grab four or five hours' sleep.'

'Me too.'

'"To bed, to bed. There's knocking at the gate."' Aiboy Ali shot him one of his questioning looks. 'Macbeth,' informed Ruud. 'My mother was an English teacher.'

'First *Sherlock*, now Shakespeare.' He cringed then glanced at his watch; an expectant expression stole across his face.

'You are going home to sleep, aren't you?'

'Of course I am.'

'Yeah, right. Brazil are playing tonight, aren't they?'

The detective couldn't help but smile, but before he replied, they both heard footsteps echoing in the far distance.

'I bet that's Werry,' sighed Ruud. 'Never takes a blind bit of notice what I tell him.'

They heard him all the way down the stairway, his shoes against the wooden steps. Backlit against a window at the far end of the long corridor, a solitary man emerged from the stairwell. He took three paces towards them and stopped.

Aiboy Ali removed his police ID card from his drill pants pocket and held it up. 'D.W. Soeprapto?' He took a step forward. Ruud stared. The man stared back. He was carrying plastic grocery bags in each hand. Ruud could just about decipher the shape of a fruit juice carton and some green vegetables with their leafy bits sticking out. The man was about forty feet away, and in the dim light it was difficult to make out whether he was curious, confused or scared.

Everyone froze.

Ruud's heart became a fist.

'Show me your hands!' shouted Aiboy Ali.

Ruud, eyes fixed frontwards, slowly reached to unclip the Heckler from his belt. The man dropped his bags and grabbed at his waistband.

There was a muzzle flash and gunfire erupted.

Bullets tore apart the wall by Ruud's head and took a bite out of the doorframe.

Showered with splinters, Ruud recoiled in shock. He knew instantly that Aiboy Ali had been hit. He dragged his eyes from the man with the gun and saw the wound, liquefying at the edges. Fuck! Aiboy Ali dropped to the floor, firing wildly, a burst of slugs smashed into the ceiling.

Move Goddamn it! Move! Move! Move! Ruud spun, rolled onto his side and squeezed the Heckler. Four pops fired in an arc. Spent shells spilled onto the floor. His ears rang.

A detonation of sound.

Of air exploding.

And ugly cries of pain.

He saw the man racing away, hurtling off the way he'd come.

Ruud moved fast. He yanked free his belt and wrapped it tightly round his friend's leg, above the entry wound. Then he was up on his feet, keeping low, crouch-running at first, Heckler & Koch aimed straight ahead as he scampered forward.

Doors nudged open. Curious expressions stared through the cracks.

Haring down the passageway now, hurdling the scattered groceries, Ruud shouted at people to get back inside. 'Call an ambulance!' he screamed. 'Police officer down! Get the fuck back inside! Police officer down!'

He dialled 118 as he ran. 'Emergency assistance required!' He barked the address into his phone.

Left, into the stairwell, he snuck a quick look over the balustrade. Three yards away, on the turn of the stair, a gun muzzle swung round and pointed directly at his face. *Move!* He reeled back just as a string of bullets slammed into the partition above him, pinging and ricocheting, showering him in debris and plaster. *Shoot back! Now! Shoot the fucker!* Ruud stuck his automatic over the side and opened up, firing blind. Four blasts. Panic fire. The sound of glass shattering resonated from below. He heard running and was immediately up, leaping down five teeth-juddering steps at a time, then over the banister at ground level.

He burst out onto the main road, into a chorus of beeping. An explosion of light hit him; headlights blinding him. A dozen cars flew past.

THERE!

A man in the distance, blurred but in frame, bolted down the road.

Ruud galloped after him.

Sprinting, splashing through puddles in a cross-alley, Ruud banged into a dawdling motorcyclist. A car braked hard with a screech of tyres and fishtailed. Ruud charged across the road, feet pounding, gun swinging. He was closing on him. He could make out the back of the man's head. A scalp, shaved at the sides, braided at the top before elongating to cornrows down the back.

Ruud's eyes centred on the cornrows now, watching them flap and bounce and coil.

A pedestrian skidded across the pavement. Ruud clattered into a crowd – a blur of shocked faces and gaping mouths. Voices shouted behind him, hollering.

A car alarm shrieked.

Horns blared.

Across another busy road.

The man zigzagged past a maze of traffic. Ruud was on him. Four feet away. Three feet. Almost in reach.

BANG!

An oncoming car smashed into Ruud. He thumped into the bonnet and his pistol butt smacked against the wind-screen, carving a spider's web of fissured glass. Despite the pain, he held onto the Heckler.

'*Tepi jalan lah, bodoh!*' screamed the driver, pounding the steering wheel with his fists. 'Get out of the damn street!'

Tumbling to the ground, Ruud was back up within seconds, pumping his legs. Everything happened so fast he didn't have time to think.

His ears rang. He could no longer hear the car horns resonating or the shouts. All he could hear was the heavy panting coming from his open mouth.

Wheezing hard, he saw the back of a cornrowed head disappear into another side alley and a new block of flats. Rushing headlong, Ruud ploughed into darkness. His vision fuzzed then cleared.

He tore through and found himself in a rear courtyard. Graffiti-plastered walls. Dripping air conditioners. Dogs barking. Up ahead, he saw a backdoor with washing hung in the open windows to dry. He didn't slow down.

The man with the cornrows ducked under the washing and hared into someone's home, stopping to slide shut a transparent screen. The screen closed with a staccato rattle. Ruud, sprinting, was going too fast to stop. The pane looked solid and thick. Elbows up, head down, chin tucked in, he crashed right through it and out the other side, the collision almost knocking him unconscious. Staggering, he thanked Christ it wasn't safety glass. Toppling, rolling, he spat out silica fragments and blinked splinters from his eyes, cannoning into a faceful of clothing hanging on a line. He kicked pyjama tops away from his legs and tore shirts and socks from his face. Where was he?

A flowerpot thudded against the wall by his ear, clay and earth exploded, catching him on the side of the cheek. He saw the back of Cornrow's heels, heard the slap slap slap of feet.

Clattering and skidding, Ruud pounded to the other end of the kitchen. Crockery smashed and broke everywhere. A woman carrying a basket of laundry screamed out in terror. Ruud didn't look back, streaking through the room and crossing a cluttered floor, leapfrogging toys, plastic chairs and an elderly couple watching TV.

A door flung open. Past the front entrance now, into the fury of the night, into the din and racket of the street. His calf muscles burned hot. He fired a shot but missed.

The man, half-spinning, aimed and returned fire. Ruud ducked and bits of brickwork went flying, splintering and shattering in the distance.

They were back in the open, charging hard, really legging it up the road, like a 100-metre dash for glory. A police siren cried out in the background, growing louder. Ruud thought he should slow down, steady his arm and take aim at the figure in front. He reckoned he had six rounds left in the magazine. The WEEE–WOR howls grew louder and louder. He was sure he had a clear shot. He stopped and planted his feet. He had him in his sight lines. And then, suddenly, he was airborne, spinning, his hands clutching at the blackness.

He experienced a second of bewilderment, after which his body somersaulted, head over heels, sending him sprawling, crashing to the ground, tumbling, scraping skin off his chest and forearms. It felt like someone had taken a knife to his face – cheekbone, nostrils, eye socket, forehead yielded to asphalt.

His jaw smashed against something as he landed with a thud. A white-hot pain shot up and down his left hip.

The lagoon-blue car with the flashing lights came to a squealing stop.

Blinking through the blood, he saw Werry Hartono climb out of the driver's door. The young second lieutenant knelt by his side, apologizing over and over again. A high-pitched whine droned in his ears. Ruud couldn't hear the words pouring from the young man's mouth; instead he stared at his face, which was blued by the emergency lights.

The left side of Ruud's body felt numb and hot and grew wet to the touch. A shard of glass stuck out of his arm.

All Ruud could do was try to get to his feet. He wanted to see if he could stand, if any part of him was broken. He clung onto Hartono's shoulders. He ran his hands tentatively over his legs, bent and cocked his knees. His limbs were rubber. 'Jesus!' Ruud said quietly to himself, realizing just how close he'd come to being killed. 'Jesus bloody Christ!'

Hartono kept apologizing.

Ruud wanted to murder Werry Hartono.

He lunged at him, but another figure moved to intercept. It was Vidi.

Ruud swung again at Hartono, wincing at the pain in his arm.

Vidi grabbed Ruud by the wrist to stop him. The man with the beard had the grip of someone accustomed to wringing the necks of *kampung* chickens. Hartono retrieved Ruud's gun and Vidi ordered him to call for an ambulance.

Ruud, eyes wild, hunched over, hands on knees, heaving for air. Glass slivers spilled from his hair and scattered by his shoes. There were cuts all over his body – some deep – and the tops of both arms leaked blood.

The man with the cornrows had got away.

Grimacing, Ruud slumped to the floor and screamed at the night sky.

Chapter Twenty-One

Thursday. 11.40 p.m.

Panting hard. I pause in the shadows to catch my breath. I must be more careful. I was careless. Next time I won't be so lucky. Now is not the time to be reckless.

Friday. 3.33 a.m.

My brother tells me he has plans for our newest lady. Big plans. He speaks in a low, cracking monotone. I listen and decide I had better buy some more plastic sheeting. Things are going to get messy. He giggles aloud. He cannot wait for the sun to rise tomorrow.

Friday. 6.58 a.m.

We approach the high-rise building and take the service stairs to the third floor. The watchman is still asleep. Nobody else is about. At the back of the building, the outer gangway is dark. We settle on the floor below the ventilation grate to her bathroom.

Several moments pass. My brother hears light shuffling footsteps from within. A shower is turned on. I imagine the kimono sliding from her shoulders; I imagine her stepping into the stall, which is covered in pink faux-marble tiles.

There is splashing and soft singing. Steam escapes through the grating. Two minutes later, she turns off the tap. Water gurgles down the drain. She must be towelling herself now with one of the velvety turquoise towels she clips to her retractable clothes line each morning. I saw it yesterday, flapping in the wind, drying in the sun. Like a prayer flag fluttering from the third-floor window.

My brother removes a thin blade from his pocket and inspects it, before securely and delicately replacing it in his jacket. He gets to his feet and makes his way down the service stairs.

Friday. 10 a.m.
The doors to SOGO department store open on the hour. We approach the Guerlain kiosk and the smell of skincare products threatens to overwhelm me. *'Bagaimana mungkin saya bisa tolong?'* she asks, her tone polite. 'How may I help you?' I recognize her at once, dressed in her smart beauty counter uniform. I tell her I am looking for a men's fragrance. Without hesitation she shows me a pale bottle, sprays a paper strip with scent and waves it under my nose. 'Héritage,' she says. 'Or perhaps you like Guerlain Homme?' She lifts a square black frosted bottle and squirts eau de parfum on a fresh testing strip.

We buy two bottles. One for each of us. She is pleased to earn a sales commission so early in the day. I smile at her and she is flattered. She is almost old enough to be Mother. I tell her I know a good place for *Lontong Balap* and if she is free later I would like to share a meal with her. I slip her a couple of crisp 20,000s as a tip, together with a gentle squeeze of her arm. It's that easy.

Friday. 9.40 p.m.

Aduh, how gullible such women are when a younger man with an eager smile comes into their lives!

The night is here. My brother has bound her and he observes her, watching this woman with a kind of reverence. Wondering if the larynx will pop, whether the hyoid bone might snap. It is fascinating, these last moments – when their eyes bulge and nostrils flare, hearing that distinctive back-of-the-throat rattle. Waiting for that fragile final split second as vibrations in the pulse tickle then ebb away. One gets a sense of power from it. A bit like playing God.

God exacts vengeance.

My brother exacts vengeance. It is what he enjoys doing. Perhaps he reveres how vengeance is delivered, how it is made to cause pain, the way it impacts both the one inflicting it as much as the one enduring it.

But then again, what is vengeance but adulterated purity? Exquisite. Sharp. So clearly concentrated.

Since childhood there has been nothingness inside of me, a harsh wilderness, a dark centre, sometimes pervaded by chinks of turbulent light, by shards of virtue, but mostly it is a black void.

For it has been forged out of a great sadness.

Blackness. A cavity.

That is until I found out about you, dear Imke.

And now the emptiness is filled with this glittering hate, this radiant hostility. By blood, I am meant to love you. But no love can be as satisfying and enrapturing as this hatred.

I was betrayed. Mother was betrayed. There was no door-slamming, no rows. He simply left us. And that abandonment shaped our lives. It turned Mother wicked. I don't believe she was always wicked. I believe it crept up on her like a cancer. Only when he jilted her did she spit out her unique brand of fury.

It was a fury I grew accustomed to as a child.

Each night I stayed up, waiting for her to return to our tiny wasteland of a home, with barely a light on in the house. Not letting the front door out of my sight. Mother – she could have been anywhere, in some rich man's mansion, or sharing his hotel room. How was I to know? The only clue to her whereabouts lay in the little shampoo bottles she brought back with her: The Grand Hyatt, The Willtop, Hotel Fiducia, Mandarin Oriental.

In my mother's world, Western men held all the power. She was doing what she had to do to earn a living. One price for short time and double amount for overnight action, depending on the man's age and looks. And then my father came along. She did not expect to hook him the way she did. Did she deceive him? Dupe him? I do not know. But my father disowned me nevertheless. He jettisoned me. Consigned me to scrap. It is a horrible feeling to be made to feel rejected. I was a little boy with a pounding heart. A little boy who Mother blamed for all her woes. Every so often I wonder if my loathing of my father belongs to her or if it is a part of me. She was, you see, very good at poisoning my mind.

And so I find myself in this whirlpool of bitterness and hostility. In a fast-rotating mass of destructive water. Sucking me under. This inverted tornado.

I hear a voice in the far reaches.

My brother is calling.

A whisper. Followed by a shout.

There are times when I see myself in a room full of mirrors, scrutinizing the receding images of myself, growing ever smaller, ever distant, staring down a long hallway to nothingness, until I am a tiny black smudge. Dissolved under the sun. Lost. Insignificant. Tormented, with the air sucked from my mouth.

But I am crawling out of that hallway now. And the light at the end of it is my salvation. Vengeance is my only salvation.

'*Buka matamu!*' my brother commands. 'Open your eyes!' His hand is round her throat again.

Oh, dear.

It appears our female companion has lost control of her bladder.

Tsk, tsk, tsk, Fatima! What a nasty smell you've made.

Dear Fatima here works in a perfume shop. The little skunk is in the fragrance business. Works at the Guerlain kiosk at SOGO department store, so her skin is usually filmed with scents of jasmine and ylang–ylang and juniper wood.

Not any more.

Friday. 11.19 p.m.

He is becoming increasingly cryptic. For reasons that are beyond me, he has begun making fishing analogies.

Yesterday he told me he was trawling. Lobbing out clues. Playing a weighted line between his fingers to see how much the police really know.

Today, he says he is throwing out chum. It's what shark fishermen do when they're out to catch the big predators. They toss the mashed guts and bones of baitfish overboard, creating a chum slick through the water. It draws the sharks from miles away. The anglers toss it out and watch as the sea bubbles and froths.

212

The press, he says, the press, the public and the police will all be in frenzy.

He says this as he buttons up his uniform. Yes, he often wears a uniform for work, one with shiny embroidery on the sleeves. There is a pin on his lapel and other *kecil* bits and bobs to clip on. Once in a while, on special occasions, he is asked to put on his dress outfit and don a peaked cap with the gold band.

It's an illusion the eye cannot see past.

So far the disguise has worked.

Chapter Twenty-Two

The green button appeared beside the picture of Mathias Sneijder together with the words 'Video Call' and a small camera icon to the right. Imke heard the familiar Skype ringtone. Her father answered and his concerned image materialized on the screen. He was drinking a cup of coffee and she saw a worried frown. He looked as old and worn as the tatty plaid shirt he had on.

It was early evening in Amsterdam. Mathias sat with his back to the kitchen window. The low sun behind him caught the edges of his red hair, making it seem as if his head was on fire.

For several numbing moments Imke just sat in the chair, in front of the laptop, rigid. Her body language spoke volumes – all stiff shoulders and controlled hand movements.

'It happened a little after you were born,' he said. 'You must have been about two years old. And it carried on for some time.'

'How long?'

The crow's feet by his eyes stood out. The images came to him with awful clarity, tapping at the windows of his memory with long, dirty fingernails.

'I'd tried to end it after the baby was born. She came to

214

me with the child swaddled in blankets and a bag full of Pampers. I couldn't do it. I was still in shock. She said she was beaten up by her father for getting pregnant. I couldn't do it. I couldn't let her go. Instead, self-destructively, I gave her money and told her nothing would change between us.'

'How long did you carry on with her, Papa?'

'Eight years.' His gaze was brittle; he kept looking away. 'When I finally told her I couldn't see her any more the trouble started.'

A hushed solitary muteness followed.

When he continued, he talked in a monotone. And as he spoke, Imke felt a crushing disappointment as his words confirmed her fears.

The microwave beeped. He got up, removed a steaming bowl of soup from the turntable and shut the door. He sat in front of Imke and blew on the soup to cool it down.

Imke pressed her knees together, tightened the sash of her dressing gown and spoke. 'Eight years. You carried on with her for eight years.'

'I'm not proud of it.'

'Poor Mama. Where is she?'

'Upstairs watching *The Voice of Holland*.'

'That show agitates her no end. I don't know why she watches it.'

He shrugged. 'It's the blind auditions. She enjoys them. Personally, I prefer *American Idol*, but not so much now that Simon Cowell's left.'

Imke looked at her hands. Eight years. Eight bloody years! 'You know what hurts so much? You'd come home and tell me about your day. You'd make me laugh about the fellow at work who couldn't say his Rs, the type of Indonesian food you'd had at the Lebaran banquet lunch, the strange things

215

you'd seen as you drove through the city. Was any of that true? Was it? Or were you just humouring me. Telling me one thing while you . . . while you spent time with this woman.' Imke covered her face with her hands. 'Oh God, why did you do that? Why did you lie to me?'

'What I did was wrong.'

'All this time you hid yourself from me.'

'I'm so sorry, Imke. If you were here with me now, in this room with me rather than on the computer, I'd put my arms around you.'

'I don't want your arms around me.'

A long silence. The air grew pregnant with things left unsaid. Mathias Sneijder sat there under Imke's dissecting eye, fully aware that this was becoming an interrogation, hoping to God it wouldn't turn into a trial.

'You look sunburned,' she said finally.

'It was hot yesterday. I was in the garden. There was rain last night. The roses needed it.'

'Your skin is going to peel.'

'Maybe just the top of my nose.'

'When I was little, your skin always smelled good when you came home from work. I used to wrap my arms around you then. Paco Rabanne it was. But it's all so clear to me now. You'd been to see her, hadn't you, on your way from the office?' she said with a catch in her voice. 'You made yourself smell nice for her.'

'I've carried this guilt inside me for so long. I should have told you.'

'Does Mama know?'

Imke already knew the answer. Erica had told her as much. Her aunt's words played on in her head: 'Your father lost his job not because of the economic downturn, not because the company was pulling expats out of Indonesia. He was dismissed because of an indiscretion, which later became a scandal. Did your Mama know at the time? Of course she knew. She closed her eyes to it. Dutch women are good at that sometimes. Closing their eyes to their husband's wanderings. Preferring to pretend that everything was perfect. Your mother is a loyal person, a noble woman.'

A pause. 'Yes, she knows. Do you want to speak with her?'

'No,' she exclaimed, thinking he was trying to wriggle free, 'this is between you and me. How did Mama find out?'

'I told her. Not immediately. Not the whole story. Only after we left Jakarta.'

Imke wiped away an angry tear with the heel of her hand. 'You told her because she suspected something.'

'Yes. Partly that. Partly because I hoped she would understand and maybe forgive me. And because I felt so alone, so isolated by not sharing it with her.'

Incredulous. 'Bullshit. You felt alone because you couldn't share the details of your affair with your wife? Sorry, that's complete bloody bullshit.'

'It's not like that.'

Imke wrung the tissue in her lap. She pinned him with a glare. 'You're sick.' She wanted to provoke him, so she could justify the rage coursing through her veins.

He stood up, clutching his reading glasses. The Skype image showed only his plaid shirtfront now. He took a step away from her, then returned to his seat.

He became resigned. He sipped his soup.

'I'm sorry, Imke.' His eyes were downcast.

Imke swallowed and pulled her gaze from the screen. Her focus fell on Kiki sleeping by the door, feet twitching with dreams.

'Why did you do it? Were you lonely, is that why you had an affair?'

'It helped fill this hole in my ego. It was wrong. I knew it was wrong even back then.'

Imke jutted her chin out angrily, feeling foolish for admitting such anger, particularly over something that had happened so long ago. No, she thought, it wasn't foolishness; she felt cheated, hollowed-out. She breathed carefully through her mouth to control her words.

'Did you never think that I would find out?' She catapulted forward from her chair, banging her elbows on the table edge. 'Did you not wonder what it would do to me, what it would mean to me? What it would do to us?'

'Of course I did.'

'But you still carried on for eight years!'

'I realized too late what an ass I'd been.'

'So you dispensed with this woman, shed your past like a snake shedding its skin. You abandoned her and you abandoned the child she bore you. You rejected your own baby. You rejected them both to save your career.'

'And to save my marriage.'

'Your marriage?' She sounded incredulous. 'Tell me, what happened to the boy? Did he stay with his mother? Was he fostered?'

'He stayed with his mother for a time. I sent her money in the early years, for his upkeep. Later, I found out he was passed around from one family member to another. I last saw him when he was six or seven. A timid little boy. After that, I can't say what happened to him.'

'Didn't you try to meet him?'

'I did, but his mother didn't encourage it. The last few times I saw him, I found bruises on his arms and legs. I confronted her about it, but she denied everything, blamed the neighbourhood bullies. I contacted the child welfare office, but this was Jakarta in the late nineties, and, well, it's different in Indonesia. Different laws, different rules, different morals. This was before the KPAI, the child protection commission, was formed.'

'I have a brother and you never ever told me.' Her voice shook. 'You washed your hands of your own son.' And if you could do that to him, she thought, you might have chosen between us and done the same to me.

'Yes.'

It took all her self-control not to lash out and strike the screen with her fist, as if shattering it would break the spell.

'I can't believe this. That you could do something like this.'

She heard him draw in his breath. And then, feeling as though all the energy had simply drained from her body, she settled her hand woodenly on the mouse. He started to speak but she clicked the red button at the bottom of the window and ended the call.

Half of her needed to learn more. The other half wanted to sweep the sinuous, toxic news under a carpet, close up the room, bolt the front door, burn the house down and run for the hills.

A knife-cut across your palm, they say, hurts more than you can ever imagine. It will heal in time, as all things heal, to form a scar. And when it does, it becomes a part of you. It becomes part of your fate line or your heart line, a ribbed white stripe between Moon and Upper Mars. Perhaps the scarification will change the course of your destiny, alter your emotional state or reshape your psychological make-up.

There is no surefire way of knowing. Indeed, even the leading chiromancers in the world don't know.

Yet Imke was sure about one thing now: you can try to dismiss that acid feeling in your gut, you can try to dismiss all those negative sensations and suspicions of self-doubt, and you can even try to dismiss that questioning look you give yourself in the mirror. But you will never dismiss the pain in your heart when the person wielding the knife is your own father.

It's the disappointment only a child can feel when abandoned by a parent, of a front door being shut, of a car driving away, the needling panic when it dawns on you that they may never come back and get you.

Later, in an email, he wrote:

Since you've been in Indonesia I have been in a state of abject self-loathing. I've been up all night sitting at the computer, not sure what to write. There is so much I want to say to you, so much I want to apologize for.

Imke read the long message. She hated every word he wrote, but it was the following paragraphs that made her seethe:

After work, every Monday and Wednesday, a few of us from the golf club would go out. We'd go to one of the nightclubs on Tanah Abang Timur. Either Tanamur or JJ's next door. It was seedy, smoky and loud. We'd get drunk. Have a laugh. The girls were freelance. I'd buy them drinks. They meant nothing to me. And then I met her and my life changed.

She had me spellbound. I guess you can say she got her hooks into me. I know it must be awful for you to read this, yet I feel it necessary to explain myself. And as for your mother, well, soon after you were born things changed between us. She shunned intimacy. She blamed it on hormones. After a while we became like two strangers occupying the same house but whose paths rarely cross. It took the summer we spent in Zeeland to save our marriage. Do you remember Zeeland? Remember our trip to the Iguana Reptile Zoo and that huge hotdog we shared?

Steamrolled. The Skype ringtone sang and it took a while before Imke trusted herself to answer. She clicked on the green button. Her father's face appeared. He talked and she listened, covering her mouth with her hand to keep the anger back. He told her the whole story. It took a while.

She wanted to shout, but she also wished she could curl up in a ball and hide under the covers.

'How can you sit there telling me all this? I can't believe what you've done. You betrayed me, you betrayed Mama.'

'I know.'

Imke felt her chin drop. She raised herself up, deciding there and then that she needed to be brave and firm about this.

She stared at the screen image of her father. Imke frequently heard how much they looked alike. Their likeness used to make her proud. That was no longer the case. 'How do you sleep at night?'

'I don't drink coffee after eight p.m.,' he quipped, hoping to ease the tension, attempting to diffuse her anger.

She cut him off. 'This isn't the time for jokes.'

His face flushed and he grew silent. Her eyes scanned behind her father's head to a row of ornamental mugs lined up on the shelf. She spotted the one that said 'Batik 'n Beans. Indonesia'. She had given it to him on his fortieth birthday. Now she wanted to take the mug back; some misguided sense of retribution.

'I'm having trouble talking to you,' he confessed.

'I want to know who your son is? The child you abandoned.'

Now Mathias Sneijder spoke urgently, sincerely. 'I can't tell you that. It's out of the question. I can't.'

'You can't or you won't.'

He sank his forehead to the table, thinking the hard surface would centre his thoughts. He said nothing.

'I want a name!' Her words ricocheted off the walls.

'I'm sorry, Imke.' His reply, dry-mouthed and sombre, hung in the air. 'Her name was Eny. Just Eny. I don't know any more than that. He was born in Hospital Gandaria some time in early December. I recall the month because the office was preparing for the Prophet Muhammad's birthday. And she called him "boy". Nothing else.'

Why is it that only when you've been deceived by a person do you begin to detect the shifty looks, the awkward expressions, the hollowness of their gestures? Imke kept her scrutiny on her father's mouth; she could see the pulse beating on his lower lip. Funny, she thought, how he touches his face when he tells a lie. I never noticed that before. Perhaps Ruud was right when he'd said: 'It's hard to trust anyone. It's a cynical thing to say, but it's true. You're talking to a person and within a minute you start spotting inconsistencies.'

'An address, Papa. I want an address.'

He touched his cheek and blinked twice. 'I don't remember where they lived.'

'I'm going to find out. I'm going to go to the Records Department, to the Civil Registration Office.'

'You don't want to do that.'

'He is my stepbrother. I have the right to know.'

A shadow settled on his face. 'Imke, you don't understand what this woman was like. She threatened to have me strangled in my sleep. My family, too.'

'Oh, so she's a bunny boiler now, is she?'

'Her mind snapped. She vowed she would hire someone to do it. It doesn't cost much in Indonesia. She came one morning to the office with a bucket of red paint and threw it all over the place, screaming. The girl at reception tried to stop her but was kicked and slapped. That was in April nineteen ninety-eight. She'd been to the office once before. The security guards escorted her out, scratching and kicking. The police came. She bit one of them. It was in the papers. She is dangerous, Imke; whatever you do you mustn't contact her.'

Imke sat back in her chair and crossed her arms. The lights were off and only the glow from the computer silvered her face. In the black of the night, with the sounds of the toads settling around her, Imke thought of her Mama being cut so deeply and having to carry this secret around with her like a hot stone. She suddenly pictured her Mama having to invent versions of the truth to fend off the ensuing gossip, and the married women at the tennis club, queuing up to muckrake, like a line of crows. How it must have hurt her, humiliated her. Did she argue his innocence? It was no wonder she always spoke of her last days in Indonesia in a voice narrow and clipped. She must have burned up from the inside with shame.

'What provoked these threats, *hè*?'

Sensing his hesitation, she repeated the question.

'I refused to leave your mother. Since then your mother and I have had some good times and some rotten times, but we are still together.'

'Why didn't she divorce you?'

'Because of a fierce loyalty.' A softening in his eyes. 'To you. She wasn't willing to hurt you in order to punish me.'

A deep, dense ache.

Perhaps Mama had been too afraid to get out, scared of change, scared of facing a new life free of marriage when her best years had slipped away . . .

Imke tightened the sash of her fuchsia dressing gown. To her surprise, she felt a tinge of regret that Mama hadn't left him. But she knew it was only anger talking.

'Please, do not resent me,' he mouthed, iterating the same five words over and over.

'I don't resent you. I don't like you much right now, but I don't resent you,' she said at last, before falling silent. She searched his face and then emptied her chest with a long discharge of breath. How could she resent him? He was her Papa. She was his daughter. They were inextricably bound. But this was entirely his making, his own handiwork. He deserved no quarter. She felt little sympathy, only a constriction in her throat; a crumpling, flattened sensation of being horribly let down.

Imke thought of a long-ago afternoon, when she was a little girl, climbing high onto the branch of a tall tree. They were at the park in Taman Tomang. She was five years old. She hadn't realized how high she'd climbed until it was too late. She sat on the branch, feet dangling, tiny fingers clinging to the knots in the wood. It was a long way down and she was terrified. She began to cry. Rocking to and fro, shrieking. A small circle of people congregated below her. She felt helpless, panic-stricken. As if the ground were spinning up towards her. Pini came running. Her Mama came running. And the more they shouted the more afraid she became. Eyes burning, she screamed for her father. The only person she trusted to help her from her perch was her papa. He returned to the scene with a bamboo ladder and climbed to the top rung, balancing on one leg as he reached across, wrapping her in his strong arms. His eyes locked onto hers, and he told her she was safe now and that if she fell he would catch her. He carried her down the ladder, his cheek against hers, and lowered his daughter to the ground.

Her father's voice interrupted her thoughts.

He was asking her a question. Imke blinked as if snapping from a trance. The sounds of the toads settled around her again. Mathias asked her if she was all right. They smiled at each other, a little sadly. No, she didn't resent him. But the trust she'd once felt for him was gone. She no longer felt safe in his arms. If she fell from up high, there would be nobody below to catch her.

Chapter Twenty-Three

Motionless. Hidden amongst the shadows. Eyes tracking movement like a jackal in the night.

From the narrow alley below, he watched the window for some time. He saw no signs of activity.

The man wearing the bifocals approached the high-rise building and took the stairs to the third floor. The watchman was asleep. Nobody else was about.

The two remaining women on the list lived at opposite ends of Jakarta; one allegedly shared a home with her son, this one lived alone. He approached the front door and knocked.

He waited. He knocked again, a little harder, but not too hard, fearful of waking the neighbours. Nothing stirred. The hall light did not snap on.

Satisfied no one was home, he doubled back, proceeded down the stairs and went all the way round to the rear of the property. Here he took the service stairs to the third floor. His shadow followed suit.

The streetlamps and the surrounding tall buildings ensured that the night was not completely black.

He walked along the outer gangway and found the door he wanted. It was dark as the gangway lights hadn't been switched on. Running a hand across his beard, he readied himself and clamped a thin Maglite between his teeth.

Bending and working methodically, keeping the beam steady, the man adjusted his bifocals and concentrated on the locks. His vision – already poor – seemed to get worse. There were two locks on the door. He estimated six pins in each lock. He glanced over his shoulder, tilting his chin, and his face grew tight.

At the sound of an engine, he started. A car drove by. A police car on patrol. He shrank. Its wide beam of headlights illuminated the length of road behind. It turned to the left and faded away.

He massaged his temples with the tips of his gloved fingers. The sweat prickled the skin beneath his shirt. He felt a fat, slippery drop slide down his lower back.

Using two small tools – a pick wire and a tension wrench – he went to work. First, he inserted the torque into the keyhole. The flat piece of metal entered the keyway with the short end bent at right angles. He kept the pressure light but constant. Next, he slipped in the length of pick wire. The pick wire was thin, five inches in length, and arched slightly upwards at the end. It went into the keyway above the torque.

Perspiration dripped from his nose.

He worked the pins, lifting each one carefully. Seconds later, the binding pin gave, followed by the driver pin. The lock clicked open. He did the same with lock number two.

A light push and the door eased ajar.

Advancing in a half-crouch, he entered, Maglite skimming the corners of each room, scanning every nook and cranny. As expected: no one home.

Everything remained untouched, neat and tidy, undisturbed.

In the bedroom, he rummaged through her dresser drawers and went through her handbags, coming away with some crumpled blue 50,000s and a delicate gold bracelet nestled in an interior compartment of an imitation Hermes shoulder bag. There were no inscriptions on the bracelet. He could pawn it in Tangerang Selatan. Sweeping a gloved hand under the mattress, he found an envelope crammed with Indo Rupiah under the bedsprings. He totted them up quickly – all in all, six million rupiah in large and small notes. He folded the envelope in two and pressed it into his hip pocket.

Satisfied, he made to leave. But then the Maglite skated over a bookshelf and his eye caught a three-ringed photograph album made from faux leather.

He thumbed through the stiff black pages. Each photograph was hand-mounted and protected by a sheet of peel-away PVC.

They were all in there: Mari Agnes Liem, Shireen Zee, Supaphorn Boonsing . . .

And then he came upon someone quite unexpected.

He shone the Maglite close. The white beam of light illuminated the face on the page. It had to be. There was no doubting it.

The family resemblance was uncanny.

Chapter Twenty-Four

Persahabatan General Hospital. The air around Ruud was thick with the smell of rubbing alcohol and disinfectant. He hated hospitals and didn't care for doctors much either. He'd felt this way from the age of ten. Ever since a strange man in a white coat cupped his balls and asked him to turn his head and cough.

Entering the ward, Ruud made his way to bed thirty-four and poked his head through the white privacy curtain. Aiboy Ali raised an eyebrow in welcome. Ruud drew the curtain closed behind him.

'Hey buddy!'

'Hello,' murmured Aiboy Ali; he shifted in his cot. He was attached to a nasal cannula and his voice was gravelly and meaty-jawed. 'How do I look? Do I look OK?'

Ruud smiled. 'Swell. You look swell. I brought you something to read.' Ruud placed the June issue of *Trax*, a local music magazine, on top of the blanket.

'What happened to Soeprapto? He got away?'

''Fraid so. It was one hell of a white-knuckle ride. How are you doing?'

'The bullet missed the femoral artery by a whisker. I could have bled to death. But it was a clean through-and-through shot. Missed the bone too. Still hurts like fucking hell.' In a little basket by the bed, his black leather biker cuffs sat on top of a neatly folded Burgerkill T-shirt. The bloodied drill pants with the ragged hole were nowhere to be seen. 'You? Your face looks bruised and fucked-up.'

'Sixteen stitches in this one.' Ruud lifted his left arm. 'Nine stitches in the other. And a bruise on my bum the size of Bali, thanks to Werry Hartono. He swiped me with a wing mirror.' He blanched a little; he was still very sore. Every step sent a barb of pain through his lower back. He'd stripped off at A&E and changed into a fresh shirt. He smelled of chlorhexidine and could feel the grime on his skin, but the doctors didn't want him to shower until the sutures had dried.

A nurse pushed through the curtain with a folded paper hat atop her head. She adjusted the IV catheter in the top of Aiboy Ali's left hand and removed the oximeter from his finger.

'Do you want to know last night's football results?' asked Ruud, keen to cheer him up.

Aiboy Ali lifted his face a fraction and grunted. He was in a green hospital gown and his throat was hoarse from the breathing tube they'd inserted during surgery.

'Three one to Brazil.'

There was a flicker of a smile.

The nurse put a stethoscope to her ears and wrapped a blood pressure cuff over Aiboy Ali's upper arm. Manually, she located the brachial pulse with a finger and placed the round end of the stethoscope against it.

'Vidi and I went to KFC and got a bucket with a side order of potato waffles. We saved you the chicken wings,' said Ruud, his voice high and energetic.

Aiboy Ali looked unimpressed.

Holding the pressure gauge in one hand and the bulb in another, the nurse began squeezing the bulb.

'Fancy a chicken wing?' Ruud persisted, proffering Colonel Sanders' face and shaking the bucket. 'You'll feel better for a bit of junk food.'

The man in the bed waved a hand to shut him up. Ruud was babbling and he knew it. In all the years he'd been on the force not once had one of his colleagues been shot. They'd been shot at, sure, but never hit. Ruud opened his mouth, and considered telling Aiboy Ali that this was a historic moment, before realizing he would sound absurd. He winced at the attempt at misplaced humour and shut his mouth again.

The airflow valve hissed and the nurse tore the cuff off. The Velcro made a ripping noise. Ruud waited for her to enter a figure on the clipboard and watched her amble off, pushing through the gap in the curtain.

'Alone at last,' said Ruud. He set down the KFC bucket on the bedside shelf.

Aiboy Ali motioned. 'Come here.'

Ruud, bent at the waist, leaned in over the side rails. Crisp wrinkles formed across the injured man's forehead. His eyes were all squinted up.

'Closer,' insisted Aiboy Ali, gruffly.

Ruud hovered over his colleague.

Aiboy Ali reached out and grasped Ruud's wrists, grasping them like handlebars. 'I want you to find him, *Gajah*.' He squeezed the handlebars like a man careering downhill on a mountain bike. 'Find him and kill him.'

The catheter in his hand came loose. He let go and, as his muscles relaxed, his head rolled back on his shoulders.

Ruud's mobile rang; it was the *dokter forensik*. He retreated to the foot of the bed. 'Yes.'

'Do you have a moment, Pujasumarta?'

'Of course, Solossa. What's on your mind?'

'I have a contact at the FBI office in Jakarta. Strictly speaking he's a legal attaché, but he works at the US Embassy. We swap information sometimes and it was my turn to call in a favour.'

'So what have you got for us?'

'A single fingerprint.'

'How the hell did you manage that?'

'The FBI explained how I could get latent fingerprints from a victim's skin. Latent prints are made from the sweat and oil accumulated on the skin's surface, and if the surface is totally smooth there's a chance we can "lift" it. Our third victim had completely hairless arms. We ran a Polilight over her body and found a partial fingerprint on the underside of her forearm, an inch from her right elbow. We're extremely lucky that the arm was nestled on her stomach, free from ground contamination and protected from the rain. The humidity helped too. Humidity helps to initialize the fingerprint residue, making it more responsive to chemical analysis.'

'You're losing me, Solossa.'

'I'll cut to the quick. We used a superglue fuming wand.'

'Sounds very Harry Potter.'

'We heat the superglue to form a vapour, which then sticks to the residue of the fingerprint.'

'You make it sound pretty simple.'

'I can tell you, it's not, First *Inspektur*.'

The patient in the next bed farted loudly and the smell added to the stink of his bandages. 'Sorry about that,' an apologetic voice whimpered from the other side of the curtain.

Ruud pushed on. 'Get the print to the lab and see if it matches D.W. Soeprapto's.'

'Already in the works. Are you at the hospital with Aiboy Ali?'

'Yes.'

'How is he?'

Ruud looked over to see his colleague biting into a crispy chicken wing.

'He'll live.' Ruud covered Aiboy Ali's feet with a blanket. A bit psychotic, but he'll live.

'Good. And you? Did you get some sleep?'

'A little.'

'And by the way?'

'What?'

'You left your sunglasses at the crime scene. I've kept them for you.'

'Thanks.'

Terminating the call, Ruud pocketed the phone and noticed his hands: dried blood caked his fingernails; he rubbed them against a trouser leg. 'Fucking stuff won't come off,' he cursed. He snatched a wet wipe from the bedside tray and set about cleaning his hands.

The ward sister appeared through the privacy curtain with her clipboard and told him that visiting hours had come to a close. Ruud squeezed his friend's hand gently and made his way along the corridor. At the end of it stood Hamka Hamzah with a faux leather photo album tucked under his arm. He looked dishevelled, wearing his police uniform liberally sprinkled with cigarette ash.

'We've identified the other women in Shireen Zee's

picture.' He ran through the names. 'They were part of a group that called themselves the Bintang Five. Freelance hookers who looked after one another; they used to work the clubs in Gambir district, such as Tanamur and JJs.'

Ruud asked him to repeat the names. Neither meant anything to Ruud. 'Good work, but tuck your shirt in, Hamzah, for goodness sake! You look a sight.'

The policeman coughed a bronchial cough and did as he was told, then belched loudly. 'Sorry, *neh*, this morning's *bubur ayam*, a few too many peppercorns.'

'What's that?' demanded Ruud.

'It arrived in a carrier bag early this morning. Sent anonymously and delivered by bicycle taxi. The duty sergeant had it dusted for prints. The bag too. All clean. But he wants you to see it. We are sure it belongs to one of the women from the mah-jong circle. It's very possible the killer sent it – to taunt us.'

'Whose album is this?'

'Belongs to a woman called Fatima Iswandari. Her name is printed on the inside flap. She is one of the five. She was standing second to the left in Shireen Zee's photo. It took us a couple of hours, but we got a warrant eventually. We sent uniforms to her house just now but found it deserted. Seems like she's vanished.'

'Vanished,' repeated Ruud.

'It's a huge city. The place swallows people up.'

He snatched the album and flipped through it. There was a solitary shot of Mari Agnes Liem and a few group photographs of the mah-jong circle, all dating back to the mid- to late 1990s, pasted to the pages. He recognized no one else.

Until.

'What the fuck?'

'What is the matter? Tell me,' insisted Hamzah.

'This person. I know him.'

'Who is he?'

Ruud threw back an energy tablet and followed it up with two extra-strong prescription painkillers.

The person in the photograph, it couldn't be, but it was; he remembered the face and the hair. Especially the hair.

Ruud looked again at his hands. They were shaking. And the dried blood was still under his fingernails.

The person in the photo was Imke's father.

Ruud burst through the swinging double doors and took the stairs to the ground floor. Across the road from the hospital, at the entrance to a mosque with soaring minarets, he spotted Witarsa. Looking sheepish, he stood amongst a plethora of shoes and sandals and had on a pair of tortoise-shell shades, which made his rumpled Walter Matthau face look even jowlier.

An elegant woman, upright on a pink Honda scooter with a lilac parasol, glided through the street. Ruud let her pass then cut across to the other side to a chorus of beeps. 'Bloody hell, boss, you all right? You're acting like you've been busted at the pharmacy buying mint-flavoured condoms.'

'Very funny, Pujasumarta. *Sialan*! That's some bruise on your face.'

'My face is fine. What are you doing here?' asked Ruud. 'I never pegged you as a religious person.'

'Getting away from the press,' he gasped with visible irritation. 'They're camped outside our building. They almost ate me alive.'

Witarsa was miserable. On his face was the expression people have when they've been jolted by the ferocious blast of a car horn.

He'd just got off the phone with his superiors; a conference call that lasted precisely two very harsh minutes. They wanted the case solved. Ramadan was approaching and they insisted he get his act together before the fasting month. The series of murders brought Jakarta a crapload of unwanted national and international media attention and the only thing the police brigadier general asked for now was a resolution, quickly, and for the news coverage to cease.

Witarsa held up a copy of *Jawa Pos*, one of the Indonesian dailies. The tic in his left eyelid was doing overtime. 'Have you seen this?' He giggled insanely, humourlessly.

For God's sake Witarsa, thought Ruud, don't go all Herbert Lom on me.

'Seen what?'

'The papers.'

'No, sorry, I've been too busy getting my limbs sewn back together.'

The banner took up the entire front page and read, PEMBUNUH BERANTAI!

'Serial killer!' Witarsa tossed the newspaper. 'Talk about a hysterical headline.' He rubbed his hand furiously across his face. 'Just two words. And this blasted picture of a machete underneath. It's the sort of sensationalist journalism that incites irrational panic.'

The pair of policemen stood in front of a *bungkus* cart.

A man approached on a motorcycle and offered to sell them a carton of contraband cigarettes. Ruud turned his back on him. The man pushed a packet of chewing gum under Ruud's nose, and the commissioner stepped forward and swiped it away, brandishing his badge.

The man sped off.

'The press has dubbed him the Mah-Jong Master.'

'Not very original,' said Ruud.

Somewhat absently, Witarsa murmured, 'the press are all fucking arseholes.' He collected himself. 'Well?' he challenged, cheeks quivering. 'Do you have anything to say?'

'There's an APW alert out for D.W. Soeprapto.'

'You think he's our man?'

'I have my reservations.'

'So do I.'

'Regardless, I'm confident we'll have him in custody by tonight.'

'Tonight! Twelve million people in this city and you think we'll have him by tonight. I admire your optimism. Look, I've had word from above; we're revising our priorities, Pujasumarta, adding more manpower. If you can't handle this case I want to know right this minute.'

'I can handle it.'

'You'd better. Anything else?'

'We know the identity of the two other women in the photograph.'

'Have you alerted them to the potential threat they face?'

'We are trying to locate them.' Ruud hesitated. His thoughts turned to the photograph album and the shot of Mathias Sneijder. Why was his picture in there? How was he connected? Was he in any danger? Was Imke?

'When you find them, bring them in to the station.' Witarsa whipped off his shades and ran his baggy eyes over Ruud. 'You need a shave.'

'I do?'

'You have a meeting with Brigadier General Fahruddin in one hour.'

'Shit. Why?'

'Why do you think?' He shifted to a more conciliatory tone. 'You're going to get a grilling. Just be prepared and don't argue with him.'

'Argue? I don't argue. I may have a passionate discussion with him and get a bit mouthy, but I won't argue. Where are we meeting?'

'D.W. Soeprapto's apartment. Forensic officers are crawling all over it as we speak.'

In daylight, the low-ceilinged, boxed-in tenement looked like a fortress and appeared to have been designed to shield its inhabitants from the outside world.

Ruud parked his car and approached on foot. The place was crawling with cops; uniformed flatfoots stood shoulder to shoulder comparing notes.

Ruud rehearsed what he was going to say to the brigadier general. There was no way of sugarcoating things; the investigation was at a critical juncture. From the moment he walked up the stairs he felt uneasy, and the feeling only got worse when he ducked under the yellow *Garis Polisi* barrier tape. He'd been unsettled by Witarsa's forewarning. What he found in D.W. Soeprapto's rooms was even more unsettling.

He'd expected to find a wall plastered with photographs of women, of past victims, some in their death agonies, overlapping each other. A stalker shrine. Newspaper clippings. Scrapbooks filled with paranoid, obsessive ramblings. Dolls with their heads ripped off. Vats of acid containing recently severed hands. Corpses stashed behind false brick walls. Satan worshipping. Hidden horrors. Instead he found . . .

'A meth lab,' said Vidi, pulling at his *Sunnah* beard. 'Can you believe it?'

The apartment smelled of rotten eggs and lighter fluid.

Measuring cups, Pyrex containers, buckets, rubber tubing, hotplates, clamps and funnels took up every conceivable work surface. Beakers labelled with the words sulphuric acid, MSM, trichloroethane and sodium hydroxide lined the shelves.

'This isn't right,' gulped Ruud. 'Our man isn't in the drugs business.'

'How do you know?' asked Vidi.

'It doesn't fit the profile.' Ruud watched a forensic specialist pick through a raft of starter fluid bottles, thermometers, aluminium foil and what appeared to be iodized salt. He looked on patiently as an officer in a white mask and goggles, using a spatula, scraped white crystals from a hotplate into a plastic beaker. It took a while as the crystals had set hard. Ruud covered his nose with a hand. The interior was stifling. With over a dozen people milling about and the enclosed space stinking of rotten eggs he was starting to feel nauseous.

He turned and came face to face with Timur Djamin from Mobil 27, armed robbery.

'What are you doing here, Lieutenant Colonel?' asked Ruud.

Timur Djamin removed his peaked cap and clasped it in the crook of an elbow. Brandishing his inch-long thumbnails, he sipped a cup of black tea whilst sucking on a sugar cube, keeping the cube lodged between his front teeth.

'We had a tip-off. How it happened was, I received a call just now saying they found full-face Balaclavas, some hand-guns and Seven Continents Movers overalls. Strikes me these fellows are not only making drugs but were involved in the Sawah Besar heist. I'm guessing the same guns were used at the robbery. The ballistic report should confirm it.' He sucked on the sugar cube.

'Well lucky old you.'

'That's right, First *Inspektur*, lucky me. Looks like you stumbled across the wrong *kriminal* at the right time.'

A uniformed sergeant marched in and stamped his feet. '*Hormat gerak!* Brigadier General in our company!' Everyone stood to attention.

Police Brigadier General Fahruddin swaggered through dressed in the uniform of a senior officer. He was an intimidating presence. In his mid-sixties, he had climbed progressively to the top of his profession, manipulating his way around the wreckage of political reforms, backing the heavyweights in intra-bureau skirmishes. Tall, distinguished, with varnished cheekbones and bow legs so curved you could ride a horse through them, Fahruddin was by far the poshest man Ruud had ever met, so posh his jaw didn't move when he spoke. 'A moment with you, Pujasumarta.' He looked hard at Ruud and ushered him to one side. 'A right balls-up. You had him and then you lost him. Let him get away.'

'I never *had* him, sir, I was in pursuit. He was armed. I am sure you've heard what happened to Detective Aiboy Ali.'

They were out in the corridor. The doorframe they stood next to sported a great gash of white splinters.

'Nine rounds discharged from your handgun and all misses,' Fahruddin's tone was peremptory. Ruud felt as if his insides were being scraped out. He saw the spot where his colleague had fallen; the floor was marked with blood.

Ruud's ears started ringing; he grew dizzy. Something was going on in his head, making his sightlines thin and flare, folding the room in two. Suddenly he saw the man with the cornrows again, heard his shoes against the wooden steps, backlit against a window at the far end of the long corridor. Aiboy Ali removing his police warrant card, holding it up. The solitary man, carrying plastic grocery bags in each hand. Fruit juice cartons, green vegetables with their leafy bits sticking out. A blur of movement. Gunshots. Bullets tearing at the wall, taking bites out of the doorframe. Aiboy Ali's voice screaming. A gaping wound, liquefying at the edges. The blood oozing. A thin wet sound.

Ruud went pale. He struggled for air. When he looked at the brigadier he saw glass coming at him and striking the side of his head like razor shards.

Fahruddin pursed his lips. 'Worse still, you've probably been chasing the wrong bloody man. Does this look like the hideout of a *pembunuh berantai* to you? The papers are calling him the Mah-Jong Master. That's bad press, Pujasumarta, bad, bad press. Did Witarsa have a word with you?'

Ruud was sweating; his heart pounded and he was breathing fast. All the air went out of his body.

'I *said* did Witarsa have a word with you?'

'He said something about adding more manpower.'

'You've been taken off the case.'

'Say that again, slowly.'

'Administrative leave.' He placed great emphasis on the words *liburan* and *administrasi*.

Dismayed, Ruud shook his head. 'What are you talking about?'

'On account of your injuries. Take a few days off to clear your head.'

'There's nothing wrong with me.'

'Twenty-five stitches is hardly nothing, First *Inspektur*. And it's been brought to my attention that you may be taking inappropriate medication.'

'Oh, for fuck's sake!' He whipped out his box of Head Start pills. 'You mean these? They're bloody energy boosters!'

'You're a good policeman, Pujasumarta. You've come a long way. I've read your file. Your arrest statistics are impressive and there's a great future ahead of you. But we feel you're not ready for a case like this. You need to take a few steps back, get some air. With you in charge things are a little . . . cramped.'

'What do you mean *cramped*?'

'We are passing this onto someone more experienced.'

Ruud stared at Fahruddin in open defiance. 'Who? Who are you replacing me with?'

The older man regarded Ruud keenly. His voice grew icy. He leaned in. 'You'll find out in due course when you report back for duty.' Ruud could smell the coffee he'd had for lunch.

'You're making a huge mistake!'

A superior smile. The police brigadier general rammed his peaked cap onto his imperious crown. 'We'll soon find out, won't we? Now, if you'll excuse me I think I've seen enough here. I have some other business to attend to.'

Ruud continued to shake his head uncomprehendingly. He was too bewildered and disappointed to respond. In normal circumstances, he would have argued his corner, pleaded for another chance, but his instincts told him to stand down. The top brass had lost face. The Royal Thai

Embassy was making noises following the death of one of their citizens. National interests were involved. None of this provided a positive image of contemporary Indonesia, a country currently embroiled in a tumultuous presidential election. Uncertainty like this shook investor confidence and damaged capital inflows. Ruud gave a rueful grin. He had no option but to tow the line.

Vidi patted him on the back and told him it would blow over in a few days.

The loudspeakers crackled. From the nearby mosque, the sound of the muezzin's call to prayer invaded the entire building and continued for almost three minutes.

Chapter Twenty-Five

Erica spent the early morning lying on her back, toes in the grass, staring at the sky and the wandering clouds. She got to her feet once the breakfast gong was struck.

A silver water-heated dish containing beef sausages and turkey bacon rested on the sideboard. A water-beaded jug of iced orange juice sat untouched on the breakfast table.

Imke tightened the sash of her dressing gown and stabbed a fork into a bowl of papaya chunks. Her gaze remained fixed on the fruit; she saw her father's face in the bowl; saw the old trustworthy smile, a smile she no longer believed in.

'I'm glad to see you're a bit more docile this morning.' Erica tossed her a sidelong look. The newspaper was open at the puzzle section – a teacup rested on a half-finished Sudoku grid.

'It's his life,' snorted Imke. 'But don't get me wrong, I'm still furious with him. I'm not exactly enamoured with you either, *hè*, keeping it all from me.'

'"Mine ear is much enamoured of thy note. So is mine eye enthralled to thy shape."'

'Shakespeare?'

'*A Midsummer Night's Dream.*'

'Midsummer Nightmare more like.'

'The truth always comes out – sooner or later. I'm just sorry it had to be me to tell you.' Erica pulled her close and felt the point of Imke's chin on her shoulder. They hugged. 'Better?'

'Better.'

'Forgive me?'

'I forgive you.' She kissed her proffered cheek. 'Tea?'

'Please.'

Imke filled her aunt's cup with Earl Grey. From their nests in the baobab trees the warblers sang nonstop.

'Aunty Ecks, can you do me a favour?'

'What's that then?'

'Can you not mention anything about Papa to Ruud?'

'If that's what you want.'

No, it wasn't what she wanted. She wanted to tell Ruud everything, but now was not the time – they were just starting to get to know one another again, their friendship was blossoming. If anything, it felt like the connection between them was growing stronger by the day. She didn't want to complicate that by bringing up her father's sordid past. 'I'll tell him soon, just not yet. God, it's just all too embarrassing.'

The houseboy approached dozily with a tray full of buns and toasted bread.

'Well, let's be thankful for small mercies. At least we have toast this morning to go with the butter,' announced Erica, cutting the slices into triangles.

'Oh, by the way, I got an email from cousin Peter. Your neighbour, old man Klooster, died. He left you a thousand euros in his will.'

'That bloody man! And all I gave him was a card and a stick of candy cane for Christmas!' Erica sipped the tea. 'Poor old Klooster.' She cast her eye over the morning papers.

'Holland five: Spain one. Now that's a result worth crowing over. And what's this? BBC reports that Indonesia is to be turned into regional chocolate hub! World's third-largest producer of cocoa beans ready to push into high-end confectionery market with MONGGO CHOCOLATE at the forefront.'

She paused to digest the news.

'Now, listen,' said Erica, thumbing through an old copy of *Condé Nast Traveller* and fanning out the centre spread across the table. Imke leaned in. 'Remember the town I mentioned called Jelekong in Bandung, where out of five thousand people thirty-five per cent of them are artists?' She pointed. 'Well, guess what? We are going there today. The Captain has offered to take us.'

'What, now?'

'Well, not right at this moment.'

Energized, Imke fastened the band that kept her flat, lifeless hair in place. 'What', she said in a tone of harmless jocularity, 'are we waiting for?'

'I have a session with the President this morning. We'll leave as soon as I'm finished.'

There he was, in one-third shadow: iron hair, jaw set, brambly eyebrows. Looking formal, with a bearlike poise, perhaps a little chiding in his dress uniform. Shoulders like ramparts. His medals shone bright, the nearest star a silver liquid glimmer in a scribble of wine-dark umbra.

'Please turn your head towards the light.' Erica was pleased. The work was really taking shape. She gazed at the large canvas on the easel then back at the President.

Looking pretty *verdomd* good, she said to herself. Not bad for a girl from Dokkum.

Erica often marvelled at how far she'd come as an artist. Forever regarded as a potential this or an aspiring that, it was only late in her career that a Greek art collector based in Paris discovered her. He was formidably wealthy, having made his fortune in asset management, and he bought six of her paintings. Within a year she held exhibitions in London, New York, Frankfurt and Moscow, rubbing shoulders with Jeff Koons, Damien Hirst and Cy Twombly. Fêted, applauded and celebrated, she hadn't expected it to last, but it had.

The President cleared his throat.

He'd been sitting for her a mere five minutes, but already he was starting to get impatient. Uninterested in her con-versational singsong, he'd remained positively mute from the moment he entered the room. She wondered what was the matter. Where was all the chucklesome banter, she thought, the talk of chewing tea leaves, the witty remarks regarding Affandi forgeries, the chitchat relating to his fried rice restaurant? Is he unwell? Perhaps he's disappointed I went AWOL the other day. No, he wouldn't care about that, surely. He's probably worried about his succession, what with all the smear campaigns, the fire-breathing speeches, see-sawing opinion polls and titanic name-calling going on.

'Do you think Jokowi will win the election or will it be Prabowo?' she stuck her neck out.

The President grew still. Joko 'Jokowi' Widodo was pro-jected to win by a narrow margin, but there were fears of electoral fraud and even instability. The establishment was mistrustful of Joko's reformist objectives. He was an outsider, born in a riverbank slum, a furniture manufacturer turned Governor of Jakarta. His rival, Prabowo Subianto, was a former military general, endorsed by a coalition of the country's largest political parties, with a juggernaut of media support, financial clout and campaign expertise behind him. His family could trace its lineage to Java's sultans. His father was Suharto's trade minister. Even Yudhoyono, as Chairman of the Democratic Party, had backed Prabowo.

Diplomatically, the President muttered something about maintaining economic stability.

Erica nodded. This was the moment of truth for Indonesia's democracy.

There was a sense of possibility in the air. What Erica saw was a brash, young country longing to fall in love with its future. She wanted to say she sensed an upsurge, a mood, a feeling, a geopolitical and social revolution, taking place, but for once her voice failed her.

'Let's just hope', ventured Erica, 'that whatever the outcome, we have calm and the state upholds the will of the people.'

The President's reply was to grunt and grumble with authoritarian indifference. She'd seen this reaction in important people before – happy and chatty one day, surly the next. It made her job all the more difficult, especially, as now, when something closes down in the sitter's face, like storm windows slamming shut in a typhoon.

Erica noticed a tendon bulge on his neck: irritation or fatigue. Either way, she decided to clam up and keep a solitary distance. It wasn't her job to entertain him.

Engine idling, the car sat in the drive. The sky was grey with clouds like pencil shavings.

Birds tweeted in the nearby trees. Deer grazed on the

lawn, ears twitching, tails swishing. The chorus of toads was in full cry.

'Sorry, to keep you waiting, Nakula,' said Imke, emerging from the bungalow, clad in a fruit-patterned shift and sun hat, smelling of sunblock. She sucked in the tropical air. 'Lovely day.'

'Waiting is what I do, madam. When I am not waiting, I am driving. When not driving, I am waiting. It is the chauffeur's job.' He pressed his hand to his heart and bowed his head.

The Captain, shaped like a melon, waddled after her. Today, to commemorate the road trip, the head of the household staff was dressed in a honeydew safari suit and well-shined shoes.

'Good afternoon, Miss Imke.' He salaamed.

'Good afternoon. You look very smart today,' she replied, paying attention to his shoes, which were brown with thick heels and pointed toes. The pointed toes distracted her momentarily, but she couldn't think why.

The Captain climbed into the front passenger seat. Flesh strained against cotton as he wedged himself between door and handbrake. Successfully negotiated, he yawned and nodded at Nakula.

Imke scrambled in next to Erica.

'Are we all ready for our trip to Jelekong?' asked The Captain. As usual, he twirled a silver pen between his fingers.

'Yes!' cried the two women, giggling joyfully in the back, enjoying the holiday atmosphere.

Within ten minutes, Erica was immersed in a packet of chocolate digestives. 'Would you care for a biscuit, Captain?'

'No, no. I never eat during a car journey. I do not have the stomach for it.'

You could have fooled me, reflected Erica, stifling a fresh bout of giggles. She passed the packet around.

'Very nice taste,' said the chauffeur, his mouth full of crumbs. 'Have you tried our pineapple jam biscuits, Slai O'lai? They are a national icon. Next time, I will bring you some.'

'That would be marvellous, Nakula,' said Erica.

An hour later, having survived the rural, bumpy road, they passed through the low arch welcoming visitors to the 'village of paintings'. They had stopped only once along the way, at a roadside stall, to purchase a bag of prawn crackers.

In spite of its relatively small size, the town of Jelekong attracted a fair number of foreign tourists on a daily basis. Framed by tall rain trees and bursting bamboo thickets, it was the definition of bucolic bliss.

Nakula parked the car. Erica and Imke saw a long line of red-roofed houses with walls made of coloured stone. Each house represented a painter's workshop. Imke noticed paintings in all shapes and sizes displayed outside the buildings and shopfronts. Further ahead, she observed a string of noisy Mainland Chinese tourists erupting from an artist's studio; they leaned their bodies against a studded antique door, all giving the peace sign as they posed in front of the tour guide's camera.

Imke decided to give them a wide berth. She went to admire the view of Mount Geulis. From their hilltop vantage point, she spied the valley below; the forest canopy was cloaked in mist and blue shadows. Imke also spotted a familiar blue car trundling up the road. She watched the Toyota Yaris pull up alongside, and when Ruud climbed out, her eyes shone.

Erica was the first to say hello. She eyed him suspiciously.

'Are you feeling all right, Ruud? You're looking rather louche today. A little dazed too. A bit like Harold the Hippy stumbling out of an Amsterdam coffee shop. Are those bruises on your cheeks?'

'I'd like to have a word with Imke, if that's OK.'

'By all means.' She left him and approached a group of young kids playing *semut, orang, gajah* — a local version of stone, paper, scissors.

On the long drive to Bandung, Ruud attempted to clear his thoughts, but the brigadier general's words kept ringing in his ears and he remained no less infuriated when the sign for Jelekong came into view.

He walked up to Imke and planted a kiss on her cheek. He smelled the scent of soap on her skin, a fresh fragrance of bergamot and sandalwood.

'Are you stalking me, First *Inspektur* Pujasumarta?' she demanded, appraising him. She curled and uncurled a wisp of hair around a finger.

'I'm a policeman, Miss Sneijder. We call it surveillance. The palace staff told me you'd be here.'

'And here I am. What happened to your face?'

'It got into an argument with a stretch of pavement. Stings a bit. Your hair looks nice.'

'Oh, well. I, *hnn*, I washed it this morning.' She giggled, unable to hide her delight. Nobody had ever complimented her droopy locks before. Perhaps the Pureology Shampoo was working its magic after all.

'Are those blonde streaks new?'

'That's from the sun.'

'Where is Kiki?'

'Back at the bungalow. She's used to it there.'

'And how's your aunt?' He peered beyond Imke to see

Erica with hands on knees, making faces at little children. The children hopped about barefooted, laughing and giggling.

'Theatrical as ever. She says she can feel the artistic energy in the air.'

Both of them shook their heads. They shared a smile.

She glanced down with a deadpan expression. 'Your socks don't match, by the way.'

'I was late getting up this morning. Got dressed in a hurry. I could've slept all day.'

'How's the investigation coming along?' Imke removed her sun hat and rubbed the red mark it left on her forehead.

'That's what I wanted to talk to you about. There's been a development.'

'A development? That's good, isn't it?'

He didn't mention his white-knuckle encounter with D.W. Soeprapto, or the lacerations to his arms, or the two hours spent in A&E lying across a paper-wrapped examination table. Moreover, he didn't say Aiboy Ali had been shot.

Instead, he said, 'Well, not really. It's about the investigation, that's why I'm here. I wanted to tell you something.' The photograph of Mathias Sneijder flashed once again behind his eyes. What was it doing in Fatima Iswandari's picture album? How did it get there? Why was it in her possession in the first place? And how was Mathias associated with these women? It mystified him and, like metallic voices clashing like tin pans in his head, it was driving him mad. He made as if to say something, but the words hooked at his throat.

'What?'

'I've been taken off the case.'

'Oh Ruud, I'm so sorry to hear that. Are you very upset?'

'Me? No, I'm OK . . . I'm fine . . .' He sighed, struggling.

His voice was barely above a whisper. 'Actually, yes, I am kind of upset. I'm confused.'

He realized he'd developed a habit of not looking her in the eye; rather, he peered at a spot to the left of her head.

She took his arm gently and led him to a roadside *kaki lima*, a mobile food stall. 'Come, let me buy you a fruit *rojak*.' The *rojak* vendor, a small, bare-chested man with an easy smile, greeted them jovially. He wiped his hands on the newspaper tied to his waist – a kind of makeshift apron – and presented the bowls of artisan spice blends. Ruud chose pineapple, jicama, mango, cucumber and water apple, dousing the mix in a sweet and zesty dressing.

Before tucking in, they washed their hands in a communal porcelain basin. The cold salad tasted good. They sat on a wooden bench under a wide parasol. Her fruit-patterned shift rode up a fraction, revealing her shapely thighs. 'Listen,' she confided, 'I've worked with a lot of policemen. Experienced, decorated policemen. It happens.'

'I know it happens. It just hasn't happened to me before.'

'Who are you and what have you done to my breezy, upbeat, buoyant-as-a-blimp kind-of-guy?'

He performed a Roger Moore eyebrow-cock.

They both smiled. 'Yeah. I'm still here.'

'You know what I would do?'

'What would you do, Imke?'

'Carry on working the case.'

'You mean behind Witarsa's back?'

'Yes, why not, *hè*? Get your team together, the ones you trust. Meet somewhere neutral, compare notes and simply carry on where you left off. Lurk about in the background. You're good at that.'

'Sounds like a plan.'

'I'm good with plans. And if you need my help . . .'

'Thanks. I'd better get the green light from Vidi and the others first. To them you're still an outsider.'

'I understand.'

They sauntered along the central alley and strolled into one of the galleries made of pink-coloured stone. A row of six artists sat poised at work. Imke watched a man with a grey ponytail run a palette knife along his canvas. 'Rooster fight?' she enquired.

The man nodded, made a flourish with his free hand to indicate the blur of feathers.

After a while Ruud took her elbow and led her into the sunshine.

They stood in the centre of the alley. Not far away, a gallery owner standing outside his shop casually slapped some wooden canvases together, hoping to arouse their interest. His wife, squatting nearby at the outdoor tap stand, scoured breakfast dishes in a plastic bucket.

'Imke, I'm curious, does the name Fatima Iswandari mean anything to you or your family?'

'No. Should it?'

'I'm not sure.'

Ruud told her a little about Fatima Iswandari and that the police had gone to her house in the morning but found it deserted; said that she had vanished into thin air; that he feared for her life. He told Imke all this without bringing up her father. He did not want to mention Mathias Sneijder until he could work out the connection. Fatima Iswandari and Mathias Sneijder – more than a coincidence, of that he was certain.

But it was his job to ask questions. Tentatively he asked,

'Did your father often take trips away from home without your mother?'

'He ran coffee estates in south Sulawesi. He was away every fortnight for a few days. But you knew that already.'

'Did he go alone?'

'Yes, he went alone.'

He blinked, bracing himself. 'What about when he was in Jakarta? Was he often out late?' What he wanted to ask was: Did he have relationships with local women?

She opened her mouth to answer the question but stopped herself. Instead, she said, 'What's this all about, Ruud?'

'Right now, I have no idea.'

Imke stayed quiet for some time. She was deep in thought, wondering if this had anything to do with her father's affair. Why would Ruud ask if she'd heard of a woman called Fatima Iswandari? Was Fatima Iswandari the woman who'd almost torn her family to pieces? No, that would be too weird a coincidence. She stared into Ruud's eyes as he spoke. A part of her wanted so much to confide in him, tell him how hurt she was, but she quickly decided against it. This was not the time or place.

A safe of brown ducks sauntered about nearby, attracted by a rainwater puddle. One of the ducks had three little ducklings waddling in her wake. Delighted by this distraction, Imke whirled around to catch Erica's attention, only to see The Captain loitering close by, squinting at her under the hot sun. She registered a flash in his eyes, an inexplicably haunted look, full of rage and torment. Taken by surprise, he immediately crouched down to pick up something he'd dropped. It was his silver pen. He retrieved the pen from the ground, then hurriedly walked away.

Imke's head twitched, the way a dog jerks its head to expel

a persistent fly. She could have been imagining it, but she was certain he'd been eavesdropping on them.

She leaned into Ruud and dropped her voice to a whisper. 'The Captain was hovering a moment ago, listening to us.'

'Yes, I noticed.'

'How long was he standing behind us, do you think?'

'A couple of minutes, perhaps. It's hard to say.'

'What was he up to?'

'He was simply standing there in the sun. Maybe he was trying to get a tan,' Ruud quipped. 'Strange, though, don't you think?'

'Very.' Imke watched the fat man toddle over to speak with Nakula in the shade, disappearing in a scrim of shadows. 'D'you know what?'

'What?'

'I think he might have stolen a pair of panties from my wardrobe.'

'You're joking!'

'It was the night Erica went missing. He was going through the bungalow. I'm sure he slipped a pair into his pocket.'

'Don't stare at him. Keep your eyes on me.'

'Did I ever mention the strange note I found?'

'What note?'

'On the day I arrived there was a note left by my bedside wishing me a short-lived stay in Indonesia. Aunty Ecks thinks it was a language mix-up, that I'm being paranoid.'

His voice changed – an edge of steel, a tightening in his throat. 'And you suspect The Captain wrote the note?'

'That's just it. I really don't know.' She stared at Ruud. 'What are you thinking?'

'You know what I'm thinking.'

With a gasp. 'Him? The roundest Indonesian in the world? He couldn't chop a tree trunk let alone someone's hand off.'

'Imke, I'm not suggesting The Captain is the Mah-Jong Master, but I want you to be on guard. Don't trust anyone.'

'Why? What do you think is going on?'

'Something I don't fully understand.'

'What?'

Ruud's agitation mounted. He was desperate to piece this all together, yet he couldn't think how. She pressed him again. He wasn't sure what to say, but his instincts told him things were about to turn very dark. And he knew that the most dangerous predators moved freely in the darkest parts of the jungle.

She felt the roughness of his thumb against her cheek. 'Just be careful, Imke. For God's sake, be careful.'

Chapter Twenty-Six

Wednesday. 1.20 a.m.

One night towards the end of the Idul Adha holiday, my mother cut off my penis. She took a blade to it. I was seven years old.

She shoved a piece of wood between my teeth and claimed it was a rite of passage. It was to coincide with the rainy season, she explained, when the cassavas were in bloom and before the rice leaves in the fields turned yellow.

The pain . . . I will remember it for the rest of my life.

Mother laughed at my pain. The other women – there were four of them – they all laughed too.

One of them, they called her Shireen, stripped me naked and tied my arms and legs to the bed. I was just a skinny little boy, with ribs showing through my skin. The ropes bruised and scored my flesh. The more I struggled the more my flesh tore.

Every part of me trembled.

'Stop!' I screamed, '*Tidak!* No!' But they would not stop. I prayed a neighbour would come from the village. That someone from down the path, or the *lurah* from along the way, would hear my wails. But nobody came.

It was inky black outside, the darkest point before sunrise.

All I saw when I stared out of the window was the tilting clothes line pole, which resembled an upright corpse. And the dreaded solid shapes of the kepuh trees.

The magical kepuh tree. The mysterious kepuh tree. The symbol of a Javanese cemetery.

As Shireen secured the knots she instructed me to relax, that it was an initiation, but my sobbing would not cease. I did not understand why they were hurting me, so she told me of a circumcision ceremony in the countryside that took place every year. It comprised three days of fun and entertainment, she said. A dozen boys and a dozen girls had their genitals snipped. Villagers from all around arrived with offerings of betel and sugar and sweet-smelling balms. They gathered at the *alun-alun*, the public square. Tribeswomen pounded rice and grated coconuts. Music played and puppets performed. At midnight the Sisingaan dancers danced to the shadows of the moon.

After three days of celebration, she said, the children were presented to the village elders, paraded on wooden lions and then bathed in the river.

An hour before dawn the boys laid themselves flat in the *alun-alun*, where the medicine man cut away their foreskins.

Shireen pinched my nose and laughed. She shoved a bag of ice between my legs. 'Here,' she said, 'keep this ice pressed to your pee-pee. I promise you it will not hurt.'

Then she massaged the tissue covering the glands of my penis.

The day before, I had been happily playing in the *kampung* square, drawing pictures in the soil with a stick. I liked that stick. It was short and smooth and sturdy and it felt good in my hands. I brought it home with me.

My mother shoved the very same stick into my mouth. I

bucked my hips frantically. She grabbed hold of my sex, yanked the loose skin forward and she cut me.

The ragged wound bled and bled and bled.

The sheets underneath were wet with it.

Satisfied with her work, Mother went and grabbed a bird from the outdoor cage and held it upside down by the feet. She sacrificed the rooster, slitting its stomach and releasing the entrails onto the earth.

But I wasn't meant to bleed as much as I did. It took a large towel and some bandages to stem the initial flow. I did not learn until subsequently that my frenular artery had been severed. First she took me to a local healer, who sprinkled a secret family remedy on my groin, but it only made matters worse. The infection that followed caused sepsis. My whole body became inflamed. I was taken to the community hospital where my mother accused the doctor of duping and exploiting her. Surely, it was unnecessary to remove the infected part of the organ, she argued. The surgeon explained it had to be done. But there were no beds available. She would have to pay him a fee to free one up. At first she refused to pay. She kicked up one hell of a fuss. Said it was part of a plot, that they were all in league with the jackal father. Only when someone called the security guards did she back down. She pawned her silver watch to raise the funds. The watch had been a gift from a gentleman caller.

The hospital was bleak, the stay arduous and grinding. I was fed painkillers to help me sleep. I was forced to lie on my back in order for the wound to heal. In a ward full of strangers, the nurses changed my dressings each morning. The gauze stuck to the dried blood, and no matter how careful they were, the skin always tore, ripping away the scab, causing fresh tissue damage.

Two weeks later, when I was discharged and allowed to return home, Mother beat me for getting sick, for wasting her hard-earned money. *Aduh*, how she beat me. Beat me like a rented mule. I kept my wounds to myself and, likewise, my shame.

That was before she started crushing cigarettes out on my back.

Wednesday. 2.40 a.m.
I have been left with scars. I have been left half a man. The doctors give me pills. The pills help with the discomfort, but they are the cause of my weight gain. I am fat because of the pills.

The scarring has caused urethral strictures, so it hurts when I urinate.

I now require periodic bougienage.

This is what is printed on the card my doctor gave me, to help me understand. I have a suspicion he copied it directly from medicinenet.com.

Bougienage: A procedure requiring the use of a bougie. A bougie is a narrow plastic or metal cylinder that a physician slides into or through a body passageway, such as the penis, to dilate the passageway, guide another instrument into a passageway, or dislodge an object.

Oh Mother, how I love you. May the fires of hell forever burn your stinking soul.

Wednesday. 3 a.m.
Once a week they came to play their game, slapping their noisy tiles on the tabletop.

They knew what she did to me. They knew all along what she was.

Yet, they did nothing.

She kept me locked in the dark until the end of the evening. Only then was I let out and paraded about.

She asked me who my father was.

I said I did not know.

That was her cue. Her cue to perform and play her part in our ugly little drama, where she came from somewhere exalted and I came from somewhere vile, somewhere despicable. She stripped me of my damp pyjamas. Made me stand naked in front of this murder of crows. Scolded me, humiliated me, flicked her wrist like a whip to strike my demolished cock, called me a bastard, the son of a jackal father.

And I felt it. *Aduh*, how I felt it.

Mankind's first recorded emotion, at least according to the Christian book of Genesis, is shame: Adam and his wife Eve felt dirty, violated. They cowered in their nakedness under God's eye, hurriedly covering themselves in fig leaves. Read the Holy *Quran* and the story is the same. 'O book! O blessed book! I hold out my hands before my face, palm upwards, eyes closed. I raise both hands up to my ears, palms facing the Qibla.'

For is there no shame more raw, more primitive than the shame of being stripped naked in front of strangers?

The four women watched her hit me. Watched me cringe and try to shield what was left of me down there.

Yet, they did nothing.

Then, when all the women had gone home . . .

Eyes squeezed shut. Pretending to sleep. I can still feel it. I am seven again. The dismay. The exhilaration. The fear.

Like a hornet buzzing between my teeth. Mother touching my legs, sliding her fingers up the length of my thigh. Me writhing and struggling. Her hand, hard and bony, taut as a scorpion on my penis.

She squeezes the tip hard. So hard I think it may pop.

After that, I do not resist. Not even when she directs my hand to her bare breast. I feel the tiny bumps on her nipple. Then down across her belly, over the downy hair and beyond. My fingertips dip inside. She is damp and swollen. Her breathing grows heavier and heavier. Until it becomes the loudest sound in the world.

And her teeth glint in the dark.

Afterwards, she will beat me.

She will beat me because she hates me. Because she feels guilty. Because she thinks there is nobody *real* inside of me. Because I am a timid seven-year-old child who wets himself and is the cause of all her troubles.

A seven-year-old locked in the darkness.

Chapter Twenty-Seven

Across the top of the door the name 'Kom. Pol. JOYO T. WITARSA' is etched in gilt letters. Here and there the gold paint has cracked and chipped, over the 'T' and under the 'S' especially. It was an old door. Vidi knocked and entered. The police chief held a plate of quartered oranges. He bit into an orange slice and spat the seeds into his fist.

'Meeting's about to start, boss.'

'The AKP is here?'

The detective with the impressive *Sunnah* beard made a face and squeezed the spring-loaded finger strengthener in his hand. 'He is here.'

Vidi, Witarsa, Hamka Hamzah and Solossa filed into the Incident Room.

They were all surprised to find Aiboy Ali, *sans* black leather biker cuffs, reclining on an aluminium chair with his back against the floor-to-ceiling glass. He held a crutch in his arms like a machine gun. There was a portable IV drip with a stand by his side. 'You just came out of hospital, izzenit?' noted Vidi.

The sun streamed through the window, splashing on Aiboy Ali's shoulders and elevated leg. He used both hands and pulled his hair from his eyes.

'I discharged myself. They weren't showing the football on TV. I had one hell of a time getting past the nurses' station.'

'You're not going to bleed all over the floor, are you?'

'I'll be fine so long as I keep my feet up.'

'Nothing new there then.'

The whole room laughed.

When everyone looked away, Aiboy Ali punched a number into his mobile and pressed 'speaker'. Ruud answered, but said nothing. He used a separate phone to text Aiboy Ali.

The detective's phone vibrated.

whos taken ovr frm me?

He texted Ruud back.

natsir a proper dickhead frm section 12

Three seconds went by.

u know him?

Aiboy Ali made a face.

yes rumour is hes a carpenters fan

Aiboy Ali despised The Carpenters.

bet he has a karen carpenter poster on his wall

Aiboy Ali despised Adult Contemporary more than any

other music genre, present or past. Easy Listening and Folk weren't his favourites either.

hows the sound quality? can u hear ok?

Aiboy Ali stared at the screen.

loud n clear

On cue, Ruud's replacement, Captain Natsir (AKP), stood up and introduced himself. He welcomed Police Commissioner Witarsa to the gathering and bowed obsequiously. He talked so loud the next room could hear him. He had a mouth on him like a 747.

'Now, before we start, can anyone tell me why these chairs are arranged in a circle?' Natsir asked.

Werry Hatono, keen as ever, sprang up like toast out of a toaster. 'First *Inspektur* Pujasumarta liked to have them in a circle,' he explained. 'He said people spoke more openly when seated that way.'

'Well, First *Inspektur* Pujasumarta isn't involved in this case any more, is he?'

u r right hes an A1 goose

'Everyone on his feet. Everyone apart from you with the crutches.' He rearranged the aluminium chairs into two rows. 'This isn't a *bangsat* group therapy session.'

Vidi gave a snort and ran some fingers through his *Sunnah* beard. He produced two coins from his pocket and used them like tweezers to pluck errant strands of hair from his throat.

266

'And you, Hamzah,' Natsir jutted his jaw at the little man. 'What's a Sabhara street cop doing here?'

'I've been involved in the case from the very beginning,' he replied, removing his beret to reveal his black centre-parted hair. 'And how do you know my name?' A *kretek* dangled from the side of his mouth.

'Says so on the brass nameplate pinned over your heart. How long have you been with the force?'

'Not long,' admitted Hamzah, pausing mid-drag. 'Eighteen months.' He stubbed out his cigarette.

'What were you doing before?'

'A bit of this and that.'

'Such as?' he challenged.

Hamzah fell into a hacking fit and the talk dried up as everyone waited for his cough to subside. He tore the filter off a fresh Gudang Garam, lit it, and took a deep pull.

'You smoke like it's an alternative to breathing.'

He coughed his rattling-coffin cough, which culminated in his having to leave the room.

Natsir straightened his tie. 'I assume our Sabhara street-cop friend is going to be some time, so we'll start without him, shall we? This is rumour management headquarters, gentlemen! Here are the facts. The fugitive D.W. Soeprapto is now in custody. He was arrested this morning and questioned by officers from Brigade Mobil 27, armed robbery. They have a ballistics match. One of the handguns found in his apartment was used in the Sawah Besar heist. However, there is nothing to suggest he's involved in the murders of our three victims. No reason at all to believe he is the Mah-Jong Master. Besides, his alibi is rock solid. The night Mari Agnes Liem was murdered he was in a police holding

267

cell — arrested for taking part in a brawl — which means we're back to square one.'

'Not exactly,' interrupted Solossa. The forensic pathologist stood and removed a comb from his shirt pocket. He slid the comb through his thinning hair. 'We have a latent fingerprint from Supaphorn Boonsing's skin. We used a superglue fuming wand.'

giddy up!

'It's only a partial thumb print, but we managed to transfer it successfully onto the lifting tape,' continued Solossa. 'Bad news is our man doesn't exist in our system. I've checked with Yogyakarta. Whoever is killing these women doesn't have a police record.'

tell natsir to cross-ref with E-KTP cards database

Werry Hartono, keen as ever, beat him to the punch, raising his hand. 'Since twenty eleven, the electronic ID card system for all Indonesian citizens is supposed to retain the holder's biodata, such as fingerprints and a retinal scan.'

Commissioner Witarsa immediately made a call to the Home Affairs Ministry.

'A partial thumb print will take longer to identify. It will take a day, maybe two,' said Solossa.

Natsir clapped his hands together. 'While the commissioner is making the necessary phone calls, I have another fact. CrimeLab Outsourcing in Sydney has made progress regarding the licence plate of our mysterious black Toyota Camry. They will come back with enhanced imagery tomorrow at the latest.

'Now, let's address the other women in Sharon Zee's photograph. Anything new to report, Second Lieutenant Hartono?'

'One of them passed away some months ago from natural causes. The other, Fatima Iswandari, has vanished, sir,' Hartono crowed, enjoying the limelight, 'and is presumed to be in grave danger. She didn't show up for work on Tuesday and has been absent ever since. A search of her premises showed no signs of a struggle. Bareskrim HQ sent head shots of Iswandari to the newspapers and a nationwide missing persons alert has been triggered. I am afraid we have to surmise the Mah-Jong Master is responsible for her disappearance. As of today her family is receiving counselling and police protection.'

'We're obviously dealing with someone pretty smart,' added the AKP. 'The fact that he's managed to kidnap this woman without raising the alarm is astonishing.'

'He is toying with us, izzenit,' growled Vidi.

'If this was Moriarty we'd be dead already,' muttered Werry Hartono.

'What was that?' boomed Natsir.

'Nothing.'

Hamka Hamzah resurfaced and took his seat.

Vidi's mobile buzzed. He answered it, exchanged a few sharp words, then got up to leave.

'Where do you think you are going?' barked the AKP.

'Toilet.' His voice dripped with sarcasm. 'If that's permissible.' He tossed his spring-loaded finger strengtheners onto the conference table.

Aiboy Ali watched him exit the room, but rather than head left for the loo, Vidi made his way to his desk, removed a small clear box from a drawer and set out for the elevators.

gajah sumthins up vidis gone walkies

Ruud texted back.

hes left the building?

The injured detective turned a fraction towards the window. His thumbs kept working.

yes not the frst time hes done this acting strange recently going off like lone wolf n not saying where

Aiboy Ali also kept an eye on Natsir.

seeing his sick cousin?

A pause.

could be

Another pause.

wheres he goin?

Aiboy Ali rested his head against the window pane.

not in position to trak his movements atm no wait i see him

With the window at his back, Aiboy Ali had an unobstructed view of the street below. Bus engines and lorry horns could be heard over the air conditioning.

He spotted Vidi cross the road, look around as if to check

he wasn't being followed, and climb into a parked car. He drove away in a black Toyota Camry.

Sunda Kelapa. The old docks.

A large white X painted on a red background marked the dilapidated bunker as structurally unsafe.

In the shadows of the masted freight ships, a murky profile moved in and out of the semi-darkness.

He stopped at the heavy street-door and huddled over. Flexing his fingers, he pulled on a pair of gloves.

Heat filled his chest.

Bending and working methodically in the poor light, the man adjusted his bifocals and concentrated on the padlock. Perspiration moistened his beard. He glanced over his shoulder and his face grew tight. He heard voices, but the dockworkers in the distance were far too busy loading and unloading cargo to notice him.

Seconds later, the lock clicked. He tugged at the heavy door and was inside.

He stood for a moment, listening in silence. Something in the darkness scuttled across his shoe. A cockroach.

He closed the heavy door behind him and turned on the Maglite, aiming it at the hard stone stairs.

The underground, abandoned icehouse was once used by the Dutch to store tilapia and snapper brought straight off the boats. The air smelt damp, but it was cool and grew even cooler with each descending step. At the bottom, the space narrowed to a cavern.

Here, he paused and listened again. The traffic rumbled above him; the sound jostled the walls.

He entered the cavern. The small underground space was

like a concrete cocoon and had been given over to vermin and insects, but he could smell it: decomposition. The taste of dank stale air and old blood crept into his mouth.

There were two portable studio lights connected to a 12-volt leisure battery. He switched them on and squinted as the brutal brightness seared the back of his eyes.

The man took in the space.

Over to the right, he saw empty paraffin cans, a coil of rope and sheets of styrofoam. A white bicycle sat in one corner. It was locally made with a red plastic seat. It had belonged to Shireen Zee.

Over to the left he saw a folding camp bed. The bed was empty. The only sign of its previous inhabitant was a dark urine stain and the blood on the ground. The blood had dried now and was no longer sticky to the touch. Some of it had seeped into the cracks in the earthen floor.

The man ran his hand through his *Sunnah* beard. He walked up to the near wall and gazed at the five photographs taped to the stone. Five photographs. Five different women.

But it was the newspaper clipping he wanted.

It too was taped to the wall, but off to the side. The cutting was from the *Jakarta Post* and it showed Erica and Imke Sneijder walking through the arrivals hall at Soekarno-Hatta airport.

Imke's face was circled in red.

Circled in blood.

He snatched it from the wall.

His face grew tight. The eyes behind the square bifocals took on the colour of coal.

The young Dutch woman was going to die.

272

Chapter Twenty-Eight

The next morning found Imke at the *Kementerian Sosial*. Dressed modestly and with consideration, she had on a loose, dark, long-sleeved cotton frock that covered her legs.

The clock on the wall struck noon. It was late but Imke didn't care. She was determined to get some answers from the Ministry of Social Affairs. Painstakingly, using Google Translate, she filled out another form in Bahasa Indonesia. A lady wearing an emerald green hijab pinned under her chin politely collected the paperwork.

Having spent two hours waiting in the rather tatty reception area and dealing with recalcitrant civil servants, she was prepared to spend another hour or so making a nuisance of herself. Over the course of those 120 minutes she had spoken to a junior minister's secretary, his personal assistant, several members of specialized staff and the Undersecretary of Social Rehabilitation. She had also received two phone calls – one from the palace chef, informing her that Kiki was being fed a diet of rice and corned beef for lunch, and another from Erica suggesting she stop at the Shangri-La Hotel for a box of Lindt Assorted on her way home.

An owlish man who spoke good English eventually

greeted her with a salaam and invited her into his office. He gestured for her to sit and asked how he might assist her.

'I am looking for someone,' she began, 'someone important to me. However, I don't know his real name.'

The owlish man blinked his large eyes.

'He was born in 1988 in Jakarta, some time in mid December. His mother's name is Eny. His father is a foreigner, surname Sneijder. The father no longer works here. Up until the age of eight, he lived with his mother, but after that I don't know. He may have been put up for adoption.' Her voice sounded hoarse and rushed. She took a breath and slowed down. 'Do you know how I can go about finding him? I want to help him.'

'Is this person a missing person?'

'No, it's not like that.' She cut to the chase. 'Sorry, this will sound strange to you, but my father had an affair with a local lady and this boy was the result of it. I know you will think it futile but I must try to find him. He's my stepbrother. If I can search your records, if there is a birth certificate or something . . .'

'This child has become a man now.'

'Yes.'

'Have you had any contact with him or his mother?'

'None.'

'Ms Sneijder, is it? Ms Sneijder, what you ask is both admirable yet unfeasible.'

'He was born in Hospital Gandaria.'

'I suspect, Ms Sneijder, you are swimming in waters you do not fully comprehend.'

'I'm aware of that.'

'Indonesia has one of the lowest rates of birth registration in Southeast Asia. I regret to say that Cambodia, Vietnam and

Thailand are all streets ahead of us on that front. As of last year thirty-five million of our citizens remain unregistered. So you see, unless this child has been brought up in a middle-class home, finding him will be nigh on impossible in my opinion.

'But things are changing,' he continued. 'The Indonesian Parliament has passed a law that makes certifying births less complicated. They have also scrapped the registration fee.'

Articulate and knowledgeable, he explained that there were an estimated five million abandoned children in Indonesia, some 170,000 of whom lived on the streets, 80,000 in Jakarta alone.

'What happens to these children when they are abandoned?'

'The lucky ones will be sent to a Children's Social Centre. If the police cannot locate any family members, they will become a ward of the state. There are also many NGOs trying to improve the situation.'

'In my case, with regards to my stepbrother, can we not search the hospital records? Can I look through Hospital Gandaria's data? If I can find out his full name I can place an ad in the newspapers.'

'Were we even to have all the necessary information, the chances of retrieval are low. Our system remains antiquated.'

'So there is nothing you can do?'

'I am sorry.'

Imke emerged from the Ministry of Social Affairs feeling weary and downbeat.

A dozen strides took her through the entrance, out onto the pavement, past the *kaki lima* selling fried bananas, past the two-wheeled cart offering *mie ayam bakso* (chicken noodle meatballs) and past the line of blue minibuses with the conductors banging the sides and shouting out destinations.

She needed a pick-me-up. Brooding was not going to do her any good.

She wanted to call her aunt, but Erica was busy. Today, she was at a lunch hosted by ISI, the Indonesian Institution of the Arts, in Yogyakarta. As the guest of honour, she was expected to say a few words and, later on, host a masterclass on oils.

Imke followed her nose. Chattering people were eating at tables laid out on the pavement. The smell of the fried bananas made her mouth water. She called Ruud.

'I'm starving,' she announced.

'If you're calling to order a deep-pan pizza, you've dialled the wrong number.'

'Where are you?'

'At home.'

'Home alone.'

'Actually, no. I have a visitor.'

Imke heard a female voice in the background and her heart sank.

'Oh?'

'Yes. She came over rather unexpectedly.'

His wife, thought Imke. Damn! Bugger! Fuck! *Hoerenjong!*

Miserably, she said, 'I'll call back when you're less busy.'

'Wait! I'm not busy. I'm anything but busy. Are you all right?'

'I'm fine. I wanted to see if you're free for lunch.'

'Yes, I'm free for lunch.'

The woman's voice echoed in the background again.

Imke made out the words 'ducky-waddle curry' and 'I come all this way, *neh*?'

'Who', Imke eventually asked, 'is that?'

'You don't want to know. Listen, where are you?'

She told him.

'What are you doing in that part of town?'

'Just sightseeing,' she lied. Imke still didn't feel comfortable telling him about her father's indiscretions.

'I know a great little place close by.'

More chatter in the background, followed by indistinct murmurings.

His voice grew muffled. 'What? No. The curry will keep. I can eat it tomorrow. Yes, yes. I know how to heat up the rice. Surely, you've got better things to do. Oh, for God's sake. Yes, yes, all right. I'll bring you along.'

Imke waited a beat.

'Imke? Are you still there? Grab yourself a coffee at J.CO and I'll come and collect you in twenty minutes.'

The restaurant was one of the oldest in central Jakarta. Originally called Cooky, it now went by the name Restoran Miranda. Steeped in nostalgia and full of whimsical charm, it was considered a Mentang institution and specialized in ox-tongue steaks, chicken steaks and *tahu telor*, a tofu omelette served with soya sauce-infused bean sprouts.

Unsurprisingly, it was full of office workers and lunchtime shoppers.

Ruud introduced Imke to his ex-mother-in-law. The woman smiled from ear to ear. 'You may address me as Nyonya Panggabean.'

'A pleasure to meet you,' said Imke, struggling to ignore the weighty aroma of Tiger Balm.

Cooled by fans, they sat outside under a beautiful bougainvillea trellis.

'I first come to this restaurant in nineteen seventy-eight. It was the lunch I shared with Alan Whicker.'

'You knew Alan Whicker?' Imke sounded surprised.

'Of course I know Alan Whicker. I used to work as a journalist. I broke the story about the man who lived in a palm tree. This man made a bed out of leaves and branches and never came down. He was in *Guinness Book of Records*.

'You should have climbed up too and stayed with him,' said Ruud.

Mrs Panggabean used a finger to flick him on the ear.

Imke's eyes grew wide. She gazed into Mrs Panggabean's good-natured face. 'And Alan Whicker found this tree-man story interesting?'

'When we had lunch here, the man had been in the tree for eight years already. I sat under that big-ugly tree myself for sixteen days, trying to entice him down. I had to leave eventually as I went into labour. The first of my nine children. His name Adi. Ruud's wife—'

'*Ex*-wife!'

'Whatever, whatever, *neh*? Ruud's ex-wife is called Utami. She was my baby number nine.'

'So was this story ever aired on television?'

'*Whicker's World: Indonesia*. 1979. Or so I am told. They did not broadcast the show here.'

'What was he like?'

'He dead now. But Alan was nice man. Very English. He wore navy blue safari suit, short sleeves. Handsome moustache. Not like Bollywood bandit moustache but nice, neat and trimmed. And he was always smiling, even when asking the rudest questions, with his eyebrows dancing mad. Always with twinkle in his eye. Just like my son-in-law here.' She clung to Ruud's arm. 'That is why I like him too much. My daughter hurt him and dishonoured me, but I am trying to make it up to him now.'

'What happened to the man in the tree?'

'Oh, he still up there.'

The food arrived.

Mrs Panggabean gestured with her eyes for them to dig in. Imke could not wait to attack her plate. She held her fork and spoon at the ready.

'Eat! Eat!' urged Mrs Panggabean.

Nearby, not a hundred yards away. A black car came to a stop across the road.

The man in the black car watched from behind the glass.

His eyes focused on the young Dutch woman in the dark, long-sleeved cotton frock. She lounged under a trellis of red bougainvillea, eating, chatting and laughing. For several minutes he did not pay attention to anything else.

A powerful, savage heat coagulated deep in his chest.

He removed a clear plastic case from the glove box; it contained a stainless-steel hypodermic needle, a 2-part syringe with graduation marks and a 50ml vial of Xylazine. He passed his fingers over the clear plastic case and then ran a thumb the length of the needle.

Not long now, he said to himself. Not long now.

Chapter Twenty-Nine

By four o'clock Imke was back in Bogor, reclining on the verandah in a banana lounger. Full of oxtail soup, chicken steak, fried prawns with sweet & sour sauce, melon juice, strawberry yoghurt, two cups of lemon tea and a mug of syrupy coffee, she was well and truly stuffed.

Kiki watched her eagerly, wagging her tail. The dog whined and placed a paw on Imke's ankle.

'All right, all right,' muttered Imke jovially. She had brought home a doggy bag for Kiki, and she shook the poly-styrene box teasingly. From it she fed the dog leftover bits of chicken. 'Good?'

Kiki sneezed her appreciation.

She stayed outdoors for some time, enjoying the sunshine playing on the trees and listening to the birds. Only when the mosquitoes began to stalk her bare ankles did Imke return inside, closing the sliding doors to the verandah behind her.

Almost immediately, she bumped into Erica, returning from her day at the Indonesian Institution of the Arts, in Yogyakarta.

'How was it?'

'Not intolerable.'

She held a bunch of artificial blossoms to her breast. Imke noticed more synthetic bouquets piled into several baskets by her feet.

'Plastic flowers?'

'The director handed them to me as a gift. What is the world coming to?' She deposited a particularly hideous bouquet of giraffe-print dahlias in a ceramic vase and left them in the kitchen.

Imke heard the fridge door open and close.

'Did you get my box of Lindt Assorted?'

'I forgot, sorry!'

'No matter. I'll alert The Captain that I need some more chocolate. Speaking of which, have you seen or heard from him?'

'Not since we went to Jelekong.'

'Three days and not a murmur, that's not like him.'

Erica collected the remote control and switched on the flat-screen TV. ANTV was showing Ghana v USA. She flicked to TVOne where Germany was thrashing Portugal.

'Football, football, football on every channel. Don't they know there's an election coming up?'

All of a sudden the vintage Bakelite phone in the corridor rang. Imke picked up the receiver.

A guard from the front gate told her she had a guest. '*Polisi*,' he said, his voice echoing as it bounced around the confines of the security kiosk. She replaced the receiver on the cradle.

'Who is it?' wondered Erica.

'Ruud,' she replied absently, hoping to hide her excitement.

'I'm going for a shower. Give him my best.' She blockaded herself in her room.

At the sound of the approaching car, Imke hurried to open the sliding doors leading to the verandah. The glass door slid in its track. She skipped outside.

The car drew into the driveway and the wheels ground to a stop. However, to her confusion, it was not Ruud's blue Toyota Yaris. It was a black Toyota Camry.

She looked on, uncomprehending.

The driver's side opened and a man with a *Sunnah* beard got out. His eyes were narrow behind a pair of square bifocals, his lashes long.

He stared directly at Imke.

He did not appear remotely friendly.

Captain Natsir (AKP) got to his feet and clapped his hands together, demanding attention. 'Listen up everybody! CrimeLab Outsourcing in Sydney got in touch. We have the licence plate!'

Werry Hartono stood ramrod straight in the middle of the Incident Room and flipped through the pages of his note-pad. 'B six nine eight seven,' he professed, hoping to sound like Mr Cumberbatch but sounding more like Mr Bean. 'The last two letters remain unattainable. However, we have narrowed it down to two Toyota Camry vehicles belonging to the Ministry of Defence.'

'Are either of them missing or reported stolen?' bellowed Natsir, strutting about the room.

'No, sir.'

'How curious. I want both cars impounded and swept by forensics.'

'Already being done.'

'Also check for noticeable dents on the front bumper.

Vidi can do that.' He looked about. 'Where is Vidi?' Natsir barked.

'He called in to say he's following a lead,' replied Hamka Hamzah.

'Last night he claimed his cousin was ill in hospital.' Natsir looked cross. 'Not acceptable!'

Aiboy Ali, leg propped up on a chair, raised his hand. 'How do we know they aren't false plates?'

'What was that?'

'If I was the Mah-Jong Master, I'd use false plates, then switch them back after the crime.'

'I think you are giving him too much credit,' bleated Natsir.

'Actually, he has a good point,' Witarsa attested, jowls sagging like an elephant's bottom. 'All you need is a decent drill.'

'So you're suggesting our killer purposefully pulled on HANKAM plates on the night of June twelfth, knowing he would be spotted on CCTV, just to deceive us.'

'Sounds logical to me.'

'And you think he's out there right now, trundling along in his black Toyota Camry, searching for his next victim.'

'He's got us chasing our tails, sir,' said Aiboy Ali. 'He's had the upper hand from the very start.'

The bearded man in the bifocals approached Imke and salaamed. 'My name is Vidi, from Central Police Station on Jalan Kramat Raya.' He spoke in English, with strong dry 'R's and rounded vowels.

'Yes, I know who you are. Are you here on official business?'

'Your dog, izzenit. Please, tie it up. I need to speak with you.'

'My dog is fine where she is.'

'It is *najis*. I am forbidden to touch the animal.'

Imke felt a strong inner stirring, a genesis – a kernel of fear, nascent yet alive nonetheless, sprouting, distending its tiny abhorrent roots.

'What are you doing here?'

'I have come to warn you.'

'Warn me?'

'Help you. I have come to help you.'

'I don't understand what you mean.'

'You are to travel with me in my car to the police station.'

'On whose authority?'

'Commissioner Witarsa has ordered it.'

'Why? What's going on? Has something happened to Ruud?'

No, it occurred to her that Ruud was fine; it was she that was in some kind of peril. She glanced over her shoulder and, to her dismay, found the parklands, the approach road and the paved apron around the staff quarters all deserted. The chauffeurs and gardeners were either massed in front of a TV watching football or snoozing.

'You must do as the chief asks. You will come with me.'

Imke fought to control the muscular spasms in her throat, the hardening of her upper lip. She folded her arms across her chest. 'Give me his phone number. I'm going to call him. I don't know what the hell this is about, but I'm going to find out right now.'

He butted in, his tone becoming more urgent. 'I have reason to believe you are in grave danger.'

'I don't understand.'

284

'Perhaps better if we talk inside, izzenit. Are you alone? Where is your aunt?'

The fear. She could feel it breeding in her stomach, round and hard, dividing, multiplying, spreading fast.

Against her better judgement, she let him in via the front entrance.

Once indoors, Vidi looked around to get his bearings.

'You want me to come with you to the station now? Right this minute?'

'Yes.'

Stall him, she said to herself. 'First, let me get some things. Clothes, a toothbrush, my passport.'

'As is your right.'

Imke hurried to her bedroom. She closed the door, then noted to her alarm that the doors were the type without locks. Why hadn't she noticed this before? She scrambled for her iPhone and called Ruud.

His phone rang and rang.

No answer.

Voicemail.

She tried a second time.

Again, no answer.

The silence in the room seemed unnatural. She felt more trapped than before. She wondered whether she ought to alert Erica. They could build a barricade out of chairs and tables. Perhaps both of them could take refuge in the bathroom . . . no, silly idea, he would come looking.

What about a weapon? Yes, find a weapon. A weapon? Who do you think you are, woman, Katniss Everdeen? Better to be a badass Katniss Everdeen than a pathetic Red Riding Hood. Look for scissors or a heavy ashtray! What about hairspray to the eyes! Or something I can throw, like a knife.

Imke took several deep breaths. She shook her head in disbelief and told herself to calm down. There was a reasonable explanation for all this. There was no need to panic. He was a policeman, for goodness sake. As insurance, she slipped a metal nail file into her pocket and stood for a moment in the doorway with her hand on the brass doorknob, working up courage. If you're going to do it, do it quick, she thought. She steeled herself, turned the knob, threw open the door and strode into the living room.

She found Vidi standing by the entrance to the kitchen. His expression was flat and cold, like a fortress. And as unwelcoming as Bijlmerbajes prison. For a moment the two of them stared hard into each other's eyes. Her heart skipped a beat. He asked, once more, if she was alone. A hush fell. This is not happening, she told herself. I must do something, before it's too late.

Unable to rid herself of the feeling that he might pounce at any moment, her bare toes gripped the floor, ready to flee. What was it that Ruud had said to her in the car: 'Imke, this isn't some TV crime drama, the suspect isn't one of the cast of characters.'

She shivered, as if someone had walked over her grave. Her vision blurred and all the air went out of her body. The panic returned tenfold. Her head shot round. Looking back towards the verandah, she calculated how far it was, and if she were to run, how many strides it would take to get outside. Ten strides, three or four seconds at most to freedom. But then what? Run. Sprint as fast as you can and head for the palace gates. And don't yell for help. Yell, 'Fire!' People always came running when you yelled, 'Fire!' What the hell was 'fire' in Indonesian?

She jumped as her iPhone chirped out the Benny Hill theme, startling her. It was Ruud.

'What's the matter?' he demanded, sensing the distress in Imke's voice.

'One of your detectives is with me. The one with the beard.'

'Vidi? What's he doing there?'

'I was hoping you could tell me.'

'Put him on the phone.'

She walked towards Vidi. She could hear him breathing hard through his nose.

'Ruud Pujasumarta wishes to speak with you.'

Vidi took the iPhone off her and, without exchanging a word, terminated the call. He held down the power button for several seconds and slid the red slider to off. His expression narrowed behind his bifocals. 'First *Inspektur* Pujasumarta is no longer involved in this case. I cannot share information with him.'

'You're scaring me.'

There was a bubble of froth at the edge of his mouth, like beaten egg white. It was only then that she noticed the gloves. And clutched in one of the gloved hands was a small clear box of hypodermic needles.

Chapter Thirty

Her heart thumped like hooves.

Backing away, Imke retreated very slowly into the kitchen, moving with caution, as though a serpent had entered the house. She paused, held her ground for a few seconds, decided she did not possess the strength to overpower him and continued backing up. With her focus fixed on the man with the beard, she summoned up some courage, braced herself for what was about to happen and took several retreating steps until her fingers groped the utensil rack. Blindly, she grabbed the closest thing to her — and brandished a potato masher like a weapon. *Jesus Christ! What are you going to do, woman, purée him to death?*

She pulled her nail file on him.

'Hey! Hey, hey!' Vidi held up his arms to pacify Imke. 'You must not be alarmed. I mean you no harm. If I meant to hurt you I would have used my gun.'

'Why are you wearing gloves? And what the hell are those needles for?' she roared.

Hearing the anxiety in Imke's voice, Kiki rushed from the verandah and began to growl, drawing in her black lips and baring her teeth.

'No, no, no! Keep the dog away.' Vidi removed something

288

from the tunic pocket by his heart. 'Allow me to explain, please. You are frightened, izzenit. There is no need to be frightened.' Trying to put her at ease, he told her he had something she ought to see.

He looked down, and then lifted his gaze from the square of newsprint resting in his hand.

'What is that?'

'No! Do not touch it. I found this at a crime scene. It may have the killer's fingerprints on it.'

He placed the news cutting on the kitchen worktop. Imke glanced at the black-and-white image and recognized Erica in the foreground and her own face just behind. 'This was taken the day we arrived at Soekarno-Hatta airport,' she deduced. 'Why am I circled in red?'

'The faces of every victim were pinned to a wall. This was there too. I think it's a kind of souvenir.'

Kiki continued to growl.

Imke made a clicking noise with her tongue and the dog heeled.

'It is why I have come. I think you are in danger.'

Imke kept staring at the black-and-white image. Her heart was still beating rapidly. 'Who knows about this?' Her thoughts raced.

'I received a tip-off from one of my informers. He said he saw a man dragging a body late at night and loading it into the back of a car. I followed up on it. I went to this underground, deserted icehouse. Nobody has been down there for years. Immediately, I knew. The Mah-Jong Master did things down there. I saw blood and ropes. The moment I realized, I made a call to Commissioner Witarsa. I spoke to him on the way here and he instructed me to bring you to the police station for your protection.'

Her body was still a knotted bundle of tension, but his story had a ring of truth to it.

She heard a moan.

Imke's eyes cut away from the kitchen worktop. She noticed Vidi perspiring heavily. His hands trembled and he was unsteady on his feet.

'What is the matter with you?'

'I need to sit down.'

'You're unwell.'

'I . . . I would like some privacy. If there is a wash-room . . .'

Imke watched as the man began to blink his eyelashes quickly. And all of a sudden it made sense to her: the box of needles; the reddening of the skin; the sweating and trembling. 'You're a diabetic, aren't you?'

'Please, I must take a seat.'

'Let me help you.' She took him by the arm and led him to the dining table in the adjoining room. 'You can inject yourself in front of me. You needn't be embarrassed.'

A chair leg scraped against the floor and he sat heavily, shoulders sagging.

His breathing was more audible now, trilling through his nose like tiny train whistles.

She fetched him a glass of water and set it down on a coaster.

'Pujasumarta and the others do not know I suffer from this. Makes me look weak, izzenit.'

The clear plastic box opened with a click.

Vidi hitched up his brown tunic at the waist and felt for the fatty tissue across his stomach.

'Rima used to telephone to remind me to test myself. That was before she fell ill, izzenit.' With erratic breaths, he told Imke about his wife. How she was sick in hospital with breast cancer. 'She used to control my diet, my medication. I forget all the time now. So, you see what happens to me when I forget to test my blood sugar.' The needle piercing his skin heightened the tension in his voice. 'I have not told my colleagues about my wife. I do not want their sympathy. They think it is my cousin who is sick.'

The Novolin R began to take effect. 'All right. Now give me time. Time.' Vidi straightened his back and closed his eyes for a while. The perspiration on his skin smelled sweet with insulin.

Imke sat nearby in silent respect with her hands in her lap.

Eyes shut and with a lone vein throbbing on his neck, he mopped the perspiration from his forehead.

'How long have you been married to Rima?'

'Twenty years and three months. Since we were both eighteen. We grew up in the same village in Sumatra. My father was a tractor driver and worked with a crew tasked with disposing of palm tree waste. Rima's father was in charge of the oil palm shredder. Twenty years and three months of marriage, but she has been my best friend for so much longer. And soon she will be gone.'

'Is it terminal?'

'Do you mean will she die?' He gave a sad nod. 'She is in a private hospital and the medicine is expensive. I am doing all I can to pay for it. There is so much pain in her small body.'

Imke sat watching him. His face expressed a mixture of despair and regret.

The bungalow grew quiet. Unable to take in the sudden stillness, Imke fumbled for something to say.

The sound of Kiki lapping water from her bowl broke the silence.

He returned her iPhone. 'I am sorry if I scared you.'

'That's all right. I think I overreacted.' She gazed at the giraffe-print dahlias peaking out of the ceramic vase in the kitchen. 'My aunt was given some artificial flowers. Would you like them for your wife?'

Vidi squinted shyly. 'You must not trouble yourself.'

'No, please, I insist.' She rose from her chair and brought over the dahlias.

Erica pranced into the room wearing a dressing gown and a bath towel wrapped round her head. She was humming 'Who Let The Dogs Out?'

'Hello, you're not Ruud.' Her skin was flushed pink, still warm from the shower.

Vidi got up and offered a salaam, introducing himself.

'Mr Vidi thinks I am in some kind of danger,' explained Imke. She relayed the information to Erica.

'Oh dear, that sounds quite serious. I guess I ought to change. I can't go out dressed in a bathrobe, people might think I'm a boxer about to enter the ring.'

A short time later, Vidi's phone rang.

He took the incoming call and surrendered the mobile to Imke. It was Ruud. He was in a flap. Imke told him everything was fine, that he wasn't to worry and yes, she would turn her phone back on.

'Imke, are you sure? Can you remember our secret code when we were young? Say it to me so that I know you're all right.'

'*Putri Salju*, Snow White.'

'OK, good.' He paused. 'You're not going to tell me what this is about, are you?'

'Not just now, no.'

'OK.'

'We'll speak again later, *hè*?' She rang off.

As soon as she returned the phone to Vidi, it chimed again. This time Commissioner Witarsa was on the line. The two men exchanged words.

Eventually, when the call ended, Vidi got to his feet. 'Trouble,' he said. 'Polda Metro Jaya received a report from Bogor Palace just now claiming there has been a theft.'

'A theft?' echoed Imke.

'The veterinary surgeon makes a visit once a month to check on the deer population. He says that drugs have been stolen from the palace's dispensary, situated next to the staff quarters. The entire stock of Xylazine has gone.'

The veterinary surgeon yattered in an excitable voice, tossing his arms in the air every few seconds. He walked into a sparse, bright, chemical-smelling dispensary, with Vidi, Imke and Erica in his wake. The echo of their footsteps vibrated off the polished floor and bare walls.

Imke took a quick inventory of what she saw: a fold-down consulting table, a stainless-steel scrub sink, a storage trolley, weighing scales, theatre cabinets, wash-down equipment and an assortment of jugs, scoops and containers.

'All drugs are kept in here,' Vidi translated. 'The cupboard was locked and the keys are kept in The Captain's office. There is no sign that the lock was forced.'

'Where is The Captain?' asked Erica.

'He hasn't shown up for work,' replied Vidi. 'I just spoke to Paspampres, presidential security. His absence is a concern. Security protocols have been triggered so the palace will be in partial lockdown until further notice. They have on record that The Captain signed out to attend a local food festival in Gambir on Tuesday, but he has not been seen or heard from since.'

They stood by a slightly open refrigerated cabinet. The cabinet was divided into two temperature-regulated sections: 2°C–7°C for antibiotics and 15°C for all other medications.

The vet swept a hand over the shelves, identifying and naming each bottle and vial his finger came across. He stopped abruptly at a gap in the shelf. 'The Xylazine's all gone!' he exclaimed. His words reverberated like hollow ripples of sound.

'The Captain is the only person with access to the dispensary keys, izzenit?' said Vidi.

'Yes,' the vet affirmed.

'When did you last set foot in the dispensary?'

'Four weeks ago, when I last came by.'

'This is very suspicious. Xylazine was injected into the victims of the Mah-Jong Master, which is why you, Miss Imke,' concluded Vidi, 'and you, Miss Erica, must travel with me in my car to the police station. For your personal safety. I am sure you understand.' The women looked at one another.

Vidi was right, there was no way they should risk being alone in the bungalow.

The detective regarded the scene for a moment longer. 'This may turn out to be a routine burglary, but I doubt it very much.'

Chapter Thirty-One

The police and forensic units swarmed all over the dilapidated bunker at Sunda Kelapa.

Ruud ducked under the yellow *Garis Polisi* barrier tape and hurried through the heavy street door and down the stone steps leading to the underground icehouse. A policeman handed him a pair of latex gloves, but before Ruud could pull them on Captain Natsir (AKP) snatched them from his fingers.

'Well, if it's not Captain Goose.'

'Turn around and wait upstairs, Pujasumarta.'

'But upstairs is for the Terra Formars. I'm a mole man. I live below ground with the tunnel people.'

'What part of "fuck off" don't you understand?'

'Hey, I was only pulling your leg. Let me through,' insisted Ruud.

The AKP raised a fist to stop him and his nostrils flared like a bucking bronco. 'There is no way you are setting foot in here.'

'The hell I'm not.'

For five heavy seconds they dug their heels in, neither man budging an inch.

Natsir, furious, sputtered, 'You're off the case,

Pujasumarta.' The statement took flight like a 747 from his mouth. 'Or have you conveniently forgotten?'

'Brigadier General Fahruddin told me to take a few days off and that's what I've done. I'm back now. Reporting for duty, under your supervision.'

'You will not get by me.'

'You're taking this rather personally, Goose.'

'Bloody right I am! You nearly brought this investigation to its knees. And stop calling me Goose!'

'Don't let this upset you, sir, but you're starting to act like a cunt.'

'How dare you!' the captain grabbed Ruud by the shirt collar.

'That's quite enough!' yelled Witarsa from the shadows. 'Break it up, you two.' He shoved his six-foot frame and bloodhound cheeks between the grappling men.

Ruud stood aside, panting.

'What's the matter with both of you? Have you got jack-fruit for brains? Start acting your rank. Pujasumarta, if you swear at a senior officer again I will dock you a week's pay. And Natsir, I authorized this, so I strongly advise you to stop acting the playground bully. We need all the help we can get, every asset. What's more, if you lay a hand on a junior officer again I will report you to IID.' Witarsa paused to make sure everyone was listening. 'Now, be a good boy, Captain, and give the man his gloves.'

The AKP clenched the latex gloves in his fist and shoved them at Ruud.

'To hell with this!' bellowed Natsir, stomping up the steps towards the slice of daylight.

It was a hollow victory.

Witarsa ran a hand across his jowls. The nerve under his

eye jumped like fleas on a cat. It was a sight Ruud had seen countless times. He shrugged a naughty schoolboy shrug and followed the commissioner through the dark tunnel. What were they going to find down here, Ruud asked himself, a room with the scraps and skin of slaughtered women? He shuddered at the thought. The two men entered the cavern and joined the knot of detectives and forensic specialists.

Despite the light rigs generating heat, it was cool.

'Chilly down here, isn't it,' said the First *Inspektur*, 'down in the spider's lair.' Taking his time, he slowly and methodically took in the panorama. Intuitively, he began to trace every line, every length and configuration of the crime site, like an animal marking its territory.

He saw the empty paraffin cans, the coil of rope and the sheets of styrofoam. A quick glance told him the white bicycle in the corner belonged to Shireen Zee. And a closer examination confirmed the folding camp bed with the dark urine stain as the primary crime scene. 'So this is where Shireen was killed.'

Ruud crouched to inspect the blood on the ground. 'But it seems to me she wasn't the only one. The blood right here looks fresher than over there.' He gestured to a spot of earth several inches away. 'See this bit where it has seeped into the cracks? Looks like a day or two old at most.'

He straightened up, approached the near wall and gazed at the five female faces taped to the stone. One of the crime scene investigators dusted each one for prints, dabbing lightly with a feather brush. Another agent guided a portable ultraviolet light over the area.

'Still no sign of the other two?'

'None,' said Witarsa. 'But there is evidence he might have kept them captive here before moving them.'

'Which suggests he has two lairs.' Ruud cricked his neck to the left and right. 'What the hell is that?' He pointed at a thick dark curtain.

Witarsa approached it and whipped it to one side. '*Alhamdulilah!* It's a type of shrine.'

Plastered on the wall, one on top of the other, were dozens upon dozens of photocopies of the same image. Ruud snatched one free and studied it. He saw a Caucasian man with a beard, aged about thirty-five. It was a prison mugshot and the prisoner was dressed in blue overalls with a black plaque identifying him as TDOC 255783.

'Who is this?'

'I have no clue, sir.'

'Find out!'

The commissioner's phone buzzed. He bent forward at the waist to take the incoming call and then stalked off in search of a better signal.

Ruud returned to stand next to the investigator with the feather brush. 'Anything?' he asked.

The investigator nodded. 'We're in luck. See that? Appears we have a clear thumb print and a partial digit on specimen three, and another partial digit on specimen four.'

'Excellent.'

Ruud kept staring at the photographs. When his gaze fell on Fatima Iswandari, he immediately thought of Imke's father and the same old questions rattled about inside his head. Why and how was Mathias Sneijder connected to these women?

The police photographer named Arief stepped into view. Ruud threw him a look and watched him for several moments. There was something odd about his demeanour today. It took a while for Ruud to work it out.

He called Hamzah over. 'What's the matter with Arief? He looks shell-shocked.'

'No idea.'

Standing to one side, the one they all called Old Crackpot Eyes stared into space, hands limply folded, cameras dangling from each shoulder.

'He's usually all elbows and arms, shoving his lens up everyone's arse,' said Ruud.

'Maybe, like me, he hasn't slept in three weeks.'

Ruud averted his gaze. He squeezed the bridge of his nose, thereby covering his mouth to stop anyone from reading his lips. 'I've got a job for you, my friend, but I need you to keep quiet about it. Don't tell Natsir, OK?'

The little policeman flexed his shoulders.

'When Arief leaves, I want him followed. Stick to him, but keep your distance. I want to know where he goes and what he does and everyone he speaks to.'

'Will I get overtime?'

'Yes.'

'And double overtime if I work past ten p.m.?'

Unbefuckinglievable. 'Whatever, whatever. Just make sure he doesn't see you.'

'You can rely on me.'

The matter was settled. At which point his chest began to rattle like a gourd full of seeds, forcing the little man out of the cavern and up the steps to suck on a Gudang Garam.

Thirty minutes later, Ruud was still underground when his phone rang. The caller display told him it was Hamka Hamzah. 'Yep.'

'I've lost him.'

'What do you mean, you lost him?'

'I followed Arief when he left the crime scene. He hopped into a taxi and I caught a Bajaj, but we couldn't keep up.'

'Which way was he heading?'

'Out of town, southbound. Something tells me he was going towards Bogor.'

'Bogor? Why would he be heading that way?'

'Search me.'

'We have something!' cried Witarsa from across the hollow. '*Alhamdulilah!*'

'Go to the palace, Hamzah, and wait for my call.' Ruud rang off. 'What is it, boss?' He turned, but the other detectives obscured his view.

'Pujasumarta, come look at this!'

Ruud burrowed past the sea of huddled bodies. The commissioner and three forensic officers circled a urethane insulated box. The bottom of the box was filled with partially sublimed bricks of dry ice.

'He stored the hands in here,' said Witarsa.

Ruud leaned in to get a better look. He covered his nose and mouth with a sleeve to stave off the carbon dioxide gas.

'But where are the hands now?' Witarsa wondered aloud.

'Probably at the Mah-Jong Master's secondary lair.' Ruud leaned in even closer and something caught his eye. A glint of metal shone from beneath a wad of newspaper by the foot of the camp bed. 'What's that?'

A forensic officer reached under the bed with gloved fingers. 'It's a pen. A silver pen.'

Ruud's heart bunched into a fist. 'Shit. I think I know who that belongs to.'

Chapter Thirty-Two

Imke and Erica packed an overnight bag and prepared to leave the bungalow.

'How long do you suppose we will be gone for, Imke?'

'A couple of days I should think, Aunty Ecks.'

Outside, they met Nakula, his chauffeur cap set at a jolly angle, playing fetch with Kiki by the sweep of the drive. The dog was having a great time retrieving a stick that the driver threw across the lawn. Each time Kiki bounded back, tail wagging, to drop the stick at his feet, Nakula rubbed her ears and rewarded her with a treat from a clear cellophane bag.

As soon as he saw the women approach he pressed his palm to his heart and dipped his head.

'Will you be requiring my services today, madam?'

'Not this evening, thank you,' Imke replied, linking arms with her aunt. 'We will be taking Detective Vidi's car.'

He had a small box of Slai O'lai cookies in his hand. 'Do you recall the pineapple jam biscuits I mentioned? I have some for you.' He bowed.

'Why, thank you, Nakula. That is very sweet of you.'

The sun began its descent, blazing on the brilliant lake, and they each shielded their eyes.

With the air conditioning on full blast, Imke, Erica and Kiki climbed into the rear of the Toyota Camry. They took the Jalan Jalak Harupat roundabout and headed north along Jalan Raya Pajajaran, wordlessly.

One police detective, two women, and a dog were in the black car racing through the advancing dusk and the silver mist of exhaust fumes. With a dark cloud hanging over The Captain's head, talk was not forthcoming.

The light faded fast and the shadows began to hide among themselves in the twilight. Vidi drove for about five miles before mumbling something about the suspension. 'A problem,' he said. He's right, thought Imke, the vehicle was wobbling, swaying to and fro as they cruised along Jalan Raya Pajajaran. He turned off the busy road and bumped along a quiet side street that bordered an open field, then he flicked on the indicator.

Imke saw scruffy trees and tangled grass.

His face unreadable, the police detective pulled the car into the wayside, along a rubble wall, switched on the hazard lights and engaged the handbrake. He snatched the keys from the ignition; the air conditioning stopped abruptly and the dashboard lights were extinguished. Only the digital clock and ambient air temperature gauge showed.

'Where are you going?' asked Imke.

'Maybe we have a puncture.'

He got out and paced up and down one side of the car before stopping alongside the front wheel. Despair deadened his voice. 'Flat tyre,' he groused.

The broad leaves of a cashew tree fanned over the hood, blocking out the glow of the streetlamps.

The policeman knelt down and frowned at the punctured

rubber. He prodded it with a knuckle and bared his teeth. The slash was the length of a finger and cut right through.

Retired in the back seat, Erica, predictably, bit into another biscuit, enjoying the heady taste of the pineapple jam.

Vidi hoisted himself up and retreated to the rear of the Toyota, popping the boot in search of the spare tyre, the jack and lug wrench. Ten seconds went by without a sound. In her mind's eye Imke could see Vidi assembling the scissor jack and placing it under the frame of the car, yet when she pressed her face against the window she saw no sign of him. She waited for him to appear. Weaving her fingers together, she laced and linked them restlessly. Apart from her heartbeat, the silence was total.

A metallic rattle interrupted the hush.

Up ahead were sparse woods and stunted shrubs. The fields to the west were recently turned, the grass upside down. Not another soul in sight. There was a school about a hundred yards away, a playground with swings and slides, and a warehouse in the distance, but no one was out and about.

Night had fallen and the sky was dyed indigo. There was little traffic on this particular side route; only the twin yellow beams of a distant truck scarred the expanse of road.

Drawn by curiosity, Imke craned her neck to see what was going on behind her, but the car boot door hid Vidi and all she saw was a shield of black metal. She felt uneasy.

Fidgeting, she laced her fingers together once again, weaving and winding them nervily.

It was getting warm in the car. Imke looked at the

temperature gauge on the dashboard. The outside air temperature was 27°C, but despite the warmth her hands and feet were cold. And the cold continued to creep up to her knees and elbows. She tried to calm herself and gave Kiki's hind leg a squeeze, but the dog didn't respond; Kiki lay curled up and fast asleep by her side. Erica too looked drowsy and heavy-lidded.

Strange.

Suddenly, a burst of gold warped the darkness. Headlights – striking the wing mirror and assaulting her eyes. She heard an engine growl to a stop behind them. A car door opened and slammed.

Footfalls.

Voices.

A silhouette glided past her window. The talk ceased abruptly.

In the same instant, Imke placed her hand on Erica's sleeve, but her aunt had drifted off. She shook her by the arm, but she didn't stir.

Confused, Imke shook her even harder. 'Erica! Wake up. Something's wrong.' Biscuit crumbs fell from her aunt's limp mouth.

And then Imke heard a thump and a gurgled cry.

'Vidi?' she yelled. 'Vidi, what's happening? Vidi!'

Scrambling, she fell out of the car.

Her eyes cut to the detective's supine body.

Blood spread over the ground like a red lake, seeping into the dark grey asphalt.

The bifocals had tumbled from his face. An ugly crimson gash ran across his severed throat and his eyes were open and bulging, his mouth frozen in a scream.

★ ★ ★

304

Transfixed, Imke's gaze locked on the dead policeman, mesmerized by the blood. No, she mouthed. No, this cannot be real.

Growing pale, she felt a tremor in the air.

A faint movement at her shoulder.

Wild, heavy steps, rushing at her from behind.

Every muscle in her body screamed out, Run! Get out of here! But the fear froze her. Her legs became rigid and wooden.

A gloved hand clamped on her mouth. A snap of pain. Her lips crammed against her teeth. The smell of synthetic rubber filled her nostrils and she tasted latex.

The earth tilted. She landed on her face.

Then she was pinned. Sharp knees crushed into the small of her back, slamming the breath from her.

Frantic, she clawed and scratched, jerking and bucking, desperate to fight him off. She struggled, but he was too strong.

Her dress looped up. One of her shoes flew off.

Her senses took everything in all at once: the hazard lights flashing orange; the heat from the car's radiator; her limp legs scuffing against the damp road; the feel of grit and dirt and sun-crisped asphalt against her mouth.

A cold sting of metal speared her neck. 'No!' she screamed.

Her assailant emptied the contents of the syringe into her blood stream.

Numbing. Heaviness.

The air solidified. Her body floated. The sedative froze her eyelids shut.

Everything went black and quiet.

Chapter Thirty-Three

The giant outdoor speakers of the Great Mosque of Sunda Kelapa popped with static. The muezzin coughed into his microphone, forcing a colony of birds to take flight in the gloom. The *Isha* prayer was about to begin.

Witarsa punched in Vidi's number again.

Ruud stood nearby, his face stained yellow by the spotlights of the forensic unit. 'Anything?'

'He's not picking up,' explained the police commissioner.

'Fucking hell!' cried Ruud. He'd already attempted to call Imke countless times, but her mobile was switched off.

'Calm down, Pujasumarta. I've already sent three squad cars to the palace. Go and brief the others. I'll keep trying Vidi's number.'

'Where's Natsir?'

'I sent him to Bogor too.'

Ruud took a deep breath and inhaled the smell of cigarettes, human sweat and diesel exhaust fumes.

Agents dragged metal barricades into place, closing the road to traffic, and there was a line of uniformed police prohibiting access to gawking onlookers and reporters, all armed with long lenses. From down the street a commuter bus braked at a red light, giving a low lament.

Ten minutes flew by, then twenty. There was still no news of Vidi or The Captain or Imke.

Ruud's mind burned with trepidation.

Finally, the fingerprint analysis came back, confirming his worst fears.

On the margins of the police barrier, by a railing, Ruud held up the evidence bag containing the silver pen. All eyes were on him. Detectives and forensic officers strained to see what it was, where the secret lay. They were all galvanized by the breakthrough; he could see it in their faces.

Ruud swallowed; his mouth felt so very dry. 'We have here.' The words wobbled in his throat and fell from his bloodless lips. At first Ruud thought the ground was shaking, that an earthquake was swaying the buildings, the streets. He stamped his feet, as if to wake up his toes, and tried again.

This time his vocal cords responded properly and his voice was steady. 'We have ourselves a manhunt, gentlemen. In my hands here is a pen that we believe belongs to the Mah-Jong Master.' He held it up to the artificial light. 'The prints on the pen are also consistent with the prints on the set of photographs pinned to the wall downstairs. Our technicians have edited the fingerprint images to remove dirt and digital noise and overlaid the sample with everything we have on file. And we have a match. Our prime suspect is a man called Chalid Ismail. He is also known as The Captain. He has no previous record. He is an employee of Istana Bogor, and has been for the last five years. Conforming to security protocol, he signed out from Istana Bogor on Tuesday. He applied for forty-eight hours' leave to attend a local food festival in Gambir. He has not been seen or heard from since.

'Furthermore, we have recently confirmed that the black Toyota Camry used by the perpetrator belonged to the Ministry of Defence car pool. Licence plate B 6987 PJ. On the night Shireen Zee's body was dumped in the alleyway behind HERO, a meeting was held at Istana Bogor by *Kabinet Republik Indonesia*, attended by eighteen council ministers. Three ministers stayed overnight, so the chauffeurs spent the evening playing cards and watching television in the staff quarters. Nobody noticed when our man pinched a set of keys and borrowed one of the vehicles. We caught the car's movements via Automatic Number Plate Recognition. The roadside cameras confirmed the licence plate at the electronic toll road on the Jagorawi highway and the e-toll collection point on the Bogor Ring Road exit.'

'Any images of the driver?'

'None. Now, if it turns out that Ismail is indeed our man, I needn't remind you that he is armed and extremely dangerous. The Police Commissioner has put out a shoot-on-sight order with immediate effect.'

Werry Hartono raised his hand. 'What is our next move, First *Inspektur*?'

'Our immediate responsibility is to secure the palace and everyone within the grounds.'

'Is it a hostage situation?'

Ruud stiffened. Something hot churned in his stomach. His thoughts turned to Imke and fear stole into his chest. Was she safe? What if she wasn't? He didn't want to think about what might happen next.

'A hostage situation? Not for the moment. We have no reports of any trouble in Bogor. The Istana is in lockdown. And I can confirm that President Yudhoyono is safe. Now, if the detectives and all ranks above sub-second lieutenants can step forward I will pass you your individual responsibilities.'

A police department helicopter hovered overhead. The dull whump-whump-whump of its rotor blades drowned out the muezzin's prayer.

All the while, Witarsa had his mobile pressed to his ear. He broke off from his telephone conversation to walk over to where the men stood. His face was serious.

'They found Vidi's car off Raya Pajajaran. He's dead. His throat's been cut.'

'Jesus Christ.' Ruud's knees went weak. He wasn't prepared for this. 'Tell me who was with him?'

'The Dutch woman, Erica Sneijder, and the dog. Both still unconscious.'

'And Imke? Where's Imke?' Panic erupted like fireworks inside Ruud's head.

'We don't know.'

'What are you telling me, Witarsa?'

'She has been taken.'

The four words chilled Ruud to the bone.

A voice inside him was screaming.

Ruud couldn't remember much of what happened immediately after that. It felt as though he'd been hit by something hard and dropped into a black nebulous hole. He recalled Witarsa shaking him by the shoulders and his nostrils stinging with the inhaled smell of sweat and nicotine and the stink of his own vomit. He called to mind the frantic telephone conversations to the Special Response Unit and 2nd Regiment BRIMOB, the wail of sirens as they raced to the Hotel Borobudur, the dash to the hotel roof and helipad. There was a hailstorm of commotion and shouting, the sounds vanishing into cotton wool, followed by the loud, dull swish of metal blades in motion. Headsets were clamped over his ears. A seat belt buckled. A man's voice on the intercom seeking permission for take-off clearance and confirming the flow of fixed wing traffic. And then being pushed down into his seat as the helicopter lifted off – the sensation of riding up an elevator and a limp perception of flying.

This is what it must be like to suffer acute sleep deprivation, he thought. To be conscious of your surroundings yet feel you're living in a dream, with impaired cognizance and foggy coordination.

None of this mattered to Ruud. The only thing that mattered was that Imke had been taken. And the clock was running.

Twenty unendurable minutes later, the chopper landed on the palace lawns, touching down on the eastern side of the lake where landing flares were lit. The propeller blades were still spinning, thumping the air, when the doors flew open. Ruud was still in a state, but his head had cleared sufficiently for him to remember to duck as he got out of the helicopter.

Floodlights lit up the grounds and a throng of uniformed guards with rifles met him.

Witarsa led the way, tall frame bent forward as though battling a stiff wind. He strode forward with his splayfooted walk.

Ruud forced himself not to run ahead.

They entered via the back door of the palace and barged into the offices of the official staff. Both Natsir and Hamzah were already there.

'I have to talk with Erica,' insisted Ruud. 'Did she see

anything? Does she know where Imke was taken? If Imke is hurt?'

'She's still woozy and acting quite confused. She's resting in the bungalow, under observation, trying to sleep it off,' said Natsir. 'There's a nurse with her. She claims to know nothing, but she thinks she was drugged. Something about some drug-laced sweets. The dog is still unconscious, so I suspect she gave the dog some, too.'

Ruud checked his watch. Three hours since Imke vanished. The first twenty-four hours were crucial. Most murder/abduction cases were solved within that time frame or not at all.

'Let's run a trace on The Captain's mobile and try to track it.'

Natsir shook his head. 'He's too clever for that. He knew we'd trace it.'

'What about Imke's mobile?'

'Imke Sneijder's iPhone was found in Vidi's car. But we think he took her laptop.'

'Can you track it?'

'No, she didn't have any tracking software installed.'

'Did you unlock and check the boot of Vidi's car? Imke might be—'

'Give us some credit, Pujasumarta.'

Ruud's thoughts turned to The Captain. 'What do we know about him? Where does he live?'

'He lives on the Istana property. Has done for the last five years. He has one of the larger rooms in the staff quarters. The boys are going through it as we speak.'

'Does he have any other residence? Parents or family to speak of? A proper home address? Where does he go on his day off? Does he have a girlfriend? A boyfriend?'

'Uniformed police have been over his mother's flat in Jakarta. There's no sign of him. Apparently he hasn't been there for some time. She claims they don't get along.'

'He might have a second home, a lock-up, a garage, a warehouse, something!'

'Trust me, we're looking.'

'We found this on Vidi's person,' said Hamzah. Ruud reached for the newspaper clipping.

Ruud stared at the black-and-white image of Imke with her face circled in red.

He should have seen this coming. He should have been there to protect her. How could this have happened? He forced himself to resist the rotten lure of self-recrimination.

'What do we do?' His voice cracked. He didn't care if he sounded brittle. Ruud looked pleadingly at the police commissioner. He felt completely helpless and inept. He ran his hands through his hair and pulled at the roots. 'Jesus Christ. Imke's out there. I'm going crazy thinking about it. God only knows what's happening to her.'

Witarsa's jowly face grew dark. He rubbed his fingers furiously across his brow. 'I'm going to have to inform the Netherlands Embassy. Their ambassador is going to kick up one hell of a shitstorm.'

This can't be happening, Ruud said to himself. He steadied himself against a chair. In the office window he saw the reflection of an angular figure behind him. He shot round but it wasn't who he thought it was.

Ruud turned to Hamzah. 'Did Arief show?'

The little policeman shook his head.

'Natsir, what did the police photographer look like at Vidi's crime scene?'

'How should I know?'

312

'Think! Was he a tall, gangly fellow?'

'No. He was short and bald. Someone from the Bogor unit, I imagine.'

'Hamzah, put an APW alert out for him.'

'Does it matter where Arief is?' Hamzah questioned. 'Now that we know The Captain is the killer.'

'Just do as I say!'

Hamka Hamzah reeled back at the force of Ruud's words. Natsir took exception. 'What the hell are you playing at?'

Take it easy and get a bleeding grip, Ruud said to himself. You still have a job to do. Organize your thoughts. Ruud paused to choose his words and recover his bearings, but his frustration got the better of him and a fuddled sentence spilled from his mouth. 'We have to keep tabs on him. On Arief. There's something here that doesn't add up.'

'What do you mean?'

He took a deep breath.

'I think there's an accomplice.'

'An accomplice? Nonsense. There's every indication The Captain worked alone.'

'I don't buy it.' Ruud fished into his pocket and pulled out a piece of paper showing prisoner 255783.

'Listen up, everyone! Come and look at this person. Dozens of these were plastered on the wall, one on top of the other, in the bunker at Sunda Kelapa. A Caucasian with a beard, aged about thirty-five. Try and find out his identity. I want to know how he's connected to any of this.'

Natsir looked at the photocopied mugshot.

'There's something else. I think,' said Ruud, 'Imke Sneijder's father is linked to the murderer. His photograph was in Fatima Iswandari's photo album. Mathias Sneijder knew these women, perhaps intimately. I just don't see how

313

The Captain fits the profile. And until we have The Captain in custody with a signed confession I'm going to follow my gut and pursue every other angle.'

'What other angle? That a police photographer is behind all this?' taunted Natsir. 'What are you going on?'

'Instinct.'

'So you're going to waste hours of police time on folly.'

'I've been thinking about The Captain. It's just too easy. The pen being left behind, fingerprints all over the place. This guy has been so careful in the past, why slip up all of a sudden?'

'Everyone makes mistakes. He obviously believed we would never find his underground bunker. And the pen and the photographs are evidence, Pujasumarta, admissible as testimony in a court of law. Substantiated proof, not conjecture.' His voice softened momentarily. 'Look, I know Imke Sneijder is your friend. And we all liked Vidi. But let's be professional about this, OK?'

Ruud slumped down in a chair and put his head in his hands. It's just too easy, he said to himself. Why would he slip up now? Why?

Chapter Thirty-Four

Saturday. 1 a.m.
Your turn, he says.
    'No,' I say.
    'YOUR TURN!' he bellows.

Saturday. 1.10 a.m.
My head is so full of his words. So full of his words. So full.
They come at me from all angles. It is like four different TV
stations blaring out the news all at once.

The remote control in my brain switches channels. White
noise. Atmospherics. Interference. Fuzz. A crackle of electric
snow.

The panic hits like a wave.

Choking. Sucking at the air. Cannot breathe.

Charlie Chaplin in a factory; he is assembling screw nuts
on an assembly line, a wrench in each hand, but everything
comes at him too fast. The conveyor belt is relentless. It
speeds up. The screw nuts keep coming. I cannot cope.

The neurotransmitters in my skull are burning hot.

Nina Bo, Nina Bo! Nina Bo! Nina Bo! NINA BO!
NINA BO!

White noise.

I am a tiny child tucked into a dark place, curled into a foetal ball. I put my hands over my ears and sing the lullaby, the song I always sang when mother made me afraid. 'Nina Bo, Nina Bo, bitten my mosquitoes,' I sing, chanting it aloud to drown out my brother. Stop it! Stop inserting words into my mind!

Faster and faster flows the blood.

He is growing impatient with me. Says I am slowing him down. Earlier he threw me the parang. He insisted it was time I proved myself to him and forced me to face the bound-up woman. 'Do it, or I will cut you up like a Kalimantan chilli.' I said I didn't want to, but he pinched me and bent my thumb back, and I realized I had to act before his anger solidified, so I gripped the horn handle of the machete. The blade was sharp enough to cut newsprint. It had a distal taper and a convex edge. I raised it high in the air, felt a white-hot surge of pure savagery, then brought it down hard.

It took two attempts. An arc of arterial spew sprayed up, misting like a red sneeze, and I am now bright with blood. I kneel and wait and watch the life drain out of her.

She is limp. Her eyes cloud over.

But he will keep her alive.

For now.

Saturday. 2.05 a.m.

Something oozes from the lifeless hand. The mucous sheaths of the tendons leak from the back of the wrist. Bits of fibrous tissue, like shiny, translucent thread, spill out.

And I can smell that she has soiled herself.

His voice starts encroaching again. Loud enough to wake

the dead. I lean forward, curling myself tighter, singing louder to make it go away.

Hunched with my forehead pressed to the floor, my mouth wide, growing wider, the saliva catching between my teeth.

The laminate flooring is sticky and wet with blood.

I blink once, twice, and moan aloud. And then I stop with a jerk and go quiet.

The white noise, the fuzz, it has cleared.

Chapter Thirty-Five

Hour by attritional hour, fuelled by caffeine and *kerupuk* crackers from the presidential kitchens, the investigators worked deep into the night. They ransacked The Captain's office, emptying drawers and cabinets, combing through correspondence and official-looking letters, searching folders and box files and ring-binders, scouring phone records, hunting for a clue, any clue that might suggest where Imke was being held. Earlier, two tech officers carried away a pair of computer hard drives and several USB flash drives for examination. Social media accounts were scrutinized, text messages downloaded, voicemails, photos and videos analysed. So far, the search had yielded nothing.

A fresh pot of hot coffee arrived from the kitchens.

Witarsa burned his lips on the scalding coffee and swore.

At 3.20 a.m. Hamzah called to say they'd picked up Arief, the photographer, in an all-night pool hall in Thamrin. Witnesses confirmed he'd been there for hours. When questioned about his skittishness earlier in the day, he admitted he'd been acting strangely. He was sick and tired of the blood, he said, fed up with photographing corpses; he wanted to branch out and stage fashion shoots, interact with models, make a name for himself.

'Fashion shoots!' cried Hamzah. 'Old Crackpot Eyes! Can you believe it?'

Ruud rang off and flung his phone across the floor.

He sifted through payroll forms and a file for the annual housekeeping budget as he and Witarsa sat, thighs spread, with their backs against the far wall, going over The Captain's documents. The others were in the adjoining room, having set up their workstations where there was more space.

Ruud snapped the file shut. He cricked his neck left and right.

'Learn anything new?'

'Apart from how much the head chef is paid, what the monthly electricity bill comes to and how many litres of mung bean juice the President drinks? Nope.'

The police commissioner tossed the papers aside. 'Same here.'

Frustrated, Ruud put his head between his knees. 'Where is Vidi's body?' he asked at length.

'They took it to the mortuary.'

'He came here to protect Imke. I can't believe he's gone.'

The police commissioner shook his head. 'Poor Vidi.'

Ruud gave Witarsa a searching look. 'I worked out what he was up to.'

'Who? Vidi?'

'I know he broke into victims' homes to steal cash and things he could pawn.'

Witarsa let the words sink in. 'He did it to pay for his wife's treatment.'

'I gathered that much,' said Ruud. 'When did you find out?'

'Last week when the photo album turned up. I'd suspected it for a while. He was always the first to get hold of the deceased's address. My guess is he only did it a few times. And always if the person lived alone.'

'Why didn't you write him up?' challenged Ruud.

'I did.'

'But you didn't file the report.'

'No.' Witarsa wriggled in his suit. 'He was a good detective.'

Ruud drained his coffee cup and peered at the grit. 'He was stealing from the dead.'

'I'm exhausted, Pujasumarta.' The police commissioner blinked hard and rubbed his hand furiously across his hang-dog face. 'This job has sucked the life out of me. You have no idea what it's like with all the political backstabbing and intra-divisional pettiness. People are out to get me. I have the higher-ups leaning on me all the time. Firing Vidi and exposing him was the last thing this department needed. I was planning to have a strong word with him.'

'A strong word?' snorted Ruud, turning the page in his lap. 'Protecting your own arse, more like. Very noble of you.'

'That's enough, Pujasumarta.'

Ruud's attention returned to the figures on the page and his eyes lit up. 'You fucking beauty!'

Witarsa puffed out his cheeks, but before he could remonstrate. Ruud jumped to his feet. 'Look at this!' he brandished a sheet of A4.

For a moment Commissioner Witarsa was at a loss. Then it clicked. 'A water bill.'

Ruud felt the blood rush to his head as his boss raised his voice to the team in the next room. 'On your feet! We have an address! It's in Kramat Jati, East Jakarta. Number twelve, Jalan Al Amin. Move it, people!'

★ ★ ★

Witarsa hared out of the room, shouting clear, concise instructions into his phone. 'I want an armed response unit. Encircle the building, cover every exit.' He sent Natsir and Ruud ahead in the chopper.

Exactly half an hour later they came in to land on the roof of Lippo Plaza Tower. Down on ground level, both Natsir and Ruud climbed into a squad car and were handed a walkie-talkie each. A crackling voice announced that snipers were in place.

Natsir bellowed into his walkie-talkie for the armed response team to go in.

The squad car, siren screaming, raced through red lights. 'ETA eleven minutes,' the driver assessed.

'Make it eight!' yelled Ruud, tipping his body forward in a half-seat position, as if riding a galloping horse.

The car accelerated harder.

Ruud held his breath.

The walkie-talkie crackled. Ruud expected to hear gunfire.

One minute and fifteen seconds. That was how long Ruud held his breath.

'Captain Natsir?' came the voice over the walkie-talkie. 'We have secured the premises. No shots discharged. I regret to say we were too late.'

'Please elaborate!'

'Two bodies. A man and a woman. Both dead. You are going to have to see this for yourself.'

Chapter Thirty-Six

Great, black thunderheads gathered. Black as the insides of hell. They blew in from the west and dumped their load.

The rain broke with such ferocity that people on the streets of central Jakarta felt they were being shot with a water cannon as they rushed in and out of buildings, dashing for cover.

The tempest left the downtown area flooded up to the knees. Monitor lizards and snakes writhed out of the open channel storm drains and splashed through the floodwaters. It was five o'clock in the morning and the Jakarta Education Agency was about to close all affected schools for the day.

In Kramat Jati the water levels were yet to rise, but the wind made the windows of the squad car creak as it pulled into Jalan Al Amin, a narrow residential street with a mosque at one end and a tiny food outlet offering *Masakan Padang* at the other. Ruud saw that the entire street was cordoned off; police and other emergency vehicles were parked in helter-skelter fashion. Red-and-blue lights flashed. Neighbours watched from their porches.

The driver pressed his badge to the inside of the windscreen and motorcycle cops in yellow jackets waved them through.

'This way!' signalled a Sabhara street cop, his beret soaked through. He led them to a cluster of low-roofed homes, their footfalls landing with swift panicky claps. The rain slashed down. At the edge of number twelve two officers from BRIMOB appeared at the smashed-in door. The officer on the left carried a breaching ram. The officer on the right lifted his tinted plastic goggles to reveal washed-out eyes; he spoke through the ventilation holes in his mask. 'Prepare yourselves. It's not a pretty sight.'

He waggled his thumb in the direction of the skinny staircase. 'Follow me.' The police lights winked off his chin strap.

Ruud nodded, as if to say he'd seen it all before, but the expression on his face betrayed the silence – the world was collapsing around him.

The heavily armoured lieutenant guided them up a flight of stairs, Heckler & Koch MP5 swinging from a shoulder, Glock 17 semi-automatic at his belt. Ruud followed, taking short, quick steps. And then he was on the first-floor landing. They pushed through a set of plastic curtains erected by the forensic unit. 'In here.'

Ruud, his brain twitching and buzzing, steeled himself. Imke's face flashed before his eyes. He heard her laughter in his ears. Imke, his *Putri Salju*, his Snow White. Ruud felt the bile rise in his throat. He had to do this; he needed to summon every ounce of courage. All the gruesome things he'd witnessed in the past played through his head: the transvestite found in a cardboard box, eyelids removed, arms and legs bound with bicycle tyres; the Filipina cannibal who served her victims to her friends; the catwalk model stabbed to death with the sharp end of a high-heeled shoe.

He'd felt sick with fear before, but nothing could compare to this.

Natsir entered first, then stopped abruptly.

Ruud blinked hard. An imprint of violence scarred the air, like the fizz and crackle of static electricity. He had to clasp his hands under his armpits to stop them from shaking. He swallowed, dry-mouthed, and stepped over the threshold.

The moisture on his brow chilled.

The bodies were right there.

He saw legs and ankles and feet. But the woman's face was hidden from view. He would not look. He could not. But what if . . . ?

'Is it Imke?' he asked, voice cracking.

No reply.

Ruud took another step forward. What he saw was straight out of a slaughterhouse. There was blood all over the place. Shimmering off the walls, the floor, everywhere.

Still he refused to look at the woman's face.

Solossa, the *dokter forensik*, crouched over the bodies.

Mute, Ruud slammed shut his eyes. Terrified.

He wanted to rush ahead, but his legs refused to shift.

Solossa talked into a handheld recorder. '. . . face caked in blood, sprawled across the laminate floor. Her left arm is a raw stump with the bone showing through. Attached to her right hand is a carving knife. And attached to the sharp end of the carving knife is her assailant.'

The smell rushed towards Ruud and he dry-heaved. It smelled as if he'd stuck his nose into a jar of old copper coins mixed with shit; the sweet effluvia stink of raw metal and wet earth made him gag repeatedly.

'Is it her, Solossa?'

'Is it who?'

'Imke Sneijder. The Dutch woman.'

'No.'

Ruud opened his eyes.

Two people, a man and a woman, lay in a crimson heap in the centre of the kitchen, almost butting heads. He saw The Captain, naked but for a pair of gore-stained briefs and a set of rubber gloves. The rubber gloves were fixed on the woman's throat, as if clutching onto a life-saving rope.

The Captain's mouth was open, sprung wide in a kind of death grimace, his teeth stained red. There were tiny black curls sprouting from his lumpy legs and stodgy shoulders. His prize watermelon of a paunch was split asunder like a burst balloon with guts spilling from the cavity, seeping across the synthetic flooring. More butchered manatee than man.

'Who is she?'

'Fatima Iswandari.'

Ruud exhaled audibly. He needed fresh air. It was stifling in the house. Windows were unopened and the fans and air conditioners were off.

Natsir dropped low and settled on his haunches, eyes level with the claret-smeared knife. The spatter had left a tidemark of deep red against the wall. Nothing stirred. The house was quiet but for the humming of the fridge.

Solossa continued his commentary. 'We have a solitary hand, coarsely severed and resting in a shallow metal pan. Next to it, a machete lined up on a newspaper encrusted with dried blood. And a bottle of water, still sweating with condensation.'

'She fought back,' said Natsir. 'He had her tied down but she got free of the bindings. Courageous girl. They both bled to death. A nasty way to die.'

Ruud blinked hard. He was angry with himself for being so close to cracking.

He went straight to the adjoining room. It was empty.

'Is she here?' asked Natsir, trailing behind. He flicked on the ceiling fan and the fss fss fss fss of the blades spun overhead. Closet doors gaped to reveal nothing but clothes.

'No,' Ruud heard himself say. 'Imke's not here.' A cold edge ran down the small of his back. Where was she? If not here, then where? He shook himself to derail the spasm of panic. He returned to the kitchen and stared at Fatima Iswandari's stricken face. 'Are there any good ways?'

'What?'

'You said it was a nasty way to die. Are there any good ways?'

Tap, tap, tap. Ruud was dreaming. A blind man's white stick struck the ground three times. The sightless figure meandered down a skinny street, disappearing in a swell of mist. Tap, tap, tap. A mah-jong player rapped the top of the square table with the edge of a tile. He had a good scoring hand – a knitted straight and a dragon *pung*. He rapped the tabletop again. Tap, tap, tap.

Ruud's eyes cracked open. Blinking through the sunlight, it took him several moments to work out that he was in the uncovered car park behind the Central Police Station on Jalan Kramat Raya and that the events of the last twenty-four hours weren't part of a horrible dream. The appalling truth that Imke remained missing hit him hard; it was like a punch to the gut.

Ruud hefted his sleep-stiffened arms and uncurled his body. He was slumped in a heap in the driver's seat of his Toyota with his knees drawn up. His lower back and left hip ached. Instinctively, he checked that his Heckler & Koch was still tucked into his waistband.

Werry Hartono's pinky ring struck the window one last time.

Ruud turned to behold the front of Hartono's slacks at belt-buckle height. He climbed out and stretched his legs, sending muscle tremors down his thighs. Gingerly, he pulled an elbow toward the opposite shoulder and held it to the count of five. He repeated with the other arm.

'Where have you been?' complained the second lieutenant. 'We've been calling your mobile for ages.'

Ruud fished into his trousers and pulled the errant phone from his pocket. 'Battery's dead. What's the time?'

'Twelve o'clock. Almost lunchtime.'

'Shit.' He finger-brushed his hair back into place. 'I've been asleep for three hours.'

'Captain Natsir wants to talk to you urgently.'

'Any new developments regarding Imke Sneijder?'

'No.'

Ruud took the lift to the second floor. Slumped in his office, he ran his hands over his tired face and stared ahead without seeing the parsnip-coloured walls, the large map of South Jakarta and the portrait of General Sutarman, the Mighty Overlord.

There was a yellow Post-it note stuck to his computer. Ruud recognized Aiboy Ali's writing. 'Call Solossa. And charge your bloody mobile!'

The first thing he needed to do was contact Erica, but he needed to prepare himself mentally. He pulled a litre of Bell's from his desk drawer and took a fortifying swig from the bottle.

He had to pause twice to collect his thoughts before he picked up the handset of his desk phone to call Istana Bogor. Seconds later, he was put through to Erica.

'Have you found her?'

'Not yet.'

'I can't bear it. Oh, Ruud, what do we do?' Her voice was a croaky warble. 'Nobody will tell me anything about Imke. I badger the staff yet all they want to know is whether I want cream with my coffee and if I have any laundry that needs doing. There's a nurse with me. And your little policeman Hamzah is still here but he's no help whatsoever. It's driving me spare. Should I call Mathias and tell him?'

'No, don't speak to Imke's parents just yet.'

'But they must be informed, Ruud.'

'I'm going to get her back, Erica, but you have to trust me. Speaking to Mathias will only jeopordize things. He's involved, but I don't know how. Have you spoken to anyone else about Imke?'

'I've contacted the Dutch Embassy but they are at a loss too. They are personally checking hotels and hospitals. I'm worried senseless. Poor Imke. I was going to surprise her tomorrow and treat her to a seaweed scrub at the Intercontinental Hotel spa.' She mewled, struggling to maintain the precarious balance between poise and hysteria. 'Have you any news at all?'

Ruud told her he had none.

She began to sob.

The corkboard in the Incident Room was covered with photographs of all four victims. On an adjoining board, a map of the city was cobwebbed with red marker-pen lines, connecting the home addresses of the four victims and the locations where the crimes occurred.

'Everything is a match,' announced Natsir triumphantly. He jutted his jaw at a crumpled-looking Ruud. 'The Mah-Jong Master, Chalid Ismail, aka The Captain, is dead. His reign of terror has ended. His fingerprints were on the machete. The machete was the same weapon used in the previous dismembering. And in his house on Jalan Al Amin, we discovered urethane insulated boxes filled with dry ice. Each one had a padded hole in the middle shaped to fit a single hand. Case closed.'

'But we never found the hands?'

'Maybe he fed them to feral dogs.'

'Four dead and mutilated,' said Ruud. 'Yet there were five women in Sharon Zee's mah-jong group.'

'The fifth person was a lady called Eny. She died earlier this year of a cardiovascular illness.'

'Natsir, think about it, please,' Ruud implored. 'Just for a minute, just . . . just think about it. There is nothing here to link any of these people with Chalid Ismail.'

'What are you talking about? We caught him red-handed.'

'It was a stage set.' The claim sounded unreasonably bold.

'Let it go, Pujasumarta. You had your moment. This is mine. I know you hate the fact that I've led a successful investigation—'

'Motive!' interrupted Ruud with a shout. 'The one vital thing we don't have is a motive. Strange, don't you think?'

'Maybe there was no motive. Maybe he was merely broken. The man was a sexual deviant. Tech found all sorts of pornography on his hard drive.'

'But none of the women were raped or sexually inter-fered with. How do you explain that?'

329

'He was a lunatic. A disease.'

'And now he's been eradicated.'

'Look, Pujasumarta, sometimes we never get the full picture. Yes, there are holes in the case that we cannot explain, but the top brass are overjoyed and relieved that the whole nasty business has been put to bed.'

'And Imke Sneijder?'

'Right now, all we can do is issue a missing persons inquiry and refer her case to the Tourist Police.'

'No, no, no. You can't call off the search now. Imke Sneijder is not "missing", she's been locked away somewhere. He has her in another location – some cellar or abandoned warehouse. In a cage. Or in a fucking cardboard box, suffocating. She'll starve to death or die of thirst. For God's sake, you can't do this!'

The police captain straightened his tie. 'I'm sorry, First *Inspektur*. I'm simply following official protocol. If you wish to make a formal complaint you will have to put it in writing and send the communication to the Internal Affairs Division.'

Chapter Thirty-Seven

It was strangely quiet. Imke was sure she was alive. She was sure because the pain inside her head couldn't exist in death.

For several hours she strayed in and out of wakefulness. The first shapes she made out on opening her eyes were skeleton arms. They dangled in the sky, like the scabby limbs of zombies. Confused, she tried to make sense of the scary outlines, and after several seconds the zombie limbs became the thick, dark boughs of a kepuh tree.

She did not immediately comprehend what she saw, though she thought she did. At first she imagined she was in the cabin of a boat because everything seemed to be swaying. She felt a slight drifting. And then she realized she was staring out through a crack in someone's curtains and became aware that she was in an unknown room.

How did she get here? Her brain throbbed dully with the effort of remembering. She sucked in several life-affirming breaths through her nose and wrenched her eyes from the trees. The trees looked unfamiliar, and yet she sensed, by the angle of the sunlight, that she'd been lying there for a while, because she was mindful that half the day had elapsed, even though she had no recollection of it doing so. It was like when she woke after having her tonsils out.

Her thoughts grew clearer. Gradually, she took in her surroundings, aware of the mosquitoes on her skin and of the stale air in her lungs.

She was face down on a single bed; a metal bedstead with four brass posts, one in each corner. The mattress was damp and sticky beneath her body. By her right breast a metal spring poked through the ticking, digging into the tissue. Gingerly, she attempted to move her arms, but the moment she drew them in, they locked at the elbows. She tried again more forcefully and got the same result, only this time the bed shuddered and shook. She bucked and jerked her body, tugged her hands.

The handcuffs clanged on the brass bedposts. The steel shackles dug into her wrists. She attempted one more time to free herself, pulling her arms together like a bird taking flight. 'Do the butterfly! The pec deck! Come on!' Her trainer's macho voice boomed inside her head. She'd done this exercise countless times in the gym. 'Do it! Heave!' She strained with all her might and then flopped onto her face. It was hopeless.

Twisting her neck muscles, she peered down the mattress at her feet. She saw ankle restraints with a locking buckle over each foot. They were attached to chains that pulled her bare legs wide apart.

And there was something jammed in her mouth, something hard between her teeth that made her jaw ache. A tear of saliva trickled down her chin.

Away to her left she spotted a large mirror on the wall, angled to catch her reflection. She heaved her upper body a few centimetres off the mattress and caught her face in the mirror. A round black object seemed to be growing out of her mouth. And there were leather straps traversing her cheeks and forehead, holding the black object in place.

It was only then that she realized she was naked.

Naked and spread-eagled.

That was when she sensed the presence behind her, an unshakable sensation that someone was watching her.

She heard the yawn of a door and the pit-a-pat slither of slippered feet. Perceived the sound of someone breathing. Breathing, watching, listening.

And then someone's hand, cold as a marble statue, lightly brushed her calf, tickle-touching her flesh.

She screamed through her nose.

The ball gag stayed in place. The taste of the rubber was bitter against her tongue.

Chapter Thirty-Eight

Ruud spent over an hour staring at the identical A4 photocopies of the mystery man. All in all, they removed 365 duplicates from the wall at Sunda Kelapa. The same image over and over again: a thirty-something Caucasian with a beard, dressed in blue prison overalls with a black plaque identifying him as TDOC 255783.

'Who the fuck was this guy?' he wondered aloud what TDOC stood for, and before long began listing in his head the states and major US cities that start with the letter T: Texas, Tennessee, Tallahassee, Trenton, Tampa, Tulsa . . .

Less than ten minutes later he'd worked out that TDOC meant Tennessee Department of Corrections and 255783 was the prisoner's TOMIS ID number.

He sat at his computer and went to a site that allowed him to look up a felony offender's identity by typing in his TOMIS ID.

The website spat out the name Thomas Dee Huskey, the Knoxville serial killer, the one everyone called 'The Zoo Man'.

* * *

'I just don't buy it,' said Ruud, shaking his head in bafflement. Everything was in a muddle. They were seated on office chairs, wedged into Aiboy Ali's narrow cubicle, with only a melamine partition separating them from the rest of the world. The partition was adorned with Burgerkill memorabilia and a vintage Iron Maiden picture disc.

He and Aiboy Ali lobbed scrunched-up paper balls at one another. The latter wasn't able to stretch very far to retrieve any errant throws owing to his wounded leg.

'There are two of them,' said Ruud, 'I'm sure of it. Working in tandem.'

'What makes you say that?'

'Either The Captain has a partner,' he closed his eyes to think, 'or the killer took him hostage, too, and staged the whole thing at Jalan Al Amin. And why the hell does he have a serial killer's image plastered all over his wall.'

'Why does anyone plaster anything on their walls?'

'Hero worship.'

'Who is this Thomas Huskey?'

'He's a convicted rapist who also killed four women, but maintained that they all died at the hands of an alter ego called "Kyle". He claimed he was insane and suffered from multiple personalities. Although he claimed "Kyle" was responsible for the murders, Thomas was found not guilty by reason of insanity.'

'What do you think this has to do with our case? Are you saying our guy has dissociative identity disorder? Come on, *Gajah*, that sort of stuff only happens in the movies.'

'I'm trying hard to figure it out.'

'What do you suggest we do?'

'I'm not sure,' replied Ruud. One thing he was certain of was that they'd glossed over something. He caught the paper ball and threw it angrily into the waste bin. The chair's caster wheels squeaked.

He reached across to grab the phone to call Erica again. 'Erica, listen to me, there's a connection between Mathias Sneijder and the victims. He's the heartbeat of this case, I'm sure of it. And I'm sure it's the reason why Imke has gone missing.'

She told him everything she knew. Ruud sat and listened. When he replaced the handset he removed his shoes and cooled his socked feet on the concrete floor. It was suddenly starting to make sense. He marshalled his thoughts.

But so much still remained in a tangle.

He squeezed his eyes shut once more and pictured the slaughterhouse that had greeted him at Jalan Al Amin. 'But I know I'm overlooking something.' With a grunt of frustration, knuckles pressed hard against his forehead, he turned it over in his mind. The newsreel images played again through his head: red briefs, rubber gloves, tiny black curls sprouting from lumpy legs and stodgy shoulders, a burst watermelon spilling guts across the synthetic flooring, a machete, crusted blood, a bottle of water.

'The water!' he yelled, jumping up.

'Bloody hell!' Aiboy Ali recoiled. 'What the fuck?'

'It was still sweating. According to forensics, The Captain died several hours before we got there, but the bottle was still beaded with condensation.'

'Which means someone else was there. Someone else must have removed the bottle from the fridge. He must have just left.'

'Jesus.'

'Did you contact Solossa?'

'No. Why?'

336

'I stuck a note on your PC. Didn't you see it?'

'Forgot all about it. Quick!' Ruud gestured towards the desk phone.

Aiboy Ali punched the speed dial and handed over the receiver.

Solossa didn't pick up until the eleventh ring.

'Where the hell have you been?' scolded the *dokter forensic*. 'I've been calling your blasted mobile all morning.'

'What is it, Solossa?'

'The Captain's postmortem temperature taken at the crime scene at five thirty a.m. was ninety-three degrees fahrenheit. After death, as a general rule, the body loses one degree per hour, which puts his time of death at around eleven thirty p.m. to midnight. Rigor, livor and algor mortis point to a time of death between ten p.m. and midnight. Even if we take into account that he was chubby, since the amount of fat around the organs can affect the rate of temperature loss, it doesn't fit.'

'Why?'

'Fatima Iswandari's body was still warm and not stiff. She hadn't been dead more than three hours. They couldn't have killed each other.'

'I knew it. So the killer abducted The Captain on his way to the food festival at Gambir and held him at the Kramat Jati house for three days. Was he drugged?'

'There is no trace of toxins in his body, but there's a blunt force wound on the back of his head.'

'He probably got thumped on the noggin in an underground car park.'

'And there's more. The single fingerprint we found on Supaphorn Boonsing, the woman in the park.'

'Yes.'

337

'Remember the latent print we found on the underside of her forearm?'

'Yes, yes, yes. What about it?'

'It doesn't match any of Chalid Ismail's prints.'

Ruud clicked his fingers for Aiboy Ali to listen in. He almost knocked over the lamp with the sweep of his arm.

'Who do they belong to?'

'You're not going to believe this.'

'Pujasumarta wants you in the Incident Room *now*!'

'So The Captain's not the killer,' Werry Hartono's mouth fell open.

'It was a set-up,' cried Aiboy Ali, leaning on his crutches and swinging his strong leg forward. Hartono got the door and held it open. 'Before leaving the palace, the perp slashed Vidi's tyre, followed him in his own car, then hijacked the fat man and Imke Sneijder.'

'I don't understand,' he said, perplexed.

'What's not to understand? Back at Jalan Al Amin he forced The Captain to strip off his clothes and don the rubber gloves before stabbing him in the chest. Then he killed Fatima Iswandari. It was all staged to make it look like they'd killed each other.'

'You are sure about this?'

'Yes!'

'What do we do now?'

'Find the bloody Dutch woman, that's what!'

Chapter Thirty-Nine

Sunday. 2.20 p.m.

A better mood, a good mood. He has good moods, bad moods and black moods. A black mood is when the angry mist descends. Those are the days when he is as mad as a bull elephant in musth. Those are the days I lock up all the sharp things in the house.

Aduh, my brother is becalmed. He tells me to consider the bigger picture. Raindrops, he says. Look at the raindrops. Big and fat. Every drop of rain falls alone. Yet when it strikes the earth to form a puddle and the puddle becomes a stream, it reaches the river or the ocean as one. I understand the imagery, but fail to see what he's driving at.

As Indonesian philosophers go, he's no Professor Notonagoro. There ought to be a rule, oughtn't there, to prevent siblings from behaving like pompous philosophical thinkers.

But, I suppose, I ought to be happy too.

Because, after all our meticulous planning, all the sleepless night, all the hours of fretting, we have her.

We finally have the girl.

Sunday. 2.42 p.m.

This afternoon I tried to masturbate. I had my sarong by my

ankles. It is hard work pleasuring oneself with only half a penis, and as soon as I started to rise I lost momentum and it withered again.

Some people will no doubt suggest I kill out of sexual frustration.

Aduh, I can tell you this is entirely untrue.

Sunday. 3.21 p.m.

I abhor being a symmetrical twin. It is because in the common public perception I am not regarded as a distinctive individual, but rather as a parallel clone – mirror born.

But why do I hate it so?

For are we not two halves of the same person?

Sunday. 3.23 p.m.

He is salivating. My brother is as impatient as a hungry child. I count backwards several hours to calculate the time – it is mid-morning now in Holland. He should be returning from Sunday mass. It is time I introduced myself to my father.

Chapter Forty

Mathias Sneijder was happy. The wind was in his hair and sunshine warmed his face. He felt good. The Raadhuisstraat bike route was less busy than usual for a Sunday morning. He'd started in Westerkerk and headed north to Keizergracht before turning back along Herengracht. Along the way, in the nearby parks, families were setting up their barbecues; the smells of hickory wood smoke and sausages on the grill, and the sound of laughter and wine corks popping, filled his senses.

Staying within the white lines of the bicycle lane, he passed the Ambassade Hotel. Next came the familiar and imposing Bijbels Museum. He'd planned to go as far as Vijzelstraat and perhaps the flower market, although the market itself would be closed.

He rode a traditional *Opafiets*, the gentleman's roadster or grandpa bike, with its upright seat, lugged steel frame and oversized tubing. A copy of yesterday's *De Telegraaf* remained trapped in the rear rack. If he didn't fall asleep after lunch, he'd tackle the Sudoku champion puzzle a little later, perhaps in the early evening.

At the Hugo Boss store, he stuck out his arm and turned left into Koningsplein, crossing the tram rails at a sharp angle to avoid getting his wheels caught.

About a hundred yards on, he stopped to take a break. He parked his bike and found a bench overlooking the canals and sat down, feeling revitalized from the fresh air and exercise. He did this most weeks to keep his muscles active, his blood pressure low and his waist firm, and he ran a half-marathon for a children's charity every April, though his time – two hours and twenty-one minutes – was slower by seven minutes this year. He exercised to keep fit, but also because he was scared of getting old and sick.

Mathias removed his trainers and socks, and savoured the feel of the pavement against his bare feet. Nearby, a tiny green caterpillar was inching its way toward some wild flowers, arching its body into an upside-down U before elongating again. Mathias reacted by stretching his own back this way and that in response.

Church bells tolled to the east and to the west. A canal cruiser glided by. He gave the tourists a wave and they waved back, smiling.

Not for the first time this morning Mathias angled his face to the sun and thanked the clouds for staying away. He flexed his mildly arthritic fingers and admired his tan. The June rays had turned his arms conker brown – not bad for a fellow with red hair, he mused, flashing a smile. He was fifty-six but felt much younger. He thought he was beginning to look a bit like Gene Kelly, which was nice; the problem was everybody else thought he looked like Gene Wilder.

He took another deep breath, sucking in the fresh air, enjoying the scent of fresh grass mingled with ice cream. Yippee, *hoera* for ice cream. He adored ice cream – vanilla especially – perhaps not to the degree that his sister loved chocolate but it was his drug of choice nonetheless.

His stomach grumbled. He was tempted to pop into

Rogh's Deli for a *pannenkoek* as it was only down the road. His mouth watered at the idea of a warm, pan-fried pancake, filled with crispy bacon and slathered with treacle. But then he remembered he'd promised to prepare brunch for Ardy.

One by one, he mentally ticked off all the items he recalled seeing in the fridge. He decided there and then to put together a mackerel and poached egg salad, followed by Nutella and bacon-stuffed French toast. The only ingredient he needed to buy was the mackerel.

As a young man he used to buy his fish directly from the fishermen as they came into port, with the gulls singing and the smell of salt in the air. There were glistening pyramids of mackerel and long, slender herring, buckets of eel and mussels, and red, shiny shrimp straight from the net. His favourite was always the herring and he would take them home for his mum to gut and cook, but once in a while he would treat himself to *maatjesharing* served with onions and pickle in a fluffy white bun.

These days nobody bought their fish directly from the fishermen; most people went to Albert Cuyp market or Fishes on Utrechtsestraat 98, but they were closed on Sundays. It would have to be Albert Heijn, he decided, even if they were more expensive; the Koningsplein outlet was open until 10 p.m.

As soon as he shoved the mackerel fillets under the grill, he began to boil the water for his poached eggs in a wide deep skillet.

'Want any help, Thys?' Ardy called from the living room.

'*Nee, bedankt.* I'm about to make the salad dressing.' He found a mixing bowl and added olive oil, a teaspoon of honey, lemon juice and cider vinegar. Grinding in a healthy amount of black pepper, he stooped to check on the fish. He'd give them another seven minutes. Now, where were the large Waterford plates kept? He searched about for a while then gave up when he found a pair of ceramic bowls; he emptied the bags of spinach, rocket and beetroot into them and dressed the salad.

The water was simmering by now, so he deftly splashed in some white wine vinegar, broke two eggs in ramekins and slowly poured them in, separately, whites first.

The eggs hung lazily on the surface.

'Something smells good, Thys,' came his wife's voice again from the living room.

He waited with a slotted spoon for the eggs to set at the edges, ready to pull them out as soon as they cooked and transfer them to a plate lined with paper towels. But he cocked it up. There was too much water in the skillet and the heavy yolks sank to the bottom, trailing the whites behind like a jellyfish. And when he removed the mackerel fillets they were overdone.

'*Verdomde!*' he swore under his breath.

Slotted spoon in hand, he wondered whether he ought to serve it; he hoped Ardy wasn't too hungry.

'I'm starving,' she said right on cue, no prompting required, standing in the open doorway, watching him.

Mathias had a theory that his wife could read his thoughts. From the moment they'd met, it seemed they shared the same brain frequency – two minds working in synchronization, nervous systems beating in harmony. Either that or she was just plain ravenous and couldn't wait to eat.

It was a good thing he'd also bought some smoked eels from the supermarket. And he also had some deliciously sinful Nutella and bacon-stuffed French toast to fall back on. Without delay, he grabbed the breadknife and sliced the loaf, halving each thick slab into triangles.

'Ardy, set the table, will you please?'

She entered the kitchen and liberated a bottle of Domaine Sainte-Eugénie Rosé from the chiller, at the same time laying out a pair of long-stemmed wine glasses.

He was in the middle of soaking the challah sandwiches in a custard mixture when the Skype ringtone sounded on his laptop. Husband and wife stood motionless side by side, staring at the screen and the call alert window.

'Are you going to take it?'

'What matter is so pressing that it trumps French toast?'

'It's Imke,' said Ardy. With a turn of his head Mathias indicated he would answer the call. He wiped his hands on a dishcloth and approached the sideboard, where his black ASUS sat open amongst the Rudolph van Veen cookbooks.

He clicked the green 'answer with video' button, eager to see Imke's face, and pulled up a chair. '*Hallo mijn mooie dochter!*' he said jovially.

'Hello there bad, bad father who went astray.' The voice was masculine.

To his confusion Mathias found himself peering not at his daughter but at a strange, bare-chested man with vulpine features and wavy black hair. 'What is this? Who are you?'

The man, youthful and dark-skinned, laughed drily. 'Really?' he said, rolling his 'R's and elongating them in that uniquely Indonesian way. 'Nah, nah.' He leered at the camera lens, his eyes as cold and hard as a river crocodile's. 'You don't recognize me? Ha! You lie! You *do* know me, I can see the unwashed guilt in your eyes.'

'What the bloody hell are you talking about? Who are

you?' This was a mistake, he thought. Someone, somewhere had dialled a wrong number. 'And what are you doing calling me from my daughter's computer? Where is she?'

'Oh, she's here,' he said, elated, watching Mathias, 'right behind me. Can you not see?' His arms opened wide and seemed to stretch into the screen; the image juddered as he angled the camera. 'Lying on my bed, waiting for me. What a firm rear end she has, no? *Aduh*, so round, look how the buttocks bulge.'

Mathias gave a gasp of astonishment. He could hardly believe what he was witnessing. There she was, his girl, facedown and naked, arms and legs outstretched, wrists and ankles bound. A black harness crushed her face, distorting her cheeks, and something black and hard was jammed in her mouth.

The laptop rose and floated momentarily then settled on the edge of the single bed, by her feet.

Listening, Mathias thought he heard a high-pitched keening. It sounded inhuman. The strangled cry came from his daughter.

All of a sudden Mathias became aware, piously aware, of the hellfire punishment about to befall him. He understood what this was all about. He knew who this person was and, more terrifyingly, he saw what he'd become. For years he'd tried to shake him off, banish his son from his thoughts, wipe him from his memory, and to a degree he had succeeded. But he couldn't do that any longer. Now the child was a man and there was no denying his existence.

Imke howled through the rubber ball gag – an animal roar of protest, anger and fear.

'Don't be afraid!' Mathias bellowed. 'Don't be afraid, *lieveling!*'

With casual recklessness the man settled down next to

her, hitching up his sarong and nestling his bare legs and oily upper body by her glabrous rump. 'Oh, come now, sister, you must not be scared of me. I am part of the family.'

His hand went exploring. He plucked at the ridges of her spine like a harpist playing the French harp. So close she could feel his breath on her flesh.

'How about you and I get down to some recreational activity.' He laid his face against the nape of her neck, his maw an eager pout. 'Sih, so that our dear Papa', he licked his lips ceremoniously, 'can watch.'

His lips froze in the shape of that final word, mouth drooping loose and lower teeth exposed like a gin-soaked, salacious Mick Jagger.

And then he blew across the surface of her back as though cooling down a scalding cup of tea.

Imke was so scared she refused to close her eyes.

'No, please.' Mathias begged. Never before had he seen his daughter at the mercy of another human being. He felt revulsion. His expression, flayed by shock, was charged with sheer animal terror.

The man ignored the plea and massaged his genitals through his sarong. 'Your father', he hissed into Imke's ear, 'was meant to be mine. But you took him away from me.'

Mathias Sneijder's skin paled and prickled with goose bumps – the tiny muscles attached to each hair follicle on his arms contracted, pulling tight the skin, forcing the hairs to bristle. His heart felt as though it was slowly detaching itself from his chest. The room, its walls and ceiling, crowded in on him.

Over his shoulder, something thumped against the floor. He heard a sudden suck of air.

His wife, the gristle on her neck straining, had fallen to

her knees; her body was rigor mortis stiff, with arms out-stretched, as though to catch her falling child. Ardy's mouth was open, but she'd been startled dumb, as if words and sounds remained outside her mind's reach. All Mathias could make out were the two strangled syllables, 'Oh God.'

Ruud, Aiboy Ali and Werry Hartono were frantic. Each man held two telephones and tried to conduct several con-versations at once.

Aiboy Ali's land line sang. He lifted a leather-cuffed wrist, hit the button and got a blast of a hysterical Walter Matthau on steroids. '*Sialan!*' he yelled. 'WHAT'S happening?'

'The prints match someone who works at Istana Bogor. Someone other than Chalid Ismail. His name is Nakula. He's a chauffeur. Polda Metro Jaya sent over his KTP details and employment file, and guess what? His mother was one of the women in Shireen Zee's photograph, the one called Eny who died five months ago of a heart condition. We're run-ning a trace and track on his mobile. Where are you?'

'Debriefing the Police Commissioner General.'

'Tell him we fucked up. Get over here as soon as you can!' Aiboy Ali rang off.

Then, all of a sudden, the talking stopped.

'Call me straight back.' Ruud banged down his handset and waited, not saying a word to the others. A minute went by, then another.

Aiboy Ali picked at his fingernails.

Werry Hartono, hands clasped behind his back, paced the room.

'What the hell is taking them so long?'

Even though Ruud was anticipating it, when the phone eventually rang it startled him.

He pounced on the receiver, listened to the voice on the end of the line and wrote down several sets of numbers on a pad. His brain was fizzing from the fresh information.

'OK!' he shouted. 'Four mobile phone towers, all to the southeast of Jakarta, towards Setu, received signal trails. Site three one three eight, site three four eight eight, site five eight six four and site four three four five. In layman's terms, we have a navigational fix and have isolated a house near Bekasi, Setu, West Java. Roughly seventy kilometres outside of Jakarta.' He punched in the coordinates and printed out a Google map of the small village.

Hartono rushed to the gun vault to retrieve a Remington 870 shotgun.

Ruud, decisive yet still at a fever pitch, checked the magazine of his Heckler & Koch, lowered the safety lever and decocked the gun. 'You stay here', he said to Aiboy Ali with rapid gestures, 'and coordinate proceedings with Witarsa. Also, I want you to call Istana Bogor. Speak to Hamzah. Get him to bring the dog.'

No, he did not want Ardy to witness this. He grabbed her by the waist and gently escorted her to an armchair in the sitting room, opposite the wall-mounted flat-screen TV.

He kissed her and noticed that the leather necklace around her neck, the one with the jade pendant, was starting to fray. He decided to buy her a new one for Christmas. Other irrational thoughts entered his head as he soothed his stricken wife, like shouldn't he turn off the oven? And should he pass her a magazine to read, to distract her, to calm

349

her. Maybe put on some music. Verdi or Strauss. Perhaps he should fetch her slippers. He muttered a fragmented prayer.

'What's happening, Thys? What have you done?'

'I will deal with this, *hè*? You don't worry about a thing. Are you going to be all right here?'

She did not answer and he saw her face stiffen as if enclosed by ice-cold water.

'Stay here,' he insisted.

He stroked her hand and told her again to stay put, but she refused to let him go. In the end he had to lever her fingers from his forearm. He left her jerking back and forth in the armchair and rounded the corner into the kitchen.

The man on the screen was still there, watching him.

'*Maaf, maaf*, Thys Sneijder, I apologize for not formally introducing myself. My name is Nakula.'

'I know who you are.'

'Yes, I'm sure you do. I am the bastard child you left behind.'

In the background, some 11,000 kilometres away, music played from a vintage record player. The song was an Indonesian favourite, 'Bengawan Solo' by Waljinah. But the record was scratched and it skipped repeatedly, replaying the same line, '*Terkurung gunung seribu*', over and over. The recurring words sounded mechanical and frightful, straight out of a psychotic horror movie.

If it bothered Nakula, he didn't let on.

'I wonder', he lowered his voice as if to impart a secret, and leaned in close to the screen, 'if you can ever understand how it feels to be erased from your father's life altogether.'

The words were like splintered glass in Mathias's head. He strained to look beyond Nakula, to see if Imke was hurt.

Recognizing Mathias's distress, he turned around momentarily to glance at the body on the bed. 'She is fine, dear
father. You need not worry. My brother will be along soon.
He is anxious to set eyes on you.'

Not daring to speak again until now, Mathias blurted out,
'Brother? You have a brother?'

'My twin.'

'You are Eny Soleh's son. If you are Eny Soleh's son, you
don't have a twin.'

'We are twins. You of all people, dear *ayah*, should know
that.'

'But your brother, your twin, is dead.'

Nakula laughed drily once more. 'Don't play games with
me. He will be here soon. He is eager to meet you.'

Mathias kept his tone even. 'He died twenty-six years ago.
I remember. I was there when Eny gave birth at Siloam
Hospital.'

'*Nah, nah, nah.*' Nakula shook his head. Mathias watched
as the man's face twisted grotesquely. It was becoming
increasingly clear to him that Nakula was deeply unhinged.
Did he really believe his brother was alive?

'Where is he now, your brother?'

The man buried his face in his hands and stayed like this
for some time. Then slowly, decisively, he lifted his chin. But
there was something subtly different about his mouth and
his eyes. 'I am here, father.' He spoke in a creepy child's voice.

Mathias felt the hairs on the back of his neck stand
on end.

'Who are you?'

'Budi.'

Was he bluffing? How in hell did he change his voice like
that? Could it be that he suffered from a mental illness, some

351

kind of split personality? Something resembling dissociative identity disorder? He'd read about a woman in south London with multiple personalities – over 100 in total – all wrapped up in one body. She'd been horribly abused as a child and her mind, traumatized beyond repair, fashioned a legion of different characters, or 'alters', to protect herself from what she'd endured.

'What', said Mathias through gritted teeth, 'are you going to do with Imke, Budi?'

His eyes, with their tiny black pupils, watched Mathias for several seconds, and then turned around 180 degrees.

'What are you going to do with Imke, Budi?'

Silence.

'Budi?'

Silence.

He tried again. 'Nakula?'

'Yes.' A man's voice once more.

'Nakula, what are you doing with Imke?'

'That is for my brother, Budi, to decide.'

'Listen to me, your brother, Budi, is dead. He died the day you were born.'

'Lies! Don't treat me like a fool, father. Do you think a fool could have planned all this? Evaded the police for so long? I am not a fool. The moment I saw the article in the *Jakarta Post*, announcing Erica Sneijder's appointment to paint the President, I went to work. That was five months ago.'

'Nakula, listen to me.'

'Five months ago, I applied for a chauffeur's position at Bogor and was told there were no vacancies.'

'Nakula—'

'So what did I do? I poisoned one of the drivers. Just a mild dose of rat poison in his Milo. Nothing to arouse suspicion. And when he fell ill I applied again for the job. I had a clean driving licence. I had no criminal record. I spoke English and a mouthful of Dutch. I had the ability to utilize tact and diplomacy when necessary. And I paid the administrator a little bit on the side to highlight my name. It's not so difficult to do in Indonesia.'

'Listen to me.' Mathias was still looking at the back of his son's head, but sensed that this was his chance to wrestle the initiative from him. He spoke assertively. 'You came out second. Budi came out first. Blue. Stillborn.'

'That is what Mother says,' he rasped. 'It is not true! She says I killed him inside her womb, when her belly was *besar* and *bulat*. Says I strangled Budi, *hnnn*, with the cord attached to my tummy, and turned him so he was pushed out feet first.'

Wanting to seize control of the situation, Mathias's voice grew assertive. Talk to him and address him by name, he told himself, get him to trust you. Keep your tone firm but calm. Don't allow your pitch to rise or let your speech pattern quicken. 'Nakula,' he said, staying composed. 'Whatever Eny said, it's not true. What happened was tragic and devastating, but it wasn't your fault.'

'That is not what my mother says. She blamed me for everything.'

He decided on direct confrontation. 'Nakula, your mother was a cruel person. I saw what she was capable of. This Budi personality is someone you made up, to protect yourself from her. He may seem real to you, but he lives inside your head. You are obviously ill. You need help. I can get you the help you need.'

'You? When have you ever helped me? You stripped me from your life!'

353

'And I am sorry for doing that to you, son. I truly am.'

'Oh, now all of a sudden you change your mind.'

'Nakula, believe me, I wish I could change the past. I cannot do that, but I can shape the future.'

Half-hearing Mathias's words, Nakula went on speaking. He raised his left hand. 'See here?' He waggled the fingers playfully. 'Left hand, Nakula. Right hand, Budi. Right hand mirrors the left hand. Right hand talks. Right hand talks with Budi's voice. He talks to me. He says left hand is unclean. His voice always in my head. *Sih*, always in my head. Whispering into the rotten parts of my mind. So how is it', he paused, searching for the right word, 'possible. How is it possible he is dead? You know what Nakula means? It means "one of a twin". That is me – one of a twin. That is why he is inside me. For balance. Left hand balances right hand. Without me he is only half a thing. Disabled.'

There was suddenly some distortion to the image as he got up to place the laptop on a different work surface. The camera took in more of the room now, capturing the action from a distance some seven or eight feet back.

Sweating profusely, he turned again to face Imke. He began to unshackle her. The harnesses clinked as he released them. That was when Mathias saw the knife in his fist. A six-inch blade with a black handle.

Mathias held his breath, terrified of what might happen next. 'What are you doing, Nakula?' The abdominal muscles in his stomach recoiled as though anticipating a punch to the gut. 'What,' he asked, 'are you going to do with that knife?'

Nakula did not reply. Mathias watched the man's rhomboids glisten with perspiration as he worked to free the harnesses. All across his back, trailing down to his coccyx, were ancient cigarette burns, ugly red-rimmed welts forming a procession of irregular circles.

They looked like war wounds, as if shrapnel had hit him.

'Nakula, listen to me. Talk to me. Tell me what happened to your back?'

'Mother, when she got angry.'

The bare-chested man gouged the ball gag from Imke's mouth with a thumb and forefinger, and sat her directly in front of the camera. She folded her forearms across her breasts with a shudder. By now he had undone all the cuffs and restraints. He wrapped his left arm around Imke's naked shoulder blades, tugging her close to him. He pulled her forward so that she faced the lens. Her cheeks were rippled with strap marks. Her eyes were bloodshot and damp. She had clearly been crying, but you could see she wanted to rend and bite and scratch.

'Now, now, do not struggle. Look at you, *aduh*, all teeth and claws. I could smash both your kneecaps to make sure you will not run. Do you want me to do that? No, I didn't think so.' He took her face in one hand and squeezed it like a tube of Thomy mustard. 'I wonder,' he said, 'if I squash really hard, will her head pop like bubble wrap?'

'You want an audience,' said Imke's father matter-of-factly. 'The best thing for me to do is end the call now.'

'And then you will never know how your daughter died.'

A tense quiet settled. An animal quiet.

Mathias swallowed. For now he had to play by his son's rules – take this one second at a time. He stared at his daughter. Do something, her eyes pleaded. He saw the pulse at the base of her throat and knew he had to steer the conversation away from Imke. 'Where,' he asked, his voice rigid, 'is Eny?'

355

'Mother? Mother is like the grit between my teeth.' He spat on the ground, shooting a strand of spittle from his mouth.

'Where is she?' repeated Mathias.

'She is with her friends. You remember her friends, don't you? No? Let me reintroduce you.' He reached down. 'This is Marie Agnes Liem.' He waggled a clear polyurethane bag in the air. 'Here is Supaphorn Boonsing. And surely you must remember Shireen Zee. Dear old Shireen.'

Mathias stared in horror at the amputated hands.

'There is a joke,' Nakula sniggered, 'I heard not long ago.' He moistened his lips with his tongue. Why did the one-handed girl cross the road? To get to the second-hand shop. Funny, no?'

'What did you do to Eny?'

Nakula's eyes turned inwards, converging on the past. 'She had a heart condition. A little pinch of barium chloride in your coffee each day for two years will do that to you. I would visit her each morning and make her a cup, pretending to be the dutiful son. Barium is such a handy chemical. When absorbed into the bloodstream, it disappears in twenty-four hours. *Sih*, it is deposited in the muscles and the lungs, but no doctor will look there, and even then it stays in the muscles for only thirty hours.

'Eventually, she was admitted to hospital. Her blood pressure was dangerously high and she was getting chest pains. PGI Cikini Hospital, her final resting place. They found me a chair and settled me by her bed. I hardly said a word to her; I just stared out of the window. The two nurses spoke softly under their breath as they checked on the tubes sticking out of her arms. And when she slipped into a light sleep,

356

the nurses moved on to the next patient, leaving me to my thoughts.

'Later, when the ward grew quiet, I closed the privacy curtains and woke her. She was groggy, of course, poor thing, but I could tell she could hear me. That was when I told her my plans, what I was about to do to her friends, to her. She was too weak to cry out but her hand reached for the call button. Naturally I anticipated this and stowed it out of her reach. There was a nervous stillness in me as I leaned my entire weight on her with a pillow to her face.' He smiled. '"Shhh-shhh-shhh!" I soothed. "That dark swirling figure approaching is only *Shaytan*, coming to usher you to the gates of Jahannam, to the abyss, where you will break into pieces and join the other shameless women and companions of the left hand in the blazing fire."'

Nakula squeezed Imke's throat. 'They said she died of heart failure.' He stared into the camera, straight at Mathias. 'Bup-bup-debup. Bup-bup-debup. And then it stopped. But you know what it's like here in Indonesia. When you're dead, you're dead. They rarely look into the reasons why.'

He paused, spread his lips to wet his tongue and smiled a messianic smile. 'But of course, you want to see your old sweetheart, don't you? Oh, you do, do you? No problem. I expected you to want to see her. Oh father, we are going to have a wonderful afternoon together. The family is reunited at last.'

With cat-like grace he reached down with both arms, momentarily releasing Imke. '*Aduh*, it was hard finding a jar big enough. But thank the heavens for the internet, *hnnn*, thank the heavens. Only nineteen dollars and ninety-nine cents, with thirty per cent off international shipping if I

357

bought two' – he grinned – 'which was nice. And they packed them with such care.'

He lifted the object up for all to see, cradling it against his chest. It was shaped like a cocoon and covered with a large red handkerchief.

'So,' he gabbed like a game-show host, 'shall we see what awaits us behind cloth number one? Are you paying attention?'

He nipped the crown of the red handkerchief between fingers and thumb and whipped it away with a magician's flourish.

The jar was large and made of glass; a ghostly grey 256 oz was stencilled across its face.

And inside, staring out, was a dug-up skull with bug-ravaged eyeballs, patchy black hair and the dried remains of stringy flesh.

'Say hello to Mama.'

Mathias's gag reflex triggered, forcing thick acid to the roof of his mouth. Every muscle in his anatomy strained. Beetles and blowflies had turned Eny Soleh's cheeks to mush. Only dry decay remained.

The bare-chested man licked his fingers and worried the knife blade, running the fleshy pad of his middle digit down its length.

He hugged Imke tight, proprietorially.

Mathias slammed his fists down, rattling the sideboard and toppling the Rudolph van Veen cookbooks to the floor. 'Listen to me, Nakula!' he commanded. 'I am your father.'

'Shut up, father.'

'Don't you dare hurt her!'

The knife jabbed against Imke's throat. Her entire body tensed. A teardrop of blood spilled and dribbled down to her collarbone.

Then, in the distance, a sound. The sound of a dog barking.

'Nakula!' cried Mathias.

The dog was right outside the front door. Barking louder. Scratching the wood. Howling. Baying. Growling.

Mathias cried out again, 'For God's sake, don't you dare touch her!'

Snarling. Whining. Barking.

Nakula blinked hard. The pressure-crushing weight came from all directions, squashing the insides of his brain. Eyes popping, he held both hands over his ears, not to drown out his father's voice, not to muffle the sounds of the dog, but rather to drown out the yowling revelations in his head. 'Quiet!' he yelled. 'I cannot hear myself think! Shut up, Budi! Shut up, shut up, shut up!'

'Nakula!' Mathias yelled, ratcheting up the volume.

'QUIET! I need quiet!'

He jabbed the knife deeper into his sister's throat.

And then realization hit Mathias hard.

There was a second glass jar.

Nakula was going to cut off Imke's head and stuff it in the jar.

Imke struggled, skewing round her head, trying to sink her teeth into the man's hand.

His fingers dug into the hollows of her face, twisting the muscles of her neck, exposing an expanse of throat. She felt the blade cool against the point of her chin.

Steel scraped skin. Skin gripped the blade.

When, all of a sudden, he broke off. Half crouching, he raised his head to sniff to the left and right of the room, up and down. 'Someone is coming.'

There was a dog barking at the door. Barking and scratching.

Imke heard the thump thump thump of approaching feet.

He grabbed a handful of her hair. The knife slashed at the front door. 'Circle the flame, circle the flame.' Eyes bulging, he repeated the words three times, four times, again and again and again.

The house with the slanting roof stood at the edge of the *kampung*.

A fierce storm had broken and it was raining heavily. Water cascaded noisily from gutters and poured from downpipes. Despite the rain, Ruud could hear the sound of his own breathing. It came in gasps.

Using the leaves of a bush for cover, Ruud studied the single-storey dwelling. He saw three windows and a door. The door looked flimsy. Could he risk a frontal assault? Part of him hoped to hear screams coming from inside. The screams would mean Imke was still alive. The other part of him, the one that was scared to death, listened for any sounds at all. But all he heard was silence amidst the rainfall. He used his sleeve to wipe his face dry. The gale flattened the fabric of his wet shirt against his chest, outlining his nipples. The smell of damp earth clung to his clothes.

He moved forward, arms extended, Heckler & Koch 9mm raised to eye level in the firing position. The dog was barking at the door, its forelegs rising to scratch at the wood.

Keeping the entryway in his sight lines, yet hidden by thick trees and a dark weave of creepers, Ruud took a quarter-circular route around the house via the dirt road that snaked through the cassava fields and bamboo groves.

He stopped about ten yards from the weather-darkened bricks of the rear wall. From his new position he watched the windows, which were covered with screens and curtains He was confident that nobody had seen him approach; no movement came from within.

Equidistant to the west, Werry Hartono waited, squatting low with his shotgun at the ready, barrel level to the ground. He gave Ruud a thumbs-up sign.

The only thing more dangerous than a machete-wielding psychopath was a machete-wielding psychopath with hostages. When backed into a corner, they killed indiscriminately, like a fox in a chicken coop. Usually all that was left behind were bodies.

Ruud assumed there was only the one hostage – Imke – but he could be wrong. There could be more. The idea was unlikely but he couldn't dismiss it.

The truth about killing somebody is that you can't be sure you're capable of doing it until you're about to do it. Ruud had never killed anyone before.

Werry Hartono repeated the thumbs-up gesture. Ruud drew on whatever reserves of courage he could muster and rushed forward through the creepers and across the rutted path. The dirt trail in front of him danced and popped from the downpour impaling the ground. Flying ants rose up in a thick swarm as he ran. Blood rushing in his ears, his face wide with terror, he flew at the door and slammed into it with his body.

Chapter Forty-One

The story Werry Hartono relayed to PROPAM, the internal affairs division, was like a sequence of freeze-frame images from a film, played to a deafening soundtrack of hoarse shouting and a child's high-pitched shriek:

Still 1: First *Inspektur* Pujasumarta rushes forward, weapon raised. The lightweight wood of the doorframe splinters on impact and the door bursts open, violently.

Still 2: A wide-angle shot with barrel distortion sees a man's mouth elongate in the form of an angry hiss as he grabs a fistful of the woman's hair. A metal blade digs into her flesh.

Still 3: Muzzle flash from a gunshot blast.

Still 4: The knife slices into a soft throat, ripping through the trachea and vocal cords, causing cricotracheal separation.

Still 5: Another muzzle blast.

Still 6: The walls grow slick and slimy with blood.

Still 7: First *Inspektur* Pujasumarta's mouth opens in a scream. But there is no sound emitted. Only a terminal hush.

There was a fleeting silence in the interview room. Behind

wired safety glass doors, the five PROPAM investigators sat in a semicircle around the youthful Werry Hartono, scrutinizing his every word, analysing every gesture, tic and facial expression.

They had very few questions. As Second Lieutenant Hartono's concise version of events correlated with First *Inspektur* Ruud Pujasumarta's, there was little to add. Pujasumarta's typed report spoke of a household snarled in secrets; a childhood scarred by physical abuse, emotional cruelty, insanity, isolation and loathing.

With a rubber stamp they marked the internal file with red ink and ticked several boxes on evaluation forms. The officers had followed protocol. Rules of conduct had not been breeched. The investigators made some jottings in their notepads and agreed that Nakula Soleh was a particularly perverse type.

'Who was responsible for hiring this Soleh madman?' one of them asked. 'Security protocols at Bogor must be tightened. This cannot happen again. It's a blessing the President wasn't harmed.'

The air conditioner hummed.

As the PROPAM people turned to each other and deliberated, Werry suddenly felt lost. His arms went rigid and the slush of jumbled recollections flitted once more inside his head.

When he looked at the lead interrogator he saw the house with the slanting roof again, the fierce storm, the water cascading from gutters and downpipes. His breathing became laboured, arriving in sticky gasps.

Over to the east, he saw Pujasumarta, crouching low, hidden by thick trees, waiting with his Heckler at the ready. He gave Ruud the thumbs-up. Instantaneously, the first *inspektur* jerked upright and rushed through the creepers. Werry was on his feet too, six paces to his left. There were wet leaves everywhere. The damp earthy smell of bamboo filled his head. Werry galloped across the rutted path, running through the rain along the dirt trail. His breathing was hard, his teeth rattled, his feet pounded the puddles of mud.

Bang! The door flew open. Lunging, Werry was inside the house.

His vision wobbled. He saw a man in a sarong. The man in the sarong was shouting. Perspiration glazed his torso. The man clutched a knife and used the woman as a human shield. He shouted but his voice sounded like a young boy's. 'I will kill her! Kill her!' he shrieked. The cries reverberated, piercing the room. 'Stay back!'

The Remington 870 shotgun was heavy in Werry's arms as he levelled it. He was aware of the Dutch woman's nakedness.

Ruud was screaming, 'Drop the knife! Drop it!'

The dog was barking and snarling.

The First *Inspektur* fired his pistol. The report knocked the wind from Werry's lungs.

The man remained standing. Still, he held the knife to the woman's throat.

'Listen to me, Nakula!' Ruud yelled. 'You don't really want to hurt her. It's your father you want to punish, not Imke.'

'But I am punishing him,' Nakula exclaimed. He turned to the laptop, but saw the shattered screen. 'You shot it! No! No! No! What have you done? Now he cannot watch!'

The man shoved the Dutch woman to the floor, releasing her, and held the blade to his Adam's apple.

'Don't! Don't do it, Nakula!'

Reeling, the man plunged the knife into the triangle of his neck, just as the first *inspektur* discharged the Heckler again. The bullet struck the man in the leg.

Werry dropped the shotgun. He slid onto his knees and tilted Nakula's head forward, thrusting his hands against the severed jugular, applying pressure to the gaping wound, pinching his thumb and forefinger together. Werry stared into the man's round eyes, at the amber flecks in his irises, watching the life force pour out. There was a momentary alertness, the hint of a farewell smile.

He saw the expression on Nakula Soleh's face. It resembled that of a child's – one of incalculable sadness and innocence, as if his soul had gone missing in the woods for a very long time but was finally finding its way home.

Until then, Werry Hartono, twenty years old and only months out of the Semarang Academy, had never held a dying man in his arms. It was only when he heard his name that he gazed up at the semicircle of investigators and found himself back in the interview room.

His throat tightened and he took one despairing drag of air. Then, quite unexpectedly, and much to the surprise of the PROPAM detectives, Hartono began to weep.

Epilogue

Sunday, 27 July, the last day of Ramadan. It was the night before *Hari Raya Idul Fitri*, a night the locals called *Takbiran*.

Mere moments to nightfall.

The Witarsa family home was full of revellers. They strung coloured fairy lights around the window frames. They wound bows and bouquets along curtain rails. Raya stars, bright cut-out decorations symbolizing peace and harmony, made of bamboo sticks and transparent pink-and-red paper, hung from the ceilings and doors. The largest, a twenty-one-pointed star, flared from a light-emitting diode lodged in its centre. And like any family get-together a slow-moving uncle was fast asleep, slumped in the corner like an overfed Alsatian.

A cheer went up. Some of the men, Aiboy Ali included, were watching reruns of the Germany v Argentina game on the television.

Out on the ninth-floor balcony, Imke and Ruud sat on a bench, hip to hip, thigh to thigh, lost in thought. Imke's gaze was on the Jakarta skyline, but her mind was miles away. She was thinking about Erica.

'My aunt's finished the portrait of SBY.'

'Is she pleased with it?'

'It took her longer than expected, not surprising given what's happened, but yes. She's happy with it.'

Ruud nodded his head slowly, and leaned in so his chin touched her shoulder. 'I was so scared.'

She seemed momentarily paralysed by his words. Then, as if to break the spell, she ran some fingers through her hair. 'So was I. But it's over now, *hè*?' She slipped her hand into his. 'I don't want to think about it or talk about it.'

'In my experience you shouldn't bottle this up.'

'For a start, he didn't hurt me or do anything except drug me and tie me up.' She touched the side of her neck, tracing the red-raw scar. A shadow fell across her face. 'Apart from this little blemish, I don't believe he ever intended to harm me. He could have killed me anytime . . . when I was at the bungalow . . . or when he drove us about. He wanted to punish the women that hurt and humiliated him. And he wanted to punish my father.' The thought burned hot in her mind.

Ruud held his tongue. She was wrong but he didn't want to say so. Ruud was convinced Nakula had planned to kill Imke all along. He was going to execute her in front of Mathias, dispose of the body, then melt away, disappear. There would be no evidence of a crime committed and no one but Mathias would go looking for him. Why would they? Why should anyone believe the Dutchman's story? As far as the police were concerned. The Captain was the Mah-Jong Master. Case closed.

And Imke? Well, she'd be classified as *Orang Yang Hilang*, a missing person. Poor Mathias would travel to Indonesia in search of her remains, where he would receive little police assistance. Perhaps he might hire a local private investigator. But where would he start looking? In this country of

17,000 islands and 222 million people, it would be an impossible task. Yes, the plan was to kill Imke. And for Mathias Sneijder to suffer the hell of searching for but never finding her body. He would never find his daughter; never give her a Christian burial; never lay flowers on her grave, and never say his final goodbyes. He'd carry the burden for ever.

'Well, thankfully,' said Ruud, 'we'll never know.'

She crinkled her nose and bit her bottom lip.

'He must have been pretty far gone,' he continued, 'to dig up his mother's body and remove her head. Do you think he was as crazy as he made out?'

Imke furrowed her eyebrows. She had long stopped wondering what made Nakula tick. For days she'd asked herself why he'd written that note and left it on her night-stand, and whether he was sane or insane, if he suffered from dissociative identity disorder or schizophrenia or borderline personality disorder, if he hated everyone in the world or just the people who injured him. And of course she never got the answers. And because she never got any answers she'd had to harden herself. At the end of the day she was alive. She had survived. So what if he killed The Captain and Vidi? So what if he murdered Sharon Zee and Mari Agnes Liem and the others? Who gives a shit if he dug up his mother? Maybe he had a thing for Norman Bates and Hitchcock films. The fact was it was over. The nightmare had ended.

At least that was what she told herself.

Her brain had witnessed extreme traumatic stress. Re-adjusting was a daily struggle. It would take time. The doctors prescribed a course of tablets – Fluoxetine: a 'mood elevator' – to be ingested once a day, preferably with food.

'Yes,' she said at length. 'Technically, I do think he was crazy. But exhuming his mother, that was a cry for help.'

'He slit his own throat right in front of us,' Ruud said quietly, with the deliberation of a man who hated sensationalizing violence. 'So perhaps he was suicidal all along.'

'And then you shot him.'

'In the leg.'

She closed her eyes and took several long, deep breaths. 'Yes, I know. I was there.' She pushed the images away.

'I think you should talk to someone, a professional.'

'I don't need a shrink.'

'Yes, but . . .'

'Hey. It's been five weeks. I'm fine and I know,' she said softly yet firmly, 'that I can cope.'

Ruud looked at her. She was strong and confident, and not at all diminished by the recent trauma.

In the distance the sun was setting. The sky was bright orange with wisps of red. 'Ahhh, another smoggy, petrochemical sunset. Don't you just love 'em?' He peered heavenward. Storm clouds were rushing in from the east. He put an arm round Imke. 'Looks like it's going to rain cats and dogs,' he said.

'Do you know that in Holland they say it's raining old women?'

'Rubbish.'

'And in Bosnia they say it's raining crowbars.'

'Absolute bollocks!' he howled.

'It's true!' Her body shook with laughter and immediately he felt her relax, casting off any lingering tension.

Kiki stirred, raised herself and licked Imke's hand. Imke patted her head and she settled back down by their feet.

Spits of rain blew in on the breeze. 'I suppose you'll be heading home soon,' said Ruud. 'Back to Amsterdam.'

'Aunty Ecks has arranged to fly the day after tomorrow. She says she can't wait to walk the canals again. She wants to grab a picnic hamper from Marqt greengrocers, take it to Vondelpark and spread it out on the grass.'

'She.'

'Hmm?'

'You said *she*, not *we*.'

'Well, as it happens, First *Inspektur* Pujasumarta, I've decided to stay on in Indonesia for a while longer.'

'Stay on?'

'Yes. Stay on.'

'Because of me?'

'No, because some friends back home have asked me to a Viking re-enactment weekend in Utrecht. I'm not sure I want to don a leather breastplate and a horned helmet on a wet Saturday morning, pillaging villages for breakfast. I'm not really into swords and shields and learning about Norse blacksmithing skills.' She elbowed him and grinned. 'Of course because of you.'

Imke closed her eyes and pictured a future life spent with Ruud. The images came freely, without complications.

'And, besides, Witarsa has offered me a job.'

'Wow!' Ruud scratched his chest through his shirt. 'He's stupider than he looks, which is saying something.'

Another elbow to the ribs.

'And your father . . . ?'

Ruud let the question hang in the air.

'Papa's most unhappy that I'm not heading home with Erica. But after what he's done and all that I've been through, I think I can handle the weight of his disapproval.

370

In a weird way, I kind of want to disappoint him. Perhaps it's my way of punishing him. Anyway,' she sighed, 'I think right now he needs some time to himself, to fight his own inner demons.'

In her mind, her father's hand – the one she clasped as a toddler, the one that stroked her cheek each morning before school, the hand that held onto hers when she fell off her moped and was rushed to A&E, the hand she kissed when singing *Sinterklaas* songs at Christmas – slowly slipped away.

'Well, as Gandhi once said—'

'You're not going to quote Gandhi, surely,' Imke challenged.

'I am.'

'Please don't. It's so cheesy. Almost as bad as quoting Confucius.'

Ruud cleared his throat theatrically. 'As Gandhi once said: "The only devils in the world are those running around inside your own hearts, and that is where all our battles should be fought."'

'Bravo.'

Ruud bowed his head, acknowledging the mock praise with a twirl of his fingers. 'So, you'll need a place to crash, I suppose. I have a seven-foot-by-nine-foot cell – er, sorry, spare room – with cold running water available for rent.'

'Sounds tempting. What about Arjen?'

'What about him?

'Won't he mind?'

'Nope.'

'How is he doing?'

'Pretty good, but he's still prone to the odd panic attack.'

'Bad ones?'

'He doesn't have a big red button by his bed which sets off an ear-splitting klaxon when pressed, but, yeah, once in a while he has a bad one. He gets overwhelmed. The good news, however, is he's finally decided to give Australia a try. Mum and Dad have persuaded him to go and live with them in Melbourne. He'll receive better treatment for his Asperger's there, and Mum will be happier that he's with them.'

Imke smiled. 'I remember the time your mum came prancing out in a white tennis skirt and top, flaunting a copy of "A Streetcar Named Desire" and crying, "Anyone for Tennessee?"'

'Yep, that sounds like her all right.'

'So you'll be hunting for a flatmate.'

'Could be.'

'I'll send over my references.'

'Only if you're ready to face dodgy plumbing, kitchen humiliation and stray cats serenading you at three in the morning. You any good at ironing shirts?'

'Sure, if you like the scorch-mark effect.'

Erica tumbled out of the apartment and onto the balcony, hooting with laughter. 'Who would have thought you could do that with liver paste? God, can you believe that story?' She wore several paper-chain necklaces garlanded round her neck, like Hawaiian leis.

'I know, who would have thought it!' cried Ruud, amused. He mouthed an aside to Imke. 'What story?'

She shrugged and gave him a wink.

Erica pulled a Milkita wrapper from a pocket, tore it, closed her eyes and took a bite.

'What's that?' asked Imke.

'A new pleasure. Try one.'

'I think it would be polite if we waited another fifteen minutes.'

'Nonsense. Nobody will mind. Go on, have a bite.'

Imke tasted the offered sweet, relishing the soft, chewy texture. 'Mmmmmm!' she moaned. 'My goodness, mmm-mmm-mmmm!'

'You're having sex with your food again,' mused Erica. 'Speaking of sex, what have you two lovebirds been chatting about out here?'

'Nothing,' Imke replied.

'Relationships? Marriage? I'd drag her down the aisle in double-quick time if I were you, Ruud. Before her looks go.'

'Aunty Ecks!'

'What?'

'Why must you keep blurting things out? Don't you ever think before you speak? Are you that insensitive?'

'I'm sorry,' she said with a gasp. 'I had no idea that talking was like crossing the road, that I had to take a moment to look both ways before advancing.'

Erica took another bite of Milkita before stomping back indoors.

Imke banged her foot against the metal railing. 'God, she's infuriating.' Ruud began to laugh. Imke squinted at him, rolled her eyes and started laughing too. She felt buoyant inside. Happy. Light-headed. A huge yellow smiley face throbbed warmly in her chest.

She retrieved a tiny package from her bag and placed it on his lap.

'What could this be?' he said, fiddling with the colourful wrapping paper.

'Open it and see.'

It was a carved agate pebble; midnight blue with speckles of pumpkin, salmon and gold.

'This is beautiful, Imke. Does it mean anything?'

'It does to me.'

She bought it at Rawa Bening market. It was a friendship stone, but in her heart she hoped it might turn out to be so much more.

To the west, under the setting sun, crowds gathered at the mosques for prayers and to give thanks ahead of Lebaran day. Within the apartment, the police commissioner's relatives gathered, sharing smiles and good wishes, eager for the moment to arrive when the patriarch beat the *bedug* drum. Only then could they break fast after Ramadan and enjoy the early-evening family feast.

For a long while Imke and Ruud sat on the bench, side by side, watching the sunset, gazing at the narrow stretch of water known as Ciliwung. She leaned in and kissed him on the lips. He held onto the heat of her body; his arm draped over her shoulders, pressed up against her, feeling her breathing pattern, slowing his own breaths until they became evenly matched.

His eyes went to the agate pebble. He stared deep into its midnight centre, at its hypnotic colours, at its moon shadows and tie-dye spirals, and seemed inexplicably transported back in time.

He and Imke are seven years old. It's Boxing Day. They are outdoors in the communal garden shared by the residents of Majestic Heights. Wall's sausages and chicken wings are grilling on the barbecue. Lars Ringstad, big and meaty, swigs from a glass of beer. He laughs and guffaws in a mixture of broken English and tipsy Norwegian. Watching transfixed, only a few feet away, the two children giggle as the angry wasp buzzes and fizzes each time he takes a sip. It is yellow and black and really, really huge, with a shiny black stinger. Lars takes a ferocious swig, knocking his head back. His mouth is like a cavern. Will he or won't he? What if the wasp stings his tongue or his lips? Will it fly out of his nose? And then it's gone! 'It was still alive when he gulped it down!' cries Imke, hopping about in bobby socks.

Ruud, still staring at the stone, at the displacement of pumpkin and gold, giggled at the ludicrous memory. And, to his delight, he felt Imke's body shake with laughter too – as though she could read his thoughts.

Acknowledgements

As ever, I am grateful to Kate Hordern, my wise and wonderful agent. Thank you Kate for your guidance, unfailing encouragement and occasional nudge when I stray off course.

Thanks must also go to everyone at Constable, especially Krystyna Green.

Lastly, I want to thank my family, particularly my wife, for allowing me to pursue my passion.